THE NUMBER *121* TO PENNSYLVANIA & OTHERS

Kealan Patrick Burke

ISBN: 1481030094
ISBN-13: 978-1481030090

BOOKS by KEALAN PATRICK BURKE

THE TIMMY QUINN SERIES

The Turtle Boy
The Hides
Vessels
Peregrine's Tale
Stage Whispers
Nemesis

NOVELS

Kin
Master of the Moors
Currency of Souls

NOVELLAS

Thirty Miles South of Dry County
You In?
Midlisters
Seldom Seen in August
Saturday Night at Eddie's
Underneath

COLLECTIONS

The Number 121 to Pennsylvania & Others
Ravenous Ghosts
Theater Macabre
Dead Leaves: 8 Tales of the Witching Season
Dead of Winter
Digital Hell

"The Grief Frequency" originally appeared in *Subterranean* #1.

"The Number 121 to Pennsylvania" originally appeared in *Cemetery Dance* #47.

"Mr. Goodnight" originally appeared in *Cemetery Dance* #51.

"Empathy" originally appeared in *Corpse Blossoms*, ed. R.J. & Julia Sevin, Creeping Hemlock Press.

"Peekers" originally appeared in *Horror World*, ed. Nanci Kalanta. Reprinted in *Eulogies: A Horror World Yearbook*, ed. Nanci Kalanta

"High on the Vine" appears here for the first time.

"Tonight the Moon Is Ours" originally appeared in *Inhuman* #3. Reprinted as "La Lune est a Nous Ce Soir" in *Borderline*, ed. Lionel Benard

"Prohibited" originally appeared in *Shivers IV*, ed. Richard Chizmar.

"Underneath" originally appeared in *Shivers III*, ed. Richard Chizmar.

"Snowmen" originally appeared in *Cemetery Dance* #54.

"Will You Tell Them I Died Quietly?" originally appeared in *Shivers II*.

"The Last Laugh" originally appeared in *Dark Discoveries* magazine, ed. James Beach

"Cobwebs" originally appeared in *Shivers VI*, ed. Richard Chizmar

"Saturday Night at Eddie's" originally appeared as an e-serial on the Subterranean Press website.

TABLE OF CONTENTS

Introduction
7

The Grief Frequency
9

The Number 121 to Pennsylvania
29

Mr. Goodnight
43

Empathy
56

Peekers
79

High on the Vine
87

Tonight the Moon is Ours
109

Prohibited
122

Underneath
135

Snowmen
160

Will You Tell Them I Died Quietly?
168

The Last Laugh
176

Cobwebs
191

Saturday Night at Eddie's
208

Story Notes
248

INTRODUCTION

I grew up around the memory of trains. Those memories weren't mine, but that didn't make them any less vivid, or any less intriguing to me. There were images on the signs outside grocery stores and pubs, and old black and white and sepia-toned photographs in the museum showing the town a hundred years before, people going about their business with a huge black train in the background, thick white smoke billowing from its chimney, as if it was fueling the sky with clouds. My mother recalled the years in which she and her friends would stand atop the bridge a few short yards from our house looking down as those monolithic giants tore across the tracks and burrowed beneath them with all the urgency of blood through a vein.

I'd like to have seen them.

Today that bridge looks down on nothing but a gravel path, narrowed for the passage of people, and nothing else, but in following it, one can retrace the journey of those steel dinosaurs, from one end of the town to the other.

But I don't live there anymore.

These days I live in a small rural area in Ohio, and every night, no matter what the weather, no matter what the season, the trains come rumbling along the track not far from our house. When I tell people this, they groan in sympathy and ask: "How do you sleep at night?" And my answer is this: "Like a baby." In fact, I have come to suspect that if I were to lie in bed at night and those trains didn't come, if the air went undisturbed by their lonesome cries, I would have trouble sleeping at all.

On those nights, on the verge of dreaming, on the threshold of sleep, when the trains unleash their sorrowful wails and send them echoing across the fields toward our house, toward me, I wonder who else is lying awake, listening, and what it might mean to them. Does that forlorn sound remind them of past loves, past lives, or past regrets? Does it summon to mind ghosts they've struggled to forget or longed to recall?

And sometimes I tell myself those freight trains, ferrying their loads to parts unknown, are nothing less than the specters of those dinosaurs I missed as a child.

The stories herein are train tickets for you.

Use them. Take your seat. Watch through the windows as life passes by, endure the darkness of the many tunnels, meet your fellow travelers, and see what's waiting for you at the next platform, when you get there.

If you get there.

All aboard!

The train is leaving the station.

—Kealan Patrick Burke
Summer, 2011

THE GRIEF FREQUENCY

We hit the guardrail at sixty-five miles an hour.

Fast enough to send Caitlin through the windshield.

Not fast enough for me to avoid seeing it.

Fast enough to snap the seatbelt around my father-in-law's chest, eliciting a low but audible grunt of pain from him in the back seat as he was thrown forward, right leg colliding with the coffee holder hard enough to crush his kneecap.

Not fast enough to stop me from thinking, as the steering wheel rushed into my face like a black hole, that if we'd waited for the storm to pass, the road might have held us better.

The black hole shrank away, replaced by a supernova that spewed stars and red gas clouds into my eyes. The vehicle bounced away and Caitlin flopped on the hood as it accordioned around her.

One blazing wet blue eye found me and rolled.

My seat slammed into the back of my head just as I turned away to try and wake up from what was certainly a dream. I closed my eyes against the raging thunder of stampeding elephants; the shriek of hungry birds and almost gasped as the window shattered, splashing diamonds in the air. Dynamite charges exploded in my ears; the mirror tumbled without gravity trailing the cheap pine tree air freshener Caitlin had bought at a gas station on our trip to Maine and as it flashed toward me I saw the little boy in the back seat. The child who wasn't there.

Just a fleeting glimpse.

Fast enough to know I'd imagined it.

Not fast enough to believe it.

* * *

9

We buried my wife on Sunday. It seemed the proper day to conduct such affairs. I stood motionless, staring down at the casket, wondering what was in there, for it was certainly not my wife. Only her body, a broken, stitched and made up thing, a puppet with severed strings, totally devoid of what had once made it mine.

On the opposite side of the grave stood Bill, my father-in-law, his shoulder braced to support Caitlin's mother's weeping face, his knuckles white around the handles of the crutches. His eyes were on me and from them radiated a cold hatred of the kind I had only just learned to apply to myself. So clear and raging were they it seemed the harsh wind blowing through the fir trees behind us swept around his glare rather than risk being scorched passing through it. I was not surprised; I was enraged. Over the grave, our hatred collided in silence:

— You killed my daughter. You took my beautiful daughter away from us you dirty sonofabitch!

She was my wife, *Bill. I loved her more than life itself. She's gone because I fucked up and I'm alone and dying inside because of it. I understand your grief, empathize with it, but don't try and make me feel any worse you bastard, because it isn't possible.*

— You killed her.

It was an accident.

— You murdered her.

Bill, I loved her.

— Murderers don't know how to love, Paul.

The priest, an oversized raven with a scabrous pink beak and silver crown, gestured in the air over the grave, dispelling our unspoken ire and blessing the puppet below. A shimmering eye framed by a snow-white fall of hair, peeked out from Bill's sleeve and regarded me with a confused look that I knew would graduate to hatred once Bill told her what I was. But for now, all that look said was: *I cooked you dinner, Paul. You were in my house. We cared for you. Why did you have to drive in the storm? Why, Paul? Look what you've made happen to our lives. You've put our precious little girl in the ground before us. Why? So you could make it home in time to watch the football game? I want her back, Paul. Can you bring her back? Make right what you've done?*

The assemblage of mourners, few of whom could manage anything more than awkward smiles, shrugs and shoulder thumps, broke up, muttered words in my face I didn't hear and went to Caitlin's parents, perhaps seeking a more sympathetic audience for their well-rehearsed speeches.

I dug deep into the pockets of my overcoat and grabbed fistfuls of patience as I watched them queue for the opportunity to be sorry.

Then, at last, there were only the three of us.

Bill hobbled his way toward me. His wife seemed to grow smaller, the gravestones rearing up behind her, as if eager to inform her how soon she'd have one of her own.

Although I knew what was coming, I dared hope otherwise. My world had become a terribly lonely, fragile and frightening place. Caitlin's parents were the only remaining connection to what my life had once been, anchors keeping my raft from going over the waterfall. I needed them and hated them, but the latter would inevitably fade with time, if allowed to.

Bill stopped before me, his plastered foot upraised and resting on a stone sphere marking the corner of a stranger's gravesite.

I waited.

He stared. Then said: "If I didn't think I'd fall, I'd break your fucking face, you bastard."

Ice water filled my belly. "Bill I—"

"I hope the game was worth it."

His cheeks were flushed, a glistening bulb of spittle nestled at the corner of his mouth, lips working desperately, trying to choke out the words that were caught in the thorns of his mind. "I hope—"

His breath caught as if I'd punched him in the stomach, and for one crazy moment, I wondered if I had, perhaps blinded to my actions by the sheer hopelessness of my situation. But then his lower lip began to tremble and tears welled in his eyes. He tried to maintain the rage but the tears washed the severity from his glare and he mentally waved me off and turned away.

"Bill I'm sorry," I said, too low for him to hear over the wind. Just as well. I wasn't sorry. What was there to be sorry for? For the rain? For trying to drive them home before conditions got really bad? For stealing everything that was good from myself? The football game had been a joke between Caitlin and I. A long-running joke. I hated football and she knew it. Her father knew it too, but as it had been the last thing she'd said before I lost control of the car and my life, Bill had seized it. In a way I could understand. Last words are important to survivors.

"Slow down, Paul," — a sigh— *"I guess the magnetic draw of Ohio V Michigan should not be underestimated."* She'd smiled then and raised her eyebrow.

But of course, Bill hadn't seen that.

Bill *had* seen the other car fishtailing into our lane up ahead and his cry led us inside the snow globe.

Now, I watched him leave, carefully negotiating the graves and stopping by his car with Agatha as they took one last long look back at that rectangular hole in the grass. An unkempt man with a shovel hovered around the grave, trying not to look too eager to get on with the task of filling in the hole and failing miserably. He dodged and weaved and inspected his nails, leaned on his shovel and stared at the sky. To me he looked like a kid trying to make himself small so the teacher won't ask him a question he doesn't know the answer to.

Then my dead wife's parents cast another look back. I felt about as animated as the stone angels behind me.

Bill and Agatha.

Fire and Ice.

And then they were gone, leaving me to listen to the wind hissing through the pines and the first few *schnicks* of the caretaker's shovel.

* * *

In the days afterward, grief stayed with me like a nagging aunt, probing my wounds at the slightest sign I'd forgotten them, whispering *can't forget, never forget* in my ear whenever I tried to distract myself.

I haunted the house, drifting from room to room, trying to avoid the image of Caitlin. But she was there, sitting on the sofa, legs crossed, foot bouncing as she clicked through the channels on the television, muttering her disdain for infomercials and sighing at the compelling insanity of talk shows. She was in the kitchen, playing with her hair, brooding over a woman's magazine or rolling her eyes

(*One blazing wet blue eye found me and rolled*)

at my culinary ineptitude. She was in the shower, pulling back the curtain and smiling coyly, moving to cover up her nakedness despite seven years of marriage and when I kissed her, her lips were soft and warm and wet. In the bedroom mirror, she stood in her business suit, preparing for another joyless day in real estate, the cute curl on her forehead reversed as I watched her reflection smile back at me in response to the same question I asked every morning:

"Can't you come back to bed for another ten minutes?"

"You know I can't. Besides, I'm dressed now."

"So stay dressed. Just lose the panties."

Smile. "Ten minutes? Isn't that a little ambitious?"

"Ingrate."

I saw her in bed then, sleeping on her side, her hair obscuring her face; hand flat on the pillow beside her, other hand resting on her hip, her breathing like the ebb and flow of a gentle tide. She was in the bedroom and that's where I found her again.

At first I thought I was dreaming it.

But she was there. Real. I mentally pinched myself, chastised the scowling aunt for being so callous, and closed my eyes for as long as I could bear it, until the blindness inspired panic. And when I looked again, she was still there. If not her, another woman, remarkably similar in size, shape, sound, but of course I knew no other women remotely like her. And no other woman knew me well enough to dare sleep in my wife's memory. I stood in the bedroom doorway, sagged against the frame and wept. Madness. There could be no alternative solution. I was *seeing* her. She was there and my conviction was so great it could only mean I'd lost my mind for I do not nor have I ever believed in miracles.

I wanted her back, yes. I wanted to wake up and find this was all just an awful, awful dream, a Dickensian view of what might have been. But I did not want the shady promises illusion wrought. No, not that. The inevitable comedown would obliterate whatever light was left.

And so I left her there, took cautious steps backward, hurrying only when she stirred. If she got up, if she shrugged off the binds of imagination and approached, smiled, spoke or touched me, I might die where I stood.

I gently closed the door and made my way, head in hands, into the living room where my sole comfort awaited me in a bottle with a turkey on the front.

I never made it to the bottle.

I made it to the sofa and stopped when I saw someone was already sitting there.

Small. Blonde hair. Legs kicking in child-like delight.

Giggling.

I ran from the house.

* * *

I found a bar a short walk from the house. I didn't want to be there but I wanted less to be home with the ghosts or the canvas for my madness. So I settled for the spirits and somehow managed to tune out the raucous noise from the crowd of revelers at my back. An occasional slam of a jaunty fist against a table tugged me from myself but it was quickly dismissed, as was the barmaid, a girl who had the shape and face of a teenager but the eyes of someone older. Once or twice she attempted to penetrate my veil of misery but my responses were curt and soon she gave up.

I stared down at my glass, at my left eye swimming in the amber depths and told myself I was going to be all right sooner or later. But I didn't believe it.

I come from a hard family, hard meaning *we hit you only because we love you* and as a result I have a short temper and a high physical and mental pain threshold. Between Caitlin and I, I was the strong one, always ready with the innumerable solutions to quandaries she considered hopeless. I rolled with the punches, she curled up in a ball and waited for me to make it better. But now all my strength had left me. I felt like a man who'd missed the last train home and was stranded on the platform watching it dwindle in the distance. Every flame I tended was quickly smothered by the dark, every smile splintered by Auntie Grief, who, appalled that I would dare attempt such a gesture of contentment, doubled the dosage of debilitating sorrow in my head.

Hope was gone.

And I was sure at that moment—a dim revelation that made me feel neither better nor worse—that what I had seen at my house today was not my wife come to tell me she had gone on to a better place or that I should live on and not worry, but rather my memory projecting reminders purely to torture me. *Self*-torture, in other words and the surest path to total, unbridled, dance-naked-on-the rooftops insanity.

And I was too weak to resist it.

Besides, who knew that insanity wasn't the answer to everything? Perhaps then I could accept those projections without fearing what they implied about my condition, sleep once more with my wife, hold her, kiss her, smell her, *have* her.

Perhaps, but I was not ready to take that step yet, if indeed it was within my power to take it at all.

* * *

I drank too much and by the time I left the bar Auntie Grief was screaming and jamming her nails into my temples. I squinted at curious passers-by who regarded me with ill-concealed suspicion and sometimes amusement, and tried not to weep. And yet she screamed and screamed at me until I couldn't help but scream right back.

Finally she did stop, though the throbbing she'd inspired in my brain continued. I was standing at my front door, nose pressed to the oak, staring at the cracks and stabbing the wood with my key, hoping I could torture it into revealing the lock. And now, ironically, I yearned for her to scream again. For though it was quiet, I was now gripped by the paranoid certainty that it was silent not because the house was empty but because whoever was inside had stopped talking, stopped *breathing* at the sound of my approach.

Inside was as I'd left it, hollow and draped in blue-black shadows like oil paintings of bruises. With more courage than I could claim in daylight or sobriety, I peeked over the back of the sofa and found no one there. Just the cushions and the small black Sanyo remote control, which was comforting — though I was not at all sure I had left it in exactly that position.

I sat down on the sofa and felt the energy drain from me, switched on the television with no intention of watching it. Just for company. Ambience. To dissuade whatever nightmares might be crouching behind my eyes waiting for lights-out.

I dozed fitfully, waking only occasionally to probe the extent of my burgeoning hangover, to straighten my crooked neck, or to check that yes, life was still a horror show.

My mouth was dry, tongue lying like a baked worm behind my teeth; every swallow made a clicking sound. I groaned.

Darkness danced a merry dance as I drifted away on a stormy sea of slumber.

And when a child's cool hand slipped into mine, I did not pull away. Nor did I scream.

But the child did.

* * *

The next morning I awoke slowly, in no hurry to leave the blissful ignorance of sleep, the task made all that more difficult by the golden fire of the sun streaming in on top of me. As I opened my eyes and blinked away the grains of muddy sleep, I waited for the pain to hit me. It did not disappoint.

Like codependents, the sorrow and the hangover came hand in hand, sprinkling ground glass into my eyes and kicking at the walls of my skull with no apology. Rising only incited violence, my insides revolting at the mere idea of standing, and so I sat, leaned forward and cradled my head in my hands. A thin membrane of old cigarette smoke clung to the inside of my mouth. My clothes felt like too-tight bandages, constricting my breathing and trapping night sweat beneath.

The shrill sound of the phone ringing was akin to someone on the other side of the room screeching and throwing javelins at my temple. In response, the twins Sorrow and Hangover launched a melee attack, intensifying their efforts as I got to my feet. The good aunt's nefarious whispers wound round my brain once more: *all your fault, all your fault. Suffer now, as you should.*

I saw stars and white sparks, fireworks in my vision as I made my way with painstaking slowness to the phone. I didn't care who was calling. I needed to pick the damn thing up. To silence it.

"Hello?" I breathed into the mouthpiece, the word feeling foul and cumbersome as it slid out of my mouth. *Never drinking again.*

There was no reply but I could tell someone was on the line. Traffic roared by in the background, footsteps clacked and receded. I concluded that whoever the caller was, they were calling from a payphone.

"Hello?" I closed my eyes, ran a hand over my face and heard the rasp of stubble. When had I shaved last? More than a few days. The morning of Caitlin's funeral, maybe. I couldn't remember.

"Paul." The word was spoken flat, a statement not an inquiry, and totally devoid of any emotion.

"Bill?" I felt the acidic mass in my stomach do a full cycle. *Great,* I thought. Not only had I awakened to an assault by Sorrow and Hangover, now Rage was on the line. I was seriously considering throwing up.

"We need to talk," said Bill, his breath sounding like a herd of rhino rumbling over the Serengeti. "I'll be at Hoffman's Café in about an hour. Meet me there."

A demand, not a request, which left only one response.

"All right. I'll be there."

"Good." He hung up.

Confused, I glanced at my watch. Almost noon. I stood for a moment looking at the sharp edges of this new reality that had grown to loathe me, then took two Excedrin and trudged toward the shower. I wondered why Bill wanted to meet me. I hoped it was to make peace. After all, we had once been good friends. But I didn't think that was it. His voice had not sounded apologetic, or even remotely forgiving, which led me to believe another unpleasant confrontation was on the cards, and that I could most certainly do without.

The shower sluiced some of the drunken caul away, but not enough. I dressed as respectably as I could muster without being sick at the effort it required and downed two cups of scalding hot coffee before I headed out the door.

* * *

The aroma of honey and coffee grounds filled the air inside the café and as it was still lunchtime, the place was packed. I spotted Bill sitting at a table with his back to the wall in the no smoking area, his crutches leaning in the corner. He looked ancient, back hunched, eyes little more than dark screw holes in a chalk wall. I had seen road maps with less lines and wrinkles.

As I approached, he looked in my direction, then slowly down at his fingers. The message was clear. He didn't want to be here any more than I did. Which got the hornets buzzing again.

I was intercepted on my way to the table by a painfully thin girl who informed me of the specials like a drug dealer desperate to get rid of her last dime bag. I wondered if they had her working on commission. I ordered a coffee ("sadistically strong with nothing but coffee in it, okay?") and tried not to take her disappointment too personally.

Bill was making the world's tiniest paper airplane out of an empty sugar packet when I finally reached the table. A small scattering of white grains surrounded his elbows. He did not look at me as I took my seat.

"Hi," I said at last.

"Wasn't sure you'd come," he replied, biting his lower lip as he struggled to fold back the final wing on the origami stealth fighter.

"You didn't give me much time to argue. Besides, why wouldn't I come?"

He shrugged. "Any number of reasons."

"I figured it was important."

"You smell like liquor."

I reddened at that, a warm cocktail of shame and irritation. "Do I."

"Yeah. Been hitting it mighty hard I imagine."

Here we go. "Yeah well, it helps."

"How?"

"Is that what you wanted to talk about? My drinking?"

"No. It isn't."

"Then why am I here?"

Bill set the plane down on the table between us and watched it unfolding itself. He sighed and finally those dark eyes met mine.

"I want you to know something," he said, lacing his fingers together. "I want you to know that I won't ever forgive you for what happened. In some, probably more rational part of me, I know it was an accident and I know you're hurting too and that you'd never have intentionally harmed her. But that's just a little whisper and it won't ever be loud enough for me to fully accept it. You were driving. Caitlin died. That's fact."

I wanted to argue then, but stopped myself. There was something in Bill's face, something written in the new lines there that kept me quiet.

He continued. "I wish it could be different, but..." The last person to say those words to me had been my old boss at Kelvin's Auto Body and Repair. He'd used them after announcing things were going badly and that I had to be let go. Bill was not only using the same words now, but the same insincere tone too.

"So do I," I told him and sat back as the reed-thin waitress deposited my unimaginative cup of coffee before me. I thanked her, watched her pretend she hadn't heard, then sipped the oily brew. It was only a shade better than I remembered it. I grabbed the sugar.

"There's something else," Bill said and now he looked decidedly uncomfortable. I paused, spoon mired in the coffee, sugar unstirred. "The reason I asked you to meet me here."

"Bill—"

"No. Let me say this. Don't interrupt me, this is hard enough."

That made my heartbeat slow to a crawl.

He sighed and it seemed most of the strength of his bones emerged on dusty clouds. "There's something about the accident you don't know."

The hair prickled on my neck. Hornets buzzed.

"The doctor told me while you were getting your nose set. He wanted to tell you too but I told him not to. Threatened him not to actually, because he said it was your right. I told him it would destroy you. Like it destroyed me. Like it would destroy Caitlin's mother if she knew."

"Bill." I swallowed dryly, my hand creeping across the table to latch onto his arm. My skin was cold though sweat ran freely from my pores. I could smell the liquor now too.

"She was pregnant Paul."

"You're lying."

I knew he wasn't.

"You're a fucking liar, Bill."

I knew it all along, deep down inside where the sun don't shine, my mind cried, but my mouth said: "Why are you doing this to me?"

Bill closed his eyes and shook his head. "I wasn't going to tell you at all. But I realized it's something that shouldn't be kept from you. Not—" He examined his fingernails. "— knowing how much you loved her."

"No."

"You're mourning her right now. No matter how much I might detest the sight of you, it's only right that you should mourn your child too."

Hot breath filled my throat. My fists clenched involuntarily, reacting to my overwhelming need to hit him, to knock that impassive expression right out through the back of his lying hating skull.

But I didn't. I simply sat, stunned, and tried to keep the tears from coming. My head felt stuffed with cotton. I covered my face with my hands, embarrassed and when I looked up, the seat across from me was empty and an old man was hobbling his way to the door.

I picked up my cup, stared at it for a moment, then flung it at the space where just a few seconds before, my dead wife's father had told me a truth I could have died never knowing.

The cup smashed against the wall, but it was not enough. I rose, catching my thighs on the underside of the table. Like a maddened animal, I pushed away and kicked at the flimsy pine until it tumbled and landed on its side, condiments and imitation porcelain bowls skidding and clinking across the tile floor.

Breathing heavily, I turned, teeth clenched. All faces were on the lunatic in the corner. Behind the counter, the thin waitress stood with a phone to her ear.

I murmured a quiet, useless apology and hurried to the door unchallenged.

The unscheduled entertainment was over.

* * *

The last time she'd mentioned it was the night of our three-year anniversary.

We were lying in bed after making love, our bodies cooling in the breeze from the open window. Her arm was thrust across my chest, fingers playing with the hair there, her chin against my shoulder, her breath tickling my ear as I drifted in and out of pleasurable dozing.

"Is now a good time?" she said softly and I opened my eyes.

"Mmm?"

"Remember the last time I wanted to talk about having kids? It wasn't a good time for you."

And I was awake. It was a subject that sent currents of unease through me every time I thought about it. Hearing her bringing it up now increased the voltage.

"Yeah."

"You said you wanted to wait until we got settled. Until you were sure your boss wasn't just dicking you around. Remember?"

"Yes I do." I stared at the ceiling, imagining tactful prompts written there.

"Well?"

"Well what?"

She raised her head and threaded her fingers through her hair, dark face searching mine. "Well...I think we're pretty settled now, don't you?"

"I guess."

"I mean, we have the house, the car, we're in pretty good shape financially. Work is good for both of us...so why not try for one now."

"One what?" I said and she nudged me. Hard.

"Don't act like an idiot." She sighed and when she spoke, I could hear the smile. "I think we're ready."

I said nothing. Had nothing to say. I didn't want a child and although I had promised her before and after we were married that we'd have lots of kids, I dreaded the idea of it. Until now, I had successfully warded off conversations like this, but there was no escaping it now and that meant one of us would be going to sleep unsatisfied.

"I don't think *I'm* ready yet," I said and braced myself.

"Why not?"

"I just...I just don't." Truth was, I didn't have an excuse other than fear and I knew that wouldn't cut it at all. I never had anything against kids. I just didn't want one. Maybe a psychiatrist could have unearthed some complicated reason for that, traced the fear back to my own childhood and put a check mark in the appropriate box on his Freudian chart, I didn't know. I was afraid, more afraid than I'd ever been in my life.

"I'm thirty-four years old, Paul. How much longer are you going to make me wait? Until it's too late?"

If honesty had had a mouth of its own at that moment it would have told her *yes, that's exactly what Paulie here wants.*

But in the absence of that second mouth, the first stayed shut.

"Paul?" She shoved me, harder than was necessary. "Answer me."

"I don't want children, Caitlin, and I'm sorry I ever led you to believe otherwise." There, it was out but as I lay there almost *hearing* it register in her mind, I had the unsettling impression that the light in the room was fading, that the shadows were crawling down the walls. Coming for me. Coming to make me pay for stealing her hope.

"Why?" she whispered then. "Why didn't you tell me?"

"Because I couldn't. I didn't know how. And...I didn't want to hurt you like this."

She lay back down then and turned away from me. "Nice job, you bastard."

The shadows continued leaking from the corners of the ceiling, running like tar down the walls. It was exhaustion, I knew, but I couldn't bear to watch them stalking me. Couldn't bear to share the bed with a woman I knew hated me at that moment.

I got up and went into the living room, where I watched *Abbot & Costello* hamming it up on television, and tried to pretend the sound of crying was only in my head.

* * *

I half-expected to see the police at the door when I got home, perhaps accompanied by an outraged coffee shop owner. But the street was deserted.

The early afternoon sunshine had been lost in a veil of gray and apart from the distant drone of an airplane navigating the clouds overhead there was silence.

I let myself into a house that reeked of alcohol and quickly undressed, taking great care not to look at the sofa or in any of the dark corners.

After my second shower of the day, I crawled naked into bed and slept.

I did not dream but sometime in the night, I heard the phone ring and someone called my name from the answering machine.

Sometime in the night, I heard a woman crying.

Sometime in the night, I was not alone.

And at dawn when I awoke, there was a child in my arms.

He was facing away from me, unmoving, his thinly haired head moving only to accommodate his gentle breathing. I smiled, and hugged him to my chest and was rewarded with the smell of talcum powder and freshly bathed skin.

"Why did I ever fear you?" I whispered to the child and kissed the top of his head. He stirred and my mouth filled with dust.

It was coming back. All of it. Even the things that had never happened.

I turned my head as much as I could without waking the child and saw Caitlin in the mirror. She was fixing the collar of her business suit, her face scrunched up in concentration.

My beautiful wife.

I cleared my throat softly and said: "Can't you come back to bed for another ten minutes?"

She looked at me, smiled. "You know I can't. Besides, I'm dressed now."

I felt the sorrow thicken in my chest. "So stay dressed. Stay. Just lose...just lose the panties."

"Ten minutes? Isn't that a little ambitious?"

"Ingrate."

I looked down and saw that I was cradling a drifting sea of dust motes lit by a spray of fire from the morning sun, though for a moment, the weight and warmth of the child remained. I kept my hands in place for fear the sensation would dissipate and mourned it when it did. Caitlin was gone too. The air had changed and the shadows were shrinking.

I was alone as before. With one difference.

Now I knew what to do.

* * *

I waited for the rain and it came on Tuesday. Four days after waking to find the child in my arms (a boy, I knew, from what I'd seen, though even the doctors wouldn't have been able to tell.)

A fine rain, less severe than the one that had guided my car into the guardrail, but it would do.

After making sure the house was clean and smelling of something other than sweat, fear and alcohol, I showered, shaved and dressed in the suit I'd worn on my first date with Caitlin. Back then, it had been stylish, worn to win the approval of a woman I feared losing even before I had her. Now it was too short at the sleeves, tight across the shoulders and had a button dangling from the cuff. None of which mattered. I complimented the dark suit with a crimson tie, splashed on some cologne (Hugo Boss—Caitlin's favorite) and combed my hair.

Before I left, I called Bill.

"I wanted to thank you," I told him.

"For what?"

"For telling me about the baby."

"It wouldn't have been right not to."

"Well thank you, and for what it's worth, you and Agatha were always good to me. I want you to know that I loved your daughter with all that was in me, and I love her still."

There was nothing but the sound of his ragged breathing for a moment.

Then: "Paul?"

"Yes?"

"What's going on?"

"Nothing."

"What are you going to do?"

I had to smile. Before she introduced me to her father for the very first time, Caitlin had imparted a caveat: *Don't try and pull the wool over his eyes, Paul. He can see through a lie at twenty paces.*

"Goodbye Bill," I said, the sound of his worried voice trailing from the phone until it met the cradle.

Next I took a cab to the Avis outlet in Delaware and spent a ridiculous amount of time filling out forms and answering questions, some of which had little or nothing to do with car rental. But I kept my patience, even smiling at the clerk who had no idea as he handed over the keys that he would never see the car or me again.

* * *

I stopped at the Kwik 'n' Go, a small grocery store-cum-gas station on the outskirts of Delaware, then took Old State Road 21 to the highway. In the opposite direction, the traffic formed an endless unmoving parade with lights like glaring eyes as workers returned home from their jobs in Columbus. The rain fell like molten silver, my wipers squeak-thumping to keep the windshield of my rented Toyota clear.

The car smelled like disinfectant, reminding me of the item I'd picked up at the store and smiling faintly, I removed the pine tree freshener from its plastic wrapper and with one hand on the wheel, looped it around the neck of the rearview mirror. There was no immediate scent from the freshener so I flicked a nail against it to set it swinging and relaxed back into my seat, slowing for the red light at the intersection.

We'd been coming back from the doctor's office that day. Bill's back had been at him again and he'd been in too much pain to drive himself. Agatha couldn't drive or she would have obliged. *Got in an accident once and never drove again,* she proudly proclaimed. *Sometimes you don't want to play chicken with the reaper.*

Knowing my fear of hospitals (I'd watched my aunt die a horrible, spluttering death in one as a kid), Caitlin had told me to wait in the small cafeteria while she took care of her father. Which I did. Gladly. They weren't gone long, but when they returned, Caitlin was a deathly white.

Concerned, I'd gone to her but she waved me away, claiming the smell of the place had just made her queasy. She hadn't eaten all day, she said, which didn't help. Her father followed, looking stoical and much straighter than before. "Good as new," he announced and herded us back out to the car.

He *knew*. Bill had faked the pain in his back (though he did have a history of them – just not this time) so he could be with Caitlin when she learned if she was pregnant or not. I still didn't understand why she didn't just go alone or why she confided in him before me? Granted, she knew I wouldn't be thrilled by the news, but Jesus...

Caitlin and my child were dead. But they had come back to me somehow, detached themselves from the fabric of the rational world to force me into thinking outside my own self-imposed limitations. Our world is fluid; I know that now. Nothing solid is really solid at all. Everything has levels. Bill, Agatha, even the Avis kid and the gravedigger exist on one, the dead on another and sometimes grief can shake the core of those levels and send the habitants of one tumbling into the next. The dead can be among the living; the living, among the dead. Normal rules no longer apply. But not everyone is tuned to the required frequency, the one I had come to know as the Grief Frequency — that special line of communication that exists so the lost can be found, as I had been found.

"Makes you long for the summer again, doesn't it?" Caitlin said then, startling me and I jerked on the wheel, almost ending it there and then. As it was, I had to struggle to get the car back in lane, my heart thudding furiously, awash in the sudden flow of adrenaline. And fear. Which worried me. In that few seconds, a thought had spiked its way to the forefront of my brain: *I don't want to die.* Would it come again when I reached that dented guardrail, preventing me from doing what I knew deep down had to be done? No, it couldn't. I wouldn't let it.

With a shaky sigh, I turned to look at Caitlin. She was sitting in the passenger seat, chewing on a strand of her hair and peering intently out at the road ahead. She was dressed in one of my denim shirts and navy sweatpants. The clothes she'd worn the day she died.

Somewhere behind me, a car horn pierced the air.

"Even with all the blasted mosquitoes," she continued.

And then I knew what I was doing was right. These were Caitlin's words from before the accident and though I couldn't remember, I would have bet anything that our car was in the same place on the road now as it had been when she'd first said them. That's why she was here, to lull me into the memory, to show me I was on the right track. To guide me there.

I looked in the rearview mirror, expecting to see Bill grinning back at me, but there was no one there, just beads of rain racing each other across the back window.

"I love you Caitlin," I told her, aching to touch her but afraid of what might happen if I tried. No. It was best to not interfere. I leaned on the accelerator and the engine whirred. The road was clear ahead, the rain steadily drumming against the hood and splattering against the windshield.

Closer.

A car honked in the left lane. I ignored it. I was in my lane and if the bastard was trying to pass me, he'd have to drive a little faster.

On impulse, I checked the mirror again to see if Bill had appeared to play his role. He hadn't.

The car honked again and I squinted through the rain-smeared glass as the offending vehicle drew level with mine, matching my speed. I saw the pale blur of a face, too clear for it to be behind its own window.

I put more weight on the accelerator. Swallowed.

The pine freshener filled the car with its sickly sweet scent.

No turning back now.

I saw Caitlin brace herself, felt the rigidity infecting her body.

The driver in the next lane drew level again, beating a staccato rhythm on the horn. Trying to get my attention.

"Slow down, Paul," Caitlin said, with a sigh. "I guess the magnetic draw of Ohio V Michigan should not be underestimated."

I rolled down the window, allowing the rain to spit in my face.

Allowing me to see the pale face screaming at me from the other car.

Bill, in the passenger seat, window down, hands gripping the door. Agatha driving. The beginnings of a smile creased my lips. The old woman was hunched over the wheel, face stark white, eyes wide and fixed on the road. *Sometimes you don't want to play chicken with the reaper.*

And then Caitlin screamed. I looked from her to the black oblong looming in the windshield. A semi, stopped at the lights. I wrenched the wheel to the right, the muscles in my arms protesting with fiery bursts of pain but it was much too late for such concerns.

I stomped on the brakes. *I don't want to die.*

But it was much too late for that too.

We missed the semi by inches.

We hit the guardrail at sixty-five miles an hour.

* * *

They came to see me this morning, Bill and Agatha, dressed up to the nines and smiling genuine smiles, something I will never tire of seeing. I guess tragedy and loss are recyclable after all.

Agatha sat with me for a while and we reminisced about Caitlin, gone a year ago today. We laughed, we cried and we sat in silence when no words were needed.

"When you get out," she told me as she prepared to let Bill have his turn, "you have to promise you'll come see us. I might even take you for a ride." She winked and turned away before the tears came. I'm still amazed she drove that day, and so damn *fast*, after all her proclamations to the contrary.

I watched her shuffle down the long white hall toward the restrooms, then looked up at Bill, who removed his hat and hunkered down next to my chair. His face was close enough that I could smell the cologne he'd dappled on that morning. It was not an unpleasant smell. The lines seemed to have faded too. Time is treating him well.

"How are you son?" he asked, a hand on my arm.

I would have shrugged, but had I managed such a thing, the nurses would have proclaimed me a miracle case.

"Better," I said, though we both knew different.

"That's good," Bill said, his smile dropping a notch. He looked down at the floor then up at the wall as if searching for notes to draw from. "They tell you yet when you might be ready to get — "

"Not yet," I interrupted. "Soon though."

Another lie. The second accident left me with a severed spinal cord and a gunny sack for a body. The surgery does little but add years and more gray hairs, and the therapy for my 'ongoing delusions' only threatens to drive me back inside myself where the hours of questions and condescending smiles cannot reach. I exist in a twilit place, never fully awake, never fully asleep, and that suits me fine, because that's where I see them the most.

"Have you made many friends here, Paul?"

"Some."

My only real friend here is Nurse Limner. She doesn't talk much, but she can write fast and if you're reading this right now, you have her to thank. Nurse Patricia Limner, who sits with me for hours and transcribes my thoughts and never judges me by them. You should know she's smiling now.

"We think about you a lot," Bill said. "About what happened and why. I can't help but feel responsible...I mean...the grief I gave you when...when..."

"Bill."

He looked up, eyes watery. "What?"

"If you cry I'll kick your ass."

He laughed then, a clumsy snort that produced a bubble of snot from one nostril. He quickly sniffed it back in, embarrassed, which in turn made me laugh in my hideous grinding way.

"I'm sorry," he said. "I guess that's what I wanted to say."

"You have nothing to be sorry for. We lost a lot. Both of us. That much hurt can change people, bring out sides to them they never knew they had. I think I'm living proof of that."

He looked away. "Do you...still see them?"

I waited for his eyes to find me again before answering. "Only in dreams."

He nodded, squeezed my hand, then looked at it and rose, knees popping.

As if they'd prearranged it, the restroom door squeaked and Agatha appeared, a mangled tissue poking out of her fist. She gave me a coy wave and Bill nodded to her. "I better go," he said with an awkward smile. "We're holding a mass for Caitlin and Paul tonight."

They told me a few months ago they'd decided to name the child though were hesitant at first because the sex of the child had never been determined. I told them it was a boy and they were kind enough not to ask how I knew. The boy needed a name. Everyone does. At the end when the lights go out, it may be all you have left in the world. And survivors need to label their memories somehow.

He clamped a hand on my shoulder. "We love you Paul. You'll never be alone as long as we're around."

I thanked him with as much sincerity as I could muster, then watched them leave with more than a pang of sadness in my chest. They are good people, always will be.

But they just don't get it.

They're not tuned into things the way I am.

I don't blame them for that. Not everyone is so lucky.

My nights are spent lying in a bed with various machines singing an incessant chorus in my ear. I want to move, to walk, to run but can't and chances are I never will. But I'm learning to deal with that too. In fact, I'm starting to need it.

Because they never visit me when someone's here. They wait until the door is shut and the curtains are drawn and the only sounds are the machines and my breathing. Then they come, stepping from the walls and smiling, sitting by my side and stroking my hair. They stay until dawn.

Things will get better. I really do believe that. I have to believe it.

Because there are things I must see, things of which every proud father wants to be a part.

Like last night, in the dark, when Paul took his first step.

THE NUMBER 121 TO PENNSYLVANIA

You know those stories I used to tell you about the Number 121 to Pennsylvania, Rusty?
Yes. S-some of them.
Well tonight you're going to see it for yourself.

* * *

Arnold sat on his porch, watching the sun die a phoenix death, bruising the clouds as it struggled to stay afloat in the evening sky. The shadows grew bolder; the trees hissing like tuneless flutes as the breeze strengthened. It would be a calm night full of sparks both earth and heaven bound; stars and fireflies fighting for the attention of anyone who cared to look upon the scene as more than a little majestic. From the old man's pipe, a tendril of smoke drifted as far as the breeze would allow before shredding it into a lingering scent of contentment. Arnold rocked himself forward, paused with his heel on the rocker, then let it roll back before stopping again.

The screech of the screen door made him flinch and he sighed around the stem of the clay pipe. "Scared the life out of me," he grumbled as his wife Trish, a picture of happiness with gloves of flour up to her wrists and unkempt strands of hair as silver as winter moonlight, set a clinking glass of lemonade on the porch railing next to where his elbow rested. "Mind you don't tip that over now," she said cheerfully and left ghostly fingerprints on his sleeve. When he said nothing, she turned to see what had caught his attention. Once, the trains had been the objects of his scrutiny but now that they were taking up the rails, she had discovered the most banal of things; a twig, a leaf, a chipmunk or squirrel frolicking in the garden, could court his fascination. Though a harmless pastime, it sometimes worried her, perhaps because she could not always share his appreciation for the commonplace.

"Beautiful sunset," she said and he hummed a response. "How lucky we are they never built a bunch of houses in that field or we'd be looking at someone else looking out at *their* sunset."

"True," he said and sucked on his pipe. "One of the benefits of bein' too far away from proper civilization, I guess. Too much of a jaunt for young folk into the city, and of course, that's where all the work is. Nothing to do out this way, 'cept of course," he said with a wistful sigh, "tearin' up them tracks."

Trish smiled, rubbed more flour into his sleeve. "It'll be okay as long as they don't put a highway in its place."

"Why else would they tear 'em up but to make it more convenient for people to get on I-39? I tell you, pretty soon they'll be knocking on our door asking us to kindly move on out of here to make room for a Wendy's."

Trish clucked her tongue. "I reckon we'll be long in the ground before that happens, sweetheart. It isn't worth the worrying."

She stooped to kiss his grizzled cheek, warmed only briefly by the smile he offered her, then went back inside.

Arnold nodded slowly to himself, his eyes lit by the magnificent inferno the sky had become as dusk consumed the horizon and sundered the last of the day's clouds, then he set his chair to rocking. The slow creak vied with the chorus of crickets for a rhythm to sing the sun to rest.

* * *

"Gotta do somethin' about the painnnn! Them bones shouldn't be pokin' out like that. I know they shouldn't. Oh God it hurts. H-hurts real bad..."
"Sssh. Say nothing, Rusty. Just stay real quiet."

* * *

The dream fragmented, its edges blunted by the solemn song of mourning haunting the midnight air. He lay there, willing away the persistent skeins of a sleep so restless it had to have been sewn by the turbulent night around him. Disorientated, he struggled to regulate his breathing; wondered for a panic-stricken moment if he were having a heart attack, then eased the tension from his muscles and let the bed reclaim him into its folds. *Nothing wrong.* The thunder rumbled somewhere in the distance, snagged on the threads of lightning that flickered its impressions of daylight through the small window to his left.

Trish's peaceful breathing slowly drew him back to sleep and he listened to the combination of sounds as the numbing hands of exhaustion wrapped around his mind.

The night sang a lullaby through the latticework of the ozone-drenched air and thunder. And in that sweet distant latent music was the clackety-clack of a train.

The curtains danced.

Fading into sleep, Arnold smiled.

* * *

"Where's the music? Oh Holy Christ, where's my music?"
"Gone, Rusty. It's gone, but I can sing to you if you like."

* * *

Over breakfast, the bright light of morning already steaming the dew from a yard caressed by the night's rain, Arnold hunched over his coffee, seeing impossible things in the steam rising from the cup. The jigsaw remnants of a disturbed slumber floated around his brain, refusing to fit into anything even remotely rational. He blew the shredded clues away and sipped the scalding brew.

"Good morning, sweetie," Trish said as she came into the kitchen, lent a glow by the sun peering in the window. "You look tired." She set about boiling the kettle for tea. "Sleep okay?"

He shrugged, sipped. "Not nearly enough. Lotta noise last night."

"Was I snoring that much?"

He grinned but it was as weak as the tea his wife favored. "The storm kept waking me."

"Oh yes," she said, joining him at the table. "I thought I'd dreamed it." She fished the tea bag out of the cup and placed it on a small plate on the table. "By the way…who's Rusty?"

Slowly, Arnold lowered his cup. Black sparks coruscated across his vision. "What?"

"Last night, in your sleep you said 'Rusty's dying'. Anyone you know?"

"I don't think so. Just dreaming."

"Well I'm sorry you had such a rough night. You should try and grab a nap later today."

"Actually," he said, staring into the night-dark depths of his cup, "I was thinking of taking a walk back the trail."

She raised an eyebrow. "Oh? What for?"

"Just to see what's left before they tear the rest of it out."

Trish stared but said nothing, hoping perhaps her worry would reach him without the medium of words.

"It's been a while," Arnold said at last, tearing a ragged wound in the quiet.

"I don't think there's anything back there you need to see. Nothing but bad memories anyway." She looked at him then and he was filled with a wave of love for her he seldom took the time to bask in these days. He reached a hand out to her and she caught it midway between them and granted him an uneasy smile. Her skin, though wrinkled by years neither of them had felt slipping away from them, was soft and supple and cool. Arnold winked at her and she sighed. "Go then, but don't be too long."

"Back before you know it." He shoved the chair back and got to his feet with a groan.

"I mean it," Trish chided as he straightened with a wince. "Be careful. If you fall and hurt yourself I'm not carrying you home."

He scoffed. "Gee, thanks a bunch. Sometimes I wonder what I married you for."

He was ushered out on a wave of false outrage corrupted by laughter.

As soon as the door was shut behind him, he looked toward the sunlight, at the faint metallic gleaming between the copse of trees at the far end of the field behind his house and his smile vanished.

Nothing there anymore, he told himself but felt a chill all the same.

* * *

The sun pulled a blanket of clouds over its face and hushed out the warmth as Arnold pushed aside thickets he was sure hadn't been there before. Thorns pricked his skin, picked his pockets and tugged for his attention as he fought through to the rails. A low breeze ran along the abandoned sleepers, whispered along the remains of tracks and scattered old dust from the backbones of steel dinosaurs mired in the earth. In the hazy light, broken glass from tossed beer bottles twinkled in the dirt.

Off in the distance to his left, where the dark line of the Oakland bridge mimicked the horizon, he could see where the men had begun their work. From where he stood, he could follow the rails halfway to the bridge before the gaping craters of progress disrupted the normality of the view. Old tracks were now replaced by fresh treads—the muddy footprints of machinery.

A dull ache—as of improperly digested resignation—throbbed in the pit of Arnold's stomach. He blew air through his nose and looked away, turned to his right where the tracks curled away from him on a passage of bone-white gravel and out of sight around a wavering mass of vegetation.

They hadn't come this far yet, but they would. Soon.

He dropped to his haunches, a process that required more effort than he could ever remember, and closed his eyes. The wind strengthened, buffeting his coarse gray hair. He could smell the grass that sloped down from the hills to meet the trail.

His eyes opened and he focused on a patch of rust no bigger than his hand, an almost spherical tattoo of corrosion on the rail nearest him. A dime-sized shard of glass next to his shoe gleamed in the half-light and in the shadow of a moment he was submerged in remembrance.

Where are you? I can't see you. Please don't leave me here...
I'm right here, buddy, right here.
Thank God, oh thank God. Where's Mom? Is Mom here?
She's at home in bed, son. She doesn't know.
You should tell her. She should know. She-she should know I love her. Will you t-ell her for me?
I'm sure she already knows.
Will you tell her? P-please?
Stop that talk Rusty. You can tell her yourself when you get better.
Ugh... I'm dying. I'm not gonna get better. Help me. Don't let me die, please God in Heaven. Don't...let me die, Daddy. PLEASE!

He gasped, stood to the tune of his knees popping in synch with the starbursts of pain.

"Shit," he whispered, his sudden fear muted by the wind, making the tears swim in his eyes.

There came a rumbling.

He looked skyward, frowned. Silver-edged thunderheads rolled across the vacant canvas of the morning sky. The grass bowed beneath the weight of invisible fingers as the stormwind combed its way west. Then an involuntary and unwelcome shudder danced across his nerves with the realization that the rumbling was not from above, but from the left. From the bridge and the ruined tracks. A movement brought his attention back to the ground before him. A spent shotgun casing, crushed and worn, rattled atop the stones between the rails. The ground was vibrating beneath him.

Confused, he took a step back, crushing a long fringe of switch grass beneath the heel of his battered leather shoes. The air rushed down his throat, painting the insides of his mouth with the faintest trace of smoke. The rumbling, faint but most definitely there, continued.

He looked back to the narrowing track, to the gaping wounds in the earth and thought he saw the air shimmer; worried it might be his eyes or his mind finally giving way under the pressure. The track twisted in imaginary heat and Arnold turned away, turned his back on all of it and plunged back through the weeds and the snare of thorns, not caring when they snagged like hooks in his skin, not caring when the *shrickkk* of fabric tearing reached him through the partial deafness lent him by his own thunderous heartbeat. He was through and flailing and in view of his house when it happened, when the nightmare he thought abandoned rushed past, shrieking and moaning, ripping at the weeds, grinding earth and stone beneath itself as it tore through the wormhole man had created for it.

Arnold was knocked to the ground by the tremors and his own unwillingness to be struck and killed or…or worse. On his back, elbows dug into the ground, he saw it but did not, would not believe it was there. Even as madness suggested itself in cold whispers, he watched the rusted black leviathan whipping and snapping the branches from trees that had grown in its absence. The air swelled around the machine, a giant, scabrous beetle-like thing rushing to its burrow in a world that seemed to have forgotten the rules. A column of oily black smoke, tinged with glowing embers like flaming dice, corkscrewed back the way it had come.

It called to him. In the lullaby sound he had missed for fifty years, it called; sang a song of loneliness he more than understood. Trembling only a little less than the ground beneath him, his elbows dampened by the moist earth, he stared at the coal black darkness rushing through the trees, listened to the clackety-clack of the wheels pounding the rails, watched the world roll to accommodate its presence.

And then it was gone.

The wind died down, smothered the imagined sound of a final farewell note from the train. The ground ceased its quivering. In the wake of the train, a queer nothingness hung in tattered veils of quiet as far as Arnold could hear.

At last he found his breath, only to have it stolen again when he saw the crooked, rotted figure standing beyond the weeds, waving at him.

Don't let me die here, the grass whispered.

This time he screamed.

* * *

"I'm calling the doctor," Trish told him.

"I don't need a doctor. I'm fine."

"Don't be absurd. You're shaking like a leaf and sweating to beat the band. I'm calling Doctor Moore and you can complain all you like to him."

"Honestly I…"

"Honestly you can just keep your trap shut unless you're about to tell me what happened back at the tracks."

He sighed. "Nothing happened back there and I don't need a doctor. You're being ridiculous."

Trish scoffed. "No more ridiculous than you going back there clambering and climbing through the scrub like a man half your age." She picked up the phone and silenced him with a hand when he opened his mouth to protest. "It won't do you any harm to have a checkup anyway. How long has it been since the last one?"

He shrugged.

"Exactly."

Arnold watched her douse her inner fire as someone spoke on the other end of the phone. She smiled at the voice and chuckled at what was undoubtedly the old doctor's wry wit. Sitting at the table, he struggled to bury the dark coiling inside his gut, tried desperately to push away what the hallucination at the tracks had been designed to make him remember.

Hallucination. Yes, of course it was. But that didn't explain the acrid taste on his tongue, the furious trembling in his aching knees or the ringing in his ears which sounded more and more like a summons the longer it remained.

He felt as if his own train were circling a rusted track around his brain, looking for the overgrown tunnel wherein remembrance lay. He swallowed sourly and shook his head. There was nothing to remember.

Nothing except the night your father died.

He jerked in his seat as if stabbed, his knee thumping painfully against the underside of the table. His cup jumped, sloshing coffee over the rim and leaking like muddied blood down the sides. Trish glanced at him, frowned and went back to her conversation.

Arnold took a deep breath and ran a hand over his scalp.

His father.

The tracks.

His father.

The accident.

Like a lock turning, the train burst through the undergrowth and shot through the tunnel, the massive main light illuminating everything, shattering the dark.

"Oh God," he whispered into a white-knuckled fist.

His skin crawled. His eyes widened.

The Number 121 to Pennsylvania.

* * *

Forty minutes later, Doctor Moore blustered his way into the house at the head of an angry wind. Dry leaves and the severed heads of newly mown grass skidded in ahead of him until he shut the door, cutting off their dance in mid song. The tall, frighteningly thin man straightened, his hat almost touching the low kitchen ceiling, and smiled a mouthful of gleaming teeth. Silver hairs poked out from beneath the brim of his hat and he displayed two sweeping wings of fringe when he raised the hat to Trish. "My dear," he said. She grinned and leaned back against the range, arms folded above her apron.

Moore's hollow, startlingly blue but sunken eyes found Arnold and he quickly approached the table. He took the chair opposite and set his black leather bag down next to his feet. "So," he said, "you've been off adventuring and scaring the wits out of that foxy woman of yours, eh?"

Arnold shrugged. "This is really all for nothing. I just went for a walk."

"Uh-huh." Moore nodded pointedly. "And decided to rest in some brambles, right?"

Arnold looked at the myriad red lines on the backs of his hands. "It's overgrown. I wanted to go see how they were coming along with the railway track, so I had to cross some thorns."

The doctor stared for a moment, then swiveled in his chair to face Trish. A smile spread across his face. "Do you know Millie Farrow at the post office in Harperville never quite got over your husband? I mean, he really broke her heart and not a day goes by where she doesn't talk about him as if he were God's gift to women. Now what exactly do you suppose it is about him that makes women swoon over him like that?"

Arnold frowned. Trish laughed. "It isn't his sense anyway. I thought when he retired he'd be taking it easy. But no," she threw her hands up in the air in exasperation, "he has to become Indiana Jones and scare me half to death."

They both looked at him and he shifted uncomfortably, felt a tremor ripple through him.

"Patricia tells me you came home shaking and in a cold sweat. It could be a fever. Did it come on you all of a sudden?" He raised his bag, set it atop his knees and opened the gold clasp.

"I just got out of breath. It's a long walk. I guess I just underestimated the distance. You know how it is when you're old; you forget your limitations."

"Amen," Trish chimed in.

"Uh-huh," said Moore, as if he hadn't heard at all. "Any pains in your chest?"

"No."

He raised a thermometer and shook it in front of him, then offered it to Arnold. When he didn't take it, Trish crossed the kitchen and snatched it from the doctor's hand. "Open," she commanded and with a sigh, Arnold sat back and obeyed. She slid the thermometer beneath his tongue.

As he sat brooding, Moore watched him with interest. "You know, Arnie...I may be completely out of line for asking this but I genuinely don't understand something about you. Now feel free to tell me to shut my yap and I will but..."

I may very well do that, thought Arnold.

"...I can't figure, what with your history of trains and all, why you'd want to go back there so much. Your wife tells me you've gone back to those rails at least once every week since you retired from the post office. I mean, it's not my aim to drag up bad memories but you lost your father there, didn't you?"

After a moment in which only the clock over the stove made a sound, Arnold nodded.

"He was hit by a train."

Again Arnold nodded, his face stark white.

Not any old train, he thought. *A ghost train. The same one he used to tell me about when I was a kid. It came out of nowhere and took him away.* He almost dared to speak his thoughts aloud, but was afraid that doing so would only feed their suspicion that he had started to crumble.

"Then why go back there?" Moore asked, looking genuinely perplexed. Trish came and retrieved the thermometer, gave it a cursory glance and said to the doctor: "Because he likes to torture himself. At least he doesn't have a fever."

Moore nodded, then fished a stethoscope from the bag before placing it back down on the floor. "Let's see how the ticker is." He stood up, his scarecrow-like figure casting an even thinner shadow over Arnold, and hunkered down next to him. His knees crackled. "Raise your shirt for me."

Arnold paused, then tugged his shirt up and watched as the surprise registered on the doctor's face. To Moore's credit, the look passed quickly as he decided the intricate network of thick scars and puckered skin written across Arnold's chest were not his concern. Not today, at least. Trish sighed. Trish, who had traced those scars with her fingers, with her lips for an eternity and knew they were as much a part of him as his heart.

The doctor placed the stethoscope to Arnold's chest. "Take a deep breath." He listened. "Okay, now let it go. I gotta tell you old boy, from the look of you and from what Patricia has told me about these inexplicable excursions, I'd have to say you're wearing yourself out. Breathe in. Okay, and out." He unhooked the instrument from his ears and sighed. "You need rest, Arnie. Thankfully there's nothing seriously wrong with you apart from a terminal case of stubbornness. Rest for a couple of days; lay off the long walks and you'll be good as new." He turned to Trish and winked. "Millie will be relieved."

As he was readying himself to leave, Arnold muttered something.

Both Trish and Moore turned to look at him. "What was that?" the doctor asked.

"Answers. You asked me why I go back there. It's for answers. Nothing about the night my father died was right. I managed to forget for so long, but now it's coming back, the sheer, unbridled *wrongness* of what happened that night. I go there to try and remember it all, every detail, to see if I can make it right in my head."

No one spoke for a few moments. Trish came to Arnold and put her hands on his shoulders, began to knead the tension from the muscles there. At the door, Moore gave a somber nod. "I understand. We all have our ghosts. But killing yourself won't help put them to rest you know."

The old doctor tipped his hat and fought the claws of the wind to keep the door held open. Then he was gone.

Trish ran a cool hand along Arnold's cheek. "Will you be all right, sweetie?"

He offered her a weak grin. "Eventually."

* * *

"Son, can you hear me?"

"Yessss...so...tired."

"No, no. Listen to me goddamn it. Stay awake. I'll sing your favorite song to you but only for a little while. The train's coming. You know those stories I used to tell you about the No. 121 to Pennsylvania, Rusty?

Yes. S-some of them.

Well tonight you're going to see it for yourself.

How?

Faith, Rusty. I called it...

* * *

...with faith.

The hollow moan of the train began in the dream but outside of it, it was even stronger. As Arnold's eyes searched the room, a shape woven from darkness walked past the bedroom window, momentarily stealing the moonlight and slashing a grotesque shadow on the wall. Arnold watched. Waited. And was not afraid.

He swallowed, turned on his side and looked at Trish. She was in deep sleep, oblivious to the murmuring of a distant train, her hair backlit by the bleached light of the moon against the wall.

For a moment he considered waking her. After all, scarcely in his life had he had anything so important to share with her, but the more he watched her, her mouth slightly open, the sweet smell of her as she lay sleeping, a soft drift of silver hair obscuring one eye, he decided instead to write it down. She would understand. But first he had to find the photograph, to make it as clear to her as the dream—directed by the capable hands of his unraveling memory—had made it for him.

* * *

He had never been here at night. The rain-dampened thorns were crystal snakes in the moonlight and the broken glass sparkled like ice between the gleaming rails. The wind hushed him, demanding he listen to the rumble somewhere further down the track, from the gaping holes perhaps, of the Number 121 to Pennsylvania as it drew nearer.

The cold ran its fingers over his skin and he hugged himself. Waited patiently, hoping Trish wouldn't wake too soon, find him gone and follow. But somehow he didn't think that would be allowed to happen. A tear spilled from his right eye and he quickly sleeved it away. He could not think of her now, could not think of what he was doing, or what he was leaving behind. He could do nothing but stand here by the rails and wait.

A short time later, a new wave of cold brushed against his arm and he jerked out of a reverie he hadn't realized had taken hold of him. Without looking, for it was better not to, he sensed the figure at his side.

"Do you remember now?" it said and Arnold cleared his throat.

"Most of it. I remember the trade. I remember seeing you die. I remember you stayed with me and you kept me from sleeping."

His father sighed, a hollow sound, and still Arnold would not look. "But do you remember what happened to *you*?"

Arnold shook his head. "I think so."

"The music?"

"Yes. I remember that. It was Elvis. *Heartbreak Hotel.* You sang it to me after I lost the radio." He paused. "And I remember the pain. It was awful."

"You remember the train?"

Arnold felt the tears returning and crammed his knuckles to his lips.

"What were you doing up here?" his father said.

"I was mad at you. You wouldn't let me take Katy Arden to the Lookout, wouldn't let me go anywhere. I came up here with the radio and…"

Down the tracks, the train sounded its horn. They could see it now, the light, a star blazing through the murk toward them.

"Go on."

The ground trembled; the air began to swell.

"I ran beside the train. I…I got sucked underneath it." "When I found you, there wasn't a scratch on your face. I thought…I thought you had fallen over until I opened your shirt. You should have been dead."

Arnold sniffed, wiped his nose. The night trembled. Frightened birds transformed into fleeing silhouettes against the sky. The chill deepened.

"You were fading, dying on me. I was furious. Furious at me, at you, at everything and I called it. I called that goddamn train even though I only half-believed in the thing, only half-believed those stories the guys told at the cookouts and campfires and taverns. Except I knew at the back of it all it would come. When I watched the blood shooting from your heart and screamed for it…I knew it would come and I knew I could save you."

"By killing yourself." Arnold wept and dropped to his knees in the grass beside the track. "Jesus. I told myself it was a dream, that I hadn't been there at all."

The rattling began to ebb away as gears ground together, a screech shattered the cold hazy air and the train, a magnificent horror of rust and twisted metal, emerged from the specters of smoke it had coughed into the air.

A hand fell on his shoulder. "We have to get going. We have to put the pieces back where they belong."

The train shrieked to a halt before them, then hissed and spat, clanked and groaned as it waited. The blackness of it fought with the moon for dominance as Arnold stood, took his father's hand and, in the swollen shadow of the train, followed him up the uneven steps of the Number 121.

* * *

The following morning, Trish woke alone to a sunrise that settled like molten lava on her windowsill. It was not odd for Arnold to be up before her, but when she didn't find him in the kitchen, a knot of worry formed in her throat. But just as she had resolved to walk back through the field to see if he was down by the railroad track, she noticed the note on the table.

It was a sheet of her own rose-colored notepaper and written in Arnold's inimitable scrawl was:

WE'LL BE BACK AROUND THIS WAY SOMEDAY.
LISTEN FOR ME

LOVE ARNIE

Clipped to the note was a color picture snipped from a high school yearbook long lost of a freckled teenager with a shock of unruly red hair, grinning toothily at the camera.

Beneath it was written:

Arnold "Rusty" O' Connor
Hayes High School, 1956

Trish sat at the table and wept for Arnold; wept as loneliness settled on her shoulders like the dust motes falling in the morning sunlight. She had known he was lost by the feeling in her chest as soon as her eyes opened and he was gone. She had known when she'd woken in the night to hear the most peculiar sound carried to her window, a sound they had grown to think of as alien.

The sound of a train.

MR. GOODNIGHT

The field behind the house had been overgrown for months, alive with grasshoppers, rabbits and a whole host of hidden creatures.

When Kevin's dad finally got a day off, he borrowed Jed Taylor's tractor and industrial mower, donned his ragged work clothes and set out to conquer the army of weeds.

Days later, the high grass little more than golden stubble, Kevin and his best friend Joey emerged from the cool shadows of the garage, shovels in hand, solemn purpose etched on their youthful faces.

The sun was high in the sky. Hot work lay ahead, but neither the effort nor the heat could dissuade two boys, free of school and hungry for adventure, from their task.

"What if we find buried treasure?" Joe asked, his eyes bright with the excitement.

"What do you mean?"

"Well, would you tell your parents?"

"Why wouldn't I? They'd probably have to help me lift it into the house."

"Yeah, but then you'd have to share it with them. Or worse, they might take it and put it into the bank and not let you spend it until you're a grownup. That'd suck. But it happens. My cousin Ron—you know, the kid who visits us at Christmas?—well, his grandmother died last summer and left him a lot of money, I mean, *a lot*. Enough to buy ten of those electric scooters at least! But his parents won't let him have it until he's eighteen! That stinks."

"Yeah, you're right" Kevin said, thoughtful. "Maybe we could hide it."

"Or bury it!"

"Don't be dumb, Joey. What's the point in digging it up just to bury it again?"

"Well, no one would find it then, would they? We could bury it someplace we know we'll find it again."

Kevin smiled. They passed beneath the shadows of the large sprawling walnut tree in the middle of the yard and paused for a moment, shovels over their shoulders like rifles. The slightest hint of a breeze cooled the sheen of sweat on their brows and they welcomed it.

After a moment of stomping a furrow in the grass most certainly left in the wake of a gopher, Joey sighed. "Do you think they'll ever find Toby Roberts?"

Kevin scoffed. "Dunno. But I sure hope not."

"Yeah. He's a jerk. I wonder where he went though. It's kinda weird isn't it?"

"Suppose. I bet he just ran away. Probably got in trouble and hopped on a train."

"You think?"

"Sure."

"But they said he didn't take any clothes or food or anything."

"Yeah right. Toby'll steal clothes and food off some poor kid he meets along the way to wherever he's going. That's what bullies do."

"I guess. Hey, at least he won't be picking on *us* anymore, right?"

"Right."

"Cause I'm all wedgied *out!*" Joey said and they moved on out of the shade and down to the bottom of the yard, where the remains of Mom's vegetable garden stood like unkempt green hair.

"Yikes," Joey said, laughing. "How come your Dad didn't cut *that* down? It looks like a jungle!"

Kevin smiled. "He wanted to but Mom wouldn't let him. She says there's still some good in it. Thinks there might be some potatoes or something the deer and rabbits didn't get. Dad wasn't happy about it, but Mom gave him one of her looks and he left it alone."

"Maybe we could hide the treasure in *there?*" Toby suggested and they both laughed.

Just past the nightmarish tangle of weeds and vines, the yard opened out onto the field. The golden earth seemed to catch the sun and hold it, making both boys squint.

Kevin kicked the earth and nodded. "We should dig here."

"Why here?"

"Why not?"

"Why can't I pick where we dig?"

"It doesn't matter!"

"Sure it does," Joey protested. "I know what you'll say if you pick the spot and we find treasure. You'll say you picked the spot so you get more treasure than me."

Kevin clucked his tongue, a habit he couldn't remember picking up but which was driving his parents crazy, especially given that it only occurred whenever he was asked to do something he didn't want to.

"So what if *you* pick the spot? You'll do the same thing!"

Joey mulled this over. Then: "Okay, how about we ask your Dad to pick a spot. That way no one gets a bigger share."

"What'll we tell him we're doing? If we say digging for treasure, then *he'll* want some."

"Tell him we're trying to build a pond."

"Nah, then he'll want to help. He'll probably come back with a big bulldozer or one of those trucks with a great big shovel on front."

"How about your mother then?"

Kevin thought for a moment, hands on his hips, the shovel lying at his feet and then smiled.

Joey followed his gaze. "What are you looking at?"

Kevin beamed. "Mia!"

"Your dog?"

"Yeah, c'mon!" Kevin started racing back toward the garage. Joey, puzzled, followed close behind.

"How is your dog going to help?"

"I'll show you! It's perfect!" Kevin said and skidded to a halt as they reached the concrete apron where Mia, his Black Labrador was lounging in the heat, tongue hanging from the corner of her mouth.

"I think she's dead."

Kevin shook his head. "She always looks like that when she's asleep. C'mon. I'll hold her, you take off her chain."

"Okay, but I don't understand what you're doing. Is she going to dig the hole?"

"No, c'mon, untie her."

The dog raised its head and regarded the boys with disinterest. A single wag of her tail in greeting was all she managed before lowering her head.

"Why do you keep her chained up the whole time anyway? She can't even run. It's mean."

"I know," Kevin said. "But when those new people moved in across the way Mia went nuts and tried to bite them all. The guy said he'd shoot the dog if we didn't tie him up." He stroked the dog's belly as he spoke and the dog rolled over to accommodate him. "Man, that guy was mad. He came over here shouting and cussing. Made my dad real angry. My dad said the dog had a right to run free and that Mia had been pooping right where the guy's kitchen table was before they built the house there. I nearly laughed at that but I was afraid someone'd get mad at me."

Joey unclipped the steel catch from the hook buried deep in the ground, so that only the short stretch of chain in his hand was attached to the dog. This would serve as a leash to keep the animal from bolting.

"It's not fair," he said. "Dog must be bored out of her brains."

"Yeah. You got her? Okay, let's go."

Sensing she'd been untied from her moorings, the dog ran, almost jerking Joey's arm out of its socket and he yelped as she dragged him back down the yard. Kevin doubled over with laughter as Joey cried out for help.

They met in the field, Joey leaning back at an impossible angle as the dog wheezed and coughed and tried to pull away from him. "Take your...stupid dog, will ya?" he pleaded, sweat dripping down his strained face.

Kevin took the leash from him. "Mia, come!" he said and the dog instantly turned and padded back to him.

"Aw man," Joey said, chagrined. "Why didn't you tell me she did that?"

"She probably wouldn't have listened to you."

"So what did we bring her down here for?"

Mia sniffed at the shovels and began to circle, breaking the pattern and doubling back as she followed a scent, huffing at the earth, then abruptly changing course.

Joey frowned. "What's she doing?"

"Watch."

The dog tugged on the chain and Kevin moved forward until Mia stopped and squatted.

Joey's eyes widened. "Aw man! That's gross!"

The dog leered at him as she voided her bowels. When she was done, Kevin led her to the nearest tree and tethered her there, where she watched for a moment, then lay down and dozed in the shade.

Kevin picked up his shovel and motioned for Joey to do the same.

He indicated the curly brown turds lying in the dirt. "*That's* where we dig," he said.

* * *

"So does this mean the mutt gets a share of the treasure?" Joey asked, pausing for breath and squinting at the sun. His hair was damp with sweat, hands dirty from pulling out clumps of earth too heavy for the shovel to handle.

They had been digging for an hour, their shirts pasted to their skin. The hole was wide, but not as deep as they'd hoped. Still, it was a respectable crater and they had no intention of giving up on it yet.

"She'd probably buy a car and drive somewhere where there aren't any neighbors."

Joey wiped the sweat from his eyes and drove the shovel down into the hole with all his might. At the instant of impact, he farted and immediately looked at Kevin for a reaction.

"Aw, *skunk!*" Kevin said and they both broke into laughter, loud enough to send a pair of blue jays shrieking out of their perch atop the walnut tree. Any attempt to stop the hilarity for the next few minutes only made it worse, so they dropped the shovels and staggered around until their bellies ached.

When they finally caught their breath and the laughter faded to contented smiles, Kevin scooted close to the hole. It was deep enough now that it would come up to his knees if he stood in it.

"Maybe we won't find anything," Joey croaked, a hand still clamped across his stomach from laughing so hard.

Kevin adjusted his position until he was on his hands and knees and brought his face closer to the hole.

"What is it?"

"I don't know but we should keep digging."

"You see something in there?" Joey crawled over and tried to see what had captured Kevin's attention.

"No. I don't see anything, but I have a feeling something's down there."

"A feeling? I have a feeling you've been out in the sun too long. Next thing you'll be yarfing your guts up all over the place."

Kevin looked up and grinned. "Better than farting."

They got to their feet, grabbed their shovels and resumed their attack on the earth.

Some time later, with the sun crawling westward through an unblemished blue veil, as the shadows of evening poked their heads out from beneath the trees and tested the air, something happened.

The hole was now deep enough and wide enough for both boys to stand in it up to their waists. A hill of dirt sat a few feet away, punctuated by bits of broken bottles, shredded plastic bags and rocks.

Kevin lifted his shovel and brought it down where the hole narrowed at the bottom. The earth gave way easily beneath the shovel.

Far too easily.

As he slowly withdrew the tool, he saw the earth crumble away into darkness that oozed like oil, staining the dirt and lapping at the sides of the hole in the wake of the disturbance the shovel had caused. He stood there, overcome by a sudden unpleasant sensation deep within him that what he had discovered shouldn't have been discovered at all.

"Hey, Kev. You getting tired?" Joey asked as he prepared to heave his own shovel back into the hole. He stopped when he saw the black liquid at the bottom. "What's that?"

"I don't know."

"Maybe it's oil! Maybe we struck oil, Kev! Man, if we did then we're rich!"

But Kevin couldn't bring himself to share Joey's enthusiasm and couldn't understand why. It was just black stuff. Nothing special. Probably oil. But for some unknown reason, he knew that it was *not* oil, *not* nothing special. *Not* just black stuff.

And worse, he felt he had done something incredibly, terribly wrong by finding it.

"Kev," said Joey, dropping his shovel and shaking him by the shoulders. "We gotta go tell your Dad! I think we found oil! We'll be millionaires, Kev! Millionaires!"

Kevin tried to smile and wasn't sure if it worked or not. He couldn't take his eyes from the hole and the black liquid slopping around down there.

Joey ceased his happy dancing and came around to Kevin's side. "Are you okay?"

"It's not oil."

"How do you know?"

"I just do."

"Yeah, right. You're ten years old. You don't know if it's oil or not. You're just trying to make me believe it isn't so I'll go home and then you'll have it all to yourself."

"No," Kevin said. "I'm not. I don't know how, but I know it isn't oil."

"Then what is it?"

"I don't know."

"Maybe we should get some of it out and put it into a jar or something. We can show your dad and see what he thinks it is? You know? Cuz I think it's oil. Really."

"It's not oil. I don't wanna touch it either. Let's just cover it back up."

Joey looked appalled. "After all the work we put into it? And what happens if it is oil? What happens if we forget about it and some other kid finds oil around here? What then? How many electric scooters can you buy on *your* pocket money, huh?"

But Kevin wasn't convinced. In fact, he thought going any closer to that black stuff than they already were was a terrifying idea. Not knowing why he should feel that way frightened him all the more and he backed away from the hole.

It wasn't so warm anymore. His skin rippled with a sudden chill, even though the sun was still clear and bright. He gripped his shovel tighter.

"C'mon, Kev. What's the matter with you? It's just some gunk!"

Without a word, Kevin dug into the hill of dirt and began to fill the hole.

"Hey, don't!" Joey said and put out a hand to stop him.

And down in the hole something grabbed Kevin's shovel.

"Oh God," he cried and stumbled backward, his feet tangling, sending him sprawling into the high grass of his mother's vegetable garden.

"Kev!"

Green darkness.

Grasshoppers sang their dismay at the intrusion and hopped across Kevin's face, danced on his lips and hid in his hair. Mosquitoes rose to drain his blood as tiny winged beetles mapped out his skin. A small stick, once used to mark the boundary of the garden, stabbed into his thigh and he moaned, batted away the insects and grabbed the hand that burst through the overgrowth.

He was out in the air, in the light, and sobbing. He dropped to his knees, wincing at the stones that bruised them. Mia barked and pulled her leash taut as she struggled to get to him. "It's all right," he told her and after a moment she whined and returned to her spot beneath the tree. This time however, she did not sleep, but watched him.

"Wait, Kev. I'll go get your Dad," Joey said, panic thrumming in his tone. He started to leave but Kevin raised his hand.

"No. I'm...I'm okay."

"What happened? You scared me to death!"

Kevin cleared away his tears and looked toward the hole. The shovel was sticking straight up as if lodged in the earth, but he knew better.

"We need...to fill in the hole," he said and knew by the look on Joey's face that he would not argue.

"Okay, but this sucks. All our hard work and..." He trailed off, and retrieved his shovel from where he had dropped it to help Kevin.

Kevin slowly rose and brushed himself off. The cold feeling seemed stitched to his bones; he couldn't shake it.

It got worse when he noticed Joey, facing the hole, back turned to him, standing motionless with shovel in hand.

A tangy, cloying smell like rotten apples wafted from the hole.

"What's wrong?"

Joey didn't answer.

A slight breeze ruffled his hair. It was the only movement.

"Joey, what's wrong?"

Joey trembled.

Mia started to bark again.

"Answer me!"

"Did you see me?"

Mia stopped barking and sat, head hung low, eyes forward as if chastened by an angry master.

Kevin looked toward the house, then at the field around him, searching for the speaker. But even before he heard it again, he knew it was coming from Joey, even though it was not his voice. It was an adult voice, a man's voice, hollow and unfriendly.

And now he was paralyzed with terror.

"Did you see me? Was it you who ran and told?"

Kevin shook his head, tried to back away but his legs wouldn't move. "I..."

"Was it you who told them where to find me, where to find me and the child? Did you tattletale on poor Mr. Goodnight?"

Joey continued to tremble and Kevin was struck by the immediate need to help him. But how?

"Joey?" he called in a feeble voice. The sun had moved behind the trees on the far side of the field, peering through them with a solitary red eye and making a shuddering silhouette of the boy at the hole.

"Poor form," the Joey-thing said, but it sounded amused. *"Not very sporting at all. I was merely trying to fix the little girl. She had something wrong with her head you see, and if those men had given me the chance I might have told them that that was all I was up to. Simply trying to tie together the broken strands in her messed up little head. There's no sin in that, surely? No sin in cracking open the egg to inspect the yolk, hmm? I would certainly have returned her to her parents when I had made sure I'd glued her back together. Where's the harm in that? And they acted like I was a monster, like I was violating the poor thing. How horrid! No, you see their narrow minds could never understand what I was trying to do. They thought*

it wicked to split a skull open in order to release the horrors, and yet—"

"Joey!" Kevin shrieked, fresh tears blurring the quivering silhouette of his best friend.

"—they had no trouble splitting open mine."

There was no sound at all now. Nature had hushed itself, perhaps sensing something abroad that shouldn't be. The sun was a crimson-eyed voyeur, the breeze like held breath.

"Who are you?" Kevin ventured, even though his mind screamed at him to flee.

"Mr. Goodnight," the Joey-thing replied. *"And you are Kevin. But what of your friend here? He seems to have landed himself in a bit of a predicament doesn't he? He seems to be in a bit of a quandary. Shall I fix him for you?"*

"Nooo," Kevin moaned through his sobs. "No, please…"

"Shall I crack open his skull and see what has gone awry?"

"Please…just let him go!"

"Hush now, Kevin. Didn't you run and tell on me? Didn't you lead them to me all those years ago?"

The acrid stench of apples grew stronger.

"I don't know what you're talking about. I swear!"

"Come now, we all have our sins to confess. Tell me yours!"

"If I do, will you let Joey go?"

"No, but I promise to take extra special care putting him back together."

Kevin ran before he was sure he still could. A scream sailing from his mouth, he batted branches aside and ran, stumbled, ran, fell, until his feet hit concrete and his father's arms were around him and all he could hear were his own cries and Mia barking.

He whimpered, but would not speak, would not tell. Couldn't. Not as long as the fear boiled within him that as soon as he opened his mouth it would not be his voice that came out.

"Kevin, what happened? Where's Joey?"

Mr. Goodnight took him, he wanted to say but pleaded with his eyes for his father to understand instead. *Mr. Goodnight took him to crack open his skull and peer inside.*

He was shivering violently, his vision blurred with tears. His father grabbed his shoulders and held him away so he could see his face.

"Kevin, what's wrong? What's going on? Did something happen to you? To Joey? Did someone hurt you?"

Kevin nodded, choked on a sob that drowned out even the thought of words.

"Okay look. You were in the field, right? I'm going to go check it out."

No!

"You go call your mother. Tell her to bring the phone with her. We may need to call the police."

Oh God no, don't! He'll get you!

He made a grab for his father's shirt but the big man was already past him and stalking across the yard. Down in the field, Mia continued to bark, a high yelp of despair.

Kevin moved slowly up the porch steps, watching his father approach the spot where they'd been digging, the evening light sending lithe shadows sprawling across the grass. The door opened and his mother, drying her hands on a dishcloth emerged and looked from Kevin's tear-swollen eyes to his father.

"What's going on?" she asked, her voice high with concern. "Why are you crying?"

He shook his head and pointed out at the field.

"Where's Joey? Kevin, talk to me? What's wrong?"

But he couldn't tell her, couldn't make her understand, so he hugged her instead and wept openly against her apron as she stroked his hair.

It seemed like an eternity before his father returned.

"There's no one down there," he said as he mounted the porch steps. "Just a big empty hole, and of course Mia, who's going crazy. I'm going to call Joey's parents, see if he went home. If not, we gotta call the cops. Something isn't right."

They won't find him, Kevin thought as he was led into the house. *Not now, not ever.*

"Kevin," his mother said once they were inside, "why won't you tell us what happened?"

"He hasn't said anything since he came running up to the house," Dad said, picking up the phone. "Best leave him alone until we find out what's going on. Get him some cocoa or something."

Kevin sat at the table and listened to his father speaking urgently into the phone.

The silence thickened.

And then sirens and lights pierced the burgeoning dark.

* * *

They put him to bed though he knew he'd never sleep.

Beneath his pillow was a hammer he'd taken from the garage. It pressed against his head, a constant reminder of both its presence and the reason for it. He wondered if he would even have a chance to reach for it when the time came.

The sounds of garbled voices on police radios, car doors slamming and dogs barking drifted up through the open window as he stared at the cracks in his ceiling. Red and blue flashes of light sailed across his wall, turning innocent shadows into twitching malevolent things.

Joey's gone. Grief settled like a stone in his belly. It couldn't be true, shouldn't be true, but it was and he knew it. He knew no matter how much he tried to pretend he was dreaming the reality was that the glorious summer had, without warning, coughed its darkness out to swallow them all.

And that darkness, that seething evil thing they'd uncovered in the field was still there, a real live bogeyman stalking the night.

Of course, they hadn't released him into the world, he realized. It wasn't their fault that Mr. Goodnight was out there now. After all, children had been disappearing long before today.

No. Mr. Goodnight hadn't been trapped under the dirt.

He'd been sleeping.

They had uncovered his hiding place.

And he would be back, Kevin knew. The security his parents provided, that safety he had always taken for granted was gone now, torn to shreds by a simple day's digging.

No one could save him now.

And as if the thought had summoned him, the bedroom door creaked open and his father, hands stained with dirt, eyes dull and frightened, entered the room and stood looking helpless down at him.

He moved around so that he was standing next to Kevin. Red light flashed across his features, ageing them.

"I'm sorry," he said.

Kevin wanted to tell him so very badly that he knew, that he didn't blame his father. Grownups had no idea bogeymen were real and slept in the dirt. The only ones who knew were the victims, and those who'd escaped to live another hour or another day before the bogeyman returned to quiet them.

But he said nothing, only nodded slightly.

His father sat on the bed and put a hand on Kevin's chest. The light showed a glimmer of tears in his eyes.

"I don't know what happened to you today, Kevin, but I'm so sorry I wasn't there to stop it."

It's okay, Dad.

"And the police are doing everything they can to find Joey."

There's nothing they can do.

"It would really help if you could tell them what happened. Where he went or…or…who took him."

I wish I could tell them too, but I'm afraid and I don't think they'd believe me.

A sudden strange scent filled the room. Kevin's eyes widened. His throat went dry. Panic fluttered like a trapped bird in his chest. He touched his father's hand.

Hands stained with dirt…

No!

His father's face turned slowly, slowly toward him.

The shadows were thick and danced in the scarlet light.

He might have been smiling.

Oh no no no!

The room smelled like rotten apples.

Not my Dad!

In an instant, Kevin was on his knees face to face with his father, the sheets tangled around his ankles, the hammer gripped tightly in one bone-white hand. He raised it over his head, watched the shadows slip away from Dad's face. Saw the eyes widen, the skin drain of blood. Any minute now he would change and then it would be too late.

Too late.

Kevin wailed, grief, agony, and horror raging out of him as he swung the hammer.

It was over rather quickly.

Afterward, Kevin breathed huge gasps of air, the tears hot on his cheeks as he stared in disbelief down at the body on the floor, the face no longer recognizable as anyone he had ever known.

A comic strip speech bubble of blood grew ever wider around the shattered skull in the pulsating light.

And his mother was standing in the doorway, a ghost miming horror as the blood ran down the hammer and trickled over his fingers. Then screaming as she stumbled across the room and dropped to her knees next to the bed, her hands fluttering around the man on the floor, afraid to touch but desperate to hold him, to be sure he was alive.

Which of course he was not.

She looked up at her son still kneeling on the bed, his face tattooed with his father's blood.

Her lower lip trembled as she struggled to make the words come out: "Why Kevin…why?"

Kevin shook his head. *He wasn't Daddy! I know he wasn't! It was Mr. Goodnight! He tricked me! Oh God, I'm so sorry! Help me!*

But when he spoke, it was not his voice that came out.

"Hush now. I'll fix you right up, my dear," he said, helpless to do anything but watch the hammer rise.

EMPATHY

Will Chambers heard the muffled thump in the upstairs bedroom and sighed. He'd hoped his absence wouldn't wake Melanie but here she came now, trudging down the stairs, eyes narrowed at the light, auburn hair tousled, dressed in nothing but an old LAPD T-shirt and a pair of black silk panties embossed with roses. Ordinarily the sight of her--long pale slim legs, unhindered breasts pushing against the material of the shirt--would have been enough to arouse him and force the worries from the forefront of his mind.

But not now.

Dear God, not now.

He watched her shuffle to the table and yawn as she withdrew a chair and plopped down into it. "What's wrong?" she asked, stifling another yawn.

He shrugged, offered her a feeble smile. "Couldn't sleep."

"Me neither."

He suppressed a laugh at that. When he'd left her in bed, she'd been snoring softly. As always, his absence had roused her, like a silent alarm.

"You must be working too hard," he said, and took another drag on his cigarette. Smoke threaded its way upward, only to be shredded by the frantic whirl of the fan. He followed the nicotine with a slurp of coffee and sighed.

"Maybe, but what's *your* excuse?" Melanie asked again, crossing her legs and playing with a lock of her hair, her eyes filled with the memory of sleep. He knew she hadn't meant her words to sound as snide and accusatory as he took them. He'd lost his job at the *Delaware Gazette* almost a month ago now, replaced by some hotshot young kid who'd come straight from Penn State armed with 'fresh and innovative ideas,' as Will's editor had put it. So far, Melanie hadn't confronted him about his prolonged unemployment, or when he might start taking steps to rectify the matter. In truth, he was afraid to tell her his plan. Writing was all he was good at, and the thought of working as a salesman or security guard disturbed him--not because of the work involved, but because of how stifling it would be to his creativity. What he wanted to do was write a novel, but he had not yet summoned the requisite courage to announce to Melanie that she would have to support them while he tried his hand at it.

"I couldn't stop thinking, that's all. You know how it is sometimes. Stupid brain won't shut down long enough for me to get to sleep."

She nodded in sympathy. "Yeah, I know. Did you try reading for a while?"

"Yeah. I grabbed that horror novel you'd left on the nightstand. Talk about the absolutely worst possible book to choose on a sleepless night."

She grinned, exhaustion still clinging to her face like a well-worn mask, and spoke as if addressing a child. "Aw, did it scare you, honey?"

No, I was scared to begin with, he almost said, but returned her smile instead. "It was a little on the violent side."

"It's a horror novel. What do you expect?"

He stubbed out his cigarette, clucked his tongue when the air from the fan encouraged it to stay alight and mashed it until tobacco erupted from the filter.

"I think it's out," Melanie said. Her hand slid across the table to rest on his forearm. "What's the matter? Tell me." He offered her another shrug, but she squeezed his arm. "You've been walking around with a frown all week. Even when I say something funny enough to get a laugh out of you, it sounds like you're doing it to keep me satisfied. Something's bothering you and you know I'll plague you until you tell me what it is."

He slid another cigarette from the gaping box by his left hand. "It's the video."

"The one you watched on the Internet?"

He grimaced around the cigarette and nodded.

"I can't understand why this is staying with you," Melanie said, rubbing her fingertips along his wrist and across his palm. It tickled, but Will was afraid if he told her so she'd take her hand away, and right now he desperately needed her touch, needed to feel the blood, the *life*, ever so softly pulsating beneath her skin. "I mean, it was a terrible thing to see, but in fifteen years of reporting for the *Gazette*, I'm sure you've seen worse—"

"No I haven't," he said, with a bitter smile. "I've seen accident victims, murder victims, all the awful aftermaths. This wasn't an aftermath. I've never seen anything even remotely like that."

She sighed, leaned forward so her elbows were on the table. "It'll go away eventually," she said softly. "You just need to get it out of your system."

"Maybe, but what I saw on that screen isn't the worst of it."

Melanie said nothing, but waited for him to continue.

He swallowed the fear that seemed to force the words out of him and cleared his throat. "Those people...that woman who died...who they killed."

Melanie nodded somberly.

"When they...when I close my eyes, I see what they did to her, in more detail than they showed on that tape."

Stop now, he thought in one dazzling, desperate moment of panic. *Don't go any further with this. You'll scare her.*

Melanie's hand found his fingers, squeezed them tight.

Will lowered his gaze to the tip of the cigarette. "I see every minute detail, from the blade touching skin, to the blood pooling around her head as they begin to cut. It won't go away."

"Honey, don't--"

"I hear her screaming and..." He swallowed again, but this time it was bile he was forced to restrain, just like the first time he'd seen what his mind now replayed in vivid detail. "Tonight, in bed, it sounded so clear it could have been playing at a low volume on the radio." He gestured emptily. "The sound changes when they saw through her vocal chords."

Melanie's face had lost all color. Her free hand now covered her mouth. "Jesus, Will. Stop, please," she mumbled.

"She whimpers." He gasped for breath as the panic that came with remembering seized him. The cigarette began to tremble in his fingers at the realization that talking about it—something he had hoped would help—only served to make them clearer, more vivid. "She sounds so child-like, as if...as if the pain is so incomprehensible it reduces her to an infant...oh God...that *sound*...and...and when it's over...when it ended, up here, *tonight*," he whispered, tapping an index finger against his temple, "...they take her head and raise it to face the camera...but...it's not her face."

"Will..."

When he looked up, there were tears in his eyes. "...It's yours."

* * *

She stayed with him until dawn's sepia-toned fingers parted the blinds and painted bars of fire on the wall. They'd moved to the sofa, where he lay on his back staring at the ceiling, Melanie nestled against him, her hand on his chest. He stroked her cool skin while she slept, occasionally squeezing her closer to him, though they could be no closer, smiling now and then at the pleasurable moan she gave when he drew his fingers down her spine. He felt as if the only way to smother the horror that seethed within him was to pull her inside him, so perhaps she could fight the terror with him. So he wouldn't have to fight it alone. For now, she was a slender, sleeping figure, oblivious to the nightmare that danced across her husband's eyes with every breath, every blink.

He was scared, and it was a preposterous fear. But knowing the foolishness of it didn't lessen its severity and now he felt as if the simple act of watching an execution, something not meant to be seen, had broken something inside him; that a rudimentary shield, essential to the sanity of man, had ruptured under the weight of his shock, and now the world had shriveled and dimmed, become a dank dark cell.

As he watched the sunlight crawl across the walls, he squeezed his eyes shut, praying nothing but dark awaited him there.

A knife grinding through muscle...a gurgled moan...Blood plumes, squirting upward and blinding him...

His eyes flew open, blinking in time with the stuttering thud of his heart.

"Of fuck," he whispered shakily. "Oh *fuck*, God, why won't this *stop*?"

A sob so loud it frightened him burst from his mouth and Melanie jerked awake, startled, her eyes searching the room before she blinked once, twice and looked at him. "Will?"

Tell her it's all right.

But he couldn't. He could not tell her it was a dream, a nightmare, something that hurt and frightened him for a while only to flee with the realization that his imagination was to blame.

Instead he said nothing, but covered his face with his hands and wept.

"*Will?*"

But even in the darkness behind his hands, he saw shredded skin.

* * *

"I could stay home," Melanie said, standing behind him and massaging the concrete tension from his shoulders. Will shook his head, and stared at his hands, at the faint trembling there. He was coming apart.

"No, you go. It won't do you any good to sit around here looking at me feeling sorry for myself."

She was already dressed for work, and looking more beautiful than ever. In truth, he did want her to stay—the thought of being alone filled him with cold panic—but he knew it really wouldn't help. She couldn't chase away the shadows that capered behind his eyes no matter how much light her company brought with it.

She gave his shoulders a squeeze and went to fetch her purse from the kitchen counter. "Okay, but you call me if you need me and I'll come home."

He nodded. "I'll be fine. Don't worry."

She turned and watched him for a moment. "You'll get over this, Will. I promise."

He wanted desperately to believe her, but the fact remained that she hadn't the slightest inclination of what he was going through, of how much his world had changed in so short a time. If he could only let her see the nightmare that had corrupted his thoughts, if he could, just for a moment, share the images that relentlessly invaded his sleep, only then might her words mean something. As it stood, her attempts to make him feel better sounded trite and absurd in the face of his overwhelming fear.

Alone.

Melanie was a mere whisper of light in a roomful of shadow.

"Call me," she said and kissed his cheek, her lips cool against his skin.

"I will," he replied, and did not look at her as she waved goodbye from the door, afraid if he did, he might see a thin red line forming around the base of her throat.

She left and silence took her place in the kitchen.

Exhausted, frightened and already beginning to feel the dark creeping back to the forefront of his mind, Will stood and hurried to the phone.

* * *

He would not watch the news.

He would not watch a movie.

He tried to watch cartoons but even the animated violence quickly brought to mind the echo of what he had seen.

He switched to *M*A*S*H*, and quickly changed the channel when one of the characters, a surgeon, got blinded by a fount of arterial spray.

He settled on a vapid sitcom—surely a safe choice—but soon even the wisecracking characters clustered around the bar began to lose their heads and bleed into their drinks. The audience laughed.

In the end, he stabbed the OFF button on the remote so hard his fingernail cracked. He lay on the sofa, finger throbbing, struggling to fill his mind with benign images: a sunny beach, the gentle hush of waves, a parade filled with grinning clowns and people in animal costumes; then a carnival, a place taken from a box marked 'safe' in his memory: dour-looking barkers plying their trades, starry eyed children clutching prizes, spinning lights, the scent of sawdust and cotton candy, and the deafening sound of screams

of screams

of screams

Until the scream was his and the room grew silver teeth.

* * *

"Is this going to cost me?" Will said.

Don dropped his considerable weight into the armchair across from Will, and smiled. "Relax. You're one of the most together people I've ever met. I doubt this is going to have me running to write you up for the *Psychiatric Times*." He shrugged off his sport coat and scowled as he draped it over the arm of the chair. "I need a new suit."

"Heal thy friend and I'll buy you one."

"You couldn't afford the type of suits I wear," Don said. "Even I can't afford the type of suits I wear, but I have an image to maintain, you know?"

"What kind of image is that? Overweight, balding forty-something on the verge of a midlife crisis, too fond of Scotch and not fond enough of his second wife?"

"People like you negate the need for an autobiography."

They shared a smile, then Will sat back and sighed. "Thanks for coming over. I couldn't think of anyone else to call. I need your help."

"So you said on the phone. What's the problem? Nightmares?"

"It's a little more than that. Actually, it's a lot more than that."

Don relaxed into his chair and clasped his hands over his large paunch. "Tell me about it."

Will gave him a tired grin. "Now you sound like a doctor."

The big man shrugged. "I've been impersonating one for over twenty years now, my friend. Sooner or later it starts to come naturally. But, as I say to all my *paying* patients, don't think of me as a shrink, think of me as someone who owes a small fortune in alimony and has nowhere better to be right now."

"Comforting."

"Works every time."

There was a moment of companionable silence, then Will cleared his throat. "Someone sent me an e-mail a week or so ago. In it was a link to a web site called Noble Sacrifice.com"

"Doesn't sound like porn," Don said.

"No. It was a website of banned movies and images."

Don frowned. "Movies and images of what?"

"People being killed. Accidents filmed by people who just happened to be there with a video camera, footage from wars, disasters...I guess all of the things they don't...*can't* show you on the six o' clock news. There were films of soldiers being tortured and killed in various conflicts...a lot of war stuff."

"And you looked at all these?"

"No...God, no. There were descriptions beneath all the links, more or less telling you what to expect if you were brave, or sick enough, to watch."

Don grimaced. "Sounds like tons of family fun."

"Yeah, everything from celebrity autopsy photographs to videos of massacres."

"Isn't that stuff illegal though? I mean, how can something like that be available for public viewing?"

"It had a warning...can't remember what it was...and a bunch of legalese saying they were protected by FirstAmendment, one word, with a link to whatever they were talking about."

"Jesus. What kind of sick fuck watches something like that?"

Will looked at him.

Don's bushy eyebrows rose. "Ah, I see."

"If you're thinking of asking me why, don't," Will told him, dropping his gaze. "I don't know. I'm not one of those people who get a kick out of watching people being killed. I don't even know why I followed that fucking e-mail link in the first place. But I did, and even as disgusted as I was by all the videotaped atrocities I saw were available, I still, with everything in me resisting, clicked on one. It said: "Nadejda Petrovna's Execution."

"Who's Nadejda Petrovna?"

"A Russian reporter. That's all I know, except of course for the fact that Chechen rebels captured her, and videotaped themselves beheading her. "

"Christ."

"Yeah."

"And you watched this?"

"Not all. What I saw was enough though. I threw up right afterward and I haven't slept since."

"I'm not surprised. That would be enough to fuck up anyone's sleep."

Will nodded. "When I do sleep, there are nightmares, except I see the people I love being hurt, not that woman."

"That's to be expected," Don said.

"Why?"

"Well because what you have to realize is that you witnessed a murder. How many average Joes can say that? Just because you watched it on a computer screen doesn't lessen the reality of it. You might as well have been looking through a window. And as any murder witness will tell you, it takes some time for the shock to wear off. Even after it does, they find themselves unable to shake off the horror, the stark reminder of just how tenuous this life of ours actually is, and the guilt."

"Guilt?"

"The guilt of watching that poor woman die, the guilt of giving in to that morbid voyeuristic impulse that exists in all of us, and of course, guilt for not doing something to help her."

Will frowned. "But I couldn't!"

"Exactly. Had you actually been looking at her through a window, you could have tried to help, or called the police...something. But you weren't. Remember that this technology, the ability to watch such things from oceans of time and distance away, is relatively new. You wouldn't see it on the news. The movies make it fake enough for you, but when you're essentially there, when the atrocity takes place inches from your face, the mind, sitting in the front row, demands intervention. The impotency that follows as a result of inaction leaves a clear path for guilt, self-disgust and depression."

Will pondered this for a moment. Don had the complacent look of a man impressed by his own wisdom, but despite it, Will felt a swell of gratitude toward him.

There was, however, another problem.

"How does knowing all this help me to deal with it? How does it make me stop seeing death and violence every time I close my eyes?"

"It will pass eventually. That I can assure you. My advice is to find something positive in all of this." Will made to say something; Don raised a hand. "I know, I know. What could *possibly* be positive about it, right? Well, how about the fact that death, to you, is no longer something that happens to everyone else? Maybe from now on every time you hear about some tragedy you won't, like everyone else does, just shake your head and cluck your tongue before getting back to your crossword puzzle. Maybe it will actually *mean* something to you."

"That can't be all," Will said, feeling the familiar barbs of panic writhing through him. "I mean, just feeling bad about death can't be the only reason this is happening."

"No, the reason this is happening is because you watched a woman getting her head sawn off."

Will felt his hope dwindle. "So in the meantime I just sit around and...what? Isn't there something you can prescribe for me?"

"Other than patience, no. At least nothing that would do you any good."

Will rubbed his hands over his face. "Shit."

"Look, Will. You made a mistake watching that damn video. But it's a mistake you'll get over with a bit of time. The cost of it is suffering through this little nightmare show for a while."

When Will dropped his hands from his face, his eyes were hollow, haunted. "And what if that *isn't* all?"

* * *

That night, Melanie dragged him from his turbulent nightmares with her lips, and her tongue. He moaned in pleasure as she tended to him, rocked his hips as she straddled him, her hair hanging in her face, eyes twinkling in the gloom. The streetlight filled the window behind her with moonlight blue, making a silhouette of her.

"I love you," he whispered.

She didn't reply. He sat up, embracing her and crushing her heavy breasts against his chest; the nipples were hardened points against his own, her legs like a vice around him, locking him into the soft wetness of her. She breathed in short sharp gasps as he ran his fingers through her hair.

Then her breathing caught. Another silhouette rose behind her.

Will froze, his erection wilting immediately.

Slowly, slowly, Melanie threw her head back.

And her neck split with a horrendous zipping sound.

As her body fell away and rolled heavily off the bed, Will found himself staring into the still watching eyes of his wife, his fingers, still tangled in her hair, now the only thing holding her head aloft.

"*Help me*," she gurgled.

Will screamed.

* * *

"Don?"

Static crackled over the phone. Will frowned.

"Hello, Don?"

"Hey buddy, you there?" Don said. "This line sucks, let me call you back, okay?"

"Okay. Thanks."

A moment later, with Will standing in the hallway, chewing his thumbnail down to the quick and frantically avoiding his reflection in the hallway mirror for fear of the ghoulish visage he might see staring back at him, the phone rang and he snatched it up. To his relief, this time the line was clear.

"How's my favorite non-paying patient doing?" Don said.

Will's cast a glance at Melanie, who sat on the sofa in the living room, nursing a cup of coffee and looking worried. He felt such a swell of love for her he thought it might reduce him to tears, and an equal pang of regret that she should have to bear witness to whatever was happening to him. Although she hadn't said anything about last night, he had caught her more than once massaging her scalp and wincing, which forced him to wonder how hard he had pulled her hair. Guilt forced him to look away, and he turned his attention back to the phone.

"Will?"

"I've been better," he told Don. "Last night was the worst night yet."

"How so? Nightmares?"

Will sighed shakily. "No. They're more than nightmares. Hallucinations, maybe. I find myself watching..." He lowered his voice, aware that Melanie was within earshot, "...watching them killing Mel."

"Watching *who* killing Mel?"

"I don't know. Whoever I saw in that video killing Nadejda Petrovna, I guess."

A sigh. "Jesus, bud, this has really burrowed its way into you hasn't it?"

"Yeah. Big time. I'm walking around in a daze from lack of sleep, afraid to close my eyes for fear I'll see the same thing over and over again: some shadowy figure cutting my wife's head off." He heard the faint rustle as Melanie rose and moved away into the kitchen. "I can't do this forever, Don. There has to be something you can do for me."

"I suppose I could prescribe some relaxants for you. Maybe some Valium."

"Will that help?"

"Well, from the sounds of it, anything would be better than lack of sleep. If nothing else, it'll help calm you down, siphon off some of that anxiety. It could be that the apprehension and fear is prolonging these 'hallucinations'. You're expecting to see them, so your mind is obliging. I think maybe one calm, uninterrupted night's sleep will do you the world of good."

"Ok, great," Will said, relieved. "So do I come down there to pick it up, or what?"

"No need. There's a CVS around there somewhere, right?"

"Yeah, over on Sandusky Street."

"Good, I'll call them from here and have them set you up. They'll call when they have the goods for you."

"Thanks a million, Don. Really."

"Don't thank me yet, bud. There's no guarantee this will help, but it *should*."

"It'll work. I know it will." He ran a hand through his hair. "So what do I do in the meantime?"

"Hang up, light a big fire, grab a bottle of wine from the refrigerator, get Melanie drunk as hell, then take her to bed and teach her the ancient art of bang-fu."

Will laughed. "A note from my doctor might help the request. After last night, I expect she'll be a little gun-shy."

"Gun-shy? Man, Freud would have had a field day with your sorry ass. And what happened last night?"

"Coitus interruptus, in the worst possible way."

"Ah, well...say no more, and that's a command, not a request. If I start getting envious of your *failed* attempts at getting it on, it'll only serve to remind me how empty and pitiful my own sex life is."

The burgeoning strains of cautious relief threatened to turn laughter into a fit of weeping as Will wiped a tear from his eye. Melanie returned to his side, put a hand across his shoulder, her eyes wide with concern.

"Thanks, Don," he said into the phone, his voice unsteady.

"For what? I'm well aware that you do this shit just to irritate me, to get me working harder than I care to. Then you stiff me and I'm the one left depressed. Textbook emotional osmosis, pal. Thanks a bunch."

"Would you knock off the wisecracks? I'm serious," Will told him. "I think I'd have gone completely insane without you."

"Bullshit. My ex-wife said the exact same thing and now she's getting porked by pool boys down in Maui, *on my tab* I may add. Now get off the damn phone and see to business."

"Okay, okay. I owe you one."

"Right. Give Melanie one for me and we'll call it quits."

A rumble in the distance and a sea of static erupted from the phone. "Don?"

There was silence, then the dial tone stuttered in his ear. With a slight shake of his head, Will hung up.

Melanie turned him around to face her, her hands seeking his face. "Are you all right?"

He summoned the best smile he could muster and wrapped his arms around her. "I think so."

She kissed him, a long passionate kiss he didn't want to end. But after a moment he broke away, staring at the small arched window at the end of the hall. Dark clouds had obscured the sun, leeching the light from the day. A moment later, rain began to fall, pattering against the glass and tapping on the roof.

"What is it?" Melanie asked.

Will looked at her, at the slender oval of her face and grinned. "Do we have any wine?"

* * *

Sometime later, with a full-blown storm battering the house and premature night pressing against the windows, the phone rang. Sluggishly, already regretting the half-bottle of wine he'd consumed before taking Melanie to bed for mercifully uninterrupted and frenzied sex, Will strode naked to the phone. Through the staticky crackle on the line, a voice laden with false cheer informed him that his prescription was ready. He hung up, quickly dressed, and hurried out to his car, the wind wrenching and tearing at him, the rain needling his face.

As he drove the short distance to the store, the wipers working frantically to keep the windshield clear, he realized he already felt better. No hallucinations had spoiled he and Melanie's lovemaking, no shadowy specters had risen from their bedroom floor and afterward, when he'd dozed, there hadn't been any nightmares waiting to thrust him back out of sleep. The dirty feeling still clung to his skin, inside and out, however, a repulsive sensation he knew would take much longer than a day to erase.

He allowed himself a sigh and, one hand on the steering wheel, reached over and popped the glovebox. An almost empty pack of Marlboro Lights tumbled out into his waiting hand. He checked the road ahead and fished out a cigarette, then straightened and thumbed the lighter on the dashboard.

Spindly-legged lightning flashed around the car like negative images of dead branches, briefly turning the rain on the windshield to glimmering jewels. Will coughed, cigarette clenched between his teeth, and drummed his fingers on the steering wheel.

To his right, the CVS sailed out of the dark, and he flipped the indicator, letting the car coast to a stop as he reached the intersection.

The lighter clacked its readiness and he reached for it.

Then froze.

The hair rose on the nape of his neck as a chill scurried down his spine.

I didn't, he thought, fingers still poised before the lighter. *I didn't see anyone in the mirror.*

A gust of wind buffeted the car, rocking it on its axle.

Closing his eyes, but only for a moment for fear unseen hands would grab him from behind, he whispered further reassurances to himself. *The trick is to believe you didn't see it, not just to tell yourself,* he imagined Don telling him. *Force it out of your head, and you'll be okay, bud. Trust me.*

Will nodded slightly, as if Don were with him in the car to see the gesture and swallowed as he straightened.

A car honked behind him, making him jump.

"Just a second, you son of a bitch," he muttered.

The rearview mirror was inches from his face, awaiting him like the sheeted body of a loved one in the morgue. He did not want to look, for ignorance granted him the ability to deny what he thought he'd seen, to deny what might be there.

He cleared the knot of anxiety from his throat and wiped a trembling hand over his face, barely heard the rasp of stubble.

Melanie will complain, he thought. *She'll have beard rash.* He almost smiled, but another angry burst of sound from the car behind him jerked the thought from his mind. Headlights filled the window like glaring eyes, attempting to blind him, as the impatient driver let his car drift closer to Will's fender.

"All *right,* asshole," Will said, and straightened in his seat, eyes squarely on the rearview mirror.

For a moment, he saw nothing but the white light making fleeting ghosts that fled across the tan upholstery and the pebbled rain on the rear windshield. But then, there was a woman sitting there, as if she had every right to be, as if she'd dashed in for shelter out of the rain and had just forgotten to thank him, or ask his permission to invade the car.

"No," he moaned and yet could not turn away from the horror that exploded within him at the sight of her raising her bony white hands in front of a face that was slowly slipping to the side, as if she were merely nodding off to sleep. He blinked rapidly, demanding his eyelids scrub away the apparition, ghost, hallucination....whatever it was.

But the woman remained, her eyes deep dark hollows in a moon-shaped face. And "*helllllp*," she whispered, before the angry red wound that circled her neck began to yawn open.

* * *

"Sir, are you okay?"

"Valium...um, Will Chambers...My psych...my *doctor* called earlier, called in a prescription for me, for...for Valium...Don Webley...*Doctor* Webley...My name is William Chambers."

"Would you like a glass of water, Mr. Chambers?"

"Please, just the fucking pills, *please*...I'm sorry. Please hurry."

"Are you going to be all right? Sir? *Sir*, are you—?"

* * *

I'll get home, he thought in a panic. *I'll get home and they'll be in my house. Those men, those things, those* animals, *and they'll have my beautiful sweet precious Melanie kneeling on the floor before them. They'll have their hands in her hair and a saw to her throat, and I won't be able to stop them. I won't be able to do anything but regret for the rest of my life that I was fucking stupid dumb piece of shit idiot enough to leave her on her own. They tricked me...this is what they wanted...this is what they wanted to do all along...getting inside my head...invading me so I'd leave my wife ripe for them to come and cut her fucking head off...*

He got home and barely thought to put the car in park before he was racing up the driveway and yelling his way into the house, not caring that he was dripping rainwater onto the carpet, not caring that at any moment the lights might go out, the power might fail and he'd be left alone, in the dark, with the monsters who had most certainly slaughtered his wife.

The door clattered against the wall and shuddered its way back.

Then the house gloated with silence.

"Melanie!"

No answer. He put his hands to his face, nails primed to tear the skin away if it turned out that his nightmare had taken his wife away from him, if the poison that had marred his soul had reached out and murdered her, if—

"Honey, what's wrong?"

He almost collapsed with relief. Melanie, eyes narrowed at the light, hair tousled, was slowly coming down the stairs, tying the belt on her robe to hide her nakedness from the cold, or from *him*, who'd become little more than a terrible phantom standing crazed in the hallway.

"Oh Jesus," he breathed, the relief draining him, the adrenaline slowly ebbing away. He leaned back against the front door. "I thought they'd got you," he whispered and with the admission came a huge whooping sob that set Melanie hurrying to cradle him in her arms. "*I thought they'd got you*," he wept, trembling.

The tears made the dead woman behind his eyes appear to swim.

* * *

"Don will call to check on you tomorrow."

Will nodded, already feeling drowsy. The Valium would work. It would have to. The alternatives were looking grimmer by the second and the renewed onslaught of gruesome images were now sharing headspace with thoughts of institutionalization and white padded rooms with screams for cushions and dripping faucets for music.

The bed felt soft and eased the rigidity from his muscles. Beside him sat Melanie, one hand propping up her head, the other stroking his hair like a violinist playing a soundless lullaby.

"I'm sorry," he told her, as the shades began to creep down over his mind's window. "I'm so sorry this is happening."

"Hush," she soothed. "It will be better after you've had a good night's sleep. Tomorrow, we can have a nice breakfast and maybe go for a walk. How does that sound, hmm?"

He composed a smile, but it was not heartfelt. "Good," he said, feeling as if a warm tide were rising in his chest, lapping at his throat. "Good."

"Try to sleep now," she whispered, and her whisper had an echo. He wanted to point this out to her, but the tide had reached his tongue and seized it. He was not alarmed, for it felt sweet as honey and he let it fill his throat until he was lost in its thick, comforting folds.

* * *

The phone rang.

Melanie dropped the paperback she'd been valiantly attempting to read in an effort to forget what was happening to Will and hurried into the hallway. With a shaky sigh, she snatched up the receiver. "Hello?"

"Mel. It's Don. Is Will still up?"

"Hi Don. No, he's asleep. Should I wake him?"

"Absolutely not. Let him sleep. He needs it. Besides, it's you I wanted to talk to anyway."

* * *

"Wake up, pig."

Frowning, Will's eyes snapped open and he coughed, wheezed and watched in amazement as what appeared to be dust rolled away across a stone floor. He shivered as a deep chill settled into his bones. Suffused white light pulsed across his vision, quickly followed by an acrid tang that was wholly unfamiliar.

"Where—?"

A sharp blow to his stomach propelled him backward and he yelped in pain as his back collided painfully with a solid wall.

Only then was he truly awake.

*Jesus...*he thought, the now familiar terror clawing its way through him with icy nails. *Jesus, they're here. They came while I was sleeping. Melanie...oh God, where's Melanie? Where am I?*

* * *

"You're familiar with Post Traumatic Stress Disorder?" Don asked her.

"Yes, it's fairly common in soldiers, right?"

"That's right, but it's actually more common than that. Any victim of shock or trauma can suffer from it. Rape, molestation, accident victims..."

"Okay."

"The reason I mention it is because I'm starting to think that's what Will's suffering from."

* * *

Before him stood a tall thin man, dressed from head to toe in black.

"Who are *you?*" The questions pushed against Will's tongue like water through a crack in dam. "How did I get here?"

The man said nothing, but despite the headgear he wore, allowing only his eyes and the wide bridge of his nose to be seen, Will knew he was grinning.

"Get up," the man ordered then, in a clipped accent Will thought might be Russian.

"Why am I here?" Will pleaded with him. "Tell me, please. What...what are you going to do to me?" He was trembling so bad he thought he might rattle himself to pieces. The cold gnawed at him--a merciless freezer cold.

"Stop asking question." It emerged as: 'Stup asging kess-chun'. The man leveled the large assault rifle strapped across his chest in Will's direction. Distantly Will found the fact that he could discern not even the slightest tremble in the man's hands incredibly disturbing. It suggested a callousness only obtained by familiarity with violence. Whoever the man behind the mask was, this was a role he had played often.

Will moved, slowly, toward the man, and as he did so, he realized he was wearing clothes he'd never seen before, and certainly hadn't donned himself--a shapeless, ill-fitting suit of the kind he'd only ever seen on the news. Prisoners in penitentiaries wore them. His heart thumped in his throat hard enough to make his head hurt, eyes brimming with tears.

"How did I get here? Please...*tell me.*"

"Stand," said the man. "Stand *now!*"

Will quickly obeyed, the dusty floor ice-cold against the soles of his bare feet, making his toes curl. *I'm dreaming*, he thought. *Those pills did something to me and I'm dreaming.* But he knew, though he wished he didn't, that whatever was happening now was the proper end for whatever horror he'd been suffering until now, that this was where it had been leading him. And that it was no dream.

I'm going to die, he realized and felt his legs threaten to buckle beneath him.

The armed man nodded his satisfaction and thrust a hand in the center of Will's chest, knocking him back against the wall. Will, winded, looked around at the small room, at the fall of dust motes illuminated by cold white sunlight that slanted through the bars of the room's sole window.

The man spoke something unintelligible and a narrow door opened at the far side of the room.

Three men entered. All of them were dressed the same as the

gunman. One of them held a video camera by his side; another held a pistol.

Will felt his skin crawl.

The third man held a saw.

* * *

"The symptoms of PTSD are numerous," Don told her, "hallucinations, anxiety attacks, night terrors, memory loss, insomnia, erratic moods, lapses in concentration, depression...sound like anyone we know?"

Melanie sagged. "So what do we do about it? Is there a way to treat it that doesn't involve a tight jacket and a cushioned room?"

"Of course. There are Neuro-Emotional Techniques, a relatively new form of 'power therapy' that have proved far more effective than 'talk therapy.' It targets the mind through the body using systems borrowed from the Chi—"

Melanie rolled her eyes. "Don."

"Sorry. But that's your answer. There are numerous treatments available." He sighed heavily. "What I think happened Will is that after seeing that video, he almost immediately began to visualize the murder, only with *him* in that woman's place. You can imagine what persistent visualizations like that can do to the nerves. Sooner or later the brain can become convinced that it's really suffering the agonies the eyes have only witnessed. It can even start reproducing the sensations associated with such a death."

* * *

"Oh no," Will moaned, his body vibrating with fear as the tall man lunged forward and grabbed him by the collar of his jumpsuit. "*Now!*" he barked into Will's face and flung him toward the others, who had stopped in the center of the room. The one with the pistol pointed it at Will's head and said something in his own language.

The video man busied himself with setting up the camera, his ministrations oddly calm—he could have been fixing the machine for a kindly old lady, instead of preparing it to film an execution. And Will had no doubt that was exactly what was happening. What was *going* to happen, and that in a few days or weeks, his death would be appearing on a sleazy website he'd once had the misfortune to visit. A horrendous snuff site that justified its existence by claiming it had a responsibility to show the world what they were trying so hard not to see, that they had *no business* seeing, when in actual fact, it had a far more sinister purpose.

Will knew that now.

What he *didn't* know was how it had been done--how he had gone to sleep beside his loving wife and woken up in a strange place surrounded by masked men who spoke a foreign language.

He supposed it didn't matter now.

He was shoved to his knees, but on the way down, he caught a glimpse of the world beyond the window, and it was not his world at all, but a cold, stark landscape of faltering buildings and slush-laden roads.

Not my world at all, he thought with a flicker of calm. *Not my world. I'm not here. They can't hurt me they won't hurt me they can't.*

A surer voice rose like a bloated corpse to the surface of his mind.

But they will.

He thought of Melanie, stroking his hair last night, and felt a debilitating wave of sorrow at the thought of never seeing her again, of her never knowing how or why her husband had died.

I love you, baby, he thought, willing the words to cross time and space and distance so she would hear them. *So very much.*

They bound his wrists and ankles with thick heavy rope that smelled vaguely of motor oil.

"Please don't," he pleaded, trying in vain to shuffle away from them. "I didn't do anything to you. I don't even know who you are." Tears spilled down his cheeks. "Please. I have a *wife*..." Terror unlike anything he'd ever known swept through him.

Somewhere beyond the room, a church bell tolled.

Cold steel bit the skin on the back of his neck.

"Don't..." he sobbed, as he struggled.

The camera began to whirr.

* * *

"Don. Why are you telling me this? Nothing like that is going to happen to Will."

"I know, I know. I'm not saying it will. I use it only to illustrate what the mind can do to someone when it manages to convince itself it's what the body deserves. Atonement for not being able to prevent someone else's suffering. It's a remarkable and tragic condition, but all the seeds are showing themselves in Will, and that's why we have to monitor him closely. You need to stay with him. He needs you now, Mel. You're the only link he has left to the outside world."

"Outside world?"

"Yeah, the *real* world, because to all intents and purposes it would appear he's losing his grasp on it at a frightening rate. Either that, or whatever dark alternative world he envisions in his head is tightening its hold on *him*."

* * *

Melanie hung up, and hugged herself against the unmerciful cold that Don's phone call had left with her. My God, could it really be so bad? Could she wake up one day to find Will had utterly and completely lost his mind? What would she do? How could she save him?

No, she decided, brushing a single tear from her eye. She would never let that happen. Never. She was stronger than that and she knew Will was too. She'd help him climb his way back from the dark valley into which he'd stumbled.

As she made her way to the bedroom, she brushed the chill from her shoulders. It almost seemed as if the house itself had grown colder. She guessed it was her imagination but told herself to check the thermostat anyway when she returned from checking on Will. A fat lot of good she'd do her husband if she let the heating go berserk.

She cracked open the bedroom door, slicing a wedge of yellow light from the dark inside. "Honey?" she whispered.

Will didn't answer, but she fancied if she strained her ears she could hear him breathing deeply, though it was hard to tell with the rain drumming on the roof. Nevertheless, she allowed herself a slight sigh of relief. It was fiercely encouraging to see that he wasn't tossing, turning or screaming at ghosts. Perhaps the pills would do the trick after all. She prayed they would.

She opened the door a little wider and entered the room. Will was lying on his back, facing the ceiling, eyes closed. Slowly, she lowered herself down on her side of the bed, wincing at the faint squeak from the mattress springs.

I do love you, she thought, reaching over to stroke his hair. *More than you know*. Her fingers found the soft curls and lightly brushed over them.

He turned his head toward her, eyes still closed, and she quickly withdrew her hand, cursing herself for disturbing him.

"Hush," she whispered.

And watched in stunned, numb horror as Will's face met the pillow and blood began to flow from his partly open mouth.

"Will?" She quickly stood, and shook him. "Oh Jesus, Will?"

His head rolled free of his body, tumbling down beneath the covers on her side of the bed. Melanie gasped, clutched both hands to her chest as if fearing her heart would burst through it at any moment, and felt the strength leave her.

"Will?" she croaked, staggering back, away from the bed and the ragged bleeding neck still poking up from the covers. She collided with a dresser and fell heavily to the floor, a trembling hand rising to her mouth. Briefly she tried to get up, a scream trapped like angry wasps in her throat, unable to break free. And then the world went black and she fell willingly into its soporific depths.

* * *

Melanie stared into her coffee, the steam rising like sinuous ghosts from a black pond, and remembered Don's words, spoken over the phone on the last night she'd awoken from yet another hideous and terrifying nightmare.

This has to be more than a coincidence, Don. What's happening to me?

Her fingers trembled as she traced a line around the rim of the cup.

Cold white sunlight pressed against the windows of the kitchen. From the television in the living room came the sound of a solemn voice relating the details of another atrocity. Melanie put her palms to her face and closed her eyes.

An impassive, bloodless, *familiar* face shrieked at her in the dark.

She jerked upright in the chair and looked at her hands, at the intensified trembling in them and stifled a sob. Will was dead. Almost five weeks had passed and still she expected him to come waltzing into the kitchen, unshaven and yawning with a dopey smile on his face. She missed him so much, missed the smell of him in the house, the *feel* of him in the house.

Gone. And she couldn't understand why, no more than she could understand the sudden, soul-freezing fear that had possessed her over the last week or so.

Trauma, Mel. The reason it seems so familiar is because it is. It can manifest itself in different ways, but essentially it's the exact same thing Will went through.

She rubbed her fingers over her temples, chewed her lower lip.

So this is what he had to suffer. You know...I wished for his pain. When he was sick, I wished I could take it from him. Now I don't want it. What kind of a person does that make me?

Human, Don had assured her. These days she felt anything but.

Next to her coffee cup sat an unopened pack of cigarettes. She quickly tore the plastic off, discarded the foil that was all that stood between her and the panacea of nicotine, and quickly withdrew one. She lit it and inhaled deeply. She considered calling Don again, but resisted. Sooner or later she would have to conquer the fear on her own, and maybe it was better to start weaning herself off his aid now before she grew to depend on him so much he tired of her constant phone calls, and referred her to someone else. Someone less caring. Someone who didn't *understand* what had happened her husband.

I've thought long and hard about it, Mel, Don had told her a few weeks after the funeral. *And it all keeps pointing to the same thing, though professional skepticism prevents me from buying it outright.* She hadn't wanted to hear it, but let him continue. Closure, she knew, was needed, or she would forever be haunted by the mystery of Will's death. Would never be able to stop blaming herself unless someone offered proof that it hadn't been her fault. An irrational need, perhaps, but very little about her life these days was rational.

You've heard of stigmata, right? When people, usually religious folks, start showing the wounds of Christ on their bodies? Bleeding feet and palms, and all that jazz?

She'd told him she had and he'd proceeded to inform her of various examples in which ordinary people had suffered extraordinary tortures, with no apparent cause.

There was a colleague of mine in Washington who documented a case in which an eight year old boy, after witnessing his mother's arm being torn off by a Rottweiler, almost immediately began to develop bruises and small wounds, consistent with bite marks, on his own arm, the same one his mother had lost, though he'd been nowhere near a dog. Three weeks later, the arm was hanging on by strings of flesh and little else, with no physiological explanation for why it had done so. In the end, psychiatrists were brought in to study the boy; they concluded that the boy's trauma at what had happened to his beloved mother was so great, it somehow lent him the ability to experience her pain, by subconsciously willing her wounds onto himself. I imagine if a boy can 'borrow' his mother's wounds to punish himself, then a devout follower of Jesus Christ could conceivably do the same.

The phone rang, jarring the thoughts from Melanie's head. She ignored the persistent shrilling and finished her cigarette. As she'd hoped, it had calmed her, but not nearly enough. She rose and went to the bathroom, locking the door behind her out of habit. As she tugged down her panties and sat on the cold oval of the toilet, she pondered Don's theory, and, as she had when he'd first proposed it, decided it was impossible. But then, wasn't the manner of Will's death also impossible? No matter which way she looked at it, something unnatural had occurred in their bedroom that night, and yet she couldn't force herself to believe that her husband had willed his own death. Trauma could be overcome. Shock would always fade, and people didn't just decapitate themselves in the dark without a weapon.

Nothing more sinister than empathy.

She covered her face with her hands and moaned. Her body ached, the muscles in her back like taut wires beneath a trembling sheet. There had to be a rational answer to her nightmare but she was no longer sure she wanted to know it. Perhaps there was safety in mystery. At some point, somehow, she would have to start rebuilding her life, even though the mere thought of it felt like a betrayal of Will. Shaking her head, she opened her eyes.

There was a man standing before her, his shadow thick and cold.

Melanie's breath caught in her throat and she looked up, tears threatening to blur her vision, fear like a snare around her throat, tightening, tightening.

Something hit the floor, and rolled and when at last she gathered the courage to look upon it, she found herself staring into her husband's glassy eyes.

She screamed and grabbed her hair, her nails digging, then dragging down her face, drawing blood, as all the horror, the loss, and the grief erupted, spewing from her open mouth as she slid from the toilet to her knees, even as instinct tried to tug her away from the head on the floor and the still, silent form of the dead man it belonged to.

And still she screamed.

And screamed.

Until the scream became a tortured gurgle as a slim but deep wound began to draw its way across her throat.

PEEKERS

Larry Morgan's resolution to make today the first in which he didn't look upon his retirement as a curse rather than a blessing, suffered its first blow when the neighbors to the left began revving their dirt bikes at each other and howling at God-only-knew-what.

Though a short stretch of dense wooded land separated the houses, the distance and the trees proved inadequate whenever Bob Landry and his wife decided to have an obscenity laced screaming match, or, as was the case now, his three teenage sons decided to converse in the language of machines. He supposed he shouldn't complain—despite how bloody easy they made it to do just that; after all, he'd won his fight to keep the boys from using his yard as a throughway, even though the deep, hardened grooves they'd left behind would take more work to erase than he was willing (or able, if he was honest with himself) to put in. His perfectly reasonable request that the culprits tend to the damage went ignored. Bob Landry had apparently been a moderately famous dirt-biker in his heyday, and so he encouraged wholeheartedly his children's desire to follow in his footsteps. Complaints were a nuisance he had come to expect, and while he was willing to limit the hours in which 'revved up', he drew the line at forcing them to clean up their tracks after them. "Fingers leave prints; tires leave marks," he'd told Larry and shrugged.

Larry looked away from the growling woods in disgust, and spotted Zach Hoffman loping across his yard toward him. Zach was almost the same age as Larry, but looked much older, and lived in one of the crowd of sterile homes that had risen over the past two years from what had, as long as Larry could remember, been an overgrown field.

He missed the weeds.

Zach was a pleasant sort, but quiet and wispy, as if he'd been cut from delicate material that had been left crumpled too long in a dusty attic. He was rarely seen venturing outside his house except to retrieve his mail and the free ad-sponsored local newspaper some unseen deliverer left on everyone's driveway, whether they wanted it or not. It was a surprise, then, to see him making his way over to Larry's place with what looked like solemn purpose etched on his face.

"Morning, Zach."

Zach nodded to acknowledge the greeting. His brow was furrowed. "Wondering if I could ask you a favor."

"Sure." *Please don't let him ask me to dog-sit that hideous mutt of his,* Larry thought. But that wasn't it, and the look on Zach's face said as much.

"Would you come over to my place for a few minutes?" Zach asked.

"What for?"

"I need you to take a look at something."

Though Larry didn't think Zach capable of anything unsavory, he reminded himself that such opinions were often echoed on the nightly news, spoken by the neighbors of seemingly ordinary people who had gone crazy and killed someone. It didn't help that Zach seemed oddly reluctant to reveal the reason for his request.

"Well, I was just about to have breakfast. Maybe I could stop by later?"

"It won't take a second, Larry, and I didn't want to bother you, but I don't trust any of those folk—" he said, jerking a thumb over his shoulder at the houses clustered around his own, "—not to write my ticket to the loony bin if it turns out I'm seeing things."

Larry was still suspicious, but his curiosity got the better of him. "What is it you think you've seen?"

"I'll tell you when we get away from the fuss of those damn motorbikes, okay?"

Larry felt compelled to point out that he hadn't agreed to anything yet but at that moment, almost as if on cue, the roar of the bikes increased as the Landry boys began to race each other around their yard.

He sighed. "All right, Zach. Let me get my coat."

* * *

They walked the short distance to Zach's house in silence, Larry unable to keep from imagining what it was he was going to be see inside the other man's home. The few suggestions proffered by his overactive imagination—honed by years of mundane office work—were not worth entertaining, and were also, for the most part, unpleasant, so he shook them off.

Despite the similarity of the houses in the new subdivision, Zach's seemed different somehow. The roof appeared to droop like a wet cloth stiffened by the sun but still damp to the touch. The windows were perpetually veiled, and as Larry cautiously stepped inside, he saw the white walls were scalded with shadow, which made them seen tattooed by clumsy hands. The uncarpeted stairs stood to the left of the hallway, and hurried up only to abruptly run to the right and out of view. Everything was either white or off-white, and Larry, who had never been inside one of these houses before today, instantly disliked it.

Zach eased the door shut, and motioned for him to head into the kitchen, which from here was a dim oblong at the end of a needlessly long hallway. Larry didn't move. The other man's gesture had been so frantic that it set alarm bells ringing in his head.

"What's this all about?"

"I'll make us some coffee." Zach, head low to avoid making eye contact, started to move away, but Larry but a firm hand on his wrist.

"Wait." He removed the hand before Zach's troubled gaze could find it. "Tell me what's going on."

For a moment it looked as if Zach was going to make another break for the kitchen, but then he sagged and glanced up at the ceiling. When he spoke, there was a tremble in his voice. "It's my wife. She's upstairs."

Potent dread coursed through Larry at that moment, forcing an involuntary shudder out of him. He was all of a sudden certain that the man had murdered his wife, that her strangled or beaten body was awaiting him on the second floor, and that Zach, at the behest of some unfathomable madness, had fetched him to come see what he'd done. Then, on the heels of dread, came realization.

Zach had closed the door behind them, and was standing much too close. And Larry was too old to run.

But before he would let the panic that swelled up his throat consume him entirely, he needed to be sure that he imagination wasn't misleading him, as it had tried to before he'd even set foot inside Hoffman's house. So he asked, struggling to keep his tone as even as possible, "What about her? IS she hurt?"

Zach shook his head. "No."

"Then what's wrong?"

"She's upstairs."

"So?"

This time, Zach looked him straight in the eye. "So she shouldn't be."

"Why not?"
"Because she's in Cleveland visiting our daughter."

* * *

In the kitchen, Zach opened the blinds and sunlight burned long slanted shafts through the floating veils of dust. Larry sat at the table, nursing a cup of coffee that so far had failed to alleviate the murk he felt inside his head. He didn't feel quite so threatened now, more confused, and concerned that he might have been right about the state of Zach's sanity.

"I'm not getting what it is you're telling me," he told his pacing host. "I'm sorry, but if you say your wife's upstairs, then obviously she's not in Cleveland."

"She called me this morning from Linda's house. Said she'd be leaving late this evening and would be home around midnight. Told me to wait up for her."

"So...maybe she came home early."

"No." Zach stopped pacing and wrung his hands together. "I saw her upstairs not ten minutes after I hung up the phone. You know as well as I do it takes hours to get here from Cleveland."

"Look, relax. It's obvious either someone's playing a trick on you, or you're just a little confused."

"Mad, you mean."

"Have you spoken to her? The *upstairs* her, I mean?"

"No, I'm afraid to."

"Why?"

"Because of the way she looks."

"And what way is that?"

"I...I don't know how to describe it. It's not a threatening look, but I *feel* threatened. And the way she stands there, half-hidden, with a slight smile on her face...I don't know what's going on, Larry, but I'm willing to swear on all that's holy that the woman up there isn't my Agnes."

"Okay. Did you phone her again after you thought...after you saw her upstairs?"

"Yes. It was the first thing I did."

"And?"

"And she was there, just as I knew she'd be."

"So, you want me to see if I see her too, is that it?"

"Yes." Zach nodded toward the stairs they'd passed in the hall. "If you would."

"Of course." Larry was considerably relieved. It was obvious that Hoffman's wife was in one of two places—Cleveland, or upstairs—not both, and either Zach had forgotten to take some kind of medication, or he was losing his marbles. If taking a peek upstairs was all that was required to satisfy him, then Larry would do just that and be done with this foolishness once and for all.

At the foot of the oddly designed stairs, he asked Zach, who looked as if the walk from the kitchen had aged him another decade, "What if I do see her?"

"Then we have a problem."

Correction, Larry thought. *Then you have a problem.*

With a smile of reassurance for Zach's benefit, and feeling more than a little ridiculous, Larry placed his right hand on the smooth mahogany handrail and took a silent breath as he turned to face the stairs.

He looked up and was startled to see an old woman looking down at him.

Behind him Zach said, "Look! I *told* you, didn't I?"

Only the right side of Agnes Hoffman's face was visible, the rest obscured by the wall at the top of the stairs where it turned sharply away from the steps. The position of her head suggested she was lying on the floor on her stomach, her body laid out behind her on the second floor landing. A wide eye, shaggy gray hair, and the curve of a smiling mouth were all Larry could see from the lowermost step. It was a disconcerting sight, for it seemed as if she might attempt to crawl down the stairs on her hands and feet. But for now, she was still, peeking down at him like a mischievous child.

"You see her, right?"

Larry nodded, but said nothing.

"I told you, she's here, but she can't be here."

"Mrs. Hoffman?"

The woman's bisected smile broadened.

"You want me to call her in Cleveland?"

"No need," Larry said. *She's right here in front of me.* "Mrs. Hoffman? Is everything all right?"

She giggled. An old voice trying to sound young.

"Mrs. Hoffman? May I come up? Do you need assistance?"

"I'm going to call her," Zach said. "You'll see what I mean."

And before he could stop him, Zach hurried into the kitchen. Outside, clouds moved over the sun and the tattooed walls darkened, an effect that backlit Agnes Hoffman's head, making a silhouette of her.

"Mrs. Hoffman, is everything all right?"

He thought she might have shivered but couldn't be sure. Then, just as he promised himself he would inquire about her health one last time before abandoning the house and these obviously confused—if not downright mad—people, she spoke to him.

"Play with me."

"Excuse me?" Larry stepped away from the stairs and closer to the front door. He was finding it harder with every second that passed to justify his remaining here any longer. This was not a problem he was equipped or had any business trying to deal with. This was a job for professional men trained to talk people down from the lofty and unstable precipices in their own brains.

Agnes sighed and though her face was dark and he could no longer see it, he knew she was still watching him.

Another step toward the door and Larry called out: "Zach...I'm sorry, but I have to go. I think you need—"

His breath caught, the words dying in his throat.

Zach was not on the phone. He was hiding, *peeking*, only the right side of him visible in the kitchen doorway, the rest of him hidden by the wall. Just like Agnes, his face was in shadow, but Larry could feel the smile. "Play with me," he said, with no trace of the anxiety he'd displayed ever since he'd come to find Larry.

"What is wrong with you?" Larry asked. "What kind of a game are you two playing?"

"You have to find us," Agnes and Zach replied in unison. "That's what we were told. That's the rule."

And then, to Larry's horror, a frail terrified voice drifted out of the kitchen, from somewhere behind the figure in the doorway. "It's not possible. I don't understand how this is happening. He's *not* me...He's not *me*...I'm real...Please God...I'm—"

Larry spun, unlatched the door, and hurried out of the house, the gleeful giggling of mischievous children poisoning the breeze behind him.

* * *

The sun returned.

As he stormed home, Larry considered calling the police, but quickly realized he had nothing to tell them. At least, nothing they'd take seriously. *Officer, my reclusive elderly neighbors subjected me to some weird kind of hide-and-seek game. Can you send someone over to chastise them?*

Right.

Oddly, the droning from the woods was almost comforting now, and as he stepped on to the loamy grass in his yard, his shadow stretching out ahead of him, the jagged song of the engines helped to keep him from thinking about the Hoffmans, and the voice from the kitchen he was supposed to believe hadn't come from the man in the doorway.

Strange people, he thought, and shook his head. Then he wondered if instead of contemplating their curious behavior, he should call someone to check on them, just to be sure they hadn't lost their minds entirely. Would he be able to live with the guilt if Agnes took a spill down the stairs, or Zach, driven by the certainty that his wife was an imposter, attempted to be rid of her?

Ultimately, he decided it was someone else's problem.

At the steps to his deck, he glanced over his shoulder at the unusually quiet neighborhood he had just left behind. Where was everybody today anyway? Where were the irritating, pampered yip-yap dogs only yuppies seemed able to tolerate? Where were the businessmen and unhappy housewives smothered in expensive robes, waving their husbands goodbye with more relief than adoration?

Something else struck him as odd then, just as he'd been about to mount the deck.

The paper.

The pointless, unwanted local rag filled to bursting with trivial and mundane stories about trivial, mundane people. Today, for the first time in as long as Larry could recall, it hadn't been delivered, and now that he thought about it, he hadn't seen it on any of the driveways around the new neighborhood either. Not that he'd exactly been looking for it.

He allowed the roaring woods to drive him inside before his morning ponderings led him to start questioning who the real senile old fool was, and cast a glance at his neat, carpeted, and *straight* stairs while he filled the kettle and boiled some water for a cup of green tea.

As he puttered about the house, comfort and complacence began to smother the chill that he'd carried with him out of the Hoffman house, and he turned his mind toward the rest of the day. There were chores to be done. There were weeds to be pulled and fallen twigs to clear, but he'd only managed to plan as far as *tea, cigar, and television* before the telephone's shrill cry interrupted him. With a mutter of derision, he waved a hand at it and let it go unanswered. A quick check of the caller ID revealed a private caller, which made it ignoring it a guiltless exercise. Satisfied, Larry took his tea and an unspoiled cheroot into the living room.

Strange, strange people, he thought, with a grim smile, as he set his tea on the coffee table and thumbed the remote.

When the television came to the life, he groaned.

Something was wrong with the picture.

Either that, or the cameraman at the Channel 9 news center wasn't paying attention, because the congenial anchorman who greeted him at this time every morning was shoved to the right of the screen.

Larry swallowed, the unlit cheroot trembling between his fingers. *It's a coincidence, that's all.* But the anchorman wasn't talking, merely sitting at his desk, one half of his face off-camera. Still, Larry could see the curve of his smile.

What in God's name is going on here?

He rose, intending to fiddle with the picture until it returned to normal, and almost leapt from his skin when the phone rang again.

"Jesus," he whispered, hand clutched to his chest, feeling the thunderous beat of his heart as the anchorman's smile suddenly widened, the phone fell silent, and a face, more dreadfully familiar than any other he was likely to see in what little time remained, peeked out at him from behind the television.

HIGH ON THE VINE

Jack Thompson didn't notice the beanstalk at first, so distracted was he by the look on his wife's face as she stood hands-on-hips in their front yard. From the entrance to the driveway she looked like an overripe tomato. Her purple housecoat only exacerbated the impression of an oxygen-starved vegetable, and he knew he was in trouble, though a quick replay of the day's events yielded nothing he'd done from which she could have drawn such ire. Ordinarily, the mere hint that she was unhappy with him would have been enough to justify protracting the journey home, lingering longer than necessary at stop signs and coasting in the slow lane. Then, when there was no other course of action available, he would ease the car into the driveway and sneak into the house through the garage. Today, however, it appeared she had preempted his strategy, lowered the garage door and, not content to wait until he skulked into her line of sight, taken her protest to the yard. That worried him, and his anxiety wasn't helped by the fact that yet again, he would have to plead his case right there in full view of the neighbors.

The change, he reminded himself, sweat making his palms slip on the steering wheel as he guided the Pinto to a halt outside the garage. The change, that's all it is. It'll pass. She won't be like this forever. But if he looked really deep inside himself where he buried the truths best not studied, he knew Ann had never been any other way. They'd met on a blind date set up by mutual friends. Jack had found her attractive, if a little crude and loud, but the longer the night went on, the more he began to suspect she had already decided they were going to be an item, a suspicion confirmed when he found himself standing before her dressed in nothing but a pair of socks and Y-fronts, Ann laughing and asking if that was what he intended to wear when he met her parents.

When he'd suggested that perhaps it was a little soon to be discussing such things, she'd shoved him out the door, which unfortunately for Jack was the front one, leaving him to find a way home in his underwear.

Smiling somewhat awkwardly at the memory, he stepped from the car into the early evening sunshine and smoothed a hand over his tie. His shadow, infinitely braver than he, stretched toward the house. "Hello honey."

It was Thursday, which meant CBS would be showing their excellent run of crime shows, something he looked forward to every week. Ann had little interest in them, or anything on television other than soap operas, which she watched with an almost religious fervor. He could only hope that her temper burned itself out by the time *CSI* came on.

The neighborhood was quiet, despite the crowd of people slowly gathering in the driveway and the street beyond. Not one of them spoke. They just stared in a kind of shocked awe, as if they'd been told their houses would soon be demolished to make way for a strip club. Curious, Jack looked at each of them in turn, but the force of his wife's glare quickly drew his attention back to her.

"What's wrong?"

Teeth clenched, her face a crimson bubble with stark white periods for eyes, she jerked a thumb over her shoulder. "You idiot, *that's* what's wrong."

He adjusted his bifocals and followed her thumb to what his peripheral vision had tricked him into thinking was an oak tree. Of course there'd never been an oak tree in his front yard before but his vision wasn't what it used to be. And the yard was Ann's domain, not his. He never questioned the additions and extractions she made in her horticultural haven.

He took a step forward and squinted.

"Is that a vine of some sort?"

Ann's eyes widened. "*Look* at it for God's sake!"

He did, and suddenly understood the awe he'd seen on the faces of the crowd.

It was indeed a vine, a dark green ropy thing as thick as his waist and studded with nasty looking thorns which were hooked downward like beaks. Birds were perched on its twisted limbs, fluttering their feathers and jerking their heads out to feed on the insects that scurried up the thing's trunk. A squirrel sat up on its hindquarters, looking confused. But although this in itself was peculiar—that a giant vine should appear without warning where once had sat a gnome with a beaming smile and a fishing rod made from twigs and twine—it was the sheer *height* of the thing that made the blood drain from Jack's face.

Leaning back, a hand shaded over his eyes, he saw that the vine dwarfed his house. Indeed it rose up and up and seemed to keep going, threading its way so far above them that distance made it gray, then silver, until it was swallowed by the clouds. What kept it from toppling over under its own weight—for it seemed to have no means of support other than its own trunk and roots—was a mystery.

Jack shook his head, and mimicked his wife's posture. "We'll if that isn't the damndest thing I've ever seen. Where did it come from? Did you grow it? It's pretty nice. Could win you prizes at the County Fair."

Ann let her arms fall to her sides, fists clenched and marched over to where he stood marveling at the vine.

"You *utter* moron. *I* didn't grow it. You think they sell seeds for this down at the Wal-Mart garden center?"

"Well, no, but I thought maybe a rogue seed— "

"I don't know *where* it came from. Why don't *you* tell me where it came from? I asked you last weekend to check for weeds. 'Clean as a whistle,' you said. Well look at that big bastard there. Is that clean as a bloody whistle? *Is it?* It blasted my gardenias into outer space, for Chrissake!"

He raised a hand and offered her a gentle smile. "Honey, there's no need to get so upset over it. I'll just call the—"

"Call who? The police? They've been and gone. Nothing they can do but patrol to make sure no kids try and climb it. The fire department? They tried hacking at it with an ax until their boss arrived and told them to knock it off. 'We don't know how tall it is, Ma'am. No way of knowing which way it'll fall or how much damage it might cause the town if it fell,' he told me. Says we'd better wait until the experts get a chance to study it, until they can get some planes up there to measure the height of it. *Planes*, for the love of all that's holy! So you tell me, Jack, who exactly are *you* going to call?"

She'd listed off the very people he'd been considering. He struggled to come up with an alternative that might placate her, if just for the moment. He agreed it was a nuisance having a towering vine sprout up in the middle of the yard but surely she didn't think it was his fault? And what good would panicking do her?

A sensible attitude, he knew, but also knew better than to advise she share it.

He was relieved when someone called their names from the crowd and they both turned to watch a handsome, sharply dressed man with a clipboard making his way toward them.

"Good evening," he said with a pleasant smile and then glanced up at the vine.

"The name's Hughes."

"What do you want?" Ann snapped. "Are you here to take that ugly thing out of here?"

"I'm afraid not," he said with a rueful smile. "Merely to advise that you get someone else to take care of it, and sooner rather than later."

"Oh marvelous!" Ann threw her hands up in the air in disgust.

"Are you with the police?" Jack asked.

"No," Hughes said, reaching into his breast pocket for a small wallet, which he flipped open to show his likeness, grinning beneath the letters FAA. "I'm with the Federal

Aviation Administration."

"Aviation?"

Hughes nodded, put away the wallet. "Yes, you see that plant of yours is presenting something of a problem for the good folk at our local airport. When that thing popped up on their radars they thought we were being invaded by aliens or something."

He chuckled. "Problem is, it's directly in the flight path of some of their planes, which is causing all sorts of chaos for them. And we can't have that."

Ann scoffed. "Maybe not, but you're welcome to have *this*," she said, nodding at the vine. "I'll even provide the chainsaw. And a nice clay flowerpot if you need one."

Hughes sighed. "That's what *I'd* do all right, but after consulting with the mayor—"

Jack brightened. "The mayor knows about our plant?"

Ann glared. "*Our* plant?"

"—and the local authorities, it seems that that would do more harm than good," Hughes finished.

Ann stepped close to the man, until there was scarcely a hair's breadth between them. Hughes' smile dropped a notch.

"You said you came here to advise us to get someone to take care of that thing, am I right?"

"Please, call me Howard."

Jack raised his eyebrows. "Howard Hugh—?"

"No connection, I assure you."

"Am I right?" Ann seethed.

Hughes nodded.

"Then why are you standing here telling me all the reasons why I *can't* get rid of it? Reasons I've been listening to all goddamn day long from one suited genius to the next. How about a solution, huh? How about you strap a super-size pair of shears onto the ass-end of one of your precious planes and have them fly up there and prune the fucker down?"

Jack winced at her cussing. Hughes looked away, embarrassed.

The crowd had spread from the driveway all the way along the street on both sides now. Cars slowed; helicopters with various radio and television-station insignia hovered around the vine; sirens wailed. Children gasped, giggled and pointed. Adults murmured fearfully; others laughed. Lights flared and cameras whirred as people committed the plant to film for fear no one would believe them if it should vanish as quickly as it had come.

"Well?" Ann persisted. "What are you going to do about it?"

Hughes shrugged. "There's really nothing I can do about it, Mrs. Thompson, except to advise you of the situation."

"Advise me of—" Her face bulged; Jack backed up a step, sure she was going to rupture something and quite possibly explode right here on the front lawn. He could imagine the headline now:

WOMAN'S HEAD POPS AT THE FOOT OF WORLD'S TALLEST PLANT—AIRCRAFT REDIRECTED.

"Fat lot of help you are." Ann said, waving him away. "Jackass, get this idiot out of my sight."

It took a moment for Jack to realize the first insult had been directed his way, then he moved quickly to Hughes' side. "You'd better go."

Hughes glanced sympathetically at him—a look that said he couldn't imagine having to live with such a woman—and walked away, leaving Jack to stare up at the vine.

The longer he looked at it, the more beautiful it seemed. Furthermore, it seemed to possess the faintest glow as if lit from within by some natural power source. It didn't sway in the wind; it hardly moved at all and yet it exuded a faint aura of vitality, of sentience, as if very much aware of where it was and more importantly, *why* it was.

Jack liked it.

When a veritable cavalcade of police cars, ambulances, fire trucks and even a few army vehicles arrived, Ann told him she'd had enough and was going to lie down, in the hope that she'd wake up to find the vine gone and her marriage annulled.

Jack said nothing.

He simply stood and watched the vine, ignoring the hubbub on the street and the intruding feet that crushed his wife's ailing gladiolas, dismissing the endless questions and microphones in his face with a distracted shake of his head.

Unmarked cars crawled to a halt; men in dark glasses arrived muttering into their wrists about 'protocol' and 'advisories'.

The sun went down; the moon came up.

The vine began to whisper.

* * *

The phone rang endlessly. Fists pounded the front door; notes were slipped beneath it. Lights of varying colors swept across the backs of the curtains, making the living room into a funhouse. In the space of one hour, jack heard every range of voice imaginable trying to lure him from the comfort of his armchair. The house trembled under the assault of inquiring minds. He refused to answer because he had nothing to tell them, and besides, now that Ann was resting, he had the house to himself, and such occasions were too rare to be squandered by entertaining questions he couldn't answer.

He sat back with a sigh, thumbed the remote and frowned. Bad enough that his home was under siege, but now the television showed nothing but the vine on almost every station: vertigo-inducing aerial views, sketches estimating the height of the plant and its genesis, some of which were so outlandish even the interviewers couldn't keep a straight face; grainy pictures of plastic-faced reporters bathed in harsh light standing outside his door and gesturing over their heads; uniformed men and women (was that a *General?*) looking uncomfortable being filmed, keeping their heads and voices low as they speculated about the possible threats the growth represented. He watched people in white coats and facemasks excising small samples from the vine and scurrying away like children robbing apples from an orchard. The vine didn't seem at all put out by the theft.

The knocking continued; the ringing continued.

If this was his fifteen minutes of fame, Jack didn't want it. All he wanted was to watch his crime shows. But they weren't on. The vine was.

* * *

The closest Jack had ever come to intimacy with his wife had been the night of their first date when she'd thrown him out in his underwear.

Ever since then, they had slept in separate beds. While Jack never understood Ann's reasons for keeping him at a distance, nor did he challenge it. He had gained precious little sexual experience since his bygone days of adolescent self-exploration, and so did not mourn the obvious lack of carnal benefits, only the warmth and closeness he could not get by sleeping alone. He was not governed by the same urges that seemed to preoccupy his coworkers, if their washroom banter was any indication of their true feelings. He just wanted to snuggle.

Surely that wasn't so much to ask, particularly since they were married and thus allowed such luxuries?

She was turned away from him, snoring, when he entered the room and slowly made his way over to his own bed. Carefully he sat, wincing when the springs squealed, freezing when his shoe escaped his grasp and thumped to the floor, but Ann didn't wake.

He realized he shouldn't have expected her to. After all, the cacophony outside had not lessened, even though it was close to midnight, and if she'd managed to sleep through that, nothing was going to rouse her.

He finished undressing and crawled into bed.

After a moment spent getting settled, he put his hands behind his head and stared at the ceiling.

He thought about the vine and the soft, rustling whisper he was sure he'd heard emanating from it like a breeze combing through a cornfield.

He wondered why it was here, where it had come from and what they were going to do about it.

And as sleep brought grains of sand to his eyes, he wondered how tall it really was, if maybe it continued on into space (with Ann's gardenias upon its crown), ignoring the rules of physics, resisting the heat of the atmosphere, stretching up and out of the galaxy until even the Hubble telescope had to shrug in defeat.

The immensity of such a thought tied weights to his mind and tugged him down into the darkness, one final question rising like a bubble to the surface: *I wonder what's at the top of it.*

* * *

At work he was treated as a celebrity. Even the most casual of acquaintances rushed at him dribbling the same questions the reporters had blurted at him, and invited themselves over for a peek at the wonder in his yard.

"Anyone climbed up yet?"

"Anything come down?"

"You sold it to anyone? Bet there's a ton of offers!"

There was much talk of barbeques, cookouts, even keggers and tailgate parties, as if the vine had magically reduced the ages of everyone who spoke about it by two decades.

His boss, an ordinarily odious man by the name of Heckler, who seldom regarded

Jack with anything other than derision laced with pity, clapped a chubby hand on his shoulder, shooed away the gaggle of star struck employees and ushered Jack into his office.

"My, my, Thompson, it would appear I've underestimated you!" he enthused.

"You have?" said Jack, bewildered and still reeling from the assault of coworkers.

Heckler lowered his immense frame into a battered leather chair, which squealed in torment, and motioned for Jack to sit. "Oh yes. I admit I've always looked at you as a somewhat…how shall I put it…*yellow* member of our team. Your sales have never been as strong as anybody else's, you walk around looking dazed half the time and to be honest, at least once a month I consider firing you."

"Oh," Jack said.

"In fact, if not for recent developments, that's what I'd be doing right now."

Laughter exploded from the bladder-like cavity between his jowls and he raised a finger. "Got something." From a drawer beneath his desk he produced two oversized cigars and presented one to Jack with a flourish. "Cubans," he said, with a grin. "Go on, take it."

Jack did as instructed, and poked the cigar between his lips. It felt like he'd stuck a branch in his mouth. With visible difficulty, Heckler leaned over, a shiny Zippo lighter in his hand, his gut making the desk slide forward a few inches, pinning Jack's knees beneath it, and lighted his cigar for him. Acrid smoke filled Jack's mouth and he coughed.

"Stalemate Incorporated is only as good as the people who run it, Thompson,"

Heckler announced, touching the flame to his own cigar and puffing plumes of smoke into the air. "It needs a steel backbone to compete out there in the big bad world and quite frankly you're the only slipped disc in our spine. At least, you *were*."

"I don't understand."

Heckler beamed but quickly ruined the expression by jamming the thick cigar back between his teeth. He sat back. The chair shrieked. Jack jumped.

"This vine thing of yours is ingenious, Thompson. Absolutely the most ingenious thing I've ever seen in all my years in the herbicide business."

"What?"

"My father always said 'Watch the quiet ones, Del, and I never understood that until now. I always thought the 'quiet ones' were that way because they feared the rest of the world, that they were pussies, y'know?"

Jack tried to grin and gave up.

"I had you figured for the type who sits at home with a glass of wine watching *CSI* while all the other guys are at singles bars trying to cheat on their wives." He bellowed laughter. "But no. *No.* There you were, you crafty son of a bitch, there you were using that big brain of yours to come up with an unprecedented ad campaign for our little company."

"Ad campaign?"

"C'mon, man. Don't try to pull the wood over my eyes. I'm no dummy."

"Wood?"

"Give yourself the kudos you deserve, my man, because it will certainly be reflected in your paycheck."

"My pay—"

"This morning alone, I've had seven different companies call to congratulate us on our wild idea…wanting to know how we did it."

"Uh…" Jack squirmed in his seat. "Did what?"

"Oh for Christ's sake, man. *The vine!* That goddamn vine has everyone out buying up all the herbicide they can get and there you are, the quiet genius, looking as normal and harmless—and let's face it, about as interesting—as a water cooler. You devious bastard. As soon as you get back on the road and people open their doors to find Jack Thompson—he of the towering weed—standing there offering to sell them the remedy for their crabgrass, they'll simply *shit* I tell you! Can't you see it?" He put a hand on his heart as if preparing to sing the national anthem. "'Yes Ma'am, it was a nightmare all right, but this is what I used in the end. Took care of that giant weed lickety-split. What's that you say? Ten cases? Oh, I'm not sure I have enough with me but…'"—fan*tastic!*" Heckler clapped his hands together. His eyes gleamed. "You're gonna go a long way in this company, Thompson. A long way. What you've done is the single most brilliant scheme I've ever seen. Everyone wants a piece of you, but let me tell you this: they'll have to pony up the big bucks to get you out from under my wing. This isn't some scam like the time my stepbrother Juan got on TV by telling the world his poodle took a dump in the shape of Elvis. This is the real McCabe we have here."

"McCoy."

"See? A genius!" He stood and extended his hand. Jack slowly rose.

"What do you say, Jack? Can I call you Jack?"

"I guess so."

"Good, good," Heckler said, coming around the desk to escort Jack to the door.

"Before you go, tell me something."

"What?"

"I promise my lips are sealed."

"Okay."

"How the hell *did* you do it?"

* * *

That evening, there were more people outside his house than ever before. To his amazement, he saw that some of them were actually setting up tents, lounging on sleeping bags, playing music, playing cards while others poked and prodded the vine and consulted with handheld instruments that gave their faces a ghoulish cerulean glow. A nude couple with braided hair and beards danced like Indians around a small fire and chanted nonsense until they were covered up and led away by the police. They'd looked like hippies, which confused Jack, who'd thought that hippies had died out after Charles Manson shot John Lennon. Arguments, debates and futures were settled among enclaves that had sprouted up almost as quickly as the vine. Old men sat on deckchairs and nodded sagely, exchanging wisdom with each other in hushed tones. When they weren't plucking nudists from his lawn, cops shared coffee and jokes, occasionally glancing up at the vine and laughing. Military men stood in a ring around the yard, holding rifles Jack hoped weren't loaded. Children out far past their bedtime picked at noses and danced bladder dances while looking imploringly up at their distracted parents. Reporters preened themselves before the cold glaring eye of men with cameras growing out of their cheeks.

After being forced to park three blocks away, Jack fought his way through the sea of inquisition and light until he was inside, where he sighed heavily and tossed his briefcase on the sofa.

"Ann?"

The house was quiet.

"Honey?"

There was a note on the table in the kitchen.

Squinting, Jack tilted it toward the light and read:

Gone to stay with my sister. She's at least capable of an intelligent conversation. I'll do you a favor and not be concerned that you're there alone. Maybe dealing with all those crazy folk will help you grow a pair of balls. And while you're wasting your life away in front of that damned television, be thankful I'm coming back, because it's occurred to me more than once not to bother.

Ann.

P.S. When I get back I want to see that vine gone. I don't care how you do it, just get rid of it.

Jack crumpled up the note, went to the fridge and poured himself a glass of wine.

The vine was still on almost every channel, but after much searching, he managed to find one that was showing an old episode of *Perry Mason*. With a smile, he sat back and soon managed to tune out the clamor from outside.

She's gone. He was less appalled than he might have thought to realize that for now at least, and for the first time ever, he didn't care.

Peace at last.

* * *

In the dream he was climbing. Thorns tore at his skin; unseen creatures left their roosts with angry cries and the air changed, grew thinner. He found it difficult to breathe but he carried on, his hands in agony, blood dripping down the length of the vine, staining the cuffs of his white shirt, the legs of his pants. The intoxicatingly leafy smell of the plant filled his head, making him dizzy. He stopped. The whisper bade him continue.

A castle, he thought. *There will be a castle at the top, waiting for me, filled with everything I've ever wished for.* It was a childish thought, but knowing this did not lessen his conviction. It might not be anything as wondrous as a castle, but *something* was up there, waiting for him.

Up and up he went, grunting at the strain, shaking alien insects from his fingers with a grimace, panicking when he almost lost his footing, or a branch gave way with a crunch and fluttered away on the currents of air that swirled around him. He persisted, the air growing colder the higher he went, and when he chanced a look down he saw, over the flapping tail of his shirt, the clouds and the gray city below—the colorless, lifeless, meaningless prison he'd been trapped in forever. The chill air cut through him and when he shivered, his spectacles slid from his nose and he whipped out a hand, felt them smack against his clammy palm, fumbled and watched as they pirouetted on one Scotch-taped leg before they tipped forward and dropped out of sight. In seconds they were nothing but a black speck, heading straight for Nowhere. Jack blinked, deeply affected by the loss— they'd been with him longer than Ann had—but when he reached for the next branch, a U-shaped serpent, punctuated by wickedly sharp thorns, he realized to his surprise, he didn't need them anymore. The glow from the vine seemed to be guiding him now more than ever, chasing the mist from his eyes and drawing him ever upward.

And when at last his head broke through the cold mist of the clouds, his eyes widened at the sheer beauty of what stood before him. An enormous castle, white and gleaming, a multi-turreted wonder cut straight from the pages of a fairy tale, with brightly colored flags snapping their masts, sprawling lawns and a drawbridge yawning wide.

Warm light filled every window, and the shadows of people dancing threw themselves against the glass. He had come this far, and though the castle was still quite a distance away, the hardest part of his journey was over.

He pulled himself up onto the silver carpet, and the voice of a woman, too seductive and kind to be his wife's, whispered, *"Come..."*

* * *

A phone call from Heckler woke him.

He sat up, groggy, and rubbed a hand over his face. Dismayed to find himself back in the unremarkable real world, he checked the clock and with a shake of his head, brought the receiver to his ear.

"Morning sport! Glad I caught you."

"It's Saturday."

Heckler hummed. "Indeed it is, and I have a meeting set up with the folks in advertising. Say about noon?"

"Advertising? I don't know..."

"They want to step up the ad campaign, just in case that plant of yours decides to disappear without telling anyone, and they want to put you on the posters, organize some television and radio spots, that sort of thing. Strike while the oven's hot, as they say. To maximize the benefit for the company, you understand. Now I told them I'd be willing to stand in for you and give them everything they need, but they weren't having it. They want you, Jack and only you. You're the face of this company now my good man."

"I'm not sure I can make it," Jack told him and listened to the sigh thundering over the line.

"Jack, pal, this isn't a suggestion. This is big business now. You have to run with the punches and roll with the pack, my man. You've single-handedly put us back in the game and if you don't step up to the challenge, then you're letting all of us—not to mention *yourself*—down. Think about it, do you really want to go back to being a nobody, huh pal?"

Jack frowned. "No I guess I don't."

"That's my boy. See you at noon then?"

"Yeah. Noon."

Heckler said something else but Jack put the phone down. He reached out a hand, parted the curtain and saw nothing but crowds of people, busily moving silhouettes fragmenting the dawn. He looked across the room, at Ann's still-made bed, and sighed.

It was destined to be a day like any other, planned by everyone else. Still wrapped in the vestiges of a wonderful dream, Jack shook his head as if someone had relayed the sad truth aloud. "No," he said, checking his hands for blood from the thorns, just in case...

And jolted when a whisper came to him.

"Come," it said. With a flood of elation and little hesitation, Jack obeyed. He recognized the voice, had been praying for it to single him out, just as the vine had seemed to single him out by appearing in his yard. He was an unremarkable man, but what had happened to him was certainly remarkable, even if Ann didn't think so and even if Heckler agreed for all the wrong reasons. In fact, now that the voice had come and he wasn't dreaming, Jack thought it was more than remarkable. It was magic. It had just taken him a while to realize it, that's all. He'd never claimed to be, as Heckler would say, "The sharpest fool in the shed."

He dressed quickly in clothes heavier than the warm weather demanded and hurried through the house, through the sunlit kitchen and out into his backyard where a conference of journalists were interrogating a haughty looking expert on something or other. Jack shouldered through them, ignoring their excited chatter and the knife-like stab of their microphones into his face, the vapid stare of their cameras, and continued on until he reached the small wooden shed in which Ann stored her gardening equipment.

The reporters continued to scream questions at him.

He shook his head, still smiling, and searched the dank interior of the shed until he found what he was looking for.

Anticipation made a hornet's nest of his insides, but that was all right. It wasn't the kind of negative buzz he felt every time he pulled into the driveway and saw Ann's temper waiting for him. No, this was altogether different. This was euphoria, pure and simple.

Ignoring the hubbub at his back, he plucked the light blue gardening gloves from their place atop the shelf of tools and slipped them on. The insides felt grainy but that didn't matter. Nothing mattered now.

"Mr. Thompson, are you considering doing some yard work?"

Laughter.

"Mr. Thompson, are you going to wring the vine's neck?"

More laughter.

"Mr. Thompson, are you going to climb the vine?"

He turned to look at them and there was no laughter when they saw his smile.

They knew that was exactly what he was going to do.

* * *

Cameras began to roll.

Jack stared at the vine, then reached out a hand to touch it. Lights flashed and he flinched before he realized the photographers were to blame. Chiding himself, he ran his fingertips over the smooth trunk.

It felt like skin. Soft, smooth and warm, like the body of a lover.

"Mr. Thompson," someone said. "This really isn't a good idea."

He answered without looking over his shoulder. "I have to see what's up there."

"But you could get hurt."

Jack shook his head. No. If there was one thing he was certain of, it was that he wouldn't get hurt. The vine was not a wicked thing, sent to harm whoever dared scale it, but a savior, taking him from the mundane ritual of his daily life and up, forever upward to something beyond anyone's ability to imagine. The scientists with all their technology couldn't tell where the vine ended or what might be at its head, but Jack knew one thing—the vine was only the root and somewhere up there the flower bloomed. And he needed to see it. It was the only thing that mattered now. It was unplanned, unrehearsed and most importantly, *his* choice.

But considering it was unlikely he'd ever see them again, Jack decided, before he embarked upon his climb, to field some of the questions the congregation threw at him. It was a mistake. It took less than an hour, but Ann's sister lived only thirty minutes away.

She must have been watching the early morning news as it left Jack's mouth and was transmitted live to every TV screen in America, because he was less than six feet high on the vine when the murmurs of the crowd became more animated and were subsequently drowned out by a single, solitary, hideous cry of, "Jack Joseph John *Thompson.*"

Jack winced, and looked over his shoulder and down at the crowd, who had parted to let the fuming woman through.

"Parents couldn't decide which of the father's three brothers to name him after," one of the reporters muttered in answer to his colleague's puzzled expression. "Used all three."

"Jesus, Mary and Joseph on a trampoline, what do you think *you're* doing?" Ann asked, her complexion the now familiar color of beets.

Jack opened his mouth, the skin of the vine pulsating slightly, softly, beneath his fingers, and swallowed the first response to occur to him. *Nothing, dear.* Instead he smiled a small smile and frowned. "I think it's fairly obvious what I'm doing. Going for a climb."

"The hell you are. Get your sorry ass back down here right this minute."

"I can't."

"What do you mean you can't?"

"I'm not coming down. I have no reason to."

"Jack..." She clenched her teeth. "You're making a fool out of me."

"No," he replied. "I think you managed that just fine on your own. All I did was watch."

"Ten seconds, Jack, or goddamn you there'll be hell to pay."

She seemed acutely aware that this time, their argument was being monitored by more than just nosy neighbors. *This* particular exchange was being watched by the whole world, and so she would have to win it. Jack wondered if maybe showboating had been her primary objective all along. She'd sure loved those outdoor dustups. He also wondered if she'd get her own talk show out of this.

"There already has been hell to pay, Ann," he told her, "and in twenty years of marriage to you, I've paid it more than once."

"Oh, so you're the victim, are you? Is that the angle you're going to try and pull off on these people?"

"I'm not using any angle, Ann, and I couldn't care less about these people, no more than they, or you for that matter, care about me. This is a timeslot and a paycheck for them, nothing more, and for you, it's a chance to demonstrate for the entire viewing public what an incredibly cruel, cold hearted, dried up old twat you are."

If there is a level of silence beneath absolute, then the crowd reached it at that moment. Ann looked as if she'd been hit by a car, reversed over, then propped up to show a class full of hormonal teenagers why they shouldn't drink and drive. Her legs wobbled, she balled up her fists then opened them. "You dirty rotten bastard. You're not going to steal the best years of my life then climb up a fucking bean sprout to get out of it. I'll kill you before I let you do that."

At that, the cameras swiveled in her direction, microphones springing toward her like spring-loaded needles. The crowd began to whisper. Murder had been promised and the world had front row seats.

Unconcerned by the ramifications of her actions on live television, Ann stalked off to the woodshed to find a weapon, and propelled not by cowardice but impatience,

Jack began to climb.

* * *

It was just as he'd dreamed it would be, though while the pain had been vague and purely visual in his mind, it was raw and fiery and all too real now. The thorns were fish hooks in his flesh, tugging it open, tearing it wide as he struggled to reach the next branch. Outraged birds flapped and screeched at him, driven to protect a domain that only days before hadn't existed. The scent kept him going, made him aware that if he learned little else during this climb, it was that magic smelled of vegetation.

"Come..."

"I am," he answered.

The air became dense, misty. Sweat ran in rivulets from his face, soaked his back, the wind growing colder, freezing his skin.

Thirty feet from the ground, doubt began to creep in. He was already getting tired, his muscles ached, his flesh felt sore from top to bottom. Even his hair hurt, however that had happened. And though he didn't want to stop, didn't want to go back down, nor did he want to die, to wither on the vine, as the song said happened to all true love. And love was most certainly what this was. The vine, a monstrous mystery plant to most, a business or scientific opportunity to others, was nothing less than Jack's way out. It had come to take him away, to make something of him, and he loved it for that, whether or not he found God, a castle, or nothing at the top. Assuming he made it that far.

Inspiration came sometime later, while he rested in a natural (if anything about the vine could be termed as such) cradle in the trunk. He was dozing, lulled by the sigh of the wind, the steady chittering of some unseen insects he had already passed, when he heard the voice cry out, "I'm coming for you, you sonofabitch," followed by a mad cackle. "I'm right behind you, Jack, and I won't stop until you do." Instantly he was awake, alert and moving, the vine groaning as he wrenched himself out of the cradle, ignoring the acidic flare of pain that scalded his hand as a row of thorns punctured the skin. His wrist soaked with blood, he hoisted himself up, occasional glimpses down showing Ann's bulky form clinging to the vine as birds squawked and beat their wings around her. The sun made the weapon in her hand gleam, and Jack felt a pang of sorrow.

So much time spent together, so many years of self-delusion, pretending she cared when all she'd ever wanted was a husband in name only, someone who would provide for her and ensure she had enough bills in her purse to blow on Friday Night Bingo. Someone she didn't have to acknowledge or love.

Jack shook his head. So much wasted time. And yet he wondered if the vine might change her too? Awaken facets of her personality that she'd kept hidden for so long she'd forgotten how to use them, like old rooms that needed airing.

Sadly, he didn't think so.

"You no good...stinkin' pig. I'm coming for you."

At all.

"You just wait for me Jack Thompson. You just wait." She sounded breathless, as tired as he was, but no less determined.

He climbed on.

* * *

Jack estimated that he had climbed seventy feet by the time he met Heckler, who was sitting on an outstretched branch which had bent under his considerable weight. He was chomping on a cigar and apparently admiring the view of the city spread out before him. He held a Cuban out for Jack, who, remembering the foul taste of them, shook his head and asked, "What are you doing here?"

Heckler's shrug made the limb he was perched on groan. "Wanted to see what you thought was so damned special about this thing that you had to climb it. The ad folks told me they thought you were one wave short of a picnic, but I stood up for you buddy, defended my wingman. Told them to watch and learn. So..." He gestured with his cigar and the wind wrenched away the smoke. "Why *are* you climbing it?"

Breathless, Jack put his face against the stalk of the vine and closed his eyes. "Want to see what's at the top."

"Oh. Think you'll make it?"

Jack grinned wryly. "You made it this far, didn't you, and you're not exactly in shape."

"True," Heckler said. "But I'm a hallucination. Makes it easier. If I was real, then you'd have passed my fat corpse seventy feet ago."

Jack opened his eyes, frowned. "It's a good likeness."

"Shows you took notice. I'm flattered."

"You look real, but I guess I was surprised you made it this high," Jack admitted.

"Eh," Heckler said, looking at the small silver speck of an aircraft soaring up into the clouds. "I'm not proud, Jack. I'm all meat. They haven't built a crane yet that could take the job on." He chuckled and puffed on his cigar. "Anyway, you're about to pass out, so I'll leave you to it. You've got stones though, I will give you that, and quite frankly I'm a little ashamed I didn't recognize it earlier. Anyway, it's all water under the bridge, right?"

Water under the bridge, Jack thought. *He got it right.* Definitely a hallucination.

"Best of luck buddy! I hope whatever's up there proves worth it." Heckler shoved forward, so that he was holding himself aloft with only his hands and the outer reaches of his buttocks, like a kid preparing to slip into a cool pond.

"Wait a minute, I—"

Jack passed out.

* * *

He awoke in the clouds, and panicked. How had he gotten this far? He'd fallen unconscious, so surely he must have let go and fallen to his death.

Ah.

That was it of course. He was dead. His body was a shattered ruin at the base of the vine, every reporter in the state gathered around shaking their heads on the main evening news. He wondered if Ann was still clinging to the plant, or if his body had knocked her off on its way down. The thought was grimly satisfying. After all, if he hadn't seen the fruition of his labors, then why should she?

He shivered, and that didn't seem right. Then he opened palms made stiff by dried blood and strain and it hurt like hell. He winced, mouthed "ow" and leaned his head back.

It thumped against the unyielding surface of the vine and he grunted as cold pain spread across his skull.

If this was death, it was terribly uncomfortable, and he mused, terribly unfair.

He'd never imagined further pain to be part of the afterlife, unless of course one had spent the better part of their lives worshipping the devil, murdering people, or working for the IRS. And since he had done none of those things and the pain was getting worse the longer he considered it, he could only conclude that he hadn't died at all, that luck had propped his passed out body up against the trunk instead of thrusting it the other way in a graceless swan dive that would have left his corpse buried headfirst, legs poking out of

Ann's precious yard like some badly choreographed parody of the witch's less-than-noble demise in *The Wizard of Oz*.

He was alive. The clouds did not signify his ascension into Heaven. In fact, they didn't signify ascension at all other than his climb thus far. The clouds had come down.

He was shrouded in fog.

Exhausted, he flirted with the idea of further rest, but worried that Ann would catch up, or the vine would get tired of his dallying and return to the seed from which it had sprung, quashing his dreams and ending his life in one fell swoop.

So he carried on, forcing himself higher, pausing only to drink the water pooled in the vine's leaves and to check to see if Ann had gained on him. But he didn't see her. He hauled himself up the vine, until it no longer felt as if he was breathing, until it no longer felt as if he *needed* to breathe. His head swam, and when at last he did fall, this time out and away from the vine, the limbs of the plant seemed to wrap around him and bring him back, saving him again, holding him until he was ready to resume. They couldn't, however save his spectacles, which he tried to catch, fumbled, and lost. He watched them go until there was nothing left to see.

At last the vine grew narrow, the air warmer, and, feeling like a stranger in his own body, Jack climbed the last of the vine, the trunk tapering to the width of a rope, and when he reached up and found there was nothing to hold onto, he found himself standing on a silver surface, which accepted him and did not let him fall as he dropped to his knees and wept.

He'd made it after what seemed like a lifetime of climbing. He rubbed numb, trembling hands over the pate of his badly wind-burned head.

The clouds danced softly around him.

"We're waiting for you," said a voice, as the drawbridge opened.

* * *

Ann collapsed in an exhausted heap at the foot of the vine, and despite the crowd still in her yard, no one came to her aid. "Help me, Lord Jesus!" she cried, unsure, even in her delirium, just when it was she'd decided to put such stock in religion. It had never helped before, nor had she bothered to believe it would. "Help me!" she yelled again, but no one paid her any attention. Perhaps it was because in the absence of its two major players, the reporters had been given ample time to decide who the protagonists and antagonists were in this surreal little drama, or perhaps it was because they hadn't even seen her drop like a rag doll from the vine. This latter seemed the most plausible, given that every single person in the yard was facing away from her.

"I'm hurt!" she proclaimed, though she wasn't, at least not physically. Only her pride had been wounded, and it would be a long time before it would heal. She was more surprised than anything else to discover that the squirrelly little man she'd married had had it in him to defy her, to do something of his own volition other than get up, whizz, shower and shave, splash on some of that cologne he favored (which she thought smelled like camel farts), go to work, come home, take a crap and sleep. It was his routine, and she approved of it because for the most part it kept him away from her. When she needed him, he was there; when she didn't, he wasn't, and that was fine and dandy.

But today...

"I think I twisted my ankle!"

Today, he'd changed, and she was alarmed to find as she'd clung to the vine for dear life that his newfound dominant attitude had affected her in the most unexpected of ways. It had turned her on. Indeed she might have learned to embrace it, even invited Jack back into her bed (on the condition that he not abandon that dominance once he got under the covers) but only after she had given the television people the dénouement they were undoubtedly expecting, and lopped off one of Jack's fingers. She would never relinquish control, but she might be willing to share it. All of which was moot now, because Jack was up the vine and she knew he wouldn't stop climbing until it killed him.

It dawned on her then, that if this should happen, the base of the vine was probably not the safest place to be, but the strength had left her. Once more she screeched at the crowd. "Please, help me, I can't walk!"

And once more, they ignored her. She frowned and watched their shadows flicker at her feet. What were they watching anyway? What could possibly have drawn their attention away from the vine, and the spousal pursuit that had been unfolding atop it? She shook her head to clear some of the murk from her mind, and, using the pruning shears she still held in her right hand, managed to prop herself up enough to get to her knees.

Slowly, head spinning, she stood.

There were flashing lights and sirens, but she'd come to expect that. Damn parasites had moved in with no consideration for her need to sleep.

There was smoke and there was fire, which wasn't expected. With a small satisfied smile, she wondered if one of those hippies had tossed his reefer into a trash can or something. Maybe that would be enough to get the lot of them hauled off to jail.

But no, she realized, somewhat perplexed and more than a little annoyed that she was not being attended to, whatever had happened was a little bigger than that. The crowd had spread out on both sides of what seemed to be a huge crater in the street, only a few yards from her driveway. Smoke rose from tangled wreckage, she saw, as she elbowed her way through the shocked and silent onlookers. A car had been crushed, or maybe a small aircraft had crashed there. Puzzled, she all but lunged through the tight barrier of human bodies and emerged at the lip of the crater. Emergency services filled the street, but the EMS, firemen and policeman were simply standing there, staring in awe into the hole.

"I've never seen anything like that," someone said at last, and Ann gave him a withering look, unsure whether or not this latest development was ample justification for her being ignored.

"Like *what?*" she asked, and saw the speaker, a middle-aged man in a crumpled suit, recognize her with a small start, as if he'd just emerged from a daydream. "Like what?" she repeated.

He nodded pointedly toward the hole, the flames from the ruptured engine of whatever had been obliterated dancing in his glassy eyes. "Must have come from a billboard or something, though I don't understand how."

"Naw, you know that wasn't from a billboard," someone else said sagely, but offered little else.

Ann looked back at the hole, at the tar, or whatever it was that was oozing over the twisted metal of what she guessed was an Army vehicle. She sneered. Maybe there was a God after all and he didn't approve of their parking outside her house. Then she noticed the thick fragments of glass, which might have been at home in the windows of a skyscraper. They were poking up from the hole like translucent mountains, mirroring the firelight. The air reeked of melting plastic.

"He's right," said another voice in the crowd. "We all saw it."

More sirens wailed. Someone barked orders on a megaphone. Few listened.

"Saw what?" Ann demanded, exasperated, tired and wanting little more than for all this to be over. To hell with Jack and his beanstalk. She just wanted to sleep and wake to find the vine gone and with it the gaggle of gawkers it had summoned to itself. Surely that wasn't asking too much? They were goddamned fortunate she hadn't thrown each and every one of them off her property right at the start.

"Spectacles," the ashen-faced man who'd first spoken told her at last. "A giant pair of spectacles."

Ann laughed at him then, a high-pitched hysterical laugh, and this time when she collapsed, someone caught her, a cop by the looks of it, though she found it hard to tell so covered was he in soot and dirt. The idea of being led to her door by someone who looked like a confused Al Jolson made tears run down her face. Al didn't seem amused, but that was okay, she found it funny enough for both of them. It was not until she heard someone in the crowd say, "Let's hope Thompson doesn't decide to come back down to look for them," that the mirth finally gave way, and by then she had been deposited on the stoop, trembling furiously. And despite the crowd gathered in the yard, the street, the city, she had never felt so hopelessly alone.

Alone but for the faintest whisper from the vine that she told herself was only the wind, not a voice, and most certainly not the rustling of leaves marking the downward passage of a giant.

TONIGHT THE MOON IS OURS

Evan waited beneath the covers for the sound. When it came crawling down the hall, a dry rasping staccato snore unbecoming the eighty-year old woman who made it, he grinned and threw back the covers. The moon, high and round and pure, shone a spotlight through the large bedroom window, illuminating his scuffed sneakers and crumpled jacket on the floor beside him. He had gone to bed dressed to save time and unnecessary noise and in less than a minute he was ready, poised by the window, face raised to the moon.

From his grandmother's bedroom, the slumberous grinding continued. Tilting his watch to the light, he saw it was not quite eleven, and that was fine. Teeth clenched as if the expression alone might lessen the possibility of noise, he painstakingly lifted the latch, winced at the faint squeak, and eased the window open.

Night air, cool and crisp, assailed his senses, canceling out the musty air in the room. Grasping the edges of the wooden frame, he put a foot on the radiator beneath the window and pulled himself up until he was crouching on the sill. He held his breath, listening, half-in, half-out of the room. Something fluttered from the safety of the spruce trees at the bottom of the yard; the stream trickling down from the mountains chuckled its way through the ditch. His grandmother's overweight basset hound Lester grumbled in his sleep from inside the garden shed.

Evan turned his back on the moon and with hands braced on the sill, lowered himself to the ground. Again he paused, sure as he was every other night that his grandmother was going to catch him sneaking out. After a moment, he slid the window back until it was almost closed, the gap left for him to poke the latch fully open when he returned.

With a hiss of triumph, he tiptoed to where the stream was toying with the light, crossed it via a small rickety wooden bridge his grandfather had made from deadwood, and was out into the fields, the grass glittering with frost before him.

* * *

His grandmother's house was separated from the rest of the village by a two-acre field owned by a local farmer, who used it for his horses. As Evan crunched through the cold stiff grass, the moon making it seem as if he was walking on diamonds, he imagined he saw the animals, proud and dark, lurking among the shadows woven by the bare chestnut trees at the far side of the field. But of course, it was too cold for them to be left out at night now. Still, when he strained his ears, he imagined he could hear them snuffling.

Ahead of him, the land dipped and became an oblong of darkness, the moon denied by the newly built community hall—a towering structure which exuded modernity and so stuck out as alien in a village as ancient as Touraneena. Evan didn't mind it so much; they held basketball and volleyball there on Saturday mornings and chess on Sunday evenings, and as long as his parents insisted on dumping him out here every weekend, every distraction from the dreary village would be a welcome one.

Next to the community center, a strip of fir trees divided a small playing field from the low-slung school. Upon reaching the firs, Evan halted and ducked down, peering through the branches past the schoolhouse to The Shelter, a long concrete enclosure with one open side segmented by pillars, where the children sat to eat lunch or play when it rained. He warmed at the sight of it. It was here, on his fifteenth birthday, among the litter, spent cigarette butts and used condoms he'd first taken a sip of alcohol (which had been terrible, but for the sake of machismo, he'd feigned enjoyment). It was here he discussed things that would have reddened his grandmother's ears had she heard.

It was here he'd had his first kiss.

Voices. He turned his head, hands gripping the warped bole of the tree concealing him, and listened. The scent of sap assailed him and he breathed it in. On the slight breeze, he recognized the lilt of Yvonne's voice and Colm's frantic, urgent whispering. The latter's panicked susurrations resolved themselves into a warning: *There's someone over there. In the trees! Listen!*

His friends. Clearing his throat and affecting a deeper, more authoritative tone, he emerged from the trees, stiffened his gait and said:

"You there. What are you doing out this late?"

There was silence for a moment, then nervous laughter. "*Evan!*" Colm sounded deflated by relief.

"You nearly gave me a heart attack," Yvonne said. "I thought it was my father."

Evan stopped short of the threshold. He could not see Colm and Yvonne's faces. The roof stopped the moonlight at their necks, encasing their heads in shadow. But he could see enough to know that Yvonne was wearing no jacket, just the sweater he liked with the picture of an eagle caught in mid-flight. It was less the picture however and more the swell of her flesh beneath it that had gained his approval.

"Where's Bobby?" he asked.

"No idea," Colm said. "He wasn't around all day today, and there's no one at his house."

"Huh," Evan said. "You'd have thought he would've said something. It's not like him to miss out."

"Maybe he got caught trying to sneak out," Colm offered.

Evan nodded. "Maybe."

Yvonne snorted. "It wouldn't surprise me if he's still sore about you and Colm ribbing him over the fairy stone."

The fairy stone. Evan couldn't resist a smile and Colm chuckled.

"Are you serious? He asked for it, with all that crap about magical rocks. Jesus, c'mon. People stopped believing in that stuff about a hundred years ago," Evan said.

"Not in this village they didn't," Yvonne said, and he didn't like how serious she sounded. If she believed in fairy stones, then he realized he might have jeopardized his chances of ever ending up with her by making fun of Bobby.

"It's ancient thinking," Colm said. "Superstition started up by a bunch of drunk farmers with nothing better to do."

Evan agreed, but decided not to vocalize it. Instead, he sighed and turned to look out across the fields he'd just crossed. He was reaching into his jacket pocket for a cigarette when Yvonne said quietly: "What about those children then?"

"What children?"

"Alice McCabe's twins. They've been missing for a week now."

Colm chuckled, but it was devoid of humor. "Those kids were odd anyway and their mother is odder still. If I lived with her and that trumpet voice of hers, I'd run away too."

"You think that's what happened?" Yvonne asked, sounding desperate to believe it.

"Sure I do."

Evan flicked his lighter and flinched when a shadow flitted across his feet. No one had moved, so he blamed the flame and the breeze and lit his cigarette.

"What do you think happened to them?" he asked Yvonne, suddenly wishing Colm were elsewhere so he could comfort her in the manner he'd rehearsed every night in his fantasies since they'd first kissed three weeks ago.

"I don't know. Give me a cigarette."

He offered her the pack, then the flame. She took both and when the lighter flared, he saw her eyes were pools of dark. Her shadow tried to tear away but was anchored to her shoulders; it stretched up the graffiti-riddled wall until she let the flame die.

"I hate autumn," Colm said then, refusing the cigarettes when Yvonne offered it to him. "So friggin' cold."

Evan didn't agree. He loved autumn; the way the leaves turned a panoply of colors before the trees let them go; the earthy aroma the breeze ferried across the fields; the crackle of frost, the clean taste in the air, the way the streets looked after the rain had come and gone. It was second only to summer in his season of choice. Whenever he and Yvonne were alone, he liked it all the more. It seemed to swirl around them with its cape of dead leaves, hiding them from the rest of the world.

"Let's go up to the stone," Yvonne said then and he looked at her.

"The stone? Why?"

"Because Bobby was so anxious for us to see it." The moon made ghosts of her breath.

Colm groaned. "But we've seen it before."

"Not at night we haven't. Not in autumn."

Evan frowned. "What difference does it make *when* we've seen it. Doesn't it look the same all year round?"

"Dunno," she replied. "But I've never seen Bobby as excited as he was about it the other night."

"Bobby's a lunatic," Colm scoffed. "He'd be amused by a donkey."

"No he wouldn't," Yvonne said, a little too protectively for Evan's taste.

"Yeah, but..." he started to say and gestured emptily. "It's just a rock."

"How do you know? You're a city boy. I'd hardly call you well-versed in the ways of rural Ireland."

That stung him and he didn't reply. The moon was a bloated thing, cold-eyed and staring. He blew smoke at it and sagged against one of the stone columns.

"It's freezing in here," Colm grumbled. "My fingers are numb."

"So blow on them," Yvonne said bitterly.

Evan couldn't understand what had soured her mood so abruptly. They'd been up to the rock last week and he had admitted that yes, it looked funny standing in the center of an otherwise empty field and yes, by all accounts gravity should have taken it down a long time ago so narrow was its base compared to the bulk that comprised the rest of it. Bobby's theory, culled straight from the cluster of bucolic locals in Brannigan's Bar, was that the rock was held in place by the power of the fairies that lived beneath it. Like a plug, he'd said, which had elicited a particularly crude sexual remark from Colm that had set all but Bobby laughing. They'd left shortly thereafter, Evan and Colm still giggling.

Afterward, Evan had recalled the conviction on Bobby's face and found it hard to believe anyone could subscribe to such preposterously outdated notions. He'd found the mental image of the four of them standing there yelping and batting at a swarm of tiny lute-carrying winged things utterly hysterical.

But Yvonne was in a stubborn mood tonight, and he had to inwardly throttle the voice that suggested she might have fallen for Bobby instead. After all, Evan was only here Fridays and Saturdays, which if nothing else granted him two days respite from his parents' endless quarreling. But it never occurred to him that Bobby might be in the running for Yvonne's affections, or worse, that she might consider him. He wasn't what Evan would term 'handsome' if forced to make a judgment, but Bobby did live in Touraneena, which gave him the advantage, if that was indeed what was afoot.

With this in mind, Evan decided the best thing to do before the damage became irreparable, was to acquiesce to her request, to do his best to seem on her side, which of course, he was. It was the superstition fueling her request that he questioned.

"All right, let's do it," he said, dropping the cigarette and mashing it into ephemeral fireworks.

"Great. Outnumbered," Colm said with a sigh.

"You'll be okay," Yvonne said. She sounded pleased. "I'll look after you."

"Haw-haw."

Yvonne rose from the bench, rendering herself all but hidden by the dark.

"Come on then," she said. "Tonight the moon is ours."

Colm merely grumbled, but Evan wanted to ask what she meant by that. *Tonight the moon is ours.* It was a curious phrase, but he supposed she'd picked it up from one of those sickly sweet romantic comedies she liked so much. In his pursuit of her, he'd even agreed to accompany her to one. *Waiting to Exhale*, it had been called though a more appropriate title might have been *Waiting for the Credits.* He had only managed to suffer through it by stealing sidelong glances at Yvonne, who was so engrossed in the movie, she hadn't noticed.

Tonight the moon is ours.

He liked that, but when he opened his mouth to tell her as much, he realized she hadn't waited to hear it. Neither had Colm.

He was alone, but for the cataract eye of the moon.

* * *

They were already in the field across from the school when Evan reached the stand of firs.

"Hey, wait for me!" he called, trying his best not to sound nervous, which he was. The speed with which they'd left him hinted at a plot; he sensed a prank ahead of him. Why else would they have scampered so fast? The paranoia theme park in his head was growing popular, so much so that he had to make a concentrated effort not to heed the whispers that told him there *was* no prank, that the only thing he had been left out of this evening was Yvonne's heart, which she might have given to Colm. But at the sight of them halting, he felt a welcome wave of reassurance. He hadn't known any of them that long, but conspirators they most certainly were not. And Yvonne loved him, no matter what vibes she might be transmitting tonight. She was forward to a fault, something that was not always the easiest thing to bear, but at least he could be sure that if her feelings had changed, he'd already know because she'd have told him.

Unless she's waiting to get you alone before she breaks your heart.

He shook his head, and concentrated on the sound of the frost crunching beneath his shoes. The breeze strengthened and carried invisible slivers of ice to his skin. He shivered. When he looked up again, Yvonne and Colm were closer, and watching his approach.

Their faces looked like moons, bleached white and featureless but for snatches of shadow.

"Hurry up," Colm said.

"Yeah, c'mon snail-trail," Yvonne added, and they turned away, just as he was within whispering distance of them.

"Are we in a hurry?" he asked, and now the sound of them trampling the iced grass seemed almost loud enough to wake the village.

"No, but it's cold," Colm replied.

Evan jammed his hands in his pockets and found himself taking longer strides to keep up. Colm was right; it was cold, so cold he had to duck his chin into his coat for fear it would freeze and drop off. To his right, beyond the low fence, his grandmother's house could be seen – a silent shape with black eyes for windows. He felt a surge of relief, as he always did when he came home after a late night rendezvous with his friends and found the house asleep. Darkness meant he'd gotten away with it again. A burning light meant someone had woken up. A light meant trouble.

Colm and Yvonne were still ahead of him. They were close enough that he could reach out and touch them, but he found he was unable to draw level with them without breaking into a jog.

"Scare you back there?" Colm said.

"No. I just thought you guys wanted to be off by yourselves that's all."

Colm breathed laughter. "That'll be the day."

Yvonne said nothing.

At last they stopped at the edge of the field where the horse chestnut trees shattered the moon and made broken spider legs of the shadows. Here the grass became a short stretch of frozen dirt that led to a moss-skinned stone wall topped by rusted loops of old wire, presumably to keep the horses from clearing the fence when the mood struck them. Without a word, and before Evan could suggest a few moments to catch their breath, Colm was scaling the wall, carefully ducking under the fence, then gone, his feet thudding down on the earth on the opposite side.

"You coming folks?" he called back. The breeze filtered his voice through the stirring branches above.

Yvonne turned to look at Evan. The moonlight streaming through the trees made sapphires of her eyes and an unflattering gray patchwork of her skin. Her hand fell on his wrist.

"Are you okay?"

His gaze dropped to her hand. Her grip was tight. "Sure. You?"

She smiled, and the expression seemed to chase the peculiar cast from her face.

In the trees, a bird flapped its wings in irritation. On the other side of the fence, frosty earth gave way beneath impatient shoes.

Colm's disembodied voice floated over the wall. "What's going on?"

"Nothing," Yvonne said. "We're just having a tender moment."

Evan's heart kicked. He smiled. "Is that what this is?"

She stepped close and he stiffened.

"Maybe."

Colm's grumbling.

A snuffling of horses Evan knew was only in his head.

The gentle soughing of the wind.

The shadows, shifting. Stirring.

Branches tapping together like dry bones.

The kiss, soft and cool on his lips but fantastically hot inside him as wild flames poured through his chest and down into his groin, where another reaction began to take place.

And then she was stepping back, her amusement little more than a shadowy curve in the stark oval of her face.

"Easy, tiger," she said and giggled.

Evan blushed then shifted his stance when her back was turned. He watched her grab the crumbling fence, her slender wrists exposed, made ivory by a swatch of moonlight, her dark hair flowing around her...

...And knew he was in love. Knew he wanted to kiss those wrists, those hands... every part of her. Knew he would have to confront her, maybe tonight if the opportunity arose, and find out exactly how much she wanted him. If it was even close to how he felt for her, if she entertained even a fraction of the desire that raged within him, then he would be entering uncharted territory, and the idea of it thrilled him. The idea of lying with her, her milky body spread out before him, his alone, free to touch, to kiss, to taste, sent shivers coursing through him, shivers that settled in his belly and stayed there like moths in a jar.

Yvonne topped the fence, loose stones clacking to the ground in her wake. She looked over her shoulder at him, the moonlit sky over the field beyond making a simian silhouette of her lithe body.

"Hurry my love," she whispered, and dropped out of sight.

Hurry my love. A trick of the wind, he knew, but dared to hope otherwise; and though that hope was feeble, he tackled the wall like a maddened thing, barking his shins, scraping his elbows, feet scrabbling against stone, hooked hands tearing clumps of moss free, until finally he was on top of the wall and surveying the flat glistening emptiness on the other side.

In the distance, at the far side of the field, the peaked roof of an abandoned barn peered at him from between fingers of spruce. Above it, the moon beamed through scudding clouds like a headlight in the fog, bleaching out the stars.

And in the center of the glittering field, a rough triangular shape rose and shunned the light. From here it looked almost like an oversized coffin, with a head too wide and a bottom too narrow. He wondered again how the slightest breeze didn't send it toppling. He estimated the middle of it to be about ten feet across. From there it tapered to a point no more than a few inches wide. By all rights, it should be lying on its face, but according to all who knew it, it had been there for as long as anyone could remember.

"I wonder why the farmer never tried to get rid of it," Evan whispered, and waited for an answer. When none came, he squinted into the gloom at his feet and saw nothing.

"You there?"

A ruffle of feathers was the only response and it came from the network of branches over his head.

He was alone.

Fear thrummed through him but he maintained his composure, not wanting Yvonne to see his true reaction to what was almost certainly a scheme to spook him. After a few minutes of listening to the rasp of his own breathing and watching the ghosts of his breath tearing themselves asunder before him, fear became irritation. He balled his fists to keep his hands from trembling. Was Yvonne just teasing him, then? Was that all this was: a joke? He desperately wanted to believe it wasn't, that she really loved him. Maybe Colm had talked her into giving Evan a good scare. If that's all it was, then fine, despite it seeming immature, even for Colm. He wanted to creep back in his window to bed tonight and lie there knowing that she loved him. He was more afraid of discovering the opposite was true than he was at finding himself suddenly and inexplicably alone.

Then he saw them. They must have been crouching in the darkness somewhere because there they were, not ten feet away, standing stock-still and watching. It puzzled him that he hadn't spotted them before now. Still, he didn't dwell on it. Maybe a cloud had passed over the moon and shaded them from view for a few moments. Whatever. They hadn't abandoned him and that's all he cared about. It was clear they weren't trying to scare him either. There was no jumping out at him, no mournful wailing, no waving arms or hands clamping on his shoulders. They just stood there, waiting. With a sigh so heavy with relief he was sure they'd hear it, he slid down from the wall and began to walk toward them.

The wind rose, sending frost-hardened leaves skittering across the ground. A trio of ravens took to the air at the far side of the field and cawed their way past the moon.

Something whickered in the shadows.

Evan reached Yvonne and Colm and half-heartedly chastised them for being too impatient.

Colm looked back at him, only the slope of his cheek catching the light.

"We weren't sure you were coming."

"And let you steal my woman?"

The silence was deadly.

Evan chuckled to show he was joking, but the sound died in his throat.

There were two vertical strips of frost, like snail-trails, on the back of Colm's jacket, as if he'd been lying belly up on the furrowed earth.

Lying on his back.

It was nothing, he decided. He was being ridiculous. Colm might have fallen, or been loaned the crystals from a low hanging branch when he'd scaled the wall.

Or from when he'd been hiding.

With Yvonne.

Despite his resistance, the certainty that he was being deceived overcame him. A cold knot of hurt tightened his throat and he allowed himself to fall back a few steps. It wasn't hard. They were walking too fast for him anyway. Tears stung the back of his eyes. He felt hollowed out, the butterflies in his stomach raising hell with razorblade wings.

It was all too clear now what they were up to and he felt like an idiot for not having seen it before. They weren't trying to scare him, not on purpose anyway. They were trying to ditch him. So they could be alone. In the dark. Colm and Yvonne. Doing the very thing he'd hoped to find himself doing by night's end. The very thing he'd dreamed of doing.

Tonight the moon is ours.

Yes, but not *his*.

Suddenly he wanted to turn and run, back to the wall, back to his room and sleep and morning and the ride home that would await him by noon. It would suit him never to see this godforsaken village or anyone in it ever again.

The splintering of his heart might have been that much easier to bear if not for their sneakiness. Without warning, he'd been relegated to third wheel, Yvonne's flirtation with him now insulting rather than titillating. Then he thought back to The Shelter, when she'd suggested visiting the stone, and realized she might not have been looking at him when she'd said it. He remembered the ease with which they'd hurried away from him, leaving him standing there. And again at the wall. He had mistakenly assumed he was part of the equation when in reality, he'd insinuated himself into a seduction ritual that did not include him.

As he plodded along behind them, he saw ice catch the light in streaks across Yvonne's back too, and that sealed it. The image of them cavorting in the shadows, their bodies tight together while they listened for Evan's approach, for their cue to act like his friends once more, infuriated and sickened him at once.

He stopped and kicked at a nub of packed earth.

Yvonne and Colm stopped too, and turned.

"What's the matter?" Colm asked, and wasn't there the slightest touch of smug satisfaction in his voice?

"You chickening out on me?" Yvonne said and though he couldn't see her smile, he could feel it. His face grew hot. He wanted to hurt them, to show them he wasn't the poor fool they obviously thought he was. Instead, he shook his head.

"I just don't see the point of this, that's all," he told them. The wind drew icy fingers across his scalp.

"Don't be such a wimp," she said and lunged forward, her pale fingers finding the folds of his coat and jerking him forward hard enough that he yelped in surprise.

Colm laughed.

When she released him, Evan stumbled back into mercilessly cold shadow. The fairy stone: an ugly featureless rock, unremarkable save for its new identity as the place where his pride had taken its fatal strike.

"Lighten up a little," Colm said, his voice still infected with mirth.

Evan raged, trembling so violently he had to reach a hand out to the stone to steady himself. The rough surface scraped his fingers.

Yvonne, bathed in moonlight, was smiling.

"Don't ever do that again," Evan said, mustering as much threat as the pain and betrayal would allow without reducing him to tears. The night had turned rotten in a heartbeat, his hopes shattered into dust and now Yvonne had delivered the final insult by tossing him around like a lackey. He wanted to go home. Home, where his real friends were. Friends who wore only one face.

"Everyone knows," she said then, and might have added something but it was lost in the beating of wings, somewhere in the trees.

A faint mist curled at Evan's feet, the breath of the moon.

Colm was still chuckling. Evan considered smashing his face in, but decided that would achieve nothing but further trouble. And yet, he knew how satisfying it would feel to hear that bulbous nose giving way beneath his fist. Yvonne would scream and try to intervene and maybe, just maybe his fist would fly wide of its mark and…

Everybody knows.

Everyone but Evan had known how sly his two friends were. Even Bobby knew. They'd played him for a fool, getting their kicks from the city boy to alleviate the monotony of country life. He supposed Bobby's superstition had been an act also, designed to make him look silly. Well, in that, they'd succeeded.

Then he heard it again, the snuffling of horses but pushed it away. His heartbeat thundered in his ears, fists clenching and releasing. He was not welcome here and had never been. Fine. They'd had their laugh. It was time to end it.

"But no one can tell," Colm said, jovially. "That's the only rule, you see."

Back at the fence, shadows poured over the wall and lingered there.

The mist spun and curled.

Wings.

"Oh don't worry," Evan said with a bitter grin. "I won't tell anyone what conniving fuckers you people are. That's your own business. I just hope it was worth it. Next time you're in Dungarvan, look me up and I'll show you how us city folk play the game."

Yvonne was still smiling that infuriating smile.

"Bobby knew," she said, "but he wasn't supposed to tell."

The clouds tore apart in the hands of the wind and clean white light fled across the field in pursuit of the dark. It lit the trees, frosting the branches. It lit the mist, and the horses standing there held still by their riders.

Evan blinked, rubbed his eyes and looked again. The field was suddenly crowded but only in the corner of his eye. When he gazed upon them fully, the horses, lathered and snuffling, and their riders, tall and staring, were lost in the haze.

Waiting.

"The McCabe twins were here too," Yvonne continued. "They knew, but despite our warnings, they told."

"What are you talking about?" Evan said, wanting to run and be away from these awful people at last. They'd tricked him, used him for their amusement and crushed his dreams in the process. What else could they do to compound his misery?

Hooves pawed the ground.

A fluttering, but no longer in the trees.

The moon, an opaque eye.

And two figures, standing before him, smiling. Smiling at the fool, even as the moonlight turned their skin to sagging parchment tattooed with hate, even as their smiles became hooked, frozen things, even as their eyes sank in their sockets and caught blue fire.

"Stop," Evan said, stumbling back until he collided with the stone. It's shadow swept cold arms around him, held him still, but couldn't stall the trembling.

Another joke, ha-ha.

But it wasn't and he knew it.

They stepped closer. The mist rose, caressing their smooth, supple bodies, now exposed and whitened by the moon. They were sexless things, he saw as he wept. Sexless, and heartless. When Colm turned his suddenly hairless head to address the riders behind him, Evan was not entirely surprised to see translucent wings struggling outward from the lines of frost on his back. They trapped the moon and fractured it, projecting an array of colors unlike anything he'd ever seen, or wanted to see. They beat once at the air, a single flutter, and Colm vanished into the mist. When Evan saw him again, he was mounted on a steed that seemed composed of spider web and glass.

The gathering was quiet.

Evan sobbed, the cold creeping inside him.

Yvonne was standing before him, tendrils of mist drifting toward his face from her glittering lips. Her eyes were moons.

"Tonight," she said, "I'm yours."

PROHIBITED

-1-

Conor gave the chill air a light punch so the sleeve of his overcoat would retreat enough to let him see his watch. It was twenty past twelve. The bus was fifteen minutes late. He shuffled impatiently and released a long slow sigh. Public transportation. In an age where sheep and sundry other animals were being cloned, probes were penetrating the outer reaches of the universe, phones had gotten almost small enough to slip into your ear, he failed to understand why the buses in this country still couldn't manage to reach their appointed destinations on time, *ever*.

As he stood among the dozen or so people who shared his plight, he considered how very thoughtful it would be for those in charge to mount little computerized displays inside the shelters at bus stops, much like those at airports, to let people know how late the bus was going to be. With forewarning, anyone waiting could choose to trot across the street to Doolan's Bar to partake of a stiff one and perhaps a toasted cheese sandwich rather than stand in the cold for an hour. But the chances of such a thing happening were highly unlikely. That would cost money, and the way the current government was shaping up to be, those funds would likely be deemed better spent on additional guards to patrol bars and restaurants to ensure no one was violating the new smoking ban.

Conor snorted in disgust and reached into his coat pocket for a cigarette. Lighting it felt like a thumb in the nose to them, though as far as he knew they had not yet instituted any regulations against outdoor smoking, as he'd heard they'd done in the States. It was only a matter of time before the Irish government followed suit, he supposed as he pursed his lips, rocked back on his heels, and sent a silvery cloud of breath and smoke billowing into the air.

Four hours. He would be damned if he was going to suffer that long without a cigarette.

A woman standing beside him, ensconced in a woolen shawl and thick pink gloves, coughed and waved an irritated hand before her face, though the breeze had already ferried the smoke away from her and off over the harbor wall to mingle with the scent of seaweed and salt.

Conor gave her a withering look, which she returned, and he shook his head before turning his back on her to examine the timetable inside the bus shelter—which was little more than a long red bench beneath an open-fronted fiberglass hut. Another woman, this one much younger and prettier than Mrs. Pink Gloves, despite her harried expression, sat down on the bench and tucked her naked hands into her armpits. A toddler, nose caked with dried snot and eyes wet from a recent bout of wailing, tugged on her elbow and went ignored. The woman's eyes were glassy. She seemed distant, genuinely unaware of her son's—if indeed that's what he was—demands for attention. Conor sympathized. She was young, too young to be a mother, as so many of today's mothers were, and her expression appeared to be an outward indication of a desperate attempt to relocate herself, if only through her imagination. The Number 4 would soon take her away, but it would not alleviate her of her burden.

Conor watched her for a moment longer, until her glazed eyes began to drift slowly in his direction, then he looked away, puffed on his cigarette and stepped out into the road.

The sky overhead was oily gray, impatient with rain.

From inside the bar across the road, someone laughed loudly, and Conor felt a twinge of longing. If only he had some way of knowing how much time he had to kill, he could be sitting there in the warmth and gazing out at his fellow would-be passengers from behind a glass of Scotch. Again he cursed the bus, the company, and the driver for forcing respectable people to stand like fools in the cold waiting for a ride that might never come. Worse, perhaps, were the cars that frequently slowed down so the passengers could gape at them as they drove by. More than once, Conor fancied he saw them leering at him, or laughing at his discomfort, and he had to avert his gaze for fear of running at them, arms flapping, invectives flooding from between his chapped lips.

Another check of his watch and the toddler on the bench began to wail anew.

Conor groaned, and took one final drag on his cigarette before tossing it to the ground and mashing it out with his heel. Sparks flew and Mrs. Pink Gloves clucked her tongue.

Two men had moved to stand at the far side of the shelter, no doubt anticipating rain. They were arguing, but despite their raised voices, Conor couldn't tell what the source of their contention was. In fact, the more he listened, the less sense their squabbling seemed to make, prompting him to glance at the men as if some clue could be gleaned from their gestures. But when he looked, he found both men had stopped their bickering and were staring straight at him, their eyes tarry and narrow above scarves that concealed their lower faces.

Whether imaginary or not, the aura of threat radiating from the duo propelled him into action, and with a bitter mutter of *To hell with the lot of you*, Conor huffed, checked for oncoming stares, and marched across the road to the bar.

-2-

There was no one inside, but the warmth he'd yearned for from across the street melted away any curiosity he might have entertained. He stood for a moment, just inside the door, eyes closed beneath the blast of hot air from the overhead heater, and smiled.

The pub was oddly empty and quiet considering it was nearly lunch hour and Doolan's was one of the town's most popular spots, and considering the gale of laughter he'd heard before, but he was too content to be bothered. After another moment of basking in the heat, he rubbed his hands briskly together and made his way to the bar.

He pulled out one of the chairs and sat, then fumbled in his pockets for his wallet, cigarettes and lighter, all of which he placed on the polished bar. When he looked up, intending to peruse the labels on the bottles hung by their necks from optics he was startled to see a large dark-haired man standing before him, blocking his view, a not at all courteous look on his bearded face.

"You can't smoke in here," he grunted, indicating Conor's pack of cigarettes with a sharp nod. "New law."

"Oh I know," Conor told him. "I wasn't planning to. Just setting them out to take some of the weight out of my pockets. I'll be crammed soon enough into a bus, so I'm relishing the space while I have it."

"What do you want?"

Conor was again struck by the man's unpleasant demeanor. He'd posed the question as if Conor had intruded upon something. Still, he decided he was not going to let a gruff bartender disrupt the ease and comfort he felt in these placid and *warm* surroundings. And what he'd said had been close to the truth; he'd put the cigarettes on the bar out of habit, not intent to light one up. Surely that was understandable. He'd been a smoker since age sixteen, and so had forty-odd years of puffing in bars to forget thanks to the new restrictions. He doubted he was alone in that.

"I'll have a drop of Paddy's," he said, sensing the bartender's impatience. A moment later a tumbler of whiskey was slammed down on the bar. Had any of the drink sloshed over the side, Conor would have been annoyed enough to refuse to pay, or demand a replacement, but none did, as if the bartender had found a perfect medium of rudeness—enough to convey his disdain, but not enough to cause complaint.

When the man's back was turned, Conor offered it a grim toast and drained his glass. The liquid fire poured down his throat, warming him from the inside out, and he shivered with pleasure. "Another one," he said, slamming the glass down in a perfect imitation of his host's brusqueness. To avoid the sour look that was inevitably directed his way, he turned his eyes to the window and the bus stop beyond.

Conor frowned. The dozen or so people had become two-dozen, unless the single glass of whiskey had been enough to queer his vision, which he sincerely doubted. They milled about the shelter, some talking animatedly, others peering mournfully up at the gray sky. The two men he'd seen arguing were apparently trying to recruit more members for their debate. Mrs. Pink Gloves was still standing where she'd been when he'd left her, but her face, an ugly pink blob, was now turned toward the bar, toward the window, toward him, it seemed. He found it unusual that more people had showed up for the bus, especially since it was running late by—he checked his watch—half an hour. He might have expected a straggler or two, people well accustomed to public transport's unique and mysterious time zone, but so many of them? Maybe he'd missed an announcement informing those lucky enough to see or hear it that the Number 4 to Dublin would be delayed on Saturday. He wouldn't know, he hadn't read a paper, watched television, or listened to the radio in years.

He shrugged off the uneasy feeling that arose within him at the thought of sharing a four-hour bus ride with that distasteful assembly. It reminded him why he seldom took buses, or any mode of public transport. They had little to no screening process, which meant any kind of wretched thing could and was, allowed on board: screaming children, puking drunks, obnoxious pink-glove-wearing old women...

He missed his car, at present serving its second week in prison for ferrying a drunk driver into a wall. *Bastards.* It would never cease to amaze him where the police chose to direct their energy when crime and drug use was at an all-time high in the town.

And up until that incident, Conor had always been a careful driver, whether inebriated or not. Truth be told, he'd been careful on that night too until the police cruiser's lights had almost blinded him.

A dull ache in his bladder told him the first whiskey had already been processed and he slid from the chair just as the bartender slammed down the second.

"You haven't paid yet."

Conor restrained the urge to tell the man where to go and what to do to himself when he got there. "I know. I'm just going to the bathroom."

"Sure you are," the bartender sneered.

"What's that supposed to mean?"

"Might as well put your cigarettes and wallet back in your pocket while you're at it. After you pay up, of course."

Conor found his contentment buckling. "Are you like this with everyone?"

The bartender shrugged. "There's no one else here."

"That's not what I meant."

"That'll be seven Euros."

Though he wanted to argue further, Conor swallowed his words, grabbed his cigarettes and wallet, and tossed a ten Euro note on the bar. "I want change," he said, as the bartender snatched the money and headed for the till.

Conor stared for a moment, debating the wisdom in pursuing the matter. His bladder decided for him. Disgusted, he turned and made his way upstairs to the bathroom.

-3-

It was in dire need of cleaning.

As soon as he stepped inside the bathroom, he was assaulted by the noxious odor of stale urine and fecal matter, with an underlying hint of disinfectant, which was perhaps the only indication that the room had ever been cleaned. The urinals were cracked and bearded with mold, the drains clogged with wadded up toilet paper. Grimacing, Conor inspected the stalls. The first door was locked, bolted from the inside. A handwritten sign informed him it was out of order. Flies buzzed dully within. The second was unlocked, but the toilet was plugged, and full near to overflowing with stained toilet paper and clots of murky material Conor was content to let remain unidentified. He thought, as he tore his gaze away, there might even have been thick clumps of dark hair in there, and imagined the surly bartender clipping his beard over the toilet.

The last stall was also open. The toilet was unplugged but caked with filth. The seat was missing, which made him glad his business here was of a quicker kind. With a sigh of resignation, Conor quickly stepped inside, unzipped his fly and idly aimed the stream of piss at the spots in the bowl where the stains were densest. As he stood there, mulling over the despicable behavior of the bartender, and the growing crowd of travelers across the street, the first drops of rain speckled the bathroom window and a clawing need arose in him.

As he shook off the last of his water and zipped up, he realized the taste of whiskey on his tongue and the hot pulse in his throat demanded to be complimented with a smoke. He lingered in the stall despite the smell, despite the feeling that every germ in the toilet would at any minute leap free to latch onto his skin, and almost absently patted his coat pocket. As his fingers traced the rectangular shape of his cigarette pack, the bartender's snidely delivered words came back to him.

Might as well put your cigarettes and wallet back in your pocket while you're at it.

Conor smiled. What an insult it would be for that brute to come up here long after Conor had boarded the bus to Dublin only to find the place reeking of smoke. *That's what I think of you and your laws.*

Buoyed by the thought of sneaky revenge, Conor took a few steps back and glanced furtively around the bathroom. He was, as he'd expected, alone. He retreated into the stall and elbowed the door shut. It was a tight squeeze, but he didn't need much room.

Ears cocked, he fumbled a cigarette from the pack, screwed it between his lips, brought his lighter up, sparked it once, twice, and lighted it. The tip flared cherry red.

The first deep inhalation of smoke was almost orgasmic. It made his nerves buzz, his fingers and toes tingle, and he grinned contentedly, letting the smoke drift on its own steam from his open mouth.

Another drag and he tipped a finger against the filter, sending ashes sizzling into the yellow toilet water.

He was thinking of Mrs. Pink Gloves and what she might have to say about his little act of rebellion when two stalls down the latch was abruptly snapped back. Startled, Conor jolted, the smoke catching in his throat. He dropped the cigarette but this time when it hit the water, the hiss seemed absurdly loud. The urge to cough was maddening and made his chest convulse, even as he tried to listen. But even the sound of his own discomfort or the thunderous beat of his heart in his ears couldn't drown out the tortured squeal of hinges as the door on the stall marked 'Out of Order' was opened.

-4-

Conor waited, eyes watering with the desperate need to cough, to release the smoke that seemed to be pinching and pulling at his lungs, until he could wait no more.

In a series of less-than-silent splutters, he doubled over, the smoke emerging in dirty spurts, saliva dripping from his mouth to the toilet, his hand braced across his chest as if to keep his lungs from bursting free of him.

Outside his stall, he heard footsteps.

"Are you okay, mister?"

Conor froze. It was a child. Only a child. He closed his eyes, relieved. "I'm fine, thank you. Just a bit of a cough, that's all."

The door behind him opened as far as it could, which wasn't very far at all. It thumped against his back. "Just a second," he said.

"I smell smoke."

"Do you?" Conor coughed once, then straightened and wiped a hand across his mouth. His chest ached.

"Yes."

"Someone must have been smoking in here, I suppose."

"*You* were," said the voice and now all concern had vanished from it. "And I'm telling."

"No, wait." Conor maneuvered himself so that he was no longer blocking the door. "Just a second, now." Clumsily, he pressed his back against the filthy wall and wrenched the door open. To his surprise, there was no one there. "Where did you go?" he asked, afraid he was too late to stop the child. "Hello?" His voice echoed around the bathroom, in which, unbelievably, he appeared to be alone.

Then, out of the corner of his eye, he caught sight of the stall door bearing the 'Out of Order' sign. It was slowly drifting shut.

"Hey!" Conor started toward it, stopping only when something slammed itself into the door from the other side, forcing it shut. From behind the door came the sound of something wet hitting the floor, a sodden mop, perhaps. It was followed by a curious whirring sound, which could have been made by the wings of a giant moth. Conor had to fight the urge to drop to his knees on the mildewed floor and peer beneath the stall.

Instead he asked, "Are you all right? Should I fetch someone?" in as gentle a tone as he could muster, even as he realized his offer would most likely land him in a world of trouble when it was discovered he'd been smoking.

When the child replied, it sounded as if he was gargling something. "I'm telling."

"Listen— "

A loud hiss obliterated the rest of Conor's response, and it took him a moment to realize that the sound had not come from inside the stall, but from the street outside the window, and the bus that had drawn up to the shelter.

-5-

He hurried downstairs and through the bar, calling out "I think there's a sick child in your bathroom," despite there being no sign of the bartender. It was a struggle to pass the full whiskey sitting on the bar, but the rumbling of the bus engine kept him moving.

He shouldered open the door and was glad to see the passengers had not yet finished filing on board, and were taking their time about it too. The rain was still falling in intermittent drops as if the swollen thunderheads had merely sprung a leak. The cold rushed to embrace him. He scowled.

The bus had stopped directly in front of the shelter. A few feet away on that side of the street, an ordinarily cheerful mural depicting the town in sunshine seemed to have darkened in sympathy with the real-world sky. Further along, the great stone buildings that housed the council offices appeared to lean away in an effort to shove the bus into the foreground. With a sigh, Conor checked his watch. Only forty minutes late. He might very well have to complain to the transport company about this. A couple of minutes could be forgiven, but close to an hour was *ridiculous*, particularly in this weather. As he stepped out into the road he was thankful for his reprieve from the bitter biting chill. The whiskey was still doing its job of heating him from the inside, and he knew the single glass had been enough to ensure he'd sleep at least some of the way to Dublin, which would make the trip seem not so long.

He looked up at the long rectangular window that ran from the front of the bus to the back, and noticed all the faces of the seated passengers were turned his way. Pale orbs behind smoky Plexiglas seemed to lean closer to the window, the eyes dark hollows, the heads hairless, mouths split in black crescent smiles.

Somewhat unsettled, but more than willing to blame the alcohol, Conor moved toward the bus, wanting but unable to tear his gaze away from the odd grinning heads.

And so it wasn't until the car horn blasted a warning that he remembered to check the road, and by then it was too late.

The last thing he saw before the Ford Focus with the missing windshield glass plowed into him, was the enraged face of the driver. He had time only to register that it was a woman, and that she was wearing pink gloves, then the world sailed away from him.

-6-

"Yes, I'm well aware of that and I apologize for the inconvenience, but another bus will be along shortly."

"And just when is 'shortly' by Bus Eireann's clock? An hour? Two hours?"

"It should be along in about ten minutes. I've radioed the station and they're sending a bus immediately."

"Bah! It'd have to have feckin' wings to make it from Waterford to here in that kinda time."

"Again, sir, I'm sorry for the inconvenience. If you call the station I'm sure they'll be glad to reimburse you the cost of your ticket."

"They damn well better."

"Step back from the door now sir, please."

"Crooks."

Conor, when he awoke, was aware only of the conversation, and monstrous pain that felt as if starving animals were gnawing on every limb and tugging on every nerve. He was sure his eyes were open, but he could see nothing, the blindness inspiring panic that served to remind him in an instant, what had happened to him.

"I'm hurt," he croaked.

A pneumatic hiss as doors were closed. The rumble and growl of an engine. The floor beneath him shuddered.

No, Conor thought. *I can't be on the bus. For God's sake—* "I'm hurt!" he cried out, and heard a chuckle in response.

"You are indeed, but we'll sort you out soon enough."

The bus cleared the shadow of the shelter and the canopy of the overhanging oak tree allowing feeble light to penetrate the trembling windows of the bus. With considerable effort, Conor blinked away the disorientation and raised his head, a move that seemed to wrench on his spine and send pain coruscating down through his body to his toes. He winced, then whined in panicked confusion when he saw that he was indeed on the bus, and that he was lying on his back in the aisle between the rows of seats. And unless his frightened eyes were deceiving him, the bus was empty but for him, and the driver, who was visible only as an overweight man hunched over the wheel.

"I'm hurt," Conor protested again. "I need a hospital."

He inspected his body as much as he was able, and noticed to his horror that his right leg was twisted completely around so that he was looking at the heel of his shoe.

His trousers had been shredded at the knee, through which bloody flesh showed.

Trembling violently now, he raised his hands in front of him. They were shredded and torn, most of the fingers on the left hand bent at odd angles. Nausea rose in him. He groaned and let his head fall back to the floor.

"Just take it easy there, Conor," said the driver. "Won't be long now."

"How..." Conor hissed pain through his teeth. Tears leaked from his eyes. "How do you know my name?"

"It's on your I.D."

"Where are you...taking me?"

"Dublin. Isn't that where you were headed?"

"Yes, but...I was in an accident. I'm badly hurt. I need to go to the hospital."

"We've gone to a lot of trouble for you today, Conor. The least you can do is be a little bit grateful."

"*What?* For Christ sake, my leg is broken, and...and God knows what else is wrong with me. I'm badly injured, don't you understand that? I was hit by a car and I should be in a hospital bed, not on my way to Dublin on a blasted bus!"

"Calm down, sir. No need for hysterics. You're only hurting yourself."

I'm dreaming, Conor realized. *I'm absolutely dreaming this. No way on earth the world has gone this stark raving mad without my noticing. And people don't bring you on four-hour bus rides when they know you're hurt.*

The very real and very hostile pain that wracked his body dissuaded such notions.

But if not a dream, then how was this happening? Terrorists, maybe? Had Dungarvan been invaded by lunatics hell-bent on plowing buses into government buildings? But why choose *him?* And where the hell where the other passengers? The ones he'd seen boarding the bus before the accident? It made no sense at all, and he had to believe this was all in his head. It had to be, and whatever that said about his mental state, he'd gladly accept, as long as it meant there would be an end to the horror.

He raised his head again and blinked rapidly in the gloom. The bus driver began to whistle a horribly discordant tune. Conor brought his gaze up to the wide rearview mirror fixed above the driver's head and saw to his dismay—though given the sequence of events he'd just witnessed he was no longer terribly surprised—that the driver was none other than the surly bartender, no longer looking so surly.

"What's going on here?" Conor asked, struggling to keep the panic from his voice.

"I'm taking you to Dublin, sir."

On the verge of sobbing, but afraid it might encourage the already flailing agony inside him, Conor reached out a hand and grabbed the metal footrest of the seat nearest him. "You know what I mean. Stop fucking with me. Who's doing this?" He tried to pull himself up, and gave up when a fresh bolt of pain struck his mangled leg.

"Doing what? I work for the government, if that's what you mean. They pay my wages."

"Please..." Conor whispered, and turned on his side, teeth clenched against the magnificent pain. "I don't understand this. I need help."

"You're right there, sir, and that's what you'll get."

"From whom?"

"From our friends in the government. It's their job to look after people like you."

Conor frowned. The government? "The new gov—"

"Oh no, sir. They're not new. Not by a long shot."

The government? Conspiracy theories raced through Conor's mind. He envisioned faceless agencies hired to stalk and hurt people, to kidnap them, and...and...He didn't know what else might be in store for him and didn't much care to think about it. But why? What had he done to—?

That's what I think of you and your laws.

His mouth popped open, lips moving to form words that would not come. Surely not? Surely it had to be more than that?

With his good hand, he searched the right pocket of his overcoat and found the cigarettes.

"Not a good idea," said the bartender/bus driver, in the same tone he'd used back at the bar. "At all."

Conor ignored him, wincing as the bus trundled over potholes, and inspected the pack.

It was not his.

Though not altogether surprised, it still alarmed him to note that he'd failed to notice such obvious differences between his regular pack of Marlboros and the thing he held now in one trembling hand.

For starters, it was not the customary red, but closer to pink, and though the usual triangle shapes were extant, the brand name was missing. But worst of all was the Surgeon General's warning, which read:

SMOKING IS HARMFUL TO YOUR HEALTH.
MAY RESULT IN CANCER, EMPHYSEMA OR TORTURE.
MAY RESULT IN THE EXCISION OF VITAL ORGANS.
MAY RESULT IN PAINFUL AND PROLONGED DEATH.

"Because I smoked a *fucking cigarette?*" Conor sobbed. "That's madness! And these aren't even mine!"

The bus driver held up one hand as the road beyond his windshield swept around him. Clutched between his thick fingers was a regular pack of Marlboros. "I snatched them at the bar, while you were busy looking at your poor suffering fellow travelers."

"Why?"

"Because eventually that illicit smoke you had, though it can have hallucinogenic side effects, will make you more docile, less...hysterical, and best of all it'll keep you awake during your procedure."

Conor felt sick. He commanded his legs to move, his body to heal itself and let him walk, run forward, just long enough for him to throttle the insane driver, or whatever the hell he really was. But there was no response and all he could do was lie there and suffer, both from the agony of his injuries and the thought of those to come.

"Sooner or later everyone will grow to understand that the new laws are there to be respected, Conor," said the driver. "Even staunch rebels like yourself. The smoking ban is just one of many changes. And it's not as if there weren't signs, but you don't watch television or listen to the radio anymore, which is a shame. You'd be surprised how convincing their voices can be. How *active* it could have made you in ensuring society learns to follow the leader."

Conor wept, and suddenly thought of his brother Roy, who today would wait patiently at Houston Station in Dublin for a bus that was not coming.

"You should rest now," the driver advised. "It's a long 'ol haul."

But Conor had a better idea. He looked at the pack in his hand and tried to grin.

At the wheel, the driver, aware of his intent, sighed heavily.

"Foolish."

Conor ignored him, and brought the open pack to his teeth. He bit down on the edge of a filter and drew out a cigarette. He didn't care now what it might do to him, or what *they* might do to him as a result.

Four hours. He would be damned if he was going to suffer that long without a cigarette.

He found his lighter and brought fire to the smoke as the bus increased its speed, the windows darkened, and the heavy clouds finally released their fury, the rain like nails against the roof.

UNDERNEATH

"This is a joke, right?"

Dean Lovell shifted uncomfortably, his eyes moving over the girl's shoulder to the stream of students chattering and laughing as they made their way to class. Summer played at the windows; golden light lay in oblongs across the tiled floor, illuminating a haze of dust from old books and the unpolished tops of lockers. Someone whooped, another cheered, and over by Dean's locker, Freddy Kelly watched and grinned.

Dean forced his gaze back to the girl standing impatiently before him. Her eyes were blue but dark, her jaw slender but firm.

"Well?" she said.

He cleared his throat, dragged his eyes to hers and felt his stomach quiver.

Her face...

Down the hall, an authoritative voice chastised someone for using bad language. Punishment was meted out; a groan was heard. At the opposite end of the hall, heated voices rose. A body clanged against a locker; someone cursed. Laughter weaved its way through the parade.

"It's not a joke. Why would you think it was?" he said at last, aware that he was fidgeting, paring slivers of skin from his fingernails, but unable to stop.

The girl—Stephanie—seemed amused. Dean met her eyes again, willed them to stay there, willed them not to wander down to where the skin was puckered and shiny, where her cheeks were folded, striated. Damaged.

"Since I've been here, only one other guy has ever asked me out. I accepted and showed up at the Burger Joint to a bunch of screaming, pointing jocks who called me all kinds of unimaginative, infantile names before giving me a soda and ketchup shower and pushing me out the door. *That's* why."

"Oh." Dean squirmed, wished like hell he'd stood up to Freddy and not been put in this position. Defiance would have meant another long year of taunts and physical injury, but even that had to be better than this, than standing here before the ugliest girl in the school asking her out on a date he didn't want.

Then *no*, he decided, remembering the limp he'd earned last summer courtesy of Freddy's hobnailed boots. A limp and a recurring ache in his toes whenever the weather changed. *Inflammatory arthritis*, his mother claimed, always quick to diagnose awful maladies for the slightest pains. But he was too young for arthritis, he'd argued. Too young for a lot of things, but that didn't stop them from happening.

The remembered sound of Freddy's laughter brought a sigh from him.

Ask the scarred bitch out. See how far you get and I'll quit hasslin' you. Scout's honor. All you gotta do is take her out, man. Maybe see if those scars go all the way down, huh?

"So? Stephanie said, with a glance at the clock above the lockers. "Who put you up to this? Is a bet, a dare, or what?"

Dean shook his head, despite being struck by an urgent, overwhelming need to tell her the truth and spare her the hurt later and himself the embarrassment now.

That's exactly what it is, he imagined telling her, *a bet. Fuck-face Freddy over there bet that I wouldn't ask you out. If I chicken out, he wins; I lose, many times over. The last time I lost he kicked me so hard in the balls, I cried. How's that for a laugh? Fifteen years of age and I cried like a fucking baby. So yeah, it's a bet, and now that you know, you can judge me all you want, then come around the bleachers at lunchtime and watch me get my face rearranged. Ok?*

But instead he said, "I just thought it might be fun...you know...go to the movies or something. A break from study...and...I hate to go to the movies alone."

She smiled then, but it was empty of humor.

"Sounds like a half-assed reason to ask out the scarred girl. You must be desperate."

"No," he said, almost defensively, "I just..." He finished the thought with a shrug and hoped it would be enough.

"Right."

"Look, forget it then, okay," he said, annoyed at himself, annoyed at Freddy, annoyed at her for making it so goddamn difficult to avoid getting the living shit kicked out of him. He started to walk away, already bracing himself for Freddy's vicious promises, and heard her scoff in disbelief behind him.

"Wait," she said then and he stopped abreast of Freddy, who was pretending to dig the dirt from under his nails with a toothpick. As Dean turned back, he saw Freddy's toothy grin widen and 'go for it, stud," he murmured.

Stephanie was frowning at him, her arms folded around her books, keeping them clutched to her chest.

"You're serious about this?"

He nodded.

She stared.

Someone slammed a locker door. The bell rang. No one hurried.

"All right then," she said. "I'm probably the biggest sucker in the world but...all right."

For the first time, he saw a glimmer of something new in her eyes and it made his stomach lurch. He recognized the look as one he saw in the mirror every morning.

Hope.

Hope that this time things would work out right. That he would make it through the day, the week, the month, without pissing blood or lying to his parents about why his eyes were swollen from crying.

Hope that there would be no hurt this time.

Way to go, Dean, he thought, *nothing quite like fucking up someone else's life worse than your own, huh?*

"Okay," he said, with a smile he hoped looked more genuine than it felt. "I'll call you. Maybe Friday? Your number's in the book?"

"Yes," she said. "But Friday's no good. I have work."

She worked the ticket booth at the Drive-In on Harwood Road. Dean saw her there almost every weekend. Saw her there and laughed with his friends about the irony of having a freak working in the one place where everyone would see her. Secretly he'd felt bad about mocking her, but after a while the jokes died down and so did the acidic regret.

Now, as she walked away, her strawberry blonde hair catching the sunlight, he realized how shapely her body was. Had he never seen her face, he might have thought she was a goddess, but the angry red and pink blotches on her cheek spoiled it, dragging one eye down and the corner of her mouth up. This defect was all that kept her from being one of those girls every guy wanted in the back seat of his car.

"I gotta admit, you got balls, shithead," Freddy said behind him and Dean turned, feeling that familiar loosening of his bowels he got whenever the jock was close. Such encounters invariably left him with some kind of injury, but this time he hoped Fred would stick to his word.

"Y-yeah," he said, with a sheepish grin.

Freddy barked a laugh. "Give her one for me, eh Bro? And be sure to let me know how that 'ol burnt skin of hers tastes."

As he passed, he mock-punched Dean and chuckled, and though Dean chuckled right along with it, he almost wet his pants in relief that the blow hadn't been a real one.

* * *

The sun was burning high and bright. There was no breeze, the leaves on the walnut trees like cupped green hands holding slivers of light to cast viridescent shadows on the lawns around the school. Dean sat with his best friend, Les, on the wall of the circular fountain, facing the steps to the main door of the sandstone building, from which a legion of flustered looking students poured. The fountain edge was warm, the water low and filled with detritus of nature and man. The bronze statue of the school's founder stared with verdigris eyes at the blue sky hung like a thin veil above the building.

"You've got to be kidding me," Les said, erupting into laughter. "Stephanie Watts? Aw Jesus..."

Dean frowned. His hopes that Les would understand had been dashed, and he quickly realized he should have known better; Les couldn't be serious at a funeral.

"Well, it's worth it, isn't it? I mean...if it keeps that asshole off my back?"

Les poked his glasses and shook his head. "You're such a moron, Dean."

"Why am I?"

"You honestly think he'd let you off the hook that easy? No way, dude. He just wants to humiliate you, wants to see you hook up with Scarface. Then, when you become the joke of the whole school, he'll look twice as good when he kicks your ass up to your shoulders. Trust me—I know these things."

Before Dean had moved from Phoenix to Harperville, Les had been Freddy's punching bag. The day Dean had showed up, he'd bumped into Freddy hard enough to make the guy drop his cigarette. Les's days of torment were over; Dean earned the label "Fresh Meat." It had been that simple; whatever part of the bullying mind controlled obsession,

Dean's clumsiness had triggered it.

"What's worse," Les continued, "is that not only will this not keep that jerk off your back, but now you've put yourself in a position where you have to *date* Stephanie Watts, and for a girl who's probably desperate, God knows what she'll expect you to do for her."

"What do you mean?"

Les sighed. "Put yourself in her shoes. Imagine you'd never been with someone. *Ever.* And then some guy asks you out. Wouldn't you be eager to get as much as you could from him just in case you're never that lucky again?"

Dean grimaced, waved away a fly. "I never thought of it that way."

"I don't think you gave this much thought at all, hombre."

"So what do I do?"

"What can you do?"

"I could tell her I can't make it."

"She'll just pick another night."

"I could just *not* call her. That'd give her the hint, wouldn't it?"

"Maybe, but I get the feeling once you give a girl like that the slightest hint of interest, she'll dog you to follow through on it."

Dean ran a hand over his face. "Shit."

"Yeah." Les put a hand on his shoulder. "But who knows? Maybe all that pent-up lust'll mean she's a great lay."

"Christ, Les, lay off, will ya? If I go through with this, it's just gonna be a movie, nothing more."

"If you say so," Les said, and laughed.

* * *

"Who are you calling?" Dean's mother stood in the doorway, arms folded over her apron. A knowing smile creased her face, the smell of freshly baked pies wafting around her, making Dean's stomach growl. The clock in the hall ticked loudly, too slow to match the racing of Dean's heart.

"Well? Who is she?"

Dean groaned. In the few days since he'd asked Stephanie out it seemed the world was bracing itself for the punch line to one big joke, with him at the ass end of it. More than once, he'd approached the phone with the intention of calling the girl and telling her the truth and to hell with whatever she thought of his cruelty. But he'd chickened out. Trembling finger poised to dial, he would remember the flare of hope he'd seen in her eyes and hang up, angry at himself for not being made of tougher stuff, for being weak. It was that weakness, both mental and physical, that bound him to his obligations, no matter how misguided, and made him a constant target for the fists of life.

"Just a girl from school," he told his mother, to satisfy her irritating smile. He hoped that would be enough to send her back to the kitchen, but she remained in the doorway, her smile widening, a look of *there's my little man, all grown up on her face.*

"Did you tell your father?"

He shrugged and turned away from her. Frowned at the phone. "Didn't know I had to."

She said nothing more, but a contented sigh carried her back to her baking and he shook his head as he picked up the phone. They were always in his business, to the point where every decision he made had to be screened by his own imagined versions of them before he did anything. It angered him, made him sometimes wish he could go live with his Uncle Rodney in Pensacola at least until he went to college and was free of their reign. But Rodney was a drunk, albeit a cheerful one and Dean doubted that situation would leave him any better off than he was now. Overbearing parents was one thing; waking up to a drunk uncle mistaking you for the toilet was another.

Shuddering, he jabbed out the number he'd written down on a scrap of paper after using Stephanie's address (he knew the street, not the exact location, but that had been enough) to locate *Julie & Chris Watts* in the phonebook.

Perspiration beading his brow, he cleared his throat, listened to the robotic pulse of the dial tone and prayed she didn't answer.

"Hello?"

Damn it.

"H-Hi, Stephanie?"

"No, this is her mother. Who's speaking, please?"

The woman's voice sounded stiff, unfriendly and he almost hung up there and then while there was still a chance. After all, she didn't know his name, so he couldn't be...

Caller I.D.

Damn it, he thought again and told her who he was.

"Oh yes. Hang on a moment, please."

Oh yes. Recognition? Had Stephanie mentioned him to her mother?

A clunk, a rattle, a distant call and the muffled sounds of footsteps. Then static and a breathless voice.

"Hi. I wasn't sure you'd call."

Me neither, he thought, but said, "I said I would, didn't I?"

"So we're still on for tomorrow night?"

There was a challenge in her voice that he didn't like. It was almost as if she was daring him to back out, to compose some two-bit excuse and join the ranks of all the cowards her imperfection had summoned.

"Sure," he told her and cursed silently. His intention had been to do the very thing she'd expected, to back out, to blame a family illness on his inability to take her out. He'd already come to agree with Les's assessment of the situation, and figured it really was a case of *damned if you do, damned if you don't*. Whatever happened with the girl, Fuckface Freddy had no intention of stopping his persecution of Dean. That would be too much fun to abandon just because he'd shown some balls in asking out the school freak. Now, not only would he suffer the regular beatings, he'd also have school rumor to contend with. Rumors about what he'd done with the scarred girl.

"You still there?"

"Yeah." He closed his eyes. "So when should I pick you up?"

* * *

The night was good to her.

As she emerged from the warm amber porch light, Dean almost smiled. In the gloom, with just the starlight and the faint glow from the fingernail moon, she looked flawless. And beautiful. So much so, that he was almost able to convince himself that she was not marred at all, that the scars were latex makeup she wore as protection against the advances of undesirables.

But when she opened the door of his father's Ford Capri, the dome light cast ragged shadows across her cheek, highlighting the peaks and ridges, dips and hollows, and his smile faded, a brief shudder of revulsion rippling through him. He felt shame that he could be so narrow-minded and unfair. After all, she hadn't asked for the scars and he should be mature enough to look past them to what was most likely a very nice girl.

Christ, I sound like my mother, he thought and watched as Stephanie lowered herself into the seat, her denim skirt riding up just a little, enough to expose a portion of her thigh. To Dean's horror, he felt a rush of excitement and hastily quelled it.

You're being an asshole, he told himself, but it was not a revelation. He knew what he was being, and how he was feeling. He'd become a display case, his shelves filled with all the traits he would have frowned upon had someone else been displaying them. But it was different, and he realized it always was, when you were an outsider looking in. Here, in the car with Stephanie, he was helpless to stop how angry and disgusted he felt. It was just another event in his life engineered by someone other than himself and that impotence made him want to scream, to shove this ugly, ruined girl from the car and just drive until the gas ran out or he hit a wall, whichever happened first.

"Hi," she said and he offered her a weak smile. Her hair was shiny and clean, her eyes sparkling, dark red lipstick making her lips scream for a long wet kiss.

Dean wanted to be sick, but figured instead to drive, to seek distractions and end this goddamn night as soon as possible. He could live with the whispers, the speculation, and the gossip forever, but he needed to end the subject of them sooner rather than later.

"So where are we going?" she asked when he gunned the engine to life and set the car rolling.

He kept his eyes on the street. Dogs were fleeting shadows beneath streetlights; a plastic bag fluttered like a trapped dove on a rusted railing. A basketball smacked the pavement beyond a fenced in court. Voices rose, their echoes fleeing. The breeze rustled the dark leaves, whispering to the moon.

Dean's palms were oily on the wheel.

"The movies, I guess. That okay?"

In the corner of his eye, he saw her shrug. "I guess."

"We don't have to, if you have something else in mind."

The smell of her filled the car, a scent of lavender and something else, something that filled his nostrils and sent a shiver through him that was, alarmingly, not unpleasant.

"Maybe we could go down to the pier."

"What's down there?"

"Nothing much, but I like it. It's peaceful."

And secluded, Dean added and remembered Len's theory on what she might be expecting from him.

"Sounds kind of boring to me," he said then, aware that it was hardly the polite thing to say but wary of letting the night slip out of his control.

To his surprise, she smiled. "I used to think that too."

"What changed your mind?"

"I don't know. The fire, maybe."

Oh shit. It was a question he knew everyone in school wanted to know, that he himself wanted to know: How did you get those scars? And now it seemed, she would tell him.

"The fire that..." he ventured and saw her nod.

"My brother started it. Funny."

"What was?"

"That he set it trying to kill me and our parents, but he was the only one who died. Hid himself in the basement thinking the fire wouldn't get him down there, and he was right. But the smoke did. He suffocated. I burned."

"My God."

She turned to look at him then and in the gloom, her eyes looked like cold stones, the light sailing over the windshield drawing the scars into her hair.

"Why did you ask me out?"

He fumbled for an answer she would believe but all responses tasted false.

"Someone dare you?"

"No."

"Threaten you?"

"Haven't we already been through this?"

"That's not an answer."

"I told you: No."

"Then why?"

"Because I wanted to."

"I don't believe you."

He rolled his eyes. "Then why are you here?"

Another shrug and she looked out her window. "I'm hoping someday someone will ask me out for real. Until then, I'll settle for trial runs. When you look like I do, being choosy isn't an option, even if you're almost certain you're going to end up getting hurt."

"Hell of an attitude," he said, but understood completely and both hated himself for being exactly what she suspected and pitied her for having to endure the callousness of people.

People like him.

"Maybe. I figure it'll change when I meet someone who doesn't think of me as a freak."

He knew that was his cue to say something comforting, to tell her *I'm not one of those people*, but he was afraid to. It would mean fully committing himself to her expectations and they would undoubtedly extend far beyond this night. It would mean selling himself to her and that was unthinkable, because in reality, he was everything she feared—just another guy setting her up for heartbreak, and as guilty as that made him feel, it was still preferable to making her think he was really interested in her. Neither were palatable options, but at least there was escape from the former.

"I don't think you're being fair on yourself," he said instead, and silently applauded his tact. "I think you look good."

She snorted a laugh, startling him and he looked at her.

"What?"

"Nothing," she replied, but kept looking at him, even when he turned to watch the road; even when he found himself angling the car toward the pier; even as he felt his own skin redden under her scrutiny. The smell of her was intoxicating, the remembered glimpse of thigh agitating him, a persistent itch somewhere deep beneath the skin.

This is a dare, he reminded himself when he felt a faint stirring in his groin. *I'm only doing it because I don't want to get my ass kicked through the rest of high school. And never in a million years would I have asked her otherwise and why the fuck is she still staring at me?*

He brought the car to a squeaking halt, its nose inches from the low pier wall, the black water beyond speckled with reflected stars, the moon gazing at its shimmering twin. Boats danced on the end of their tethers, bells clanking, announcing every wave. A rickety looking jetty ran out to sea and vanished under the cloak of night.

And still he felt her eyes on him.

After a moment in which he screamed to announce *well here we are!* he turned to ask her why she was staring—he couldn't bear the sensation of those eyes on him any longer—but when he opened his mouth to speak, she leaned close and crushed them with her lips, her tongue lashing away the memory of them.

Dean's eyes widened in horror.

Oh Jesus.

She shifted her lips, just a little and the side of her cheek grazed him. Hard skin. It was as if her nails had scratched his mouth. He recoiled; she followed, her hands grabbing fistfuls of his shirt. He moaned a protest but it only spurred her further. Her hands began to slide downward and oh God he was responding—even in the throes of horror he was responding and his hands were sliding over her blouse, feeling the softness there, the small points of hardness beneath his fingers and unbuttoning, tearing, freeing her pale, smooth unblemished skin. She made a low sound in her throat and broke away and for a terrible moment he thought she was going to stop, even though he wanted her to stop because this was a nightmare, but instead she sloughed off her blouse and smiled and now she was wearing just a bra and it was all he could see in a world full of pulsing red stars that throbbed across his eyes. She reached behind her and slowly, teasingly removed her bra and replaced it with his hands. His breath was coming hard and fast, harder and faster, an ache in his crotch as his cock stiffened even as his mind continued to protest *stop it stop it stop it you can't do this you don't* want *to do this* and she was on him again, her hair tickling his face, her mouth crushing, exploring, tearing at his clothes and he moaned, begged her, kneaded her soft, perfect breasts, then released them as she moved lower, lower, her wet lips tasting his nipples, his stomach, her fingers hooking the waistband of his pants and...

...and then the passenger door was wrenched open and disembodied white hands, large hands, leapt forward and tangled themselves in her hair, wrenching her head back to show a face with surprise-widened eyes and a gaping mouth too stunned to cry out.

Dean could do nothing, the lust that had swelled to bursting within him quickly turning to icewater in his veins. *Oh God, no.* He watched in abject terror as Stephanie was torn screaming from the car, the breasts he had held not moments before crushed beneath her weight as she was thrown to the ground face first. She whimpered and for a moment it was the only sound apart from the steady clanking of the bell.

And then Fuckface Freddy's sneering face filled the doorway.

"Surprise, shithead," he said.

* * *

It took only a moment for Dean to gather himself, but he did so with the awful knowledge that he was probably going to die and that awareness lent a sluggishness to his movements that saw him all but crawl from the car to see what Freddy was doing to the girl.

It was worse than he thought, because as he straightened himself to lean against the car, he saw that Freddy was not alone. Lou Greer, the principal's son, track-star and all-round sonofabitch was with him, giggling uncontrollably into his palm and shuffling around Stephanie, who was now sitting up, a shocked expression on her face, her arms crossed over her bare breasts.

Freddy was smiling, a feral smile that promised hurt.

"I'll be damned," he told Dean, "you're just full of fuckin' surprises, man. I was only kiddin' you about bonin' Scarface and here you were about to let her gobble your rod. That's really somethin'."

The bell clanged on, ignoring the hush of the tide.

Somewhere far out to sea, a ship's horn sounded.

The ground around the car was sandy, a thin layer scattered above concrete. Pieces of broken glass gleamed in the half-light from the streetlamps that peered between the canopies of box elder and spruce. This also provided a perfect shield from the road. Few cars would pass by tonight and those that did would not see much should they deign to look in this direction.

"Don't hurt her," Dean said, knowing as he did so that anything he said would only bring him more pain at the hands of Freddy and his comrade.

"That sounded like an order to me, Fred," Greer said, and giggled. It was the contention of most people who knew him, that the last time the principal's son had been lucid, Ronald Reagan was taking his first spill over a curb.

Stephanie was shivering, her pupils huge, the scarred side of her face lost in shadow, and while Dean was filled with terror, he couldn't stop himself from reflecting back on what they'd been doing before Freddy had come along.

But then Freddy stepped close enough to drown Dean in his shadow and the memory was banished from his mind.

"Since when do you give a shit about her?" Freddy asked, somehow managing to sound convincingly curious.

"I-I...I don't know."

Freddy nodded his complete understanding and turned back to Stephanie. She watched him fearfully.

"You do know he set you up, right?"

Greer giggled and muttered "oh shit, that *sucks*" into his hand.

Stephanie looked at Dean and he felt his insides turn cold. There was no anger in her eyes, no disappointment; just a blank look, and somehow that was worse.

"That's a lie, Stephanie," he said, stepping forward, "I swear it's—"

In one smooth move, Freddy swiveled on his heel and launched a downward kick into Dean's shin. Dean howled in pain and collapsed to the ground.

"Shut the fuck up, weasel," Freddy said, and drove his boot into Dean's stomach, knocking the wind out of him. Dean wheezed, tears leaking from his eyes. When they cleared, he saw Stephanie, her arms still crossed across her breasts, her face drawn and pale but for the angry red on her cheek.

I swear I didn't he mouthed to her but knew she didn't understand, knew she couldn't understand because the look in her eyes told him she wasn't really here anymore, that she'd retreated somewhere neither he nor Freddy and Greer could reach her.

Greer stopped giggling long enough to ask: "What'll we do with her, Fred?"

Freddy shrugged and turned back to face Stephanie.

"Can't fuck her," he said, as if he were talking about the weather, "they'd swab her scabby ass and I'd be off the football team."

"Please, leave her...alone," Dean managed, though every word felt like red-hot hooks tugging at his stomach.

"If you don't shut up, we will leave her alone, and do all the unpleasant things to you instead," Freddy said, over his shoulder and for a moment Dean stopped breathing.

Do it, his mind screamed. *Tell them to go ahead and beat the shit out of you. At least they'll leave her alone!*

But he said nothing, merely wept into the sand.

He didn't want her to get hurt, but he had been hurt so much himself that he couldn't bear the thought of more. Even if all of this was his fault. Even if the memory of the way she was looking at him haunted his sleep for the rest of his life.

He.

Couldn't.

Do it.

Incredibly, sleep danced at the edges of his mind and he almost gave himself over to its promise of peace, but then he heard a grunt and Greer's manic giggle and his eyes flickered open. The world swayed, stars coruscating across his retinas, then died.

Stephanie was no longer kneeling.

She was lying flat on her back, breasts exposed with Greer holding her wrists in his hands, as if preparing to drag her over the broken glass. As Dean watched, heartsick and petrified, Freddy grinned and straddled the girl. Still, she would not take her eyes off Dean. He wished more than anything that she would and "please," he moaned into the sand, sending it puffing up around and into his mouth.

"How did she taste, shithead?" Freddy asked and, setting his hands on either side of Stephanie's midriff, leaned down and flicked his tongue over her left nipple. As Greer giggled hysterically, Freddy sat back and smacked his lips as if tasting a fine wine.

"Charcoal, perhaps," he said and that was too much for Greer. He exploded into guffaws so irritating that eventually even Freddy had to tell him to cut it out.

And still Stephanie stared at Dean.

Oh fuck, please stop.

"I'm sorry," he whispered, and knew she didn't hear.

"Then again…" Freddy tasted her right nipple, repeated the lip smacking and put a thoughtful finger to his chin. "Maybe soot. You wanna taste, Greer?"

He didn't need to ask twice. They exchanged positions, Stephanie never once breaking eye contact with Dean and never once trying to struggle against what Freddy and Greer were doing to her. She said nothing, but bore the humiliation in expressionless silence.

Dean, unable to stand it any longer, scooted himself into a sitting position, his back against the car, drew his knees up and buried his face in the dark they provided, surrounding them with his arms. In here, he was safe. All he could hear were the sounds.

It lasted forever and he wept through it all, looking up only when a sharp smack made him flinch.

Greer was on the ground, his giggling stopped, a hand to his cheek. Stephanie was in the same position as before, but skirt was bunched up around her waist, her panties down almost to her knees, exposing her sex, a V-shaped shadow in the white of her skin. Freddy towered over Greer, one fist clenched and held threateningly at his side.

"I said *no*, you fuckin' retard."

Greer looked cowed, and more than a little afraid. "I was just goin' to use a finger."

"Get up," Freddy ordered and Greer scrambled to his feet. They stood on either side of the prone girl, the threat of violence in the air.

"You do as I say or fuck off home to Daddy, you understand me?"

Greer nodded.

"Good, now go get the car. We're done with this bitch."

Another nod from Greer.

The sigh Dean felt at the thought that it might all be over caught in his throat when Freddy turned and walked toward him. Dean's whole body tensed, anticipating another kick, but Freddy dropped to his haunches and smiled.

"Do we need to have this conversation?"

Dean said nothing; didn't know what he was supposed to say.

"Do I need to tell you what will happen if you tell anyone what happened here? Not that anyone will believe a little fucked up perv like you anyway, and I have ways of making sure the finger gets pointed in your direction if you start making noise. Capisce?"

Dean nodded, tears dripping down his cheeks.

"Good. Besides, we didn't hurt her, now did we? We were just havin' some fun. Harmless fun, right?"

Dean nodded.

Freddy's grin dropped as if he'd been struck. He leaned close enough for Dean to smell the beer on his breath.

"Because you open your fuckin' mouth, shithead and two things are gonna happen. First, we'll have a repeat of tonight's performance, only this time we'll go all the way, you know what I'm sayin'? We'll fuck that little burnt-up whore 'till she can't walk no more and then I'll get Greer to do the same to you, just so you don't feel left out, understand?"

Dean nodded furiously with a sob so loud it startled them both. Freddy laughed.

"Yeah, you understand," he said and rose to his feet, taking a moment to dust the sand off his jeans. He looked over at Stephanie, still lying unmoving where they'd left her, and said to Dean: "She's not much of a talker, is she?"

Dean was silent.

"Pretty fuckin' frigid too. Must be your aftershave got you that itty bitty titty, shithead."

Greer's Chevy rumbled to a halt a few feet away.

Freddy glanced back over his shoulder, then looked from Dean to Stephanie.

"Well folks, it's been fun. I hope you've enjoyed me as much as I've enjoyed you!"

He turned and walked to the car, his boots crunching sand.

With a whoop and a holler, Greer roared the engine and they were gone, the Chevy screeching around the corner onto the road behind the trees.

Night closed in around the pier and there were only the waves, the clanging of the bell and the soft sigh of the breeze

* * *

"Stephanie?"

He had brought her clothes, gripping them in a fist that wanted to tremble, to touch her, to help her, but when he offered them to her, she closed her eyes and didn't move.

"Stephanie, he said if I asked you out, he'd quit picking on me. He scares the shit out of me and I'm tired of getting my ass kicked and creeping around worrying that he'll see me. So I agreed, like an idiot. I'm sorry. I really do like you, even if I wasn't sure before. I do like you and I'm so sorry this happened. I swear I didn't know."

There was an interminable period of silence that stretched like taut wire between them, and then she opened her eyes.

Dark.

Fire.

Slowly, she reached out and took the clothes from him.

"Wait for me in the car, I don't want you looking at me," she said coldly, but not before her fingers brushed the air over his hand.

"Okay," he said and rose.

She stared, unmoving.

"I am sorry," he told her and waited a heartbeat for a response.

There was none. He made his way back to the car and stared straight ahead through the windshield at the endless dark sea, ignoring the sinuous flashes of white in the corner of his eye. Echoes of pain tore through his gut and he winced, wondering if something was broken, or burst.

When the car door opened, his pulse quickened and he had to struggle not to look at her.

"Drive me home," she said and put her hands in her lap, her hair, once so clean and fresh now knotted and speckled with sand and dirt, obscuring her face. "Now."

And still the smell of lavender.

He started the car and drove, a million thoughts racing through his mind but not one of them worthy of being spoken aloud.

When they arrived at her house, the moon had moved and the stars seemed less bright than they'd been before. There were no voices, no basketballs whacking pavement, but the breeze had strengthened and tore at the white plastic bags impaled on the railings. Stephanie left him without a word, slamming the car door behind her. He watched her walk up the short stone path with her head bowed, until the darkness that seethed around the doorway consumed her.

Still he waited, hoping a hand might resolve itself from that gloom to wave him goodbye, a gesture that would show him she didn't think he was to blame after all. But the darkness stayed unbroken, and after a few minutes, he drove home.

* * *

He awoke to sunlight streaming in his window and birds singing a chorus of confused melodies in the trees.

A beautiful morning.

Until he tried to sit up and pain cinched a hot metal band around his chest. He gasped in pain. Gasped again when the pain unlocked the memory of the night before, flooding his mind with dark images of a half-naked scared girl and maniacal giggling.

The clanging of a bell.

oh god

He wished it had been a dream, a nightmare, but the pain forbade the illusion. Real. It had happened and the light of morning failed to burn away the cold shadow that clung to him as he recalled his cowardice.

Jesus, I just sat there.

When his mother opened the door and spoke, startling him, he exaggerated his discomfort enough to convince her to let him stay in bed. He endured her maternal worrying until she was satisfied he wasn't going to die on her watch, and then cocooned himself in the covers.

When she was gone, he buried his face in the pillows and wept.

I just sat there.

He wondered if Stephanie had gone to school today, or if, even now the police were on their way to Dean's house, to question him. The momentary thrum of fear abated with the realization that he had done nothing wrong. Freddy and Greer were the ones in trouble if the authorities were brought into it. And still he felt no better. Doing nothing somehow made him feel just as guilty as if he'd been the one holding her down, or pawing at her breasts, mocking her.

He wanted to call her, to try to explain without panic riddling his words, without fear confusing him, but knew he'd lost her.

But what if I hadn't lost her? he wondered then. *What if Freddy hadn't interrupted us and we'd ended up having sex? What would that mean today? What would that make us?*

He saw himself holding her hand as they walked the halls at school.

He saw himself holding her close at the prom as they danced their way through a crowd grinning cruelly.

He saw the look of need in her eyes as she stared at him, the possessive look that told him he was hers forever.

He heard the taunts, the jeers, the snide remarks but this time they wouldn't be aimed at Stephanie alone. This time, they'd be aimed at him too for being the one to pity her. For being blind to what was so staggeringly obvious to everyone else.

What the fuck is wrong *with me?*

Pain of a different kind threaded its way up his throat.

He didn't like the person his feelings made him.

He didn't like who he was becoming, or rather, who he might have been all along.

I just sat there...

As the light faded from the day and the shadows slid across the room, Dean lay back in his bed and stared at the ceiling.

Watching.

Waiting with rage in his heart.

For tomorrow.

* * *

"Mr. Lovell, we missed you yesterday," a voice said and Dean paused, the only rock in a streaming river of students.

The main door was close enough for him to feel the cool air blasting down from the air conditioner, the sunlight making it seem as if the world outside the school had turned white.

Dean turned to face the principal, a tall rail-thin man who looked nothing like his son. Small green eyes stared out from behind rimless glasses. His hands were behind his back, gaze flitting from Dean's pallid face to the object held in his hand.

"Yeah," Dean muttered. "I was sick."

"I see," Principal Greer said, scowling at a student who collided with him and spun away snorting laughter. "Well this close to exams I would expect you'd make more of an effort to make classes."

"It couldn't be helped."

Greer nodded. "Where are you going with that, may I ask?"

Dean lingered, his mouth moving, trying vainly to dispense an excuse, but finally he gave up and turned away. He walked calmly toward the main door.

"Excuse me, Mr. Lovell, I'm not finished with you."

Dean kept moving.

"Mr. Lovell, you listen to me when I'm talking to you!"

Now the scattering of students in the hallway paused, their chattering ceased. Heads turned to watch.

The doorway loomed.

"Lovell, you stop *right this minute!*"

Dean kept moving.

"You…your parents will be hearing from me!" Lovell sounded as if he might explode with rage. Dean didn't care. He hadn't really heard anything the old man had said anyway.

The hallway was deathly silent as he passed beneath the fresh air billowing from the a/c, and then he was outside, on the steps and staring down.

At where Fuckface Freddy was regaling two squirming girls with tales of his exploits.

"I swear," he was saying, "the bitch told me she got off when guys did that. I mean…in a goddamn *bowl* for Chrissakes! Can you believe that shit?"

It took four steps to reach him and when he turned, he squinted at Dean.

Sneered.

"The fuck *you* want?"

Dean returned his sneer and drew back the baseball bat he'd taken from his locker.

He expected Freddy to look shocked, or frightened, or to beg Dean not to hurt him. But Freddy did none of those things.

Instead, he laughed.

And Dean swung the bat.

* * *

His parents, talking. He lay in the dark, listening. They were making no intent to be quiet.

"Did you talk to him?"

"I didn't know what to say. He says his sorry."

"Sorry? He gave the guy a broken jaw, a busted nose and a concussion! Sorry isn't going to cut it."

"He was upset, Don."

"Oh and that's supposed to get him off the hook, huh? Did you ask him what the hell he's going to do now? Greer *expelled* him. You want to appeal against that? Just so our darling son can beat the shit out of the next guy who's dumb enough to cross him? Everyone gets upset, Rhonda, but not everyone pisses away their future by taking a bat to someone. I can't wait to hear what that kid's parents are going to do. They'll probably sue the ass off us."

"He says the guy was picking on him."

"Oh for Christ's sake."

"Well I don't know…you go talk to him then."

"I'm telling you…if I go up to that room, it won't be to talk."

"Then talk to him tomorrow. He's obviously got some problems we didn't know about. You being angry isn't going to help anything."

"Yeah well, jail isn't going to do him much good either, now is it?"

He lay in the dark, listening.

Smiling.

* * *

Over the next few days he was dragged to meetings, and heard the tone, but none of the words. Voices were raised, threats were issued, and peace was imposed. There were questions, different faces asking different questions, all of them threads connected to the same ball: *Why did you do it, Dean?*

Had he chosen to answer those blurry, changing faces in all those rooms that smelled of furniture polish and sweat, he would have told them: *I just sat there.* But instead he said nothing, and soon the faces went away, the slatted sunlight aged on the walls and there was only one voice, a woman, speaking to him as if he were a child, but still asking the question everyone wanted to know and which he refused to answer because it belonged to him, and him alone.

"Dean, I want to help you, but you have to help *me*."

That made him smile.

"Tell me what happened."

He wouldn't.

"Tell me why you did what you did."

He didn't, and when she shook her head at some unseen observer, standing in the shadows at his back, he was released. No more faces, no more voices, just his parents, expressing their disappointment, their frustration. Their anger.

It meant nothing to him.

* * *

In the dark of night he awoke, unable to breathe, his body soaked in sweat, panic crawling all over him.

I'm sorry I'm sorry I'm so sorry

Look at you now, a voice sneered in his ear and when he turned toward it, Fuckface Freddy was grinning a smile missing most of its teeth, his nose squashed and bleeding, one eye misshapen from when Dean had knocked it loose. His breath smelled like alcohol. *Look at you now shithead.*

Dean clamped his hands over his eyes, into his hair and pulled, screamed, a long hoarse tortured scream that made lights come on in more houses than his own.

Look at you now…

* * *

"These sessions will only be beneficial to you, Dean, if you open up to me..."

* * *

Look at you now...

* * *

"He starts at Graham High in the fall. Let's hope he doesn't fuck that up."

"Don't talk like that, Don. He's still your son."

"Thanks for the reminder."

* * *

Stephanie kissed him, her head making the covers ripple as she worked her way down his stomach. He moaned, filled with confusion and desire. Surely it couldn't all have been a dream, but if not, then he was thankful at least for the respite, this neutral plain where no harm was done and no one had been hurt.

Not here.

And when he ran his hands through her hair, she raised her face so that he could see the scars. So that he could touch them, remember them. But there were no scars. Only a wide gaping smile from which Greer's giggle emerged...

* * *

Almost a month later, his parents left him alone for the weekend. They'd asked him to come with them to Rodney's farm; his uncle was sick, and they claimed getting away from the house for a while might do Dean some good. And Rodney would be just tickled to see his nephew.

Dean refused, in a manner that dissuaded persistence, leaving them no option but to leave him behind, but not without a litany of commands and warnings. Then, on Friday evening, his mother kissed him on the cheek; he wiped it away. His father scowled; Dean ignored it. Then they were gone and the house was filled with quiet, merciful peace.

Until there was a knock on the door.

Dean didn't answer, but his parents had not locked it and soon Les was standing in the living room, hands by his sides, a horrified expression on his face.

"Dude, what the fuck are you doing?"

"Venting," Dean said, drawing the blade of his mother's carving knife across his forearm. He stared in fascination as the cuts, deep and straight, opened but remained bloodless and pink for a few moments before the blood welled.

"Hey...don't do that okay?" Les said, his voice shaking as he took a seat opposite Dean. "Please."

"It helps," Dean said, wiping the blade clean against the leg of his jeans. Then he returned the knife to an area below the four slashes he'd already made. Blood streaked his arm and Les noticed a spot of dark red was blossoming on the carpet between his legs. Dean had his arm braced across his knees, as if he were attempting to saw a piece of wood. Face set in grim determination, eyes glassy, he slowly drew the blade back, opening another wide pink smile in the skin.

"Jesus, Dean. What are you doing this for?"

"I told you," Dean said, without looking up from his work, "it helps."

"Helps what?"

"Helps it escape."

"I don't get it."

"No. You don't," Dean said and grit his teeth as he made another cut.

* * *

There were dreams and voices, the words lost beneath the amplified sound of skin tearing.

And when he woke, he knew his arms were not enough.

* * *

Summer died and took fall and winter with it, a swirl of sun, rain, snow and dead leaves that filled the window of the Lovell house like paintings deemed not good enough and replaced to mirror seasons that surely could not move so fast.

A somber mood held court inside. A man and a woman moved, tended to their daily routines, but they were faded and gray, people stepped from ancient photographs to taste the air for a while.

And upstairs, a room stood empty, the door closed, keeping the memories sealed safely within.

Another year passed.

* * *

"Two, babe," the kid said, running a hand over his gel-slicked hair and winking at the pretty girl in the ticket booth. On the screen behind him, garish commercials paraded across the Drive-In screen and the meager gathering of cars began to honk in celebration.

The kid glanced over his shoulder at the screen and looked back when the girl jammed two tickets into his hands. Using her other hand she snatched away his money, offered him a dutiful smile and went back to her magazine.

"Chilly," scoffed the kid and returned to his car, his shoes crunching on the gravel.

The movie previews began and the honking died. Crickets sawed a song in the field behind the screen.

The moon was high, bathing the lot in a cool blue light.

"One," said a voice and the girl sighed, looked up at the man standing in front of her and began to punch out the ticket. Her hand froze.

"Hi Stephanie," Dean said.

He moved his face closer, so the amber glow fell on his face and Stephanie barely restrained a grimace.

"What are you doing here?" she asked after a moment, then tugged the ticket free and slid it beneath the Plexiglas window.

"I wanted to see you."

"Oh yeah, for what?"

"To apologize."

"Apology accepted," she said testily and glared at him. "That'll be two dollars."

He smiled, said, "You look amazing," and passed over the money.

And she did. The scars were gone, with only the faintest sign that they'd ever been there. Perhaps the skin on her right cheek was just a little darker than it should have been, a little tighter than normal, but that could be blamed on makeup. Without the scar, she was stunning, but then, through all his nights of suffering and the endless days of rage, he'd come to realize that even *with* them, she'd been beautiful. It was he who'd been the ugly one, ugly on the inside.

She stopped and stared at him, the look he remembered, the look that had haunted him, but then it was gone; exasperation replacing it.

"What happened to you?" she asked.

He put a hand to his chin, to the hard pink ridges of skin there and shrugged. "I had to let it out."

He expected her to ask the question so many people had put to him ever since the day his father had kicked in the bathroom door and found him lying bleeding on the floor, his face in ruins, his mother's carving knife clutched in one trembling hand, but she didn't. She simply shook her head.

"You destroyed yourself."

He nodded. "For you."

Her laugh was so unexpected he staggered back a step, the scars on his face rearranging themselves into a map of confusion.

Someone honked a horn at the screen. A chorus of voices echoes from the speakers.

Stephanie looked ugly again. "You almost killed him you know."

"Who?"

"Freddy."

"I know. He deserved it."

"No he didn't."

He watched her carefully, watched her features harden and a cold lance of fear shot through him.

"What do you mean? After what he did—"

She frowned, as if he had missed the simplest answer of all. "I *asked* him to do it."

On the screen, someone screamed. For a moment, Dean wasn't sure it hadn't been himself.

"You used to see Freddy hanging around all those cheerleaders and blonde bimbos at school, right?"

He nodded, dumbly, his throat filled with dust.

"Did you ever actually see him out with any of them?"

He didn't answer.

Ominous music from the speakers; footsteps; a door creaking loud enough to silence the crickets.

"He had an image to maintain, Dean. He had to fit the role of the high school stereotype. He was a jock and that meant he should be seen with a certain type of girl. But that's not the kind of girl he *liked*." She smiled, and it was colder than the night. "He liked his girl's damaged, as if they'd been through Hell and returned with tales to tell, as if they had scars to prove they were tough and ready for anything. The Barbie doll type made him sick."

Dean shuddered, jammed his hands into the pockets of his coat; wished he'd brought the knife.

"I was his girl," she said, a truth that wrenched his guts surer than any blade. "No one knew because he still had his pride. Why do you think he hit Greer for trying to fuck me? That was going one step too far. 'Course that dumbass Greer knew nothing about it and still doesn't."

Dean stared, his body trembling, his hands clenched so tight the scars on his arms must surely rip open and bleed anew.

A joke. It was all a joke.

"We didn't think you'd freak out like you did and beat seven shades of shit out of Freddy. Christ. You nearly killed him, you asshole."

But Dean didn't hear her. An evil laugh filtered through the speakers, followed by a hellish voice that asked: "Where's my pretty little girl?" And then a scream to make Fay Wray proud.

Where's my pretty little girl?

"How..." Dean began, before pausing to clear his throat. "How did you...?" He indicated his own mangled face with a trembling forefinger.

"Surgery," she said airily. "It's why I'm still working in this fucking dump. My mother refuses to help me pay for it. Too busy buying shit she doesn't need on the Shopping Channel. Of course, when I lost the scars, I lost Freddy too. I was tired of him anyway."

The sound of unpleasant death, of skin rending, gurgling screams, and bones snapping, filled the air.

"Hey," Stephanie said with a shrug, "it's all in the past, right? No hard feelings?"

Look at you now, shithead.

Dean nodded, licked his lips. "Yeah. Right, no hard feelings."

Stephanie nodded her satisfaction. "Good, so are you going to watch your movie, or what?"

Look at you now.

SNOWMEN

The two men standing in Ryan's backyard were like irises in the eyes of winter.

And they were looking right at him.

The boy stood in his bedroom, the cold licking his wrists and ankles. He shuddered. His bed stood only a few tantalizing feet away. The window was even closer.

But he couldn't move. Not yet.

It was as if those faceless men playing statues in his back yard wouldn't let him look away. Wouldn't let him call his parents.

Not that that would do any good anyway. Dad had come home drunk enough to fill the entire house with the smell of sweat and whiskey. Mom was asleep on the couch, exhausted after carrying his father up the stairs and roaring abuse at him. They wouldn't be in any mood to entertain Ryan now. Just your imagination, they'd say.

But it wasn't his imagination. Nor a dream. He had blinked his eyes once, twice, three times. He'd pinched his arm hard enough to force him into stifling a yelp – there would be an angry red welt there tomorrow. He'd gone to the bathroom to pee and splashed cold water on his face…and when he'd returned they were still there. Two of them. One large, one small.

Faces in shadow, staring at him. He knew they were staring at him, could feel their eyes on him.

It was snowing again now but that didn't seem to bother them. They simply stood, unmoving, watching him with fierce interest. Waiting for something maybe. But what?

Again he thought of rousing his parents. So what if they didn't believe him or were angry? At least he wouldn't be alone. At least then he could drag them in here and let them see for themselves that he wasn't lying, or imagining things.

But would the men still be there?

Courage bloomed in him like a warm flower and he willed his legs to move.

In a heartbeat he was padding across the cold floor. He yanked the door open and the narrow hallway beyond yawned into view. His father was closest, so he hurried down the hall to his parent's bedroom and tapped once on the door – a matter of formality – then entered the room.

And stalled on the threshold, halted by memory. His eyes searched the dark, finally straining the shape of a bed from the meager light spilling in from the hall. An uncertain pale oblong held the crumpled shape of a wild-haired shadow, open-mouthed. Gasping and gurgling. Gasping and gurgling.

Can't wake him, Ryan thought, fearful. On his cheek, the latent print of an old wound rose like a submarine from the deep and brought a flush to his skin. The sound it brought echoing inside his skull was a mere whisper but the remembered threat was enough.

Wake me again you little bastard and I'll break y—

No. Suddenly afraid his presence would be enough to rouse the sleeping man, Ryan eased stealthily back, wincing in time with the creak and groan of the floorboards. He paused once more on the threshold, listening.

The shape on the bed shuddered, fell silent. Ryan's heart stopped.

He waited, hair prickling, for a sleep-muddled grumble. *"Whhhat're you doinginhere, punkkk?"*

But it did not come. Waiting until the awful gasping and gurgling resumed, Ryan moved out into the hall, a heavy sigh momentarily drowning out the machinery of drunken slumber. He slowly turned the knob as far as it would go so the door would shut without a sound and was relieved when it did so without betraying him.

Safe. He was annoyed at himself for even thinking his father could help him. He knew all too well from past experience that Dad was a mean drunk. Worse when roused from sleeping it off. And yet Ryan had intended on doing that very thing.

Dumb jerk.

There was not a doubt in his mind that his father loved him (even if he never said as much), and would never intentionally lay a hand on his son. But when he was drunk, he changed. Became possessed. He was a monster, who forgot the people who shared his cave and lashed out at them as if they sought to invade his territory. He hurt them, then wept in the morning when he saw what he'd done. A broken finger, a bleeding nose...a cut cheek. A broken heart.

Ryan's breath whistled through his nose as he approached his bedroom. The door was opposite the stairs and now indecision cut through him. Wouldn't it be wise to check and make sure the men were still there before trying to wake his mother?

Sure it would. But what if they weren't there? It might mean they'd left, their staring game spoiled now that he'd moved away from the window, or it might mean they'd moved, looking for a way into the house to get him. The thought chilled him. But not nearly as much as the one that followed it: *What if they're* already *inside?*

Ryan swallowed, braced a hand against the wallpaper to steady himself. He listened to the sounds of the house. *Creak, groan, sigh, creak,* all in time with the soughing of the wind through the eaves. But weren't those creaks like footsteps mounting the stairs? Wasn't that groan like a stubborn door being carefully shut? The sigh the inexorable breath released at last by someone who'd been holding it?

Ryan began to tremble.

Creak, groan, creak...

Someone on the stairs.

Creak, creak, sigh...

"Hello?" Ryan's voice was tiny and quickly swallowed by the shadows hanging in the corners of the hall.

Creak. Creak. CREAK.

"Who's there?"

The wind answered him. "*Ryyyyaaaannnn,*" he was *sure* it said.

The footsteps drew closer.

This was not imagination either. Ryan felt his bladder let go, soaking his pajama bottoms as tears welled in his eyes. Not imagination at all and that was unfortunate, for at that moment, the lights flickered, just as the maker of those creaking sounds reached the top of the stairs and stepped onto the landing.

And there was no one there.

Lights buzzed. Shadows leapt, but the hallway was empty.

And from his father's bedroom, the suddenly reassuring sound of a hacking cough quickly became a gurgling snore once more.

Shivering, Ryan looked down at the puddle between his feet. He would have to clean it up before he got in trouble, but that could wait. He was already in trouble, but this kind of trouble was the very worst kind. The kind of trouble where you're not sure who's after you or why.

All you know is that they are.

He stepped around the puddle, hand still splayed against the wall, the floor creaking and cold, the wallpaper he'd always hated whispering beneath his fingers, and swung into his room. The moonlight was splashed across his bed, smothering darkness in the folds where he had thrown back the covers when something had woken him up and drawn him to the window.

As it drew him to the window now, his body tensed, eyes wide and still moist.

They won't be there, he knew. *They won't be there because they're in the house with me, probably creeping up the stairs right now.* His certainty was reinforced by years spent watching horror movies at his best friend Larry's house on Halloween. Horror movies he knew his parents didn't approve of. Larry's parents didn't care. Sometimes they even joined them in watching them. In horror movies, the Thing That Was After You always stood motionless when you caught sight of it. Then, when you brought your parents back, babbling and screaming about the monster in your closet/on the ceiling/under your bed/outside your window and pointed at where you'd seen it, it would be gone. Making you a victim of something almost as bad as the monster: enraged parents. It would wait then until Mom and Dad were sound asleep before creeping out to kill you.

Now, he slowly stepped up the window, his breath held, the feel of the wet pajama pants unpleasant against his skin.

They won't be there.

But they were.

In exactly the same positions as before. A sudden need to throw open the window and shriek *what do you want why are you standing in my yard?* down at them struck Ryan hard in the chest and he almost acted on it, until reason kicked back in and he stopped himself. That would be crazy. Opening the window might be just the move they were waiting for. His breath fogged against the glass and warmed his face.

He noticed something then, something awful, something he should have noticed before.

The air around the figures was still, unbroken.

They have no breath.

A noise in the hall made him jump. *Creak.*

Creak. Thump.

Ryan started to turn.

And one of the men in the yard moved. Ryan gasped.

The move had been slight. So slight he almost hadn't caught it. The one on the right had tilted its head at him, as if confused by his actions, or the lack of them.

But as much as it seemed he had to, he couldn't dwell on that now. Because this time, there was *definitely* someone out in the hall. The creaking of the floorboards he could have explained away as the same phantom walker he'd imagined on the stairs, but the thump could be nothing but a footfall.

Thump. There it was again.

Heart hammering madly, Ryan cast a quick glance over his shoulder, almost expecting to see the people in the yard had flown up and were leering in at him, their dead faces pressed against the glass. But no, they were still down there, watching. Ringed by leafless walnut trees.

Ryan padded slowly across the room and stopped a few feet from the door.

Somewhere out in the hall, a door opened. No attempt had been made to hide the sound of the knob rattling or the hinges creaking. Unsteady footsteps thumped one-two-three across the hall. Stopped.

Ryan's breath rasped. He shook. Folded his arms to steady himself.

Silence.

The fear within him seemed caught on the scale dead center between relief and outright screaming terror. The footsteps were too confident, too uncaring to be those of an intruder.

Dad?

Thump, thump, thump.

Again they stopped.

The only bathroom in the house was downstairs. Ryan seized on the memory of many nights waking to the sound of his drunken father struggling to negotiate the hallway, blinded by the light. His old man had even fallen down the stairs once and sprained his ankle, though the following day he'd claimed he'd twisted it while playing baseball with his cronies. But Ryan knew different. He'd heard it all, the rattling calamity, the startled cry, the hiss of pained breath through clenched teeth, the call for Mom.

The footsteps started again and he almost cried out his father's name.

But isn't that what they want you to think? a voice inside him cautioned and he clamped his mouth shut. *You've seen two of them down there. Who says there isn't a third?*

That was true. What if that was another one of them out there, pretending to be his father? Trying to coax him out by fooling him into feeling safe?

*But the footsteps…*They'd come from up the hall, from the direction of his parents' room and not the stairs.

You were asleep. One of them might have crept into your father's room.

He hadn't thought of that.

Call for Mom.

Yes. That was it. That was the thing to do.

But wait. What if that *was* one of them out there. Wouldn't calling Mom lure her right into its arms?

His thoughts felt tangled, confusion overwhelming him until he found himself crying again. Soundlessly. *Why is this happening?*

Thump, thump, thump, thump, thump, THUMP! The footsteps jerked him to attention and he hastily wiped the tears away with his sleeve and focused on the door. Something grazed the hallway wall. Close.

The thumping stopped.

Ryan's gaze fell to the light beneath the door. Twin shadows in the amber light, cast by the feet of whoever was standing outside.

"Dad?" he whispered.

Quiet, but for the wind hushing the night.

"Daddy?" he repeated and almost screamed, almost died of fright when an answer came.

"Ryyannn?"

The boy stepped forward, then back, his arm outstretched, uncertainty making a dance out of his movements.

It's a trick! They're trying to trick you!

But how could he be sure?

Don't open that door! They'll get you!

But what if it was his father, squinting at the door wondering what the hell was going on? Wondering if he'd imagined hearing his son's voice. Then he'd leave, go downstairs or back to bed. Leaving Ryan alone again.

And that couldn't happen.

"Ryyyaannn? That youuuu?"

The boy was at the door before he could change his mind.

RYAN NO!

Sobbing now, ignoring the ripple of fear that passed over him, Ryan tugged the door open. The light blazed in his eyes, momentarily making a hunched shadow of the thing standing there. A noxious odor rolled across the threshold.

The voice inside him fell silent.

The house fell silent.

Then a board creaked as the shadow moved forward a step. "Ryan? What the hell's goin' on? Why you up?"

The tears came in a torrent Ryan was helpless to stop as he rushed forward and wrapped his arms around his father's waist, almost sending both of them sprawling.

"Ryan? Hey! What's...?" Large muscular arms pried him loose and his father squinted down at him through eyes so full of red veins Ryan was amazed he could see through them. "What the hell's the matter with you? Why are you crying?"

"The win—" Ryan started to say, then wiped his eyes and rushed back into the bedroom. No. Had to check. The very worst thing that could happen now would be for him to tell Dad everything only to have the creatures in the yard vanish like they were supposed to. Like they did in the movies.

"Ryan?"

Everything was all right, Ryan realized, a surge of confidence brewing in his chest. Daddy was here now and even monsters with no breath would think twice before crossing his father. With the foul stink from the man clinging to him, a smell he now found infinitely comforting, Ryan closed his eyes and leaned forward to look out the window.

Please be there. Please be there. Please.

"Ryan? What are you doing?"

Ryan opened his eyes. And grinned triumphantly.

Relief swelled over him. "There's someone in the yard. Come look. They've been watching me all night. Two of them. They're not supposed to be there, are they Daddy? And they're not breathing!"

A weary sigh from behind him, followed by a click as his father switched on the light, casting a yellow oblong out onto the thick white snow beneath his window.

"There they are. Come look!" Ryan said, narrowing his eyes, unable to stem the excitement now that his lonely night of terror was over. Whatever those things down there had come for, they wouldn't get it now.

He rubbed his fists over his eyes. Felt the grit of forgotten sleep come away.

He looked down and pointed at the two figures, now bathed in hazy light.

And froze.

Even from here he could see the mistake he'd made in the beginning thinking there were two men down there. There weren't. Nor were they the wicked monsters of his imaginings.

One of them was a woman. The one with the tilted head

(*because it's coming* off)

166

was a woman.

His mother. Glittering in the light, ice forming a skin over her body, holding her in place, holding her still and firmly planted in the mound of snow at her feet.

"Ryan? What are you doing?"

Ryan began to tremble, a whine building in his throat, trapped there with all hope of a scream.

Daddy sounded as if he needed to clear his throat. Daddy's reflection grew bigger in the window. Beneath which, another version of Daddy, the *real* Daddy, stood in his very own mound of snow, arms pinned to his sides, skin alive with crystals, mouth open and filled with snow.

Staring.

The shadow filled the window, draping darkness over the figures frozen below.

Ryan watched it, allowed his eyes to meet the reflection of the liquid blue sparks hovering just above his head.

Gasping and gurgling, a sound he had mistaken for his father's snoring. He now realized it had been nothing so innocent. As icicles met his skin and darkness filled his eyes, all awareness of pain and death swept away from him, leaving him with one single shred of a thought.

That in the morning there would be three figures in the garden.

WILL YOU TELL THEM I DIED QUIETLY?

I tried to be like them once. I tried to stop. It didn't work. Couldn't work after your uncle brought The Yawning Thing home. That made it worse. That brought the dreams, and the dreams said I should die and die quietly. For this, I need your help. Will you help me?

Yes, if you promise not to hate me.

Of course. I could never hate you, nor should you ever hate me. Not for this. Hate them instead. All of them.

The shrieking of tires further down the rain-slicked road made Elias jump. Concerned, his uncle clamped a hand on his shoulder. "Okay?" he asked and Elias nodded, then looked up at the roiling quicksilver sky. It had been raining since her death. Endless rain that turned the earth to sludge and darkened moods already somber. He gritted his teeth until they hurt and let his uncle steer him into the crowd of walking umbrellas clustered at the churchyard gates. Autumn hissed past them clinging wetly to the wheels of a hurried driver and the stooped men hunched further away from the icy spray.

The graveyard yawned wide revealing crooked stone teeth set on green-capped gums of misshapen earth. They would put her somewhere hidden, in a plot no one else wanted, Elias knew. Somewhere she wouldn't be found unless by chance or mistake. In the weeds, perhaps, for their generosity could only extend so far after all these years spent hating.

Somewhere quiet.

He watched black heels creating echoes on the paved path, stared at the stockinged feet of their owners and felt the anger flare once more, searing the inside of his cold skin, heating his cheeks.

He watched the congregation of strangers, bustling purposefully forward through the sheets of rain; unfamiliar shapes garbed in misery they would cast off once they had muttered the words expected of them. All niceties spun from the remnants of old hatred.

This was a soulless, senseless, unhallowed place where the ground prospered on the bones of more strangers. No one mattered here, neither the living nor the dead.

He was already starting to regret agreeing to let them take her here.

A tall thin figure with a shredded cloud for hair parted the crowd and floated through the gray towards them. Elias sighed to a halt, accepted the squeeze of his uncle's hand again and nodded. Reverend Flood mimicked it, disrupted the carefully placed creases in his face with a practiced smile.

"Elias." For a moment nothing but a sad, slow shake of his head. "I'm so glad you decided to let us perform the ceremony. In times like these it is of no use to anyone to keep old feuds going, wouldn't you agree?"

Elias frowned, tautened the silence between them with a glare at the holy man, bore his uncle's attempt at a thank you and let himself be ferried further toward the grave. Inside, his guts rolled coldly. *Feuds?* Is that what they called it? Or had he missed a note of mockery in the reverend's words? His face reddened. Then he thought of Veronica. She would have laughed, and that made the first smile of the day corkscrew the corners of his mouth.

The shadow of the church dropped over them, steam rising from the skin of a crowd that had unified to become a solid, shifting mass of hushed tones and clucked sympathetic tongues. Elias hated them then, wanted to hurt them, to shriek his rage at them, to scare them into revealing the true purpose for their presence here. But instead he said nothing and let the memory of Veronica's patience carry him beneath a steeple pretending to fall in time with their advance. The wind hurried them; the rain needled them and they were inside, awash in the warmth of an alleged grace and a phalanx of candles. Heads turned; white smudges draped in hollow pockets of mourning watching for victims, perfecting solemnity.

And it was quiet.

"You should probably sit up front," his uncle said and at last his hand was removed. "She would have wanted you to."

Elias moved away from him, sparing him a glance as he did so. Uncle Travis had never been close; was no closer now despite his valiant attempts to be supportive. He had in fact been relegated to little more than a blurry figure in the background of his mother's photos and his nephew's recollections from years past. The smile he offered Elias was tired and confused. He was just as out of place as his nephew, but less equipped to deal with it. The old man lowered his painfully thin frame into a seat, next to a withered old woman whose one good eye rolled to watch him.

The carpet in the aisle was red velvet and whispered against the soles of Elias's shoes. He noticed black crescent symbols—meaningless to anyone not well versed in the way of the New World—slipping beneath his feet. Then gone. He raised his head. The altar was a morgue slab dressed in veils that clung greedily to the shadows of the candles. Behind it, set high in the old stone wall an orb of stained glass rose, a kaleidoscope of ill-formed images, fragmented faces with jigsaw skin, all bowed in supplication to some higher power Elias didn't care to know. He was not here to give thanks.

Will you tell them? Will you expose their narrow-minded ways and tell them I died because of this? Because of the Yawning Thing? It stands there, wanting me to be inside it you know, wanting me to become one with it. Such a terrible graceless thing.

At the head of the church sat a rigid cabal of imposters. To Elias, they were as loathsome as the black-clad throng who'd crawled through the churchyard like starving cats. For a moment they made no move to make room for him, but eventually a sneer was cast his way and they swept aside on a wave of grumbled whispers. He sat and ignored the fetid stench radiating from the fraternity. Sat and waited.

The candles flickered.

Reverend Flood drifted from within the ill-lit recesses, through the gloom into the fluttering light, his eyes wide and flitting from face to face. His spotless black shoes made no sound on the marble steps as he ascended the altar from the left, genuflected, and floated into position behind the slab, head bowed. Elias felt his skin ripple and tears of anger fill his eyes. *I should not have let them take her*, he thought and was answered by her voice: *There is no shame in lying with the enemy if the enemy is not aware of itself.* He nodded to himself, shuddered off the lingering skeins of repulsion at being so close, so caught inside a crowd of his family's one-time persecutors and listened.

I'm fading. Are you there? Tell me you won't leave. I'm scared. See how it watches me? See how it wants me?

Don't be frightened. I won't leave.
Will you tell them I died quietly?
Yes.
Even if I don't?
What? What does that mean? You said –
I'm fading. Quick, grab the needle...

"We are gathered here to pay our respects to a most unique and curious woman. A woman misunderstood by many. A woman who suffered under the terms of old superstitions, stubbornly upheld by the ill-educated among our parish. It is time we put an end to such nonsense once and for all." Though swathed in cloaks hewn to imbue divinity, the elderly reverend wore one too many shadows, his face one too many lines for Elias to believe him sincere. The charitable words fell from his mouth like worms from a fallen pail. As if he'd read the thought, the holy man fixed him with a hard stare, a half-smile dancing on his thin lips.

"Grief unites us all, my friends, regardless of our religion and in grief, people can be saved."

Rain thudded dully against a roof so high above them it could not be seen in the gloom.

Smoke ghosts wrenched themselves away from the candles as the front doors were heaved closed.

"Let us pray for her immortal soul," Flood commanded. "Pray for the soul of Veronica Ryman, that her body may rest and her soul find peace in the afterlife." The sudden silence prompted by the reverend's words brought a startling and impossibly obvious question hammering into the forefront of Elias's mind.

The body.

Where is her body? It should be here.

It was a burial. He had assumed the coffin would take its place at the head of the church. Had he misinterpreted the rituals of these commonfolk?

He stood and dragged the upset murmurs of the crowd up by his elbows. For the first time he noticed the thrumming, as of an engine buried beneath the church. His blood vibrated with it as around him, shadowed heads nodded in glee at his confusion. Sudden, almost debilitating fury struck him, flooding his veins with adrenaline, drowning the fear that lapped at his throat. Then he was up and out and stalking towards the altar, where the reverend's arms were held aloft as if expecting his faith to keep the roof above their heads should it deign to fall.

Elias clenched his fists to his sides and mounted the steps; cast a venomous glance at the holy man before he turned to face the congregation.

Towards the back of the church and the shadows gathered there, his uncle's hand waved objection, little more than a pale shape shifting in the gloom. He ignored it.

Thunder grumbled over their heads. Murmurs leaked from the pews and gathered in pools of dissension in the aisle.

I loved her, Elias realized. *This would never have happened if I had told her so, given her hope. Something else to think about besides that* thing.

"Son," said Reverend Flood, the abstract flow of his garments belying the benevolent composure on his fissured face. "I understand you're upset."

"Do you?" Elias said with a bitter grin. "Perhaps I'd be less upset if you'd tell me where she is."

"What? Where who is? You mean your mother?"

"Who else are you burying today?"

Shock snapped the spines of those who'd been content to bow their heads and ignore the proceedings and now all faces were raised and staring.

Flood shook his head, brow furrowed. "She's here. We'll bury her after the ceremony, like we always do. Why are you so upset?"

"Why isn't she here in the church? Is that part of your goddamned ritual? I want to know where she is. Now."

Flood leaned closer and Elias had to struggle not to back up a step. A hush rushed from the back of the church through the pews and swept against his cheek like a blow that had fallen short. There came what might have been a muffled cry of pain and he looked out at the crowd. Silent, somber faces. His uncle's hand still raised and waving.

"Would you have preferred she be displayed, Elias," Flood whispered. "In the condition you left her in?"

Elias felt his rage surge inside him. Lies wept from the open wound of the holy man's mouth, sickening him. "You said she'd be treated like anyone else," he said through clenched teeth. "Why isn't her body in the church?"

Flood looked evenly at him. "Who said it isn't?"

"Then where is her coffin?"

Incense filled the air, though Elias had seen none burning. Silence stretched out between them as it had in the churchyard before his uncle had bade him move on.

A mistake.

This was all a mistake.

He was seeing the truth now as if the opacity of their false promises had been ripped from his eyes. Elias and his family were pariahs. His mother's death should have been a triumph for them. Instead they had offered to inter her on their ground, by way of a peace offering. But what holy man would voluntarily offer to give peace and eternal life to a witch?

Elias had swallowed the hurt, the pain, the grief at her passing, had weathered their choreographed mourning despite the clear memory of their cruelty to her while she lived. He had walked among them, bristling with repulsion at the mere thought of being so close, nauseated by his willingness to accept their pitiful gestures of condolence. No longer. The charade would end one way or another. He would tear the façade down around them, then take her body away and bury her where she would have wished.

"Son," said Flood, "you didn't bring her to us in a coffin."

They called it Nocturnity, *Elias. Though on the placard at its feet it says* The Yawning Thing. *It was supposed to be a symbol of sleep, a cure for insomniacs who were instructed down through the ages to gaze upon it so that it might make them tired by looking at another man's exhausted image. It didn't though. It drove them mad, sent them into fevers, bestowed night terrors upon them, haunted them until they splintered their own bones and split their skins trying to climb inside its mouth. Your father brought it to me. Said it would look after me, help me to sleep while he was off on another of his acquisitions trips. It didn't though and he never returned. Since then, it has stood right where it is now, watching me, whispering perverse things to me in the twilight between sleep and wakefulness, telling me to die quietly before it consumes me whole. And I believe it. Don't you?*

I don't know.

Of course you do. You're such a good boy and you must help me. You must save me from it. You must ensure that I cannot see it, that I am not here to bear witness to it when it comes to tear me asunder.

But how?

You'll know.

"You murdered her," Elias said and sneered into the reverend's face. "If not for you she'd have been able to run, to get help. All of you killed her." He pointed out at the crowd and his breath caught, his finger fell. The congregation was standing, a black sea of motionless figures, faces raised and twisted in the candlelight. Watching him. Something scraped against a wall near the back of the church.

"It was you who did the murdering," Flood told him. "You and your kind."

The rain thundered overhead; the floor hummed underfoot.

Elias stared, felt the weight of the congregation at his back. "I helped her. I gave her a quiet death."

Flood gave a sad smile. "I'm afraid not," he said. "I'm afraid it wasn't that quiet at all and you know it."

I can see him, Elias. I can still see him watching. Take my eyes. Take that needle. Take them. I don't want to see it anymore. Make me blind to it. Quick, quick. Good boy. Oh God...

"It's why you brought the statue," Flood continued. "It's why you agreed to let us have her. You thought she'd gone crazy, and she had. What you didn't know was that she was right." He nodded toward the sacristy, where beside a small stained glass door, the shadows were thick. Elias followed his gaze. "Is-is she there?"

"God gives the power to those who know how to control it, my son. The statue was meant to find us. There is no room left for your kind."

Elias wasn't listening. His feet had found the steps. The doors at the front of the church rattled. He looked in that direction, saw his uncle still waving, though now his hand was free of his body and being held aloft by a stranger.

Trapped.

They'd walked right into it. It hurt his head to think about how long the machinery must had been turning to bring them here, to bring down his family, his mother. Panic seized him, siphoned the air from his lungs and he gasped and tumbled forward into the gloom. *At least she's here*, he thought frantically. *I'll see her one last time.* He could ask her forgiveness for not ushering her out as he was supposed to, for making her death anything but quiet. She had died with a guttural scream he'd had to sever with a carving knife, the horror tattooed on her face as she choked on her own blood. No. Not quiet.

He flung himself deeper into the gloom, his fumbling hands warmed by feverish breath he prayed was his own. The thrumming in the floor felt almost pleasurable now, sending a tingling up through the soles of his feet. Feeble light strained through the stained glass door of the sacristy. Beyond it figures moved, their arms dwindling into curved, raised shapes. Sharper shadows. He ignored them, continued to search the corner, met the mottled stone of the wall, kicked against the rug when it gathered like a tired dog at his feet and then…

Here.

Cold, polished marble slipped beneath his fingertips.

Nocturnity. The Yawning Thing.

Behind him the carpet whispered to him of the advance of the throng.

"Forgive me," he said as a break in the crowd revealed the face of the statue. A long thin face with wide eyes and an impossibly long mouth looked back at him. Black marble. From between its teeth, bloodstained blonde hair trailed down to its muscular, lifeless chest. Elias closed his eyes, sank heavily to his knees. "She didn't die quietly," was all he could think to say as the congregation drew a tight circle around him and hissed curses down on his head.

As one, the candles went out.

A final breeze touched his face and he smiled, imagined it was her fingertips brushing his lips.

"Neither will you," someone said as the curved shadows descended from over their heads.

THE LAST LAUGH

"Paxton, wake up."

"Ten minutes," Josh mumbled, and started to roll over, but his roommate's hand clamped down on his shoulder and halted him, pulled him back.

"C'mon man, you gotta *see* this."

"What is it?" Begrudgingly, Josh opened his eyes and shaded them against the morning sun streaming in through his window. "And so begins another day in Yawnsville."

His roommate, Rick, was a live wire of excitement, which, for a guy with hideous acne, greasy hair and bifocals, was a state usually reserved for those times when he spoke of the women warriors in online games as if they were prospective dates. To call him a 'nerd' wouldn't be capturing the complete wonder of the guy's essence. "Check this out," he said, nudging Josh hard one more time for good measure before hurrying over to the window overlooking the courtyard.

With a groan and a yawn that made his jaw pop, Josh threw back the covers and got his feet on the floor. "This better be good."

"I don't know if it is or isn't, man, but I can tell you it's pretty messed up."

The awe in his roommate's voice was enough to get Josh to stand, though he did so on legs that were no more alert than their owner. He stretched and shuffled over to join Rick at the window, where he squinted, brought his face closer to the glass and frowned. "Jesus…"

"Yeah. Weird, huh?"

"You could say that, yeah," Josh said.

The courtyard was nothing fancy, in keeping with the complex that surrounded it on three of the four sides. A small fountain, filled with crumpled up soda cans and other detritus tossed into it by the residents or the people who passed by the wrought-iron gate at the entrance, stood like a faux marble cradle with a pond scum coverlet in the center of the yard. The building catered mostly to students from the Redfield College of Arts & Sciences a few blocks away. But as far as Josh could tell, the crowd gathered in the courtyard now was not comprised of students, at least none that he'd ever seen before.

"Maybe they're demonstrators. You been using any abortion or gay stuff in your jokes lately?"

"No, but remind me that I need to start."

"Yeah, sure."

Josh grinned. "Maybe we're unwitting participants in a cell phone commercial. You know the one...where this crowd follows this guy around because he's using shitty service or something?"

"Yeah, or maybe they're like the crowd from that Bradbury story."

"Who's Bradbury?"

"Never mind," said Rick, and went silent. A moment later, he frowned and looked at Josh. "Hey...at the club last night."

"What about it?"

"Remember what you said to that Conrad schmuck?"

"Not really, no."

"You told him there wasn't an audience you couldn't get rolling in the aisles."

"So what?"

"So he had the same audience you had. You killed 'em; he didn't. I saw him leave that place and man he was like a freakin' beet."

Josh grinned. "Pickled?"

"Red. Pissed off."

"And you think he dialed Rent-A-Crowd down there as some kind of revenge ploy?"

"It's possible, isn't it?"

"Anything's possible, but this looks a tad ambitious for that little weasel. And what exactly would doing something like this achieve anyway?"

Rick shrugged. "Dunno. Maybe it's the opening salvo of a practical joke war. Which means, you'll have to go one better."

"Better than what?" He jabbed a forefinger at the window. "This? This isn't a joke. Getting a bunch of people with nothing better to do to stand in the courtyard staring up at us? Wow...I'm truly humbled. Maybe, *if* this is a prank war, I can get them to actually *do something* when it's my turn, huh? What a classic that'll be."

"Either way, you should probably find out what they want."

"Fuck 'em," Josh said, and made his way over to the coffee machine. "You find out what they want."

"Why me?"

"I'm not awake yet. Besides, we're not sure that they're actually here for me. Maybe your chess club is striking because you keep stealing their queens. Hell, could be they're here to bug someone in the apartment below us. Who knows?"

"I'm not good with crowds."

"You know what they say is the best way to conquer your fears and shortcomings," Josh said, and searched the counter for his cigarettes.

* * *

He watched from the window as Rick opened the door and stepped outside. The crowd had left pockets of space here and there, but not many. Josh estimated there were maybe two hundred people crammed into the courtyard, and although he'd been blasé about it with Rick, he had to admit he felt a small spark of admiration for anyone who could convince a couple hundred adults to drop what they were doing to go bug a two-bit comedian. Which of course, was what he was, and he didn't mind admitting it to himself, though of course he'd die before he'd let anyone else in on that little secret. He was popular at The Crooked Clown Comedy Club and that was really all that mattered at the end of the day. He got paid, and occasionally, if it was a slow night and the waitresses had been treating themselves to a few surreptitious sips, he got laid too. His grades were nothing special, but not disastrous either. He was coasting by, enjoying himself greatly in the process, and making just enough to feel smugly satisfied when his parents called to ask if he'd seen the error of his ways so they could welcome him back to the family with open checkbooks. "Fuck no," was his response to that little lure, and hung up before they started reminding him of his past transgressions. As far as he was concerned, there was no error to be seen. He'd done a chick who'd claimed to be eighteen, and turned out to three years shy. Worse, he'd gotten her pregnant and his family had been forced to intervene. They'd cut her a tidy sum to shut her up, and told Josh he was on his own. Somehow that didn't seem fair. Not that it mattered now. He knew they were keeping tabs on him though. When he got busted for possession of pot, they were all over it. Drunk-driving and reckless endangerment? Ditto. So despite their claim that they'd washed their hands of him, he knew they'd never be so far away that they wouldn't rush in to cover his missteps, all for the sake of keeping the family's hard-earned reputation intact.

And that afforded him great freedom indeed.

Puffing on his cigarette, he brought his forehead to the glass and watched Rick gesticulate dramatically to the unmoving crowd. *Christ*, he thought. *Guy should be a politician*. And while his roommate mimed away, Josh studied the faces of the gathering. Man, but they were a dull bunch. As far as he could tell, the average age was about twenty, but not a single one of them looked like they (a) knew what the hell they were doing here, or (b) had any kind of cogent plan in mind. Which seemed preposterous. Surely there had to be more to this than just showing up outside his apartment? Conrad was a loser, sure, and about as witty as a cat trapped in a barrel of fish piss, but he had to have more up his sleeve than what Josh was seeing now, assuming Conrad *was* behind this little flash mob. And if he wasn't...well, then a call to the cops was probably in order, but Josh figured Rick could take care of that too, whenever he got done playing Citizen Kane down there.

The phone rang, and Josh was glad of the interruption. The crowd and their *Night of the Living Dead* act was already starting to bore him. He transferred the cigarette to his left hand, scooped up the receiver of the phone he liked to call "The Bat-Phone" because of its hideous scarlet hue, with his right. "Lo?"

"Hey buddy."

"Hey. Who's this?"

"Jim Conrad. Your *colleague* down at th—"

"Yeah, I know who you are. What's up?"

"You look out your window yet?"

"Sure did."

"And?"

"And what? Same 'ol, same 'ol. Quite frankly I'm still pissed that they had the balls to call it 'quaint and homely' in the brochure, when it's about as quaint and homely as a penitentiary for incontinent seniors."

"Funny."

Josh took a pull on his cigarette and made sure he blew the smoke into the phone as loudly as he could. "That's what it's all about, isn't it? A few laughs. A few chuckles. So what was it you called about?"

"You know what I called about."

"Sure. You want me to hook you up with a gig where the people might actually appreciate your tired old vaudeville zingers and spinning bowties, right?"

"They want you to tell a joke."

"Who does? The stoners in the quad?"

"You have to make them laugh."

"Hell, that's easy. I'll just give them a rundown of last night's performance. *Yours.*"

Conrad scoffed. "You'll need to do better than that."

"Hey, man, c'mon…you know I can do better than that. You have to watch me do better than you every Thursday night, and while I appreciate how bitter it's made you, this…" He gestured dismissively at the window as if the man on the other end of the phone could see it. "…This isn't the answer. Making that bunch of loons laugh—which you know I could do in a heartbeat—would only leave you feeling even more inadequate. No, sir. No. I think the right thing to do would be to find an alternate source of employment, Conrad. Find something you're good at, like waiting tables, or maybe mopping the floors at a porn theater. Something that'll give you that sense of validation you so desperately require."

Conrad chuckled. "I already have an alternate source of income, Paxton. I'm a magician. And a good one."

"Really? Wow. Can you conjure yourself up some talent?"

"I can do more than that, buddy. Much more than that."

"Like convincing folks to picket outside a rival comedian's apartment? That's quite a trick, man. You're three steps from Vegas with that one, although I gotta tell ya, I'd have been a lot more impressed if you'd filled the courtyard with tigers."

"I don't know how to do that yet."

"Shame. Me and Tony the Tiger could have tied one on." Josh sighed. "Anyway, sure was a kick chatting with you, Connie, but I have better things to do, like pegging your mob with bottle tops, so—"

"You have to make them laugh."

Josh frowned. This was getting tiresome, and all joking aside, he was genuinely starting to question Conrad's health. The guy sounded completely whacko. "Yeah, you already said that. So that's what you want? I crack a joke, and crack them up? What then?"

"Then they leave."

"Man, you really need to find a hobby."

"And if you don't make them laugh," Conrad continued, "they won't."

"Then they really need to find a hobby too."

"Goodbye, Paxton. And good luck."

Josh smiled. "So long Siegfried."

* * *

He was in no hurry to rid himself of the crowd. After all, life off the stage had been pretty tedious of late, so what harm was there in having a few giggles at Conrad's expense? He found himself hoping the guy was paying his crew by the hour, in which case the moron was going to have to pull twice as many rabbits out of his ass to stay in the black. The thought amused him. He was still smiling about it when he took his shower, got dressed, and parked himself in front of the television, getting up to look out at his new audience only when it occurred to him that Rick had been gone for almost an hour.

Outside, the crowd hadn't moved, were gazing up at him with blank eyes, only their hair moving, courtesy of a light breeze.

There was no sign of Rick.

"Chickenshit," Josh said, and after running through a short and completely imaginary list of priorities, he decided to face his visitors and be done with it.

* * *

They applauded him.

He stood in the doorway, the heel of one shoe keeping the thin metal door slightly ajar should it turn out that Conrad's jealousy was of the murderous kind and this mob were here to stone him, and raised his hands demurely while he took a half-bow and told them they were being too kind. He waved down their applause and, despite the bizarre stage upon which he had found himself, began to prepare for an impromptu performance.

His eyes alighted on a pale, thin brunette three rows back. Like the rest of the crowd, she wasn't smiling, only watching him emotionlessly, but damn she was cute. Not only that, but she seemed oddly familiar. Had Conrad recruited these folks from the club's regular attendees? If so, the guy was even dumber than Josh had given him credit for. Fact was, they were regular because Josh kept drawing them back, so the odds of him knocking them dead, good to begin with, had just gone through the roof.

He looked from face to face, somewhat unaccustomed to being before an audience that wasn't making any noise at all. In the club, during a performance, you could always count on some muttered conversation from the back of the room where folks knew they couldn't be seen—something Josh detested, but strangely enough found himself missing now. People coughed, clinked glasses, shuffled their feet, adjusted their chairs, tried to sneak off to the bathroom without drawing Josh's attention. But here in the courtyard, there was only the sound of Josh clearing his throat.

"So," he began, smiling at all the unsmiling faces. "I hate to tell you this, but if you guys are from FEMA, you're a little late."

The silence deepened, and for once Josh was suddenly grateful for the little snare drum and cymbal sound in his head: *baddum-bum-chish*. He looked at the faces before him, each one so somber and serious, he found it hard to imagine them wrinkling with mirth. Okay, so topical humor isn't doing it, he thought, dismayed at the single unwelcome note of uncertainty that thrummed in his brain. "All right," he continued. "So you guys have been around. The usual fare won't satisfy you. I'm betting Connie told you to wear your best poker faces and not to crack up over anything less than the best, right?"

Unsurprisingly, no one offered him a reply.

"I'm guessing it's going to have to be a real doozy of a show to get you gusy rollin', right?"

Beyond the complex, traffic droned, horns honked, and life went on as usual, but here in the courtyard, the quiet was almost reverent, as if the crowd had gathered to hear not a joke, but a sermon.

"All right," Josh sighed, and did a quick scan of the crowd. He saw more faces he thought looked familiar, and then jolted as his gaze alighted on one he most certainly knew. The acne-ridden bespectacled man looking back at him was standing as still as the rest of them and wearing the same look of patient anticipation. *You fucking traitor*, Josh thought, but quickly regained his composure, more buoyed by the challenge Conrad had set for him than he was unnerved by the sight of his roommate standing amid the crowd as if he'd been there from the beginning.

"So who here's from out of town?"

* * *

"You're on in five minutes," the stage manager said curtly, and withdrew his head from the small, unpainted dressing room in which Josh sat looking at himself in the cracked unlit mirror. There were dark bags like healing bruises beneath his eyes, but he hadn't been fighting anything but frustration, anger, and self-doubt over the past six days since the crowd first showed up outside his apartment. Lack of sleep wasn't helping. He'd been staying up late scribbling down jokes that seemed completely ridiculous in the morning, and thinking up new material when he was supposed to be sleeping. During the few classes he still took, the words his instructor wrote on the blackboard became punchlines to jokes Josh hadn't been let in on.

And the crowd...

The crowd was still there, all day, every day, and on through the night. How they managed to maintain their vigil without eating or sleeping, or *moving*, was beyond him, and he was forced to conclude that either they were as mad as the man who had assigned them this insane task, or Conrad really was capable of magic, a theory that seemed even more preposterous. Whatever the case, they were starting to worry him, and he despised himself for letting that happen. He'd called the police, of course, when two full days passed with no sign of the mob repairing to the apartments of the other successful folks Conrad had to have on his shit list. The officers had come, and ironically, laughed when he told them, then showed them, the situation. Thankfully they'd been obliged to do something no matter how amusing they found it all. The crowd was trespassing, after all, and causing Josh undue emotional distress, and the police had seemed to understand that, so he left them to address the crowd, went back upstairs and drew the shades, only to open them thirty minutes later to find the crowd now had two new recruits, both of them wearing police uniforms. The cruiser they'd arrived in was still parked outside. The thought that people could not just abandon their jobs without someone asking questions, and eventually coming to look for their erstwhile employee, was not as comforting as it should have been. He realized the crowd would probably just absorb them too, until it grew too big to be contained by the courtyard, or the street, or the city...

The absurdity of that notion got him laughing, but the face in the mirror looked closer to weeping.

"Okay," he told himself, smoothing his face with trembling hands. "Be cool. Just pull it together. That little prick can only do this to you if you let him."

He adjusted the collar of his denim jacket, rose, and with a deep breath, headed out into the narrow hall toward the stage where the host—a bald, diminutive man by the name of Sal Rossetto—was already introducing him. The raucous enthusiasm of applause melted some of the ice from his bones, but when Josh jogged out into the lights, a forced smile plastered on his face, he realized it was only applause, no whistles, no cheers. No voices at all. Just the staccato sound of cold palms meeting.

The crowd was here.

* * *

Fifteen minutes later, "This is a first," Rossetto said, back in the dressing room. "In two years I've never had to yank you off in the middle of your show. What the hell happened out there?"

"It wasn't my crowd," Josh told him and lowered his head, palms clamped to the sides of his face. "I don't know who those fucking people are, but they're not *my* crowd."

Sal leaned back against the door and sniffed loudly, a habit everyone he encountered found annoying, and produced from the breast pocket of his lilac colored sport coat a slim cigar, which he lit with an equally slim silver lighter. Then he blew out a plume of smoke and smiled.

"Listen, kid. You're a good earner for the club. Hardly a seat empty when you're on, and tonight was no different, even if you did get the oil painting instead of the audience. Hell, I've never seen a guy who didn't get that at least once. Would you believe we had Billy Crystal do a show here back in the early eighties? I swear, you could have heard a dog fart out in the alley his jokes fell so flat."

Josh didn't believe it, was in fact almost completely certain that Crystal, or anyone else of note, had never done standup here. If they had, that little bit of history would have been used more in promoting the place, but in The Crooked Clown Comedy Club, there were no signed portraits or headshots on the walls, no Polaroids in little frames, nothing, and this was the first time Sal had referred to anything but police raids, egos, and fistfights when recounting the club's history. It was obviously an attempt to try to lessen the blow of an unimpressed audience, and on some level Josh appreciated that, but had Sal known the full scope of what was happening here, he might not have bothered.

"Who's on out there now?" Josh asked him.

"The Conrad kid."

"That asshole."

"Hey, easy. He might not be in your league, but whatever kind of…" He prodded the cigar at the air between them, as if trying to write the words in smoke, "…*Cosmic shift* …is happening here tonight, he's got them rolling. You struck out. It happens. You'll get over it. As long as *someone's* got them laughing, I don't really—"

Josh slammed a fist on the table, startling Sal. "That snake is trying to sabotage me."

Sal regarded his cigar, as if he suspected that's where the allegation had come from. "Say what?"

"He's got this…this crowd following me around everywhere. They're camped outside my place morning, noon, and night, waiting for me to make them laugh. They came here tonight. That's who my crowd was, and they're doing all of this because that son of a bitch is *making* them do it."

"Conrad?"

"*Yes.*"

Sal looked up. "You're saying he paid, or somehow, got a crowd of folks to follow you around?"

"Exactly."

"For what? To *not* laugh at your jokes?"

"Yes."

"Does it need to be said how crazy that sounds?"

"I know how it sounds, but that's what's happening."

"Huh."

"You don't believe me?"

Sal sniffed. Josh wanted to punch him. Then, "Hey," the host said. "A pirate walks into a bar with a steering wheel shoved down the front of his pants. Barman says, 'Christ, that has to be uncomfortable,' and the pirate says: "Aaaarr, it's drivin' me nuts.'" He bellowed laughter, but halted and went back to studying his cigar when he realized Josh wasn't.

"That's an old one," Josh said.

"Yeah, but there's a message in there if you think about it."

"That I'm nuts?"

Sal shrugged. "In this world, you're either the nuts or the steering wheel. Go home. Get some sleep. And lay off anything you've been messing with, all right?"

"For fuck sake, Sal. I haven't been messing with anything."

"All right, but you're wound up tighter than a fly's asshole, and you're no good to me like that. You know how it works by now, kid. You bring your A-game here and nothing less, so go home and deal with whatever needs to be dealt with. Mine it for new material. And when your brain's back in its box, when *you're* doing the steering, call me and we'll set up some more dates for you."

Josh felt a flutter of panic in his chest. "What do you mean set up some dates? I'm down for every Thursday night."

Sal gave him a sympathetic look. "Yes, you are, but I don't need trouble here and looking at you right now, that's what I'm seeing. Take some time to get your head together and we'll talk."

Josh stood, anger filling him. Sal did not back away, nor did he appear intimidated, and there was good reason for that. The guy was small, but Josh had seen him level more than one guy twice his size.

"Go home," Sal said, a warning in his eyes as he held open the door for Josh. "Now."

* * *

He left the club, fuming, but knew there was an opportunity to release that anger, and this time not in the direction of someone who didn't deserve it. Sal was right. He was a mess. He needed to get his head together. But he needed to do something else first. So he didn't go home. Instead, he waited in the parking lot underneath a dark, starless sky that seemed to hang very low, and tried to ignore the stares from the silent crowd milling in the street, their gaunt peering faces like pale balloons tethered to the parking lot wall. That they were there further enraged Josh because it meant that the reaction Conrad was getting now from the audience inside the club wasn't coming from the same one he'd assigned to torment Josh. It meant there was a chance that the laughter was legitimate, *real*, and that bothered him most of all.

They found *that* son of a bitch funny?

He waited, trembling, fists clenched, for Conrad to come out.

* * *

Magic, real or not, apparently didn't come with an advance warning system. With a forearm across Conrad's throat, Josh had him pinned against the wall opposite the club's side door before the thin man knew what was happening.

"Hey," he protested in a strangled voice, his tongue jutting out, eyes bulging from their sockets. "Get the hell *off* me."

"Conjure your way out of this, you prick."

"I said, get *off*."

"Not until you make them go away," Josh said through clenched teeth, leaning in so his forearm was pressed even tighter against Conrad's windpipe.

The other man gasped. "If…if you kill me, you'll be screwed."

"Yeah, well, maybe I'm okay with that. After all, you've taken my audience and my job. What else do I have to lose?"

"Plenty. Now let me *go*." With a surprising burst of strength, the smaller man planted the palms of his hands against Josh's chest and shoved him away, but once free, he didn't try to run. Instead he massaged his throat, wincing, and glared at Josh. "You asshole."

A quick check of the side door showed that no one had heard the commotion, or if they had, had chosen to ignore it. Josh looked back to Conrad, temper leading him to imagine all the different ways he could cause the other man great physical distress.

"What do you want from me?" he asked. "What do you want to make this stop?"

"I don't want anything from you," Conrad replied, with a smirk. "I've already got what I want. All that's left for you is to make them laugh." He nodded in the direction of the waiting crowd. "Once you do, you'll never see them, or me, again."

"How do I do it?" Josh didn't like the desperation in his voice, but he wouldn't worry about that now. He needed answers, and if he didn't get them, this little runt would be leaving in an ambulance. "How do I make them laugh?"

Conrad's smirk faded. "That's a dumb question."

"Just fucking *tell* me, all right? I'm tired of this."

"I already told you. Tell them a joke. Do something funny. You make them laugh, they leave. It's that simple."

"I've tried that. They don't laugh."

"Every audience is different. You know that. What works for one might not work for another. Try something different. Something new. Try harder."

Josh grabbed fistfuls of his hair and pulled as if the pain might override the frustration. It didn't, adding only physical discomfort to the mental anguish. "Why are you doing this to me?"

"I needed the money."

"For Chrissakes, I'll give you money to end this if that's all it is."

"Too late now," Conrad told him, with a pretty good impression of genuine regret. "Sorry. But you're a funny guy, remember? You'll figure out a way to crack them up." He patted Josh's shoulder.

It was one step too far.

Josh grabbed him, and with a cry that brought half the staff of the club running out to see what was going on, broke the man's arm, nose, and all but one of the fingers on his left hand.

And as Josh had envisioned, Conrad, who hadn't answered his questions, was taken away in an ambulance.

Josh was taken away in a police car.

* * *

The crowd was still outside, though in the two weeks since the incident at The Crooked Clown, it had vastly increased in size. Now, they spilled out onto the street, lining the pavement on both sides and forcing pedestrians to walk around them. Those brave enough to attempt to elbow their way through the throng, didn't come out the other side. Josh had watched other students in his building try to talk to the crowd, to reason with the unmoving mob. Some demanded an explanation; others tried intimidation. One of them even waved a gun in their faces, but they didn't so much as look at him. They just kept on staring up at Josh's window, waiting for him to make them laugh, and the next day, the students were part of their number.

No one called. No one came to help, or see how he was doing.

He was alone.

And when at last he confronted the crowd again, it was not to tell them the joke he hoped would win them over. It was find one of the policemen they'd claimed as one of their own, and relieve him of his gun.

Back in the apartment, he drew the shades, downed a full bottle of whiskey, and wept. He felt nothing. The fear he'd predicted was a voice at the bottom of an elevator shaft, too far away to make a difference.

He shivered and shook, muttered threats to that bastard Conrad he knew he would never carry out, and glanced at The Bat-Phone every few seconds, awaiting a call from someone who still cared. Wondering if he should call his family, and see if they could help him one last time.

No. He shouldn't have to ask, shouldn't have to come looking for them. They should care enough not to have to be called upon to save him. He'd rather die than beg them for help.

He turned on the TV and tried to lose himself in the sitcoms that thrust other people's fabricated contentment in his face until the canned laughter made him feel sick. He turned it off.

As the sun went down and the room grew thick with shadows, there was nothing but silence inside the apartment and out, and though he couldn't see them, he felt a thousand eyes watching, peering deep into his soul, where there was little left to see. The impossibility, the implausibility of this situation was not lost on him. It just didn't matter anymore.

Despair overwhelmed him. He ransacked the apartment, flung wide the shades, yanked open the window and tossed anything he could find down upon the heads of his tormentors.

Still, they didn't move, though one of them blinked at him through rivulets of blood from the gash where the corner of Josh's toaster had dug a furrow in his skull.

"Fuck the lot of you," Josh screamed at them, tearing the shades from their rails. "I'll give you something to laugh about!" He retrieved the gun, returned to the window and leveled the weapon at the impassive faces, hoping one in particular would look like they deserved the bullet more than the others.

But none of them did.

There was no malevolence in their expressions. No ill will specifically directed his way. They were merely puppets, he realized, here at someone else's request. Instruments of vengeance. Harming them would achieve nothing, just like snapping their master's bones hadn't changed a damn thing. This, was *done*.

He lowered the gun, tears streaming down his unshaven cheeks, then cocked the hammer on the policeman's revolver and slid the cold barrel into his mouth.

Only one way out now, he thought. *Only one way to win, to go out while I'm still thought of as a stand-up guy*. He smiled around the obstruction clamped between his teeth. *Good one, boss.*

He pulled the trigger. Bloody thunder roared through the apartment.

In its wake, laughter from the courtyard.

Then applause.

* * *

"What happened?" the woman asked, grimacing at his bruises.

"Paxton happened," he said, and took a seat beside her on the park bench.

The sun was high and bright, the light filtered through the canopies of oak leaves and casting watery shadows on the ground around them. A pleasant day, but one the lingering pain in his bones kept Conrad from fully appreciating.

"Here," the woman said, handing him a brown padded envelope. "And I'm sorry you got hurt."

He shrugged and the motion sent a bolt of pain from his elbow up the side of his neck. "Comes with the territory," he said, and accepted the envelope.

"Don't you want to count it?" she asked, as she watched him stuff it, with obvious difficulty, into the inside pocket of his coat.

"I trust you," he replied, and started to rise. "Pleasure doing business with you."

"Wait."

"What is it?"

"Do you think he suffered?"

He smiled tightly. "No, it was quick."

"Thank you." There were tears in her eyes.

He nodded and started walking, but she was on her feet, a hand on his shoulder, before he'd taken two steps. He turned to face her, marveling somewhat distantly at how utterly beautiful she had probably been before Paxton ruined her and carved the deep worry lines that radiated from the corners of her eyes and mouth. The breeze made her auburn hair dance and he wished he were the kind of man who'd get to brush it from her eyes someday. But he wasn't. Besides, Paxton had all but destroyed her life and left her with enough hatred for her to seek the most unspeakable kind of revenge. Truth was, casting a spell such as the one she'd been so specific in requesting, had been a first for him. Most of it had been simple direction and illusion, a matter of conjuring up the latent images of long-dead comedians, but somewhere in its conjuring, he'd accidentally tapped into something darker, more dangerous and less controllable. Not that it mattered really. The end result had been achieved to the client's satisfaction, and he'd come away forty grand richer. But those insidious threads he'd woven, however unintentionally, intrigued him. They demanded further exploration. Though comedy was his dream, he was no fool, and realized the advantage this strange power might yet afford him.

"I'm not a bad person, you know," the woman said, and he knew she was not concerned with his opinion of her, only her own, which he figured was pretty unflattering right now.

"I know," he said. "But if it makes you feel any better, it would most likely have ended this way eventually anyway, without anyone's interference. What you did for your son was an act of mercy."

"Mercy," she repeated, as if tasting the word. Then she nodded, offered him a fragile smile and turned back to the bench, where her purse, a sad deflated thing, awaited her. "Goodbye," she said, her voice trembling under the weight of tears he knew she would have to contend with for many more years to come, because no sin ever went unpunished in the world of hate, pride, and magic.

"Goodbye, Mrs. Paxton," he said, already repainting the encounter in a humorous light, so that it could be mined for jokes when next he needed them.

COBWEBS

I began to be forgotten on a dawn no different than any other I'd seen during the past few years of my incarceration at Spring Grace Retirement Home. The ever-present burning ache in my bones was no better or worse. The sheets were still too tight, the pillow too lumpy, the room a little too cold. Shadows squatted in the corners where they had no business squatting, but like silent drunks, were too harmless to justify ousting. Pins and needles made hornet-filled trees of my legs. The radiator gave its little metallic *tick-tick-tack*, and belched liquidly. Even the light, splintered by the Venetian blinds to form horizontal bars of cold fire on the puke-green wall, looked the same.

But today something *was* different. When I moved my hand down over my face, over features that had aged badly without my consent and without my noticing, the very ordinary caul of post-slumber confusion clung to the tips of my fingers, and didn't let go as I brought them up for inspection.

Like the memory of old kisses, there was a cobweb stretched across my mouth, violin-string skeins of it stretching out to my fingertips as if waiting for my horrified cry to play them. But I didn't utter a sound, even when I probed the expanse of the web with my tongue and it came away coated in sour-tasting dust. I sat up, not without effort, and beat and pulled and scratched somewhat hysterically at my mouth until all that remained of the cobweb hung in dark brownish clumps from my fingers. *Steady, Al.* My heart was beating fast enough to give me pause, to distract me from the origin of my panic. *Calm down, it's okay, it's all right*, I told myself and waited for the voltage of fear to ebb away. *It's okay.* I looked up at the ceiling. There were cracks in the plaster and cobwebs in the corners, but none on the unremarkable light shade. Of course, there wouldn't be, for it was the obvious suspect, the inanimate villain of the piece, who had shed its cotton candy cobweb skin onto my face as I'd slept.

Grimacing, I got up, every joint and muscle firing off a round of pain, and after a careful inspection of the terrycloth for more invasive gossamer threads, crept into the robe. The smell of disinfectant, nauseatingly familiar, reached me before I opened the door, before I'd cinched the belt on my robe. The smell is meant to hide the odors of age, sickness and death, of hopelessness, but for those of us who call this place a home, it is a constant reminder that we are the creatures from which the terrible stench originates, things better hidden away so the world can be spared the inconvenience of looking at us and seeing its future.

When I got to the lounge after the usual ritual of ignoring the staff's automated cheer, and waiting for mail that wasn't there, I found my friend The Cowboy's chair was empty, and he hadn't made his move. The chess pieces were as we'd left them the evening before. The only other soul in the room was Doris Randle, who had at least been capable of a smile when she'd first been admitted, but now gaped dumbly at me as a string of drool tried to connect the corner of her mouth to her paisley-patterned bosom. Two strokes had made an empty vessel of her. It was my contention another would kill her.

"Morning Doris," I said, one hand absently moving to my mouth to be sure no trace of the cobweb remained, or maybe I feared her drooling was contagious.

She stared without seeing me.

"You know him?" she muttered, and I, mistakenly assuming she was talking about The Cowboy, almost celebrated her words as the most coherent anyone had heard from her in months. But then "The kid?" she continued, and I let out a long low sigh. "The one in the classroom? They let the little bastard loose with his crayons. They asked him to color the heart." Her eyes grew more distant, dropped away from me to the chess set. "He didn't stay inside the lines."

I followed her gaze. Looked at the chair. It shouldn't have been empty. It never was at this time of day. Meeting here for our morning chess and banter was about the only ritual either of us had, and one we had come to depend on to help preserve our wits in a place designed, it seemed, to steal them. Then, as I stared at the cheap plastic-backed chair, envisioning The Cowboy with his small blue eyes, salt-and-pepper hair, and grizzled chin, the light through the room's single window changed, only slightly, but enough to make me think it should have been snowing outside. It was that kind of light. Cold and blue. It diffused the gnarled and sad shadow of the eucalyptus in the planter on the sill, blurring it, making the outthrust limbs look like the desperate arms of one of my fellow inmates, clambering for the sleeve of someone who might care.

I wanted to ask Doris if she had noticed the peculiar change in the room, but knew she wouldn't answer, at least not coherently. So, "You take care now," I told her, and left before she was able to coax her gaze back to where I'd been standing. A man could get lost if he spent too long wading through the overgrowth in her field of vision.

Back in the hall I grabbed the first nurse unfortunate enough to cross my path, and asked her where The Cowboy was. But even before that loathsome look of practiced sympathy crossed Nurse Stanford's taut face, I knew.

"He went peacefully," she said. "In his sleep. You must have been close."

It struck me as odd that she didn't know that. There wasn't enough camaraderie among the withered souls in Spring Grace for our friendship to have gone unnoticed. I thought of the slight chill I'd felt in the lounge, the changing of the light. Now it seemed like an omen. I almost smiled. The Cowboy would have been smugly satisfied to know that his passing had knocked askew some portion of the universe, however briefly

"Is everything all right, Mr. Ross?"

"Yes, why?"

"No particular reason."

Then why ask? I thought, but said instead, "I'm fine. Thank you." I started to move away, then stopped and looked back. Nurse Stanford hadn't moved. She was still standing there, hands clasped matron-like beneath her bosom.

"Can you please," I said, "if it isn't too much trouble—send someone in to remove the cobwebs from my room?"

She looked momentarily confused by the request. I didn't wait for her answer. Instead I headed back to my room, and was relieved to find the light hadn't changed in my sanctuary.

I sat on the edge of the bed for a while, hands folded in my lap, feeling unpleasantly hollow deep in my chest and alarmingly near tears. Worse, I couldn't tell how much of my burgeoning sorrow was for The Cowboy, and how much was a result of the selfish realization that I was now well and truly alone.

My last remaining friend was gone.

I wondered if he had really gone quietly into the sunset, or if, before they stowed him in the back of that quiet ambulance, they'd had to pause to remove the cobwebs from his lips.

* * *

Noon brought thoughts of a towheaded kid who'd loved magic. A kid who used to usher his Mom and me into the living room, knowing it would mean he'd get to stay up a little later than usual. He wore a top hat and a cape. He even had the white gloves and the dramatic flourish the costume seemed to instill in whoever wore it. Those gloves cut the air above a red velvet tablecloth he'd spread across a narrow workbench. Props were arranged atop that crimson surface, sleeves shirked back, face impassive but not entirely hiding the look, the barely contained smirk that told us all we were going to be astounded and amazed, whether we believed in him or not.

Beneath the cobwebs Marcia was forever vowing to remove, little Joey called upon his carefully practiced powers of prestidigitation to stun us all, and while many of his tricks were transparent numbers, more often than not, he succeeded.

But the years robbed him of magic and the need to impress. They robbed us all of a lot of things.

He still calls from time to time, but only to assuage his guilt, and to remind himself I'm still there.

Sometimes, I don't wait for his concern to lead him.

After lunch I found myself in the hallway, lamenting my choice of the mushy Salisbury steak and wishing I had some gum, or a mint—anything to rid my palate of the noxious taste. I stepped up to the payphone after patiently listening to Zach Greenburg cursing at his daughter for fifteen minutes.

The earpiece was unpleasantly moist as I listened to the connection worming its way from Ohio to Colorado.

On the third ring, Joey answered.

"Dad? Jesus, how've you been?"

"Not good enough for you to start calling me Jesus."

His laugh was strained, as always. "Nice to hear that place hasn't knocked the wit out of you."

"Not for the want of trying."

"Right."

The stretches of silence grow longer every time we talk, as we both search for something agreeable to say. It has become like trying to find change in a phone booth's coin return. Sometimes you get lucky; more often you don't.

"So how's the weather there?" he asked.

"Sunny." *Aside from a brief change to tell me my friend had died.*

"Nice. It's cold as hell down here."

"I'd still rather be there than here. The idea of stocking up wood excites the hell out of me. Better than sitting in my room waiting for something interesting to happen."

"Yeah." Pause. The rustle of papers in the background. *Multitasking.* "It was Drew's birthday last weekend. Wish you could have been here."

"I didn't know." And in truth, resented the implication in his voice that I should have. "What is he now, nine?"

"Eleven."

I whistled.

"I've been meaning to get up there to see you, you know?"

I didn't know, but as easy—and in truth, pleasurable—as it would have been to say so, I resisted and mumbled affirmation into the phone.

"But it's a long haul, Dad. Especially with Kathy working such long hours. If she takes time off now it'll look bad. She's still in training, did I tell you that?"

"No." Nor did I know what she was in training *for.*

"Yeah. If she took time off, it'd set her back, and she's busted her hump long enough."

"Why not come up here by yourself? Get me out of this dump for a night and tie one on with your old man? Like we did back in—"

"Dad?"

"What?"

"Dad? Yeah. Can you hold on, just a sec? I got a call coming in that I need to take. Seriously. Stay with me OK? I promise...just a sec."

"All r—"

An abrupt click and the phone became a conch shell, whispering to me in the voice of my own blood.

I waited ten minutes, maybe a little less, certainly no more, before I hung up.

He didn't call back, and I knew better than to wait.

* * *

That Friday, our prison was invaded by a group of high school students, led by a petite raven-haired and bespectacled teacher who seemed convinced she could alter the world and, more specifically, the universes of her charges, with frantic gesticulation and a series of high-pitched yelps. They orbited around her like lazily drifting planets until she meted out their destinations and observed them as they spun off into the hall. While she directed the flow of angst-ridden traffic, we stared with the same kind of fascination a tired dog uses to watch birds eating the crumbs from his bowl.

"Joseph Henner," the teacher wailed. "I know that's not a lighter I just saw in your hand. Make your way to Mr. Ross's room. Number 18; end of the hall. Remember why we're here."

Why we're here. I was still waiting for someone to let *me* in on that little secret. I hurried back to my room.

Henner skulked in a few moments later. He was a scrawny acne-riddled teen dressed in a black trenchcoat, scuffed Doc Martens and a T-shirt that displayed a skull-headed man wielding a knife beneath the legend: *We All Gotta Go Sometime. Some of Us Sooner Than Others.*

True enough, I thought.

"What school do you go to?" I asked him, when it became painfully clear he wasn't going to initiate the conversation.

"Crosby High."

A quip about the absence of Stills and Nash from the name rose in my mind like an image in a photographer's developer tray, but I let it pass. Any hope was ludicrous that the sullen mass of baggy clothes and attitude before me would have even the slightest idea what I was referring to.

"I'm Joe," he said.

"Alfred Ross."

"Cool." He didn't look at me. "So, do you, like, stay here all the time?"

"Yes."

"That blows. Doesn't it get boring?"

"Absolutely."

"I'd go nuts."

"Some of us have."

"You got a TV?"

"Sure, in the lounge. And my friend and I play chess." I caught myself too late and felt my polite smile fade. "Used to play chess."

"He die?"

"Yes. Just last night as a matter of fact."

"How?"

Only then, only in that very instant, with the rest home filled with the alien sound of youthful laughter and this morose kid inspecting my room and talking about death like it was an old television show he only vaguely remembered, did I realize I didn't know how The Cowboy had died. *In his sleep*, Nurse Stanford had said, and it had been enough at the time. It wasn't enough now.

Cobwebs got his heart.

"Old age," I said, at last, and knew it wasn't a lie.

"Bummer."

"Yeah. It is. He was a good friend."

"So..." he began as he looked around my room, at the bare picture-less walls and the half-full glass of water sitting on my nightstand, "How long you been here?" It sounded like something he was reading from a cue card, and all the while he avoided looking at me. Maybe he was afraid he'd see a vision of himself in sixty years.

I could have assured him that I'm nobody's future.

"Coming up on six years."

"Long time."

"Feels longer," I said, and that was the God's honest truth. It felt like the tail end of a life sentence.

The kid sighed. His patience wasn't going to hold out much longer, and I couldn't really blame him. At his age humoring old folks would have been way down at the bottom of my priority list too.

At length his gaze settled on the only picture in my room, the grainy, washed-out photograph of Meredith on the windowsill.

"Your wife?"

"Ex."

"Still alive?"

"Yes, and cavorting with the pool boys in Florida, I imagine."

He asked an odd question then, one that, given his demeanor, I'd never have expected to hear from him: "You still love her?" It was also the only question he asked during our short time together that sounded as if the answer mattered to him.

Why, I'd never know.

"Yes. She's my biggest regret. Letting her go, that is."

"Then why did you?"

"I didn't have much of a say in the matter."

He nodded, ran a finger over the cheap faux-gold frame, and I knew I'd lost whatever spark of interest had flared in him. "You have any war stories?"

"No, I never fought in any wars. Do you?"

"Do I what?"

"Have any war stories."

He jammed his hands into his pockets. "Dude...I'm in high school."

"Isn't that a type of battlefield?"

Shrug. "Whatever."

Outcast, I thought. *Probably slouches in the corners at school trying to avoid trouble, rock music blasting in his ears, then goes home and does the same there, avoids life as much as possible. Hides in his shell.*

I felt sorry for him until I realized my life wasn't a whole lot different. Both of us were in cages of different design, but cages all the same.

"How come you've only got one picture?"

"I have more. I keep them under the bed. Would you like to see them?" Only after the words were out of my mouth did I realize how creepy they sounded. I might as well have propositioned the poor kid. *Hey boy, want some candy?* Inwardly, I groaned.

"Nah. Some other time."

"We don't have to talk, y'know," I told him. "You can just tell your teacher we did."

"Suits me," he said without hesitation, and produced from his trench coat pocket a pair of earphones so small I wondered if he'd ever had to reel them out of his inner ear. A small white rectangle with silver buttons followed and he jabbed at it with a nicotine-stained forefinger. The earphones began to hiss.

It felt wrong not to say something else, for the boy looked lost, crumpled up inside himself, desperate perhaps, the true emotion in his eyes obscured by the steam from the anger at the core of him. Maybe I should have been firm instead of grandfatherly. Maybe I should have told him to sit up straight and tell me what his problem was, to have some respect for his elders. Maybe that's what he was missing in his life, someone who looked like they gave enough of a damn to listen to what he had to say. But by the time enlightenment chased away the fog in my brain, Henner had already plugged his ears and thumbed up the volume on his odd-looking player.

"Later, man," he said as he stood up and headed for the door, the angry wasp sound of the music trailing behind him.

"What will happen then?" I murmured as he stepped out into the hall, into the river of students and moved upstream against the current.

I wondered how long it would take for him to erase me and my sad little room with its single picture from his mind.

* * *

198

There was a headcount in the hall sometime later, a chorus of bored responses, and then the roar of a bus engine signaled the departure of youthful laughter from Spring Grace. I trudged to the lounge, took my usual seat at the small Formica table The Cowboy and I always shared. The chess set was still there, but someone had prematurely ended our game and set up the pieces for a new one.

"Ron," I called to a tall thin man in a chenille robe, who was sitting in a worn armchair and grumbling at the television. "Ron!" His shock of white hair rose above the back of the armchair like stuffing.

He looked over his shoulder, his silver stubble scratching against the robe, and gaped fish-like at me through bifocal lenses. "*What* for God's sake?"

"You play chess?"

"What?"

I resisted the urge to scream at him. "Chess. Do you play it?"

"Like checkers, isn't it?"

"No. Not really."

"Then, no," he said, and turned back to his show. "I don't."

No one else present in the lounge did either, and by the time I'd put the question to them all, I didn't feel much like playing anymore. Besides, when The Cowboy and I had played, it hadn't really been about the game.

"He could never do clouds." Doris was sitting by the window, staring out, her eyes like pale gems in the deep pockets of a thief. "They were always dark and crooked, even when the sky was right. Liked to draw the spiders. Made them look like small men crouching in the corners."

"Sounds like a real talented boy," I told her, but knew I was talking to myself. Still, it made me curious, as it always did, to know who it was that had ownership of such a prized lot in her brain that not even her strokes could turn it fallow, or salt the earth of recollection. Whoever it was, whether real or fantasy, living or dead, they would not truly die until she did. And for that, I envied them.

* * *

Summer tired of its sun and dance routine, and moved on. The leaves died and the voice of the wind grew hollow, playing discordant music through the eaves of Spring Grace. The sense of isolation deepened. People stayed in their houses, and we in our rooms. A few more of my neighbors passed away. Some in their sleep; some screaming, while people whispered in the hall. Others were ferried away in the night in the quiet ambulances and never seen again. I told myself they'd escaped, been granted a stay of execution and were enjoying their freedom somewhere warm, but inside I knew better. Nobody ever leaves this place, though we talk about it all the time. *The door's right there*, we'd say, *and no one would even notice if we walked straight outta here*. And yet we never do. In times of excitement, that door looks like the door to Heaven. More often, it looks like the opposite.

We don't know what's out there anymore, you see. At some point none of us can remember, we stepped off the train and it carried on without us. Years have passed, been stolen while we've slept, and beyond our windows the world has changed. The light has changed.

It's safer here, even if it means we have to endure the ghosts of our pasts, the specters of regret, with nary a distraction to keep us sane. It's safer here because the future is guaranteed. There are no surprises left for us within these walls. You pass the time. You smile at kindred spirits in the hall. Maybe one weekend you luck out and end up getting your hands on the remote control before anyone else, maybe get to watch a Western or an old MGM musical. And at night, in bed, you say a small urgent prayer to a God you don't believe in that you'll wake in the morning still in possession of all those things that have made you what you are. That you won't find yourself dazed and drooling in a chair next to Doris Randle, with the needle in your mind stuck in a groove. But most of all, you pray that someone out there still remembers you, still thinks about you every now and then...still loves you, because there isn't a dark memory or shard of guilt inside that terrifies you as much as the idea of being forgotten. *Please*, you whisper, knowing tonight might be the night that quiet ambulance comes for you, its brakes squeaking softly as it pulls up to the curb. *Please...remember me.*

And as sleep comes, you remember *them*, and all the things you did wrong that led you to this place, this desert island forever threatened by the encroaching tide of time and regret. You weep, and in the morning the cobwebs on your face are larger, denser than before.

* * *

"We did clean your room, Mr. Ross. I sent one of the orderlies in there yesterday while you were having dinner."

"Then they did a sloppy job."

"Are you feeling all right? You look pale. Maybe I should—"

"I'm fine. I need to use the phone. Please have someone go over my room again."

"Of course."

* * *

He didn't mention the last call. I doubted he even remembered it.

"Dad? Great news. I sold a screenplay to Bob Garrison at New Line."

"New Line? What's that, like the fishing channel?"

A chuckle. "It's a Hollywood film company. We're talking *big* time here."

"I see, well congratulations then."

"You don't sound impressed."

My fingers tightened on the phone. I looked over my shoulder and saw Zach Greenburg scowling at me, oxygen mask gripped tightly in one liver-spotted hand. His rheumy eyes radiated impatience. He was no doubt anxious to call his daughter for her bi-weekly lecture. I turned back to the phone.

"It's not that, it's...why haven't you been in touch?"

"I tried a few times. No one answered."

It was a lie, a poor one, and it hollowed me out like a Jack o' Lantern. The phone doesn't ring enough in Spring Grace for it to ever go unanswered. But I accepted it because the alternatives were no better. What did I want to hear? *Dad, I forgot. Sorry.* No, I would take the lie. A starving man can't afford to be choosy about the quality of meat he's given. Unless it's Salisbury steak.

"Okay," I said. "Any plans to come see me?"

"Sure, we'll work something out."

"It's been forever."

"It has. Dad, I'll get up there, I promise. This new deal will mean I'll have to travel to New York now and then. I can stop in to see you on the way back."

"That would be nice. You should bring Kathy and Drew along too."

A sigh. "Maybe. We'll see."

"Is everything all right with you guys?"

"It's fine. You'll see us soon, I promise."

Behind me, Zach shuffled his feet.

"Listen Joey, I have to get going. There's a queue for the phone forming here."

"Okay Dad. Thanks for calling. It's always good to hear from you."

"You too. Stay in touch, will you? Call anytime. It's not like I'm busy around here."

"Will do."

"Give my love to my grandson."

"Bye Dad."

I hung up and as fast as his stiff joints would allow, Zach was in my face, his breath like sour milk, hooked nose inches from mine. "How do you do that?"

I raised my hands, not to placate him, but to remind him there was such a thing as personal space and that he was invading mine. "Do what?"

"Make calls without using money? There a trick to it?"

I looked over my shoulder at the phone, as if the answer to his odd question might be written somewhere there. It was a basic model payphone, silver, with square touchtone buttons. "Collect," I told him after a moment of thought. "Dial zero first, then the number."

He considered this, then nodded sharply. "Wish someone had told me that when I first got here. I've been stealin' nickels for six years." His laugh turned into a coughing fit, then a series of strangled gasps. I waited a moment to be sure he wasn't going to end up dropping dead right there, then left him, red-faced and wheezing, but well enough to complain about the c0ntaminants "those goddamned witches" were putting in his oxygen. After poking my head into my room to ensure the nurse had made good on her vow to have the cobwebs removed (she had), I stared down at my slippers as they traced the same old route back to the lounge.

There could be grass under there, I thought, with a faint smile, *gravel or macadam. I'm the only thing keeping me here. There are plenty of people out there who I can get to know. People who would think of me as a friend, maybe, or a kindly neighbor. People who'd remember me.* And as I passed the glass doors of the main entrance and ignored the pleasant inquiry from the pretty young nurse at the station, my smile grew.

Elm trees lined the long straight path from the door to the street, which in turn led into town. A couple of dozen steps and I could hitch a ride. A couple of steps; a short walk. That was all. Anyone could make it. *I* could make it. Abruptly I was assailed by memories from my youth: of walking barefoot through the grass with my best friend Rusty O' Connor, as oblivious to the mosquitoes as I was to the nurse who spoke to me as if I'd magically reverted to the age represented in the memory. Fishing poles held by our sides, the backs of our necks reddened by the glaring sun, laughing our fool heads off at silly things as we headed for Myers Pond and the promise of catfish we would never catch. The rumble and scrape of trains beyond the pond; the honk of jaybirds warning its brethren of our approach; the low buzz of dragonflies beating us to the shimmering water...

"Mr. Ross?"

A cloud darkened the sun of memory; the color faded, as did the smile it had brought to my face. Out there lay the road, but where did the road lead? To a new life or an overdue death? Rusty had followed a path in his dotage that had erased him from the earth, never to be seen again, nothing but a cryptic message left behind to let his wife know he wouldn't be coming back. Did he choose the wrong road? Did he stand on a similar threshold, lured by the promise of something better? Of a few more years of adventure?

"Mr. Ross? Is everything all right?"

Did he go somewhere he thought he'd be remembered?

"I'm fine," I said curtly, sensing the nurse moving around the desk toward me.

Outside, beyond the glass that might as well have been an iron gate, the elm trees nodded slightly in the breeze. They almost seemed to whisper, *Foolish old man. Remember your place.*

I moved on, watching my feet tread nothing but worn tile, just like yesterday, and a thousand days before it.

Do a trick for me, Joey, I thought, with tears in my throat. *Make me vanish. I'd rather be where you are.*

* * *

The man seated at the chess set looked out of place in the lounge. He was dressed like a salesman, from his paisley blazer and yellow shirt, right down to his white socks and worn leather loafers. Beneath a thick head of curly black hair, equally thick eyebrows were knitted in concentration over a pair of silver-rimmed spectacles. His long oddly delicate and perfectly manicured fingers floated above the head of the unsuspecting black queen.

I sat down with an audible sigh, glad to be relieved of my own weight for a while. "Doctor."

He looked up and beamed. "Mr. Ross. How are we this morning?"

"Tired."

As per usual, Ron had commandeered the television and seemed hypnotized by the gymnastic bounce of a female prizewinner's breasts on some game show. I couldn't blame him really. They were far from proportionate, given the woman's slight build.

"Are you still taking your medication?"

I nodded, turning my attention to Doris. She sat in her preferred spot by the window, head tilted as if asleep, but her eyes were still open. She looked more distant than ever. While Ron gaped at his buxom contestant, I found myself watching Doris's chest to be sure she was still breathing.

"She's okay," Doctor Rhodes said.

"Good." I turned to face the board. "Do you play?"

"Not since high school I'm afraid."

"Good enough. It'll still put you leagues above anyone else in here."

He looked at me over the rims of his spectacles. "Except you."

"Except me."

"Wonderful."

I studied the white ranks before me. "The AMA relaxing their dress code?" I nodded pointedly at his atrocious suit.

He smiled and folded his arms. "It's my day off."

"And you're spending it here?"

He shrugged and blew out a breath. "Well, I've been so busy with administrative work lately, I thought it the perfect opportunity to come in and see how people were doing."

I smirked at him and advanced a pawn. "That's very sad, Doc."

"Not at all," he protested. "When was the last chance you and I had a chance to shoot the breeze?"

He copied my move, but I didn't watch it. I was too busy watching him, trying to read his face, but his pleasant expression was an effective shield.

"I hate to disappoint you," I said, moving my bishop into the space the pawn had vacated. "But I very much doubt anything of any consequence has occurred since we last spoke."

Again he copied my move. "Is that so?" He was moving toward a point and his refusal to make it was starting to annoy me, but not nearly as much as the sensation that unseen hands were slowly painting a target on my head.

"I get the feeling you don't agree."

He smiled warmly and flapped a hand at me. "Ah, it's nothing."

"Then why are you here?"

"Well..." He looked around the room, his gaze lingering on Doris longer than it had on any of the other occupants, until finally his eyes met mine. "I can't let even the most innocuous of incidences go unquestioned around here, Alfred, you can understand that. The risk is too high to just pass it off as the vagaries of old age."

My fingers had settled on the bishop. Now they released it,

unmoved.

Rhodes seemed to be searching for the right words to say what he'd come to say, and I willed him to spit them out. At length, he did.

"Nurse Stanford mentioned some weeks ago that you were shaken up by what happened to Harold Wayne—The Cowboy—is that right?"

"I was." I frowned at him, saw uncertainty flicker across his face. My unease increased. "Why? Does that make me cause for concern? A special case? He was my friend. One of the few I have...I *had* in here. Naturally losing him would shake me up, just as it would anyone else." I became aware that my voice had risen above conversational level and I was being needlessly defensive. Ron's chair creaked as he finally looked away from the game show and peered at us. Some of the men at a card table in the corner paused to watch. I dismissed them all with a disgusted wave of my hand and glared at Rhodes. "Why? And why are you looking at me like that?"

He clasped his hands together over the chessboard. "I'm worried about you, and I don't think you're telling me the truth about you taking your pills."

"Of course I am. I said I was, didn't I? And what are you worried about me for anyway?"

"I'm worried, Alfred, because The Cowboy died over four years ago."

I stared at him. He stared back, the concern in his eyes maddening. Insulting.

"You *know* that," he said in a low voice as he reached across the table, his sleeve scattering the pieces as he tried to take my hand. I pulled away from him.

"Why would you say that?"

"Because it's the truth. A truth you know, and have known for years. He died in his sleep on Christmas Eve. You were the one who found him, remember? It was snowing like crazy outside. Worst snowstorm we'd had in decades."

Cold blue light, a voice tried to insist but I slammed the door shut on it, just as I intended to slam the door shut on Rhodes and his lies. "Why are you...?" I shook my head. "I won't tolerate this. Not from you, or anyone else. You have no right."

"Alfred, listen..."

"No." I rose and winced as a bolt of pain slammed into my right knee. I braced a hand on the chair to steady myself. "I don't know what it is you're trying to accomplish with this madness, but I won't sit here and listen to it. It's one of the few privileges I have left."

I began to hobble toward the door, heard the sound of chair legs scraping against the floor as Rhodes stood.

Go, Alfred, I told myself, my arms and legs trembling so bad I was afraid I wouldn't make it to the door, *Go before he tells you the rest. Go before he tells you what happened to—*

I froze.

The room itself seemed to send waves of cold air at me, chilling my back through my shirt while heat blossomed in my chest, stealing my breath. Tears welled in my eyes. Unseen fingers squeezed my throat.

I will not hear this. I will not.

The sound of rubber soles slapping against tile and all of a sudden Nurse Stanford was standing in the doorway, blocking my way.

Despite the pain that drilled through me from the top of my skull down into my chest, I almost laughed, though on some distant level I doubted I had the strength. *It's an intervention.*

"You've been using the phone," Rhodes said, and his voice was close, cautious. "Can I ask who you've been calling?"

"My..." My breath burned in my throat. "...Son."

"Alfred...the box beneath your bed..."

"Don't touch it."

"No one has."

"Then...how do you know?"

The cheers from the television were muted. The compassion on Nurse Stanford's face made me want to throttle her, but even if I had the guts to attempt such a thing, my arms refused to move. I felt a tear trickle down my cheek.

"How do I know *what*, Alfred?" He moved to stand in front of me, but his shadow was a second too slow in following.

The fluorescent lights covered my eyes with frost as I felt the strength drain from my limbs. *I'm going to fall and they won't catch me,* I thought, pure terror surging up through me from a bottomless pit in my stomach. *I'll hit my head and die right here in this awful room with all these people here staring at—*

My mind buzzed, chased away the pain, the thought, the awareness. I turned, intending to run, driven by one last automatic impulse to flee from these insane people—

—and fell forward, tried to think my arms into action, but they stayed by my sides. I toppled like the pawns beneath the Doctor's sleeve.

* * *

A heart attack, the man in the quiet ambulance told me. *But you'll be fine*, he said.

I know different.

I've lost them all. Their faces only exist now beneath my bed, in the box that has been substituting for memory. Black and white photographs, snapshots, obituaries, and letters from long-silenced voices I have been hearing on the phone.

Doctor Rhodes stopped by in the beginning, to check on me, but as time went by his commitment to the residents at Spring Grace caused his visits to become infrequent. I haven't seen him in almost a month. I have a new doctor now. New nurses, whose faces aren't so sharp or smiles as false. I have a new room.

It has no window.

This frightens me. Because there will come a night when the small men crouching in the corners come out, dancing like lunatics, and maybe one of those small men will be wearing white gloves, and his hands will cut the air above a red velvet tablecloth, and he'll do one last magic trick for me. He'll make endless veils of cobwebs fall from the ceiling and they'll land like muslin on my face. Over and over and over again until my breath stops coming and my heart stops beating. He'll hide me as I have hidden him for so long.

But not yet. I am not done yet.

Not tonight.

There is a sullen high school boy out there who still might remember. There is a sour old man with an oxygen mask back at Spring Grace, who is thankful he no longer has to wait in line. There is a drooling woman who speaks in riddles, who has a golden field in her mind where the people she has known still run.

Maybe I'm there.

Maybe she remembers.

Maybe.

SATURDAY NIGHT AT EDDIE'S
(Excerpt from *Currency of Souls*)

CHAPTER ONE

Eddie's Tavern.

This is where I come to try to forget my pain. There's so much of it here that isn't mine, it should make me feel better, but it doesn't.

And yet here I am, same as always. Saturday night at Eddie's.

There's no neon sign out front, nothing to advertise this as a place to come drown your sorrows, and that makes sense because sorrows aren't drowned here, not all the way, only pushed under and held for a while.

The moon is a nicotine-stained fingernail as I step out of my truck, ponder the feel of my gut straining against my belt, and ease the door shut behind me. I'm getting fat, and I suppose as they say, like death and taxes, I'm shit out of luck if I expect to be surprised by it. Man eats as much chili as I do without chasing it down with a few laps around the barn, well...weight doesn't evict itself.

I start on the path to the tavern door and see pale orbs behind the smoked glass turn in my direction. Nothing slips past these people, quiet or not. The door doesn't creak, though it's old enough to have earned that luxury. Instead it sighs. I sigh too, but I don't share the door's regret. For me, I'm just glad to be out of the cold and among friends, even if they mightn't look at me the same way. Even if, in the dark of night when sleep's a distant memory, I really don't think of them the same way either.

All the usual folks are here.

The pale willowy woman with the figure that could have been carved from soap, that's Gracie. She inherited this place from her Daddy, and considers it less a gift than another in a long line of curses from a man who dedicated his life to making hers a living hell. Leaving her the bar was his way of ensuring she'd stay right where he wanted her, in a rundown hole with no prospects and surrounded by friends not her own. Gracie has no love for anyone, least of all herself. She's still got her looks, though they fade a little every day, and she'd get out of this place in a second if she thought the city would take her. I'm sure it probably would. Take her, grind her up, and spit her out to die on some dogshit-encrusted sidewalk a thousand miles from home. Chances are a pretty girl like that with little world experience would end up missing, or turning tricks in the back office of some sleazy strip-joint to keep her in heroin. No, a girl like Gracie is better off right where she is, polishing glasses that stay so milky with grime you almost expect to see smoke drift out of them when she picks them up. She might be miserable, but I figure that's her own doing. Her overbearing father's influence is just an excuse. He's dead, after all, and buried out back. There's nothing to stop her selling this dive, except maybe a burning need to prove herself to his ghost.

At the bar sits a naked man. That's Cobb. Cobb says he's a nudist, and is waiting for the rest of the colony to come apologize for treating him so poorly. What they did to him is unclear, but he's been waiting almost three years now so most of us expect he's going to die disappointed. Cobb has big ears, a wide mouth and a line of coarse gray hair from the nape of his neck to the crack of his bony ass. He looks like a hungover werewolf caught in mid-transformation, and knows only four jokes. His enthusiasm doesn't diminish no matter how many times he tells them.

"Sheriff..." he says with a wide grin.

Here comes the first of them.

"A sailor and a penguin walk into a bar..."

"You'll have to take the back door," I respond, feeding him his own punch line.

"Shit...I told you that one?"

"Once or twice."

Two stools down, sits Wintry McCabe, a six foot six giant of a man who could probably blow the whole place clear into the next state if he sneezed. He's mute though, so you're shit out of luck if you're waiting for a warning. Gracie asked him once how he'd lost his voice and that's how we all found out that even if he could talk, chances are he wouldn't say very much. Near the top of the *Milestone Messenger* (our weekly rag), in the tight white space beneath the headline, he wrote, in blue ink and childish handwriting: WENT UP THE RIVER. COST ME MY WORDS. Then he smiled, finished his drink and left. After he'd gone, we speculated what the *Messenger's* new and intriguing sub-header might mean. Cobb reckons Wintry lost his tongue in a fishing or boating incident. Florence thinks he did something that affected him spiritually, something that forced him to take a vow of silence as repentance. Cadaver believes Wintry's done hard time, was "sent up the river" and someone in there relieved him of his tongue. I favor this theory. He looks like a man with secrets, none of them good. But Wintry has never volunteered any clarification on the subject; he hasn't written a message since, and he seldom opens his mouth long enough or wide enough for us to see if that tongue's still attached. If he can't communicate what he wants with gestures, he goes without. That's the kind of guy he is. But while it remains a mystery why he's mute, we at least know why he's called "Wintry". He got the name on account of how he lives in an old tarpaper shack on the peak of Grable Mountain, the only mountain within 100 miles that has snow on the top of it no matter what the season. As a result, even when there's suffocating heat down here in the valley, Wintry's always dressed in thick boots, gloves, and a fur-lined parka, out of which his large black hairless head pokes like a turtle testing the air. Tonight, he's testing a Scotch, neat. And while may not be able to talk, he sure likes to listen.

He's listening to Florence Bright now. She's sitting sideways on her stool, her pretty ankle-length dress covering up a pair of legs every guy in town dreams about. She's wearing a halter-top to match, the flimsy cotton material hiding another pair of attributes every guy in town dreams about. Flo is the prettiest gal I know. Reminds me a little of Veronica Lake in her heyday, right down to the wavy blonde hair and dark, perfectly plucked eyebrows. Florence has the dubious honor in this town of being both a woman in high demand, and a woman feared, but guys get drunk enough they forget they're afraid of her. Everyone thinks she murdered her husband, see, and while I don't know for sure whether she did or not, it's enough to keep me from sidling up to her in my sad little lovelorn boots. Wasn't much of a justice system here at the time, and I did what I could investigation-wise but wasn't a badge inside the city limits or out that could pin the blame on Flo. Nothing added up, and I have to wonder how many male—hell, maybe even *female*—cops were just fine with that. Wonder how many she sweet-talked into forgetting themselves. After all, we had a woman obviously abused by her husband, then said abuser turns up not only dead but so dead even the coroner coughed up the last bit of grub he'd poked into his mouth when he saw the body. Something wasn't right. That, or someone didn't do something they should've. More than once I've put myself under that particularly hot spotlight but quit before I get too close to things I'd rather not see.

So that's Flo, and looking at her there, the last thing you'd ever call her is a murderer. Of course that might just mean she's cold-hearted. But whether or not she knifed Henry Bright to death, doused his body in kerosene and lit the match, I have to admit I get a stab of envy every time she laughs and touches Wintry's elbow. Long time since I made a woman laugh. Long time since I did anything to a woman but make her weep.

I take a seat at one of three round tables spread out between the bar and the door. The abundance of space and lack of furniture make the place seem desolate and empty no matter how many customers it has, though the seven people here now, myself included, is about as busy as it gets. Except on Saturday nights, of course, when we expect one more. The poor lighting, courtesy of two plain bulbs hooded by cracked green shades, does nothing but spotlight dust and crowd everybody's table with shadows.

At the table across from me, a young man in a plaid shirt sits sweating and scowling at me through his dark hair. One hand holds his bottle of beer in a white-knuckle grip; the other is under the table. Probably on a gun. That's Kyle Turner, and he's wanted me dead since the night I murdered his parents. That was last summer. Every Saturday night since, the kid's been in here, trying to talk himself into using that Magnum .357 of his to ventilate my skull, but so far he hasn't been able to draw it out from under the table. So he just sits there glaring, and has Gracie drop the beer down to him at his table so he doesn't have to get up and reveal the piece he thinks I don't know about.

Someday he might get the guts to do it, and they'll probably kick him out of here, but only for disturbing the peace, not because he'll have disturbed my brain with a few warm rounds of the kind not meant to be served in bars. I admit I get a bit of a kick out of seeing him though, and if he weren't there I'd surely miss him. His hatred of me makes me feel a little like Wild Bill Hickock.

I know nodding a greeting at him will only aggravate him further, so instead I look the other way, away from the bar, back toward the door and the table shoved right up against the wall to the right of it. Cadaver is sitting there, lost in the shadows, though I smelled him as soon as I came in. I didn't offer him a greeting because you're not supposed to unless he offers you one first. It's a tradition that precedes my patronage here, so I honor it without knowing why.

"Evenin', Tom," he says, in that voice of his that sounds like someone dragging a guitar pick over a bass string. He's got a box where his larynx would be, which I guess is the cost of sixty years of smoking, and his face has sunken so deep you can almost see the contours of his chipped fillings beneath the skin. He's got a cataract in one eye, the lid is pulled halfway down over the other, and an impressively wide scar bisects his face from forehead to cleft of chin. He's a sight, and knows it, which is why he favors the dark, where he counts the pennies from his pocket and places them in rows, over and over and over again, until the sound of those coins meeting each other starts to feel like a measurement of time.

An ugly man, for sure, but damn he smells so good he makes me ashamed of my cheap cologne. Makes me wish I'd remembered to buy a nice bottle of Calvin Klein or some such fragrance. Something expensive. You can tell a lot by the way someone smells. Cadaver uses his to hide the smell of death.

"Evening," I tell him back, and feel more than see his twisted smile.

"Wonder who's drivin' tonight," he says, each word separated by a crackling swallow. It's wrong of me to say it, but I wish he wouldn't talk. Man without a human voice is better staying quiet, and I know that grinding electro-speak gives everyone else the creeps too.

"Wish I knew," I say, and turn to the bar. "Gracie?"

"Comin' up." She tosses on the bar the soiled rag she's been using to wipe the counter. "Hot or cold?" This is her way of asking if I want beer or whiskey. A strand of her auburn hair falls across her eyes as she waits for my reply, and she whips it back with such irritation, I'm suddenly glad she doesn't have a kid to use as a piñata for her misery.

"Both," I answer, because it's that kind of night.

As if I've asked her to wash my damn car, she sighs and sets about getting my drinks.

I drop my gaze to the mirror behind the bar and see Wintry raise a hand. His reflection waggles its fingers, keeps waggling them like a spider descending a strand of silk, until the hand is out of sight, then he nods twice and goes back to his drink.

"I heard," I say to his broad expanse of back. "We could do with it." I glance over at the kid, see his puzzled expression surface through the anger before he catches me looking and quickly goes back to scowling. His arm tenses, and I wonder briefly if I'm going to feel a bullet rip through my crotch, or my knee. The way that gun is angled makes me wish he'd just take the damn thing out and go for a headshot. But I guess he wants to make me suffer as much as possible.

"Wintry says rain's coming," I explain, careful to make it seem like a general announcement so the kid doesn't decide I'm trying to make a fool out of him by implying he didn't get it.

"Started already," Cadaver drones from the shadows.

"Weatherman says it's goin' to be a storm," Cobb intones, his buttocks wriggling as a shudder passes through him. "Hope I can bed down in here if it does." This last is directed at Gracie as she rounds the bar, a bottle of Bud in one hand, a bottle of whiskey in the other.

"This ain't a boardin' house, Cobb," she says over her shoulder, puffing air up to get the errant lock of hair out of her eyes. I'm struck by the sudden urge to brush it out of her face for her, but she'd likely jerk away and tell me to mind myself, and she'd be right of course. Long ago I learned that men and women's ideas of polite isn't always the same, and never will be as long as we guys feel compelled to consult our dicks every time a woman walks into the room. "But there are plenty of empty places on Winter Street. I'm sure Horace and Maggie'd show you someplace to lay your bones. Hell, if you dog Kirk Vess's heels, I bet he'll lead you to shelter."

Vess is our town lunatic, a card Gracie has played in the past just to get on Cobb's nerves.

"I'm sure." Cobb's repulsion at the idea is clear, but everyone here knows he's fighting a losing battle if he thinks he'll get Gracie to cave. "I can pay you though."

Gracie puts down my drinks, brushes dust off my table and looks into my eyes for the tiniest of seconds, enough to let me know that the superhuman precognitive sense unique to women has alerted her to what I'd just a moment ago been considering. And the message is: *Lucky you didn't.*

She heads back to the bar, a lithe woman dressed in drab clothes designed to make her look less attractive. I'll never understand that, but then again, the day men understand women is the day we may as well go sit on our plots and wait to be planted.

Or maybe I'm just not that bright at the back of it all.

"You can pay me by puttin' some clothes on," she tells Cobb. "Maybe if you were covered up, you wouldn't need to fret about the rain."

"I'll put you up," Cadaver offers in his robot voice, and Cobb turns slowly around, his bare ass making squeaking sounds against the top of the stool. I wonder how much Pine-Sol Gracie uses in any given month on that chair alone. It's the only one she allows him use. Just that chair, or his squeaky ass goes on the floor.

There's a look of consternation on Cobb's heavily bearded face when he turns fully around, his small blue eyes squinting into the shadows, as if seeing Cadaver will lessen his distaste at the idea of spending the night with the man. His chest is a mass of silvery curls, thickest along his sternum where it leads down over a swollen belly to a frenzied explosion of pubic hair, from which a small stubby penis pokes out. We've been seeing Cobb and his tackle for three years now. We should be used to it, and I guess for the most part we are, but every time his dick eyeballs me, I want to ask him if chestnut leaves are considered clothing by whatever governing body inflicted his nakedness on us in the first place. But I keep my mouth shut and avert my eyes, to the kid, who's doing a good job of looking like he may rupture something at any minute, and finally focus on my drink.

There's a thumbprint on the shot glass too large to be mine.

"That's mighty decent of you," Cobb says eventually.

"Don't mention it."

Over Cadaver's pennies, I can almost hear the hamster wheel spinning in the nudist's head. Then he says, "But you know what...? I'll just call my wife. She won't mind comin' to get me. Not at this hour. Not at night." He claps his hands as if he's just stumbled upon the cure for world hunger. "Hell, she'll have heard there's goin' to be a storm, so she'll have to come get me, right? No woman would make her man walk in this kinda weather." He's looking for support now, and not for the first time I envy Wintry's muteness, because everyone here knows that getting Mrs. Cobb to come get her husband isn't going to be as easy as he seems to think. The day he abandoned clothes was the last time anyone saw Eleanor Cobb in town. Naturally, we worried, but a few weeks after her husband's 'unveiling' I checked on her. She's fine, just laid up with a terminal case of mortification that I don't see ending until Cobb starts wearing shorts, or that chestnut leaf. Why she stays with him at all is another one of those mysteries.

"You could always start walkin' now before the worst of it hits," Flo chimes in. Her voice is husky, perfectly befitting a crime noir femme fatale. It makes my hair stand on end in a good way. "No one ever drowned in the rain."

Cobb ignores her. He's got a drink before him and intends to finish it. He squeaks back around to face the bar. "Can I use the phone?" he asks Gracie, and this at least she's willing to allow, even though it's a payphone and no one should need permission. But this is Gracie's place, and things run differently here. Stone-faced, she scoops one of the nudist's dollars off the bar, feeds it into the till, and drops four quarters into his outstretched palm. With a grin of gratitude, Cobb hops off his stool and heads out to the small hallway that leads to the payphone, and the restrooms beyond.

No one says anything.

There is silence except for the clink of Cadaver's pennies.

A few moments later, Cobb starts swearing into the phone.

No one is surprised.

I raise my glass with a muttered: "To Blue Moon," in honor of the man who can't be here, and take the first sip of whiskey. It cauterizes my throat. I hiss air through my teeth. Flo goes back to talking to Wintry, leans in a little closer, one leg crossed over the other, one shoe awful close to brushing against the big black man's ankle, and there's that envy again. But I remind myself that she's probably only cozying up to him because he's mute, and therefore unlikely to ever ask her about her past. For the second time in a handful of minutes, I'm covetous of Wintry's condition.

Cobb slams down the phone, curses and stalks back to the bar, his flaccid tool whacking against his thigh. I close my eyes, pray my gorge can handle another night of the old man's exhibitionism and concentrate on refilling my glass.

"She weren't there," he mutters before anyone has a chance to ask, and slaps a hand on the counter. "Fill me up, Gracie," he says. "And make it same as Tom's. It'll keep me warm on the walk home."

I almost expect Cadaver to remind Cobb of his offer, but Cadaver is ill, not dumb. He says nothing, just keeps on counting those pennies.

"You make it sound like you can just walk outta here as you please," Gracie says scornfully. "You take a blow to the head, or is all the drink just makin' you dumber?"

"He ain't the boss of me," Cobb says, scowling like a sulky teen. There's no passion in his voice, no truth to his words. Everyone here knows that, just like we know a little brave talk never hurts, as long as you only do it among friends.

"You reckon he'll show up tonight, Tom?" Flo asks, twirling a lock of her hair around a fingernail the color of blood.

"I reckon so."

She sighs, and turns her back on me. Flo wants hope, wants me to tell her that maybe tonight will be special, that maybe for the first Saturday night in years, Reverend Hill isn't going to come strolling in that door at eleven o' clock, but I can't. I realized a long time ago that I'm a poor liar, and despite the gold badge on my shirt, no one should look to me for hope, or anything else.

From the corner comes a sound like a dead branch snapping. It's Cadaver clucking his tongue. Seems a coin slipped off the top of one of his miniature copper towers.

Gracie goes back to pretending she's cleaning the bar.

Cobb grumbles over his beer.

Occasionally I catch Wintry looking at my reflection in the mirror. What I see in his dark eyes might be concern, even pity, but if I was him, I wouldn't be bothering with the mirror, or me, not when Flo's breathing in his ear. Besides, I'm not looking for sympathy, only solutions, and I don't reckon there's any to be had here tonight or any other.

The heat from the kid's glare is reliable as any fire on a winter's night.

These are my friends.

CHAPTER TWO

The clock draws out the seconds, the slow sweep of the narrow black minute hand unable to clear the face of a decade's worth of dust. When at last it reaches eleven, with no sign among us patrons that any time has passed at all, there comes the sound of shoes crunching gravel.

Everyone tries real hard not to watch the door, but there's tension in the air so tight you could hang your washing off it.

Reverend Hill enters, and with him comes the rain, and not the spatters Cadaver announced, but a full-on tacks-poured-on-a-metal-roof downpour. Bastard couldn't have timed it better, though if it inspires an impromptu sermon from him, he'll have trouble getting anyone to believe God is responsible, no more than we'd buy that the silvery threads of rain over his shoulder are strings leading to the hand of a divine puppeteer.

For him, the door groans as he shuts out the storm.

He doesn't pause to regard each of us in turn like any other man would, gauging the company he has to keep, or counting the sinners. Instead, that confident stride carries his lean black-clad self right on up to the bar, where Gracie's stopped cleaning and watches him much the same way the kid at the next table is watching me. Except, of course, Kyle's not looking at me right now. All eyes are on the holy man.

The town of Milestone has rotten luck, much like the people who call it home, though to be fair, over time we may have grown too fond of blaming the things we bring upon ourselves on chance, or fate. It's more likely that bad people, or folks with more to hide than their own towns can tolerate gravitate here, where no one asks questions and they carry their opinion of you in their eyes, never on their tongues.

When Reverend Hill came to town, filling a vacancy that had been there for three years, he brought with him the hope that spiritual guidance might chase away the dark clouds that have hung over the people of Milestone since Reverend Lewis used his belt, a rickety old chair, and a low beam in his bedroom to hasten his rendezvous with his maker.

But in keeping with the town's history of misfortune—or whatever you want to call it—what Hill brought to Milestone wasn't hope, but fear.

"Rum, child," he tells Gracie, and leans against the counter right next to Cobb. He makes no attempt to conceal his disgust for the naked man. Hill has beady eyes, too focused, self-righteous, and intense, to bother with color of any determinate hue. I'm convinced those eyes can see through walls, which may explain why no one in Milestone goes to confession anymore. He has eyebrows a woman would kill for, plucked and arched like chapel naves, a long thin nose that spreads out at the end to allow him the required amount of air with which to fuel his bluster, and a thin pale-lipped mouth that sits like a scar above a pointed chin. At a guess I'd say he's about sixty, but his age seems to change with his mood. The dim light shuns his greased back hair, which is artificially black. Everything about the guy is artificial, as we discovered not long after he came to town.

Some folks think he's the devil.

I don't, but I'm sure they've met.

"Evenin', Reverend," Cobb says, without looking at the man. Cobb's afraid of Hill. We all are, but the nudist's the only one who greets him.

"What do the young children of Milestone think when they see you walking the streets with your tool of sin flapping in front of their faces, Cobb?" the Reverend asks, louder than is necessary. "Immodesty is a flagstone on the path to Hell, or were you operating under the false assumption that nakedness is next to Godliness? Think your "gift" gives you the freedom to disregard common decency?"

Cobb turns pink all over, and doesn't reply.

The Reverend grins. His large piano key teeth gleam. Gracie sets his drink down in front of him. She doesn't wait for payment.

217

I'm alarmed to find myself choked up, gut jiggling, trying to contain a laugh. "Tool of sin" is bad, even for Hill. Sure, he makes my skin crawl every time I see him, but even though I know there's nothing funny about this situation, nothing funny about what goes down here in Milestone's only functioning bar at this same time every Saturday night. As it turns out, the humor must already have been on my face, because those coal-dark eyes of his move from Cobb's pink mass to me, and his grin drops as if someone smacked him across the face.

"Something funny, Tom?"

"Nope."

"Are you sure?"

"Yep."

"Your smile says different."

"Who can trust a smile these days, Reverend? I sure don't trust yours."

That's enough to give him his grin back. He scoops his rum off the counter and saunters over to my table with all the confidence of a man who enjoys his work, who's going to enjoy knocking the town sheriff down a few pegs. He drags back the empty chair opposite me, sits, and studies me for a second. I feel like carrion being appraised by a vulture.

His face is only a shade darker than the little rectangle of white at his collar.

"Tell me something, Tom."

"Shoot."

At this, Hill looks over his shoulder, to where the kid is still sweating, but I'm willing to bet that sweat's turned cold now. The Reverend turns back and winks. "Better not say that too loud. Someone might take you up on it."

"He's confused," I tell him, and take a sip of my whiskey. Beer's a pleasant drink, and requires patience; whiskey's a straight shot to the brain, and I need that now if I'm going to act tough in front of the only man in Milestone who scares me. "He should be gunning for *you*."

Thunder rattles the rafters; the smoked glass flickers with light, illuminating the rain pebbled across its surface.

"Maybe so," the Reverend says, "But he knows better than to shoot a man of the cloth. He's a God-fearing soul. He wants vengeance without damnation."

"Bit late for that isn't it?"

His lips crease in amusement. "I'm not sure I know what you mean."

I decide not to humor him. "Who is it tonight?"

Cadaver has stopped counting his pennies.

"Straight to it, eh? I like that."

"Cut the bullshit."

He clucks his tongue. "Profanity. The mark of an ignorant man."

I wish that were true. I'd love to be ignorant, sitting here with my drink, trading barbs with a priest who may or may not be the devil himself. At least then I wouldn't see what's coming.

"So who's driving?" I ask, and everyone but Wintry turns to look. He's watching the mirror.

The Reverend reaches into his pocket and tosses a pair of car keys on the table between us. "You are," he says, and every hard-earned ounce of my defiance is obliterated. He might as well have shoved a grenade down my throat and locked me in iron skin. I release a breath that shudders at the end. No one in the bar sighs their relief but I see shoulders relax, just a little, and hear the clink of Cadaver's pennies as he goes back to counting.

On the table, there's a ring of six keys. Three of them are for the prefabricated hut that passes as my office. Two are for the front and back doors of the prefabricated hut that passes as my house. The last one's for my truck, and the keys have fallen so that one is sticking straight up, toward the Reverend. It's not a coincidence.

"You know how it goes," he says, and sits back in his chair. "And if I were you, I wouldn't be all that surprised. You've dodged the bullet for quite a while, haven't you?"

His face swells with glee. I imagine if I punch him right now, which is exactly what every cell in my body is telling me to do, his head would pop like a balloon. But no matter how satisfying that might be it won't change the fact that tonight my number's come up. I get to drive. Hill, son of a bitch that he is, is still only a messenger, a courier boy. Putting a hurting on him wouldn't make a difference.

Cobb speaks up, "Hell, Tom, I'll drive for you. It'd keep me out of the rain. Besides, I told 'ol Blue Moon I'd take him up a bottle of somethin'. Kill two birds with one stone, right?" His nervous grin is flashed for everyone's approval, but he doesn't get it. No one even looks at him, except me, and though I don't say it, I'm grateful. I know Cobb walks around in the nip for one reason only—he wants to be noticed, remembered for something other than his gift, or maybe he does it to draw attention away from it. A *hey look everybody! Underneath my clothes I'm just the same as you!* kind of gesture. It doesn't work, and I guess, like the rest of us, he's tired of trying, tired of waiting here every Saturday night to find out if he's going to have to murder someone else. Considering what he can do, and what he's had to do in the past, it's got to be tougher on him than most of us. Like being God and the Devil's ping-pong ball. I also know, even if the Reverend allowed it, Cobb wouldn't follow the rules tonight. Chances are, he'd drive my battered old truck right off the Willow Creek Bridge, be smiling while he drowned and poor old Blue Moon Running Bear would have to go without his whiskey for a little while longer.

"Very noble of you," Hill says, sounding bored. "But this isn't a shift at the sawmill. There's no trading." He looks Cobb up and down. "But don't worry. You'll get your turn. You get that car yet?"

"Wife doesn't let me drive it. Not here. Not when I'll be drinkin'."

"Then either lie or quit drinking. But get it."

"All right."

Cobb offers me a sympathetic glance. I wave it away and look hard at the priest. "Who is it?"

From the breast pocket of his jacket, he produces a pack of Sonoma Lights. "Anyone got a light?"

When no one obliges, Gracie tosses him a box of matches, which he grabs from the air without looking—an impressive trick that leaves me wishing like hell he'd fumbled it. He lights his cigarette and squints at me through a plume of blue smoke. "You want the name?"

"No. I'd like to keep what little sleep I get at night. Unless you want to take that too."

"Oh now, would you listen to this? You make it sound as if you're the victim!" He barks a laugh and swivels in his chair to face the bar. "Is that what all of you think? That I'm the bad guy, come to destroy your lives?" He turns again, addressing Cadaver and the kid this time. "That you're all just innocents, forced to do the bidding of some wicked higher power?" He shakes his head in amazement. "Don't fool yourselves folks. Until I came along you were hanging in Purgatory, waiting for a decision to be made either way. You should be thanking me that you're not all roasting in the fires of Hell."

"So that's not what this is then?"

He leans close, eyes dark, twin threads of blue smoke trailing from his wide nostrils. "Not even close, Deputy Dawg."

We stare at each other over the table. I try to will the kid to take his shot. I don't even care who he hits. But the kid isn't moving, just watching, just like everyone else. The rain keeps raining and the thunder keeps thundering, but inside Eddie's there isn't a sound, until I speak.

"This will end, you know." It's a threat that has no weight behind it. I want this to be over; I want things to be the way they were before my wife died, before the kid got it into his head that my skull would look better spread across the wall; before we all ended up here as slaves to our sins, but it's too late. There's no turning back now. Things have gone too far. Hill knows this, knows surer than shit that all of us are going to be here next Saturday night and the Saturday night after that, and the one after that until we've paid off whatever debt it is he's decided—or more accurately, whoever *controls* him has decided—we owe.

But tonight isn't going to be that night, and as blue light fills the cracks in the rundown bar, I reach across and slide the keys toward me.

"I know it will end," the Reverend answers, and pauses to take a deep drag on his cigarette. "Tonight it ends for you."

I close my fist around the keys and let them bite into my palm.

"You get a thief and his girlfriend," he continues. "The guy shot a pump jockey in the face, killed a woman and injured a little kid. The girlfriend's an addict and a whore. No one will miss them."

"Someone will. Someone always does."

The priest sits back again and smiles. "That's not for us to worry about."

"Not for you maybe."

"These missives from your goody-goody conscience are getting to be a real bore, Tom."

"This, from a priest."

His smile fades. "You'd best get moving, Sheriff. Your people need you."

I throw back what's left of the whiskey, then grab the bottle to keep me company. Hill won't object—he likes us good and drunk—and though Gracie might be pissed that she's out a few dollars, she won't say anything either. She understands the nature of dirty work.

I stand and jingle the keys in my palm. "When this is over," I tell him. "You're the only one going to Hell."

He doesn't answer. Instead he slides my glass in front of him and puts his own thumb over the print. It fits perfectly. He chuckles and turns his chair around so he's facing the bar. Flo avoids his gaze and slips her hand over Wintry's. Everyone goes back to doing a real bad job of pretending nothing's amiss.

At my back, Cobb grumbles on.

The few steps to the front door feel like a condemned man's walk to the electric chair, the lightning through the windows only adding to the effect.

As I reach the door and grab the brass handle, the lightning reveals the skeletal profile hunkered nearby, the shadows of the coin towers like knives jabbing at his chest. He's looking out the window, darkness pooling in the hollows of his eyes as, in what passes for a whisper, he says, "Someone's comin'." Then I hear it. Hurried footsteps, confused shuffling, and I move back just in time to avoid getting my face mashed in by a hunk of weathered oak as the door bursts open almost hard enough to knock it off its hinges. Rain, wind and shadows fill the doorway. Without knowing, or caring who it is that's standing on the threshold, I lunge forward, plant my hand in the middle of the figure's chest and shove them back out into the storm. "Get the hell out of here," I tell them, in as hard a voice as I can muster under the circumstances. Hill would love this, more recruits for his twisted game. But whoever it is I've just tried to dissuade, grunts, pivots on a heel, slams back against the door for balance and reaches out an arm toward where I'm standing, ready for anything.

Anything but the gun that's suddenly thrust in my face, the steel barrel dripping rainwater. "Get the fuck back inside," a man's voice says, and then a woman stumbles forth from the darkness and collapses on the floor. The rain that drips from her sodden form is pink. She's bleeding somewhere but right now all my attention is focused on the black eye of the gun that's three inches from my nose.

"Flo, Gracie…someone help the lady," I call out.

"Don't you touch her," the man says. I wish I could see his face, but so far he's only a voice and a pale sleeve with a Colt .45 at the end of it.

I'm getting real tired of having guns pointed at me.

CHAPTER THREE

"Move back," the gunman says. "Now, or I redecorate this shithole with your brains."

"God knows that would be an improvement," the Reverend chimes in, sounding not-at-all annoyed by this intrusion.

The woman is shuddering, and there's that goddamn instinctual need to help, to touch her, make sure she's okay, but that bullet blower keeps me in place.

"How come you don't have a piece?" says the man.

"I do, just not on me."

"Anyone else in there likely to act the hero?"

I consider Kyle. He's got a gun, and the guy's probably going to find that out sooner or later. But "No," I tell him, because later's better.

"You better not be lying to me."

"I'm not."

"Carla, you alive?"

On the floor, head bowed, dark wet hair almost touching the boards, the girl slowly shakes her head. She's bleeding something fierce.

"She needs help." It's an obvious statement, but considering the guy is still standing in the doorway pointing a gun at me, I figure he could use the reminder.

"Yeah, no shit. Don't suppose there's a doctor in there?"

"No, but we can at least patch her up, stop the bleeding. Give her something for the pain. You're not doing her any favors leaving her on the floor."

It doesn't take him long to realize I'm right. He waggles the gun in my face. "Back up. All the way to the bar, and keep your hands where I can see them."

I set the whiskey bottle down on the floor and do as I'm told, walking backwards, hands in the air, until I'm just about level with the Reverend's table. "You plan this?" I ask him, though somehow I know he didn't, not unless he was suddenly stricken with guilt and decided to save me gas money.

"It would seem," he replies, "that we'll have to suffer an unscheduled interlude."

"I find it hard to believe you don't make allowances for this kind of thing."

"Oh, but I do. Before this night is through, that man and his little trollop will be still be so many pounds of mashed up meat branded by the tires of your truck, Tom. Doesn't matter what they do to piss away the meantime."

"Shut your mouths," the man with the gun says. He steps into the light and at last I'm able to see the face of my intended victim. He's little more than a kid, it seems, not much older than Kyle, wearing a cream colored suit that was probably nice before the blood spoiled it, with a white shirt open at the collar. Shoulder-length blonde hair frames a face hardened by the many pit stops on the road to a Hell of his own design. He slams the door shut behind him and stands there, gun trained on me, then at everyone else in the room, before coming round to me again.

"This isn't the way to do it, son," Cadaver says, and the thief almost jumps out of his suit and the skin beneath. I wince, waiting for him to pump a few rounds into the shadow in the corner, but he manages to restrain himself. "Who the fuck is *that*?"

"Cadaver," I tell him. "He's just an old man. Leave him alone."

"The fuck's he doing hiding?"

"He's not. That's his table. Light just isn't so good. It's how he likes it."

"Yeah?" The kid doesn't sound convinced, and his fingers dance on the butt of the gun like he's deciding whether or not to illuminate Cadaver's corner with some muzzle flash. "Move out here with the others."

Cadaver doesn't make a sound, nor does he make a move.

The kid clicks back the hammer. It makes the same sound Cadaver does when he swallows.

"Look kid..." I take a step forward, and realize a split second after I've done it that it's a mistake. The gun finds me again. Now I have two of them pointed at me. If Kyle and this guy fire at the same time, I may very well hit the ground with two shadows. I raise my hands palm out. "Just hang on a second, will ya? No one needs to get hurt here." Which is a damned lie. Sooner or later, someone's going to get hurt, and satin-pillow-in-a-pine-box kind of hurt. Right now though, the question is not who, but how many, and that's not good enough.

The kid catches sight of Cobb. Frowns. "Why's he naked?"

"Because I choose to be," Cobb states boldly. "Ain't got no use for clothes."

The kid smiles, and for a moment I see the *real* kid, the one hiding deep down inside that suit, the kid who watched his manners when his aunt came to visit, said grace before meals, and shook in his shoes when he showed up at the door for his first date. An All-American kid run over on the road of life, relieved of his dreams, then fixed right up with some choice drugs, a gun and a whore and sent on his way. Only to end up here, with his would-be executioner trying to talk some sense into him.

"Some bunch of fuckin' loons we got us here, Carla."

The woman on the floor doesn't respond, but I almost don't notice because now I know her name, and it dances before my eyes in lurid neon, mocking me. I wasn't supposed to know. I don't want to know, but now that I do, their ghosts will have names too.

Wintry turns around in his seat, his huge head sheened with perspiration, and stands. The expression on his face is unreadable, but that big nose of his is flaring at the ends like a bull about to charge.

"Hey now." The kid is visibly intimidated. "Sit right back down big man, or I'm going to have to cut you down."

Wintry doesn't move, but his eyes move to the fallen girl.

"What are you doin'?" Flo asks, and grabs his sleeve. "Sit *down*."

But Wintry doesn't. He glances at me and nods one time, as if it's the cue to do something, as if he figures I'm clever enough to read those large brown eyes of his, or maybe he thinks he's already shared his strategy via some telepathic link. Whatever it is, I don't have time to figure it out because Wintry's already moving, brushing past me, his jacket making a zipping sound as it grazes my outstretched fingers. It smells of pinesap and smoke.

"Wait..."

My objection is overruled by Flo's panicked cry. "Wintry, don't!"

Wintry keeps walking.

The kid stiffens. "Hey, I said sit *down* man."

"Goddamn it," Gracie pipes up. "Do as he says."

The kid aims the gun at the big man's chest, licks his lips.

Wintry keeps walking, but he's not heading for the kid. He's headed for the girl, and surely the kid sees this. Surely he'll read the big black man's intentions, understand what I didn't, and—

There's a bang as if thunder has slipped under the door, a burst of light, and Wintry finally stops walking.

Flo screams, her hands flying to her face like a mask made of fingers.

The girl on the floor whimpers and looks up. Her face is a mass of ragged bloody scratches. The rain has smudged her mascara into raccoon-like circles around her glassy eyes. Her lipstick runs clear across her cheek. She looks at us all in turn as if she's just realized we're here.

My ears are ringing.

I wait for Wintry to look down, to assess the damage like folks do in the movies before they finally acknowledge a mortal wound and drop to the floor. Wintry'll make a hell of a thud when he falls. My mind races, trying to think of something to do or say, but that shot might as well have passed through my brain.

"Wintry..." Flo sobs.

But when the smoke that coils like low fog between the big black man in the parka and the couple by the door finally dissipates, it's the kid who staggers back and drops to a sitting position, his back against the door. On his face is shock, and confusion; on his shirt is a blossoming crimson flower.

"My, my," says the Reverend.

I hear Flo's breath catch in her throat.

Smoke continues to drift out from beneath Kyle's table. The kid came here tonight to shoot someone, but the bullet that has my name in it now sits lodged in the belly of the man I was supposed to kill. I'll wait to ponder the irony of that. There's no time now.

Silence weighs heavy in the room. At last I find my tongue. "Wintry, go on." He does, stopping by the girl, though his eyes are on the wounded kid, and the gun that's still in his hand.

Cadaver, in an uncharacteristically animated move, emerges from the shadows looking grim, his black plastic raincoat swirling around him. His hip jars the table; another coin drops from its tower. Aside from Wintry and the girl, he's nearest the kid, and knows it, and so hurries to his side, hunkers down and gives the kid a sympathetic glance before relieving him of his weapon. The kid doesn't resist. Because the little microphone that Cadaver needs to press against the metal box in his throat to enable him to be heard is back on his table, he wheezes his words, and no one but him and the kid hear them. The kid stares at the old man as if he believes Death himself has come for him and replies, "Brody. James Brody."

And just like that, my nightmare is complete.

"Fuck," I mutter and squeeze my eyes with a thumb and forefinger.

There comes a crashing sound and everyone jumps, startled, no doubt wondering what calamity has befallen us now, maybe the storm, God's Hand, has come to smite us all one by one, like we damn well deserve. But it isn't anything so dramatic. It's Flo, who has swept her arm across the bar, sending a bunch of glasses and bottles crashing to the floor.

"What the hell?" Cobb stands up, looking down at himself and the shattered remains of his Bud, but I know what she's doing and silently commend her for it.

"Bring her here," she calls to Wintry, and he lifts the girl as if she weighs no more than an empty sack.

Kyle's still watching Brody, who's gasping in the corner like he's taken a slug in the lung. If he had, I figure he'd already be dead, but it's hard to predict any man's reaction to having his body insulted by a bullet.

Cadaver, still with Brody, looks over his shoulder at me and mouths the words, "Needs fixin'."

I know he does, but the Reverend's presence is like an extra shadow at my side, reminding me of the futility of our actions. Whether we patch those two unlucky kids up or not, they're still going to die before the night ends. But Cobb is with Flo now, looking like the world's unlikeliest orderly as they lay frayed towels out across the bar. Gracie is talking in soothing tones to the girl, who I can see now has a wide gash across her chest, another somewhere in the tangle of her hair that's sending rivulets of blood down the back of her neck. Flo takes her hand as Wintry lays the girl down on the bar and heads back for her boyfriend. With the exception of Kyle, who I guess is in shock himself, the Reverend, and me, everyone is helping, even though we're all privy to the same awful truth, truth we have no business knowing.

Those kids are doomed.

But right now, that doesn't seem important. After all, they're here when they shouldn't be, and the keys to my truck, the keys to their fate, are still in my pocket.

So I do the only thing left to do. I go to Kyle.

I stop a few feet from his table, blocking his view of the wounded kid by the door. "You all right?" Another dumb question, but the only one I've got.

"What do you care?"

"You did the right thing, you know. If you hadn't, it'd be Wintry bleeding to death on the floor. Any one of us might have done the same thing."

"But you didn't."

"We would have if we'd had the opportunity."

He looks up at me slowly and blinks, all of the hostility gone from his face, along with the color. "Is he dead?"

"No, but he's hurt bad."

"He going to die?"

I consider my answer, then decide on the truth. "Hell, everybody does, but maybe not tonight."

"I'm going to Hell."

"Why do you say that?"

"Because I murdered him."

"Not yet you didn't. And even if it's too late and he expires on account of that bullet in his belly, all you did was hasten what was coming his way tonight anyway."

"We're all going to Hell."

"Probably. Doesn't mean we have to be in any hurry though."

"That bullet wasn't meant for him."

"I know, but we can either stand here debating who should be dead and who shouldn't, or we can help these kids out."

"Why?" He frowns and the sweat pools in the creases. I'm overcome with a sudden and alarming urge to hug the boy, just crush the fear out of him. But to do that I'd have to be calm myself, and I'm a long way from that right now. Besides, while I suspect he's shot the last man he's ever going to, I've been surprised before, and I'm in no rush to test the theory. Not yet, anyway.

"Because they need it."

He laughs soundlessly, a wheeze that could have come from Cadaver's mouth. "I could put this gun in my mouth right now."

"Sure you could."

"Would you stop me?"

"I reckon I'd try."

"Why?" When he looks up at me, the emotion in his eyes is more powerful than any bullet, powerful enough to make me drop my gaze and immediately feel ashamed of it.

I clear my throat, the words like glass tearing their way up my throat, slicing open my tongue. "Because no matter what you think of me, you're still my son."

He scoffs. "My father's dead."

"No I'm not, I'm standing right here. You're looking at me, just as you've been looking at me every night since your mother died."

"Since you killed her."

"I didn't kill her."

"Yes you did. You killed both of you."

"If that's true then why do you come in here every Saturday night with a gun pointed at me? Can't kill a dead man, y'know."

I'm fighting a losing battle to keep my composure. I want to hug the little son of a bitch, squeeze the hate out of him, reclaim him while I still have the chance, force him to understand.

But I don't understand it myself.

"The bullet wasn't meant for you either," he tells me and finally brings the gun out from beneath the table. I recognize it of course, seeing as how it used to have a home in my holster. No police issue weaponry in Milestone, no sir. You just take whatever you think you'll need to get the job done. Back when there was a job to do, that is.

"It was for me," he says, and I feel my heart shatter into a thousand pieces.

Whatever I might have said, whatever magic words I might have summoned from the ether are blown away by the woman's scream. Both of us turn toward the bar, and see Carla convulsing, chopping that scream into stuttered wails as Flo, wincing, presses a damp cloth to the girl's chest.

"Jesus." I give the kid one final glance, hoping he sees the plea for another chance to talk this over, then I'm gone, storming across to the girl, my heart and soul in ruins as surely as if I was the one stretched out on the bar.

I haven't gotten far, when Brody, slung over Wintry's shoulder, calls out, "Go easy on her. She's pregnant."

And that takes what little wind is left in my sails right the fuck out of them.

I turn on my heel and Reverend Hill slams his glass down on the table and stands. "Enough."

I want to kill him. Rage boils within me, fueled further by regret over Kyle and his intentions, rage at my blindness, at my cowardice, for never questioning the speed with which my world grew dark, or the pain I dealt the people fumbling around within it. "You son of a bitch. You never mentioned a child."

"What difference does it make? People who cause fatal accidents very rarely get the luxury of counting their victims beforehand. Had everything proceeded here as it was damn well supposed to, you'd never have known any different, and that murderer's conscience of yours would have been spared an extra little slice of reality." He steps close, until our noses are almost touching. "Never forget, Sheriff, that I am the only thing standing between you and eternal damnation. *I'm* the closest thing you have to God, and as such I own you, so it would behoove you to stop questioning it and accept it as truth."

"This *is* eternal damnation," I counter, "And it seems to me that God would know what the fuck was going on, which you clearly don't."

Brody moans with pain as Wintry sets him down in his own chair next to Flo. Even in times of stress he knows better than to seat anyone in Cobb's place.

The Reverend looks over my shoulder at the kid, then smiles. "Then let's find out why things *haven't* gone according to plan, shall we?"

Cadaver regains his seat amid the shadows.

Gracie spills bourbon over the girl's exposed chest—the wound is deep—eliciting another agonized shriek from her, and I know I'm right. This is eternal damnation, or at the very least, some kind of waiting room where all we get to do is sit and stew and wait for our number to be called. I decide in that moment, without even the faintest idea how it's going to go down, that more than these kid's numbers are going to be called tonight.

The Reverend stands before the kid, who has a blood-soaked hand clamped over his belly. "Well now," he says, "Looks like you're in a bit of a pickle here."

"We need a doctor," Brody says, his pallid face slick with sweat. "Please."

The Reverend cocks his head. "And why should we do something like that for a man who introduced himself by shoving a gun in a lawman's face, then threatened to shoot the only fella in here who seemed inclined to help him?"

"Gracie, call Doctor Hendricks," I tell her, but the Reverend raises a hand he'd like you to believe was made to heal sinners.

"Do no such thing."

"Reverend," Cobb says. "This ain't how he's supposed to go anyhow, so what harm is there in fixin' him up?"

I look squarely at Cobb. "Can you help them?"

He nods frantically.

"Will you?"

Everybody present knows what it will cost Cobb if he does, but damned if he doesn't go on nodding that big old shaggy head of his. For a brief moment my envy extends from Wintry to this sad old man with his sagging body, who, if nothing else, has the kind of heart most of us would, and have, killed for.

But then the Reverend glances up at him and scowls. "You stay out of this, Cobb. When we need the black magic of heathens, you'll be the first to know. "

The dying kid fixes the nudist with an odd look. "Your name's Cobb?"

Cobb, equally perplexed, nods. "Yeah. Why?"

The Reverend sighs. "Shut your goddamn mouth. Now listen here, kid. All I want from you is a simple answer. This town's reserved for the dreamless, the lost and the hopeless. You may be a no-good piece of shit, but I bet you've got ambitions, right?"

"Sure. Seeing another sunrise was one of them."

"From somewhere other than Milestone."

"Yeah."

"Why is it, then, that instead of being in the driver seat of your nice new—*stolen*—midnight blue Corvette heading North, right the hell out of this burg, maybe with that filthy whore of yours giving you a blowjob while you listen to some of the devil's music on the stereo...why is it that you're sitting here dying?"

Brody's eyes widen until they seem to fill his face. "Shit, I'm dying?" He starts to chuckle. "Fuck me, Dean. Looks like we get to do that duet after all."

The Reverend slaps him, a quick dry open-handed slap that knocks the mirth right off the kid's face. He looks stunned, his breath coming in short hard rasps, then angry. "Preacher," he says, mustering as much iron into his words as he can. "You're lucky I'm down or I'd have to beg my Momma for forgiveness for busting your nose."

And on hearing that, God forgive me, I find myself warming to the bastard.

"Answer the question, sonny," Reverend Hill tells him. "Now, or I guarantee that shot to the gut will seem like a bee sting by the time I'm done with you. You see, here we follow a strict set of guidelines. Sinners atone for their sins by ridding the world of filth, just like them. There are outposts like this everywhere. Each one has its own methods too. Here at Eddie's, you get to drive. But seeing as how you're past doing anything of the kind, and therefore, all but useless to me, you'd better start answering my questions. So, for the last time, *why* are you here?"

Brody ignores the priest and glances at Cobb again. "She had the same name as you."

Cobb blanches. "Who did?"

Brody starts shaking, worse than before, and suddenly his eyes are on me with such intensity, even Hill looks over his shoulder. "Sheriff," the kid says. "Mind if I give you something?"

"Go right ahead, as long as it isn't a bullet."

"In my pocket...two twenty dollar bills and a five."

"Okay."

"Can you give them to that man there?"

"Cobb?"

"Yes."

I resist the urge to ask him why he didn't just get Cobb to take it himself.

"Not much life in you," Hill says, dropping to his haunches. "Better start talking. Just because you die doesn't mean I can't reach you."

Brody swallows, looks at Cobb, then away. "She came out of nowhere."

Cobb takes a step forward, but is stopped by the Reverend's glare and Wintry's hand on his shoulder. "What's he talkin' about?"

"Your wife, I expect," Hill says, with no emotion at all, then reaches forward and tilts the kid's head up until their eyes meet. "Am I right?"

"We didn't see her. She must have had her lights off. And if you don't get your fucking hand off me, Preacher, I swear I'll use every last ounce of my strength...to put you through the wall."

As I'm listening, I picture Eleanor Cobb, hunched over her steering wheel, trying to look as small and inconspicuous as possible, afraid of being seen by anyone, even in the storm, lights turned off on a quiet road because she doesn't imagine she'll encounter another car, and doesn't want to draw attention to herself if she does. But she hasn't counted on a thief and his woman traveling on that same quiet road, pedal to the metal, eager to be clear of a town that reeks of death.

I lower my head. "Jesus."

"Hang on, kid," Cobb says, and his tone is both desperate and disbelieving. "You must be mistaken. She doesn't come to get me. She never does."

"She did tonight," Hill says.

"No."

"I took her wallet. Figured...with the state she was in...she wouldn't need it. Saw her name...I'm sorry...you can have the money...I'm—"

I look up in time to see Cobb lunging for the kid, but Wintry's got him in a firm hold, and all Cobb can do is struggle until the strength leaves him and he turns, embraces the big black man and weeps uncontrollably.

"Get him a drink and sit him down," I tell Wintry, and he does. I'm surprised anyone is listening to me. Nights as wild as these badges count for nothing.

All the fight has left Cobb.

Reverend Hill stands up and scratches his chin. He sighs heavily. "Sheriff," he says. "Looks like you and I have a bit of a problem."

CHAPTER FOUR

Considering the amount of blood on the chair and the floor beneath him, I don't reckon the kid has much time left. His face is the color of fresh snow and he's propped up against the bar like a guy who's had too much to drink and is trying to remember where the hell he's found himself. And, aside from the drink part, maybe that's exactly what he's doing.

The girl on the bar turns her head. Her tears are silent. Seems all the fight has left her too. She closes her eyes, jerking occasionally and gasping as Flo and Gracie tend to her. "She's goin' to die if we don't do somethin'," Flo informs me, and it's hardly a revelation, but the one man willing to do something is way past doing it now. It's not like I can waltz up to Cobb and ask him to mend the people who killed his wife. That's the saddest part of all. I doubt he'd have been all that worried if his gift allowed him to raise the dead. But it doesn't. He can heal, that's it, and only wounds, not diseases. And right now, I'm willing to bet Cobb's second-guessing the limits of his power, wondering if it might work on his wife.

The priest turns to look at me. "You've got a job to do, Sheriff. Lucky for you, there'll soon be one less victim to worry about. Your boy gets that one. It's almost poetic, isn't it?"

"What is it you want me to do, exactly?"

"You gonna just let me die?" Brody croaks. "I knew there was a reason this town stank."

The Reverend shrugs. "No more than you were planning on doing all along. I want you to get in your truck and drive through town, fast as that piece of shit can carry you."

"Might want to watch the profanity there, Reverend. It being the mark of an ignorant man an all."

"Just do your job."

"For what? The kid's dying and—"

"Quit saying that, wouldya?" Brody interrupts.

"—his girl's bleeding out on the bar."

"True..." Hill shows his teeth. "But dying means they aren't dead *yet*. I reckon if you work fast and get them in your truck, you can still take care of business. Hell, I'll give you a break and just get you to take care of the girl."

"Can't you just let this one be?" Flo asks. "She's with child, for God's sake."

Without glancing her way, Hill says, "As are you, but you wouldn't expect anyone to forgive you *your* transgressions just because you spread your legs for a man."

Flo doesn't look shocked or stunned. She looks angry, and when she looks at Wintry, who is kneeling next to Cobb at the table where I first sat down, that anger turns to shame. Wintry, however, doesn't look quite so impassive anymore. Sins, the threat of Hell, death and murder don't make him blink, but finding out he's a Daddy sure does. His mouth is open, just a little, and I reckon even though he can't talk, he's saying something.

Thunder rolls like boulders across the roof.

Lightning shows me Cadaver in the corner, counting.

Me, I feel no more envy. Instead, I feel bolstered a little, aware that all those long-winded old passages you find in the bible about life and death and retribution may mean something after all. All we know, all we have known for as long as I can recall, is death. Now there's life. Even if we can't help poor Brody and Carla, even if we can't save her baby, Flo is pregnant, and the significance of that single fact is so great it makes my head hurt and my heart beat a little faster. Flo, a creature of death, is carrying life. Untainted life. Life Reverend Hill, for all his threats and blustering, cannot reach. Yet.

Flo is pregnant.

And whether or not she ends up filling that empty vessel with hate, or sadness, or sin, right now, for me, it represents just the tiniest bit of hope.

It's enough.

And it would seem I'm not alone in feeling that.

Without any of us, even the supposedly all-knowing Reverend, hearing his approach, Kyle is standing next to the priest, and the gun that has held so much meaning tonight, is gripped firmly in his hand again, the determination I've watched for three years back on his face, the muzzle nestled firmly against Hill's temple.

"I'm not driving tonight," I tell the priest, but Kyle has other ideas.

"Yes you are."

I look at him, wondering if this is how he finally intends to rid himself of his long-dead father. A man, who, despite all the nightmares and all the people he's killed on someone else's behalf, only ever felt guilty for the death he didn't cause. Cold as that sounds, I reckon there's a lot of truth to it.

"Me and you and the Reverend are going to take a ride tonight," Kyle says. "We're going to take that girl with us, and we're going to get her to Doctor Hendricks."

The priest chuckles. "Is that so?"

"Shit," Brody intones, struggling to sit up straighter. "What about me?"

He is ignored. We're not going to abandon him. That much I know. Not if there's a chance to save him. But Kyle's calling the shots now, so we're going to play it his way for the time being. The girl looks a lot worse off, so she goes first, is what I'm guessing is Kyle's reasoning here, though it would be just as easy to take them both. Maybe I'll suggest that once the gun's been lowered.

"Yeah, that is so," he says in response to Hill. The gun trembles in his grasp. I'm not yet at the point where I'm doubting my earlier opinion on whether my son will ever shoot a man again, but I'm not confident. What I am, however, is damn proud.

"Let me ask you something, Kyle. What exactly do you think shooting me will accomplish? Do you think I'll just drop like a rock? Like all these other weaklings? In case you haven't noticed, I'm the landlord here. Everyone answers to me, just as there are higher forces I answer to when the work has been done. When their *penance* has been done. And you, boy, have a lot of making up to do."

"And when is the penance done, huh? How many corpses amount to penance in your eyes? Ten, twenty, a hundred?"

"You'll know when it's done."

"Right," Kyle tells him. "When you've had your fill, maybe, you sick fuck."

The Reverend sighs. "Is it your intention to see how much suffering you can bring upon yourself? Pull that trigger then and we'll all see just how—"

Without warning, Kyle does as he is asked. The Reverend stands where he is for a moment, then topples. The echo of the gunshot rivals the rage of the storm and the sound of blood dripping could be the rain tapping on the window. What used to be Reverend Hill's head is now spread across the wall next to where Flo is standing, spattered in his blood. She doesn't seem at all put out, merely inconvenienced. Her eyes, white periods in a gore-smeared face, widen. "There's no way it can be that easy."

"Doesn't matter," I tell her. "He's down, and that's the end of it."

And yet no one moves. Instead we watch Hill's corpse warily, waiting for some sign of the power that has kept us bound for years. We half-expect the brains splashed across the wall to fly back into the man's ruined skull, the blood to return to the cavity Kyle's bullet burst open, the wound to heal. We wait for the Reverend to rise, murderous rage contorting his sallow face as he chooses which of us to destroy first. We wait. We watch.

But what happens is infinitely more surprising.

Nothing.

The all-powerful Reverend just lies there, minus most of his head, and deader than dog shit.

"I've never in all my years seen so much blood," Gracie says, and it sounds like a comment that should be followed by tears. But this is Gracie, and I'm willing to put money down that she's already stressing over the cleanup. "Guess he was just a man after all."

"I want to go home," the girl on the bar says, and that pulls us from our trance-like state of expectancy.

"We'll get you there, honey." Flo's hands tremble as she sleeves some of the priest's blood from her face.

"It's gonna be all right babe," Brody soothes, though he's in too much pain to sound sincere. "We'll be out of here soon, then it'll just be you, me and Dino."

Kyle is still holding the gun out, still pressing it against the ghost of Hill's temple, and I put a hand on his forearm, urge him to lower it before it goes off and adds someone else to the rapidly rising number of dead. For a moment he resists, then the tension ebbs away.

"It's okay son."

"Kyle," he mutters.

"What?"

"You don't get to call me 'son'."

"Okay."

Wintry is still tending to Cobb. The old man has downed half a bottle of whiskey. I'm sure wherever his mind is, it doesn't know what just happened, and maybe that's for the best. Wintry locks gazes with me and in that brief glance, we're like two old farts trading war stories. What's happened here tonight won't ever be forgotten, no more than will the things that led us here, the errors in judgment, the wrong turns, the simple little mistakes that all add up to an express elevator ride right into a nightmare no amount of waking up can cure. But this is a lull, and a welcome one, and I figure everyone (except maybe Brody and the girl) is going to savor it before the next unwelcome development. For however briefly, this is Eddie's bar, the only functioning water hole in a near-dead town, and right now, for the first time ever, these people truly are my friends.

Wintry goes back to silently consoling the inconsolable Cobb. Gracie heads into the ladies room and emerges with a mop and bucket that are filthier than the floor but don't, to my knowledge, have human remains on them. Flo tries to get the girl to stand up. It isn't going to happen.

"We need to take him too," I tell Kyle with a nod in Brody's direction.

"No."

"Why?"

"Yeah," Brody adds. "Why? If it's because you shot a perfectly nice guy like me, and don't know how to apologize...hell...that's all water under the bridge." He grins and there is blood on his teeth. "I don't hold grudges."

"He's a murderer," Kyle says.

I lean in close. "For fuck sake, Kyle. *Everyone* here is a murderer."

"Not like him we're not. He enjoyed it. Did it on purpose."

His logic makes my head swim, and the only thing I'm really sure of is that I don't agree with it. "Listen, you have to—"

"Leave him," Cobb says dreamily, as if our banter has woken him from a doze.

Everyone looks in his direction. He, however, does not look at us.

"Cobb..."

"Leave him. I'll take care of him."

I can't be blamed for taking that like it sounds. Sure, Cobb can heal folks, but considering we're talking about the man who just killed his wife, I don't imagine healing has anything to do with it.

"Take care of him how?"

"Fix him up, Sheriff. What else?" His eyes are swollen from crying, his face almost as pale as Brody's.

"Any number of things," I reply. "He can die on his own if that's what you're figuring to help him with."

"I said I'll fix him up. Weren't like he killed Ellie on purpose."

"You don't know that."

"No. I don't." He takes another slug of whiskey. "But why are we here?"

I don't know how to answer that. Seems no one does. But for the low whimpering of the girl, the room's awful quiet.

"We come here to try to make peace when there ain't none to be had. We come here to be forgiven. Way I figure it, Sheriff, is if I don't do what every ounce of me wants to do to this kid, and instead I fix him up, like I want to be fixed up myself, like I can never be fixed up, then maybe it'll count for somethin' in this great goddamn plan we're all so fuckin' tangled up in. What do you think?"

I consider that for a moment because it's worth considering. Then: "I think you may be onto something," I tell him.

"Yeah?"

"Yeah." I look at the girl. "What about her?"

"Nothing I can do for her. Maybe Hendricks can pull a miracle out of his hat, but not me." He glances down at Brody. "She's too far gone."

Brody sighs shakily, tries to stand and fails. Although Cobb has agreed to help the kid, I figure we've just seen his revenge. Telling the kid his girl is going to die is about the only weapon he has left to use, I guess. Hurt him as much as possible before he heals him.

"All right."

Cobb nods, and goes back to his drink. "Don't leave Ellie out there on the road, Tom. She deserves better."

"I'll see to it."

"You're leaving me here with *him*?" Brody asks, appalled.

"It's the one good option in a dump truck full of bad ones," I remind him. "Take it or leave it."

Gracie comes around the bar, flips that lock of hair out of her face and sets the mop and bucket down by the priest's body. "Think we should burn him?" she asks, as casually as she might inquire about the weather. "Bury the ashes and salt the earth?"

I understand her concern completely. No one wants to see that son of a bitch get back up. "If he was anything as dangerous as he led us to believe he was, he'd already have done something. And if he still plans to, then I don't reckon cooking him or seasoning the mud's going to do us a whole lot of good."

She sighs, and it's the most human I've ever seen her look. There's the urge again, to hold her, but this time I know it's because I need it, not her. So again, I restrain myself.

"Why didn't we do this three years ago?"

It's a good question, but I leave it unanswered.

I walk to the center of the room, Cobb and Wintry's table to my right, Cadaver still lost in the shadows by the door to my left.

"You okay, Cadaver?"

"Just countin' what's left," the electronic voice from the dark replies, followed by that familiar clink of pennies.

"Let's get this done," Kyle says behind me, and I'm glad to hear it. It means two things to me: First, he's still in control. The shock of shooting two men in the space of twenty minutes hasn't yet reduced him to the wreck it makes of others, and eventually will make of him when he least expects it, and second, it represents action, movement, right when my bones are threatening to turn to jelly and leave me a quivering, sobbing mess on the floor.

We move.

I'm stronger than Kyle, so I slip my hands beneath the girl's arms; he takes her feet.

"Hurry, for God's sake," Brody moans. "Don't let her die."

We carefully time the move, and with Flo ahead of us, we're out the door and loading Carla into the back seat of my truck before the second hand of the clock has made a full sweep.

We leave a trail of pinkish blood behind us.

CHAPTER FIVE

The rain is pelting down like machine gun fire, the wind trying its best to wrench the truck doors right off their hinges as we bundle inside. Makes me wonder if this is the Reverend's 'boss' gathering his fury, preparing to blow us all to whatever the alternative hangout is for the kind of deities that would consider Hill a valued employee.

I'm still too scared to believe this is over. It's an ugly feeling I know well, and can only hope will abate as soon as we have Carla at the door of the good doctor, provided she lives that long. As I gun the engine into life, and look at Kyle, who's wiping the condensation clear and peering out at the rain, it occurs to me that if this is really the end of the nightmare, I have no idea what to do with myself. There won't be any glorious sunshine through my window in the morning, marking the equally glorious beginning of a new chapter of my life. I'm still a murderer; there's still the guilt, and there's my son, who thinks I'm dead and doesn't mind. All that will really change will be the venue into which I bring my suffering. I don't imagine next Saturday I'll be at Eddie's. Instead I'll sit at home without those faces to act as mirrors for my own self-loathing.

I guide the truck out of the parking lot, careful to avoid the other cars, and turn out onto the road that will bring us to town, and to the doctor who I know won't take too kindly to being roused at this hour of the night, especially to tend to an injured whore with needle marks parading up her emaciated arm.

"Faster, she's not looking too good," Kyle says, looking over his shoulder as if he's been peeking in on my thoughts. "Think the baby'll make it?"

"Hope so." I resist the urge to remind him what Cobb said about her chances.

It's damn near impossible to see anything beyond the glass, the high beams like swollen ghosts staying three steps ahead of the grille. I'm going fast, aware that at any time I might inadvertently fulfill my obligations to the dead Reverend and run somebody over, or mash the truck into some poor drunk driver's car as he struggles to make his way home.

"C'mon for Chrissakes, she's bleeding bad."

It isn't a long drive, but the storm buffeting the truck and Kyle's endless needling make it seem like hours. Lightning turns the world to rainy daylight as I turn off the main road onto Abigail Lane, where the good doctor has his home.

Hendricks' place used to be a farmhouse, through the windows of which long gone farmers watched the world fall victim to the voracious appetite of progress. Mining companies bought out the land for the families of their employees, and people got greedy. Then the money ran out, and so did the people. Hendricks, an M.D. from Alabama who claimed he was "just passing through," saw no reason to move on when he caught sight of the sickly state of those who'd stubbornly refused to leave Milestone in the great exodus of '79, and when he heard the asking price for a house nobody wanted.

As we pull into the drive that slopes upward to the block-shaped two-story house, there are no lights in the windows, which doesn't come as a surprise. I find myself wondering, if we had kept going instead of turning into Hendricks' drive, how long it would have taken us to come upon the twisted wreck of Eleanor Cobb's Taurus.

Despite the forbidding darkness of the house that looms over the car, Kyle's already hurrying to get the girl out. Not the smartest move considering the Doc might not even be here, so I leave him to his grunting and trot to the door.

Knock, knock. No sound from within.

"Leave her there," I call back to Kyle, who's as good as invisible behind the car's lights.

"What?"

"I said leave her *be*. If Hendricks doesn't answer, what good will dragging her out in the rain do?"

"What else *can* we do?"

"I don't know. We'll deal with that if and when— "

"Sheriff?"

The front door is open; the storm deafened me to the approach of the bespectacled man now standing there squinting out. "That you, Tom?"

He's a reed-thin man and heavily bearded. I've always suspected that, just like the deceased Reverend, vanity has driven the doctor to dying his hair to keep from looking his age. And though in this light he doesn't look much healthier than the girl in the back of my truck, I'm glad as hell to see him.

I summarize the situation as calmly as I can. It doesn't sound calm in the least by the time it reaches my lips, but Hendricks steps back, his face a knot of concern. From upstairs, his wife calls out a demand to know what's going on. The doctor turns on the hall light. It's the warmest looking light I've seen in quite some time, and the shadows it casts are gentle. "Bring her in. I'll see what I can do." He reaches the stairs and yells up, "Queenie, I'm going to need your help down here."

And in what seems like a heartbeat, the doctor is bent over the girl where she lies prone on the couch and swaddled in comfy looking blankets. The towels wrapped around her head make it look as if she's being prepped for a massage, nothing more. The blood running between her eyes spoils that illusion though. She's shivering, which is good. Means she's still breathing. "Lost a lot of blood," Hendricks says, pressing the cup of his stethoscope to her chest. "You said an auto wreck?"

"Yeah."

"Anyone else hurt?" He appraises Kyle and me. "How about you guys? You look pretty shook up."

"We're fine," Kyle says. "She going to be all right? She's pregnant, you know."

Hendricks frowns.

"She told us," I add quickly, covering Kyle's blunder. "Right before she passed out."

I can't tell whether or not he's buying it, but he says nothing, just presses that stethoscope to the girl's breast and breathes through his nose. His wife stands off in the corner, arms folded over her dressing gown. She looks pissed, and I can't blame her.

When at last the doctor looks up, his face is grave. "I'm sorry to say I don't think there's a whole lot I can do for her, boys. The baby's gone. That I can tell you right now for certain, and it's only a matter of time before she follows. I'd have to open her up to say for sure, but my guess is she's busted up pretty bad. Judging by that blood and the way she's breathing, seems she's got a punctured lung too. Pupils are dilated. Head's cracked open almost clean through to the bone. Frankly I'm amazed she's not dead already." At the looks on our faces, he continues, "But you fellas did real good. Wasn't much more you could have done for her. She'd have appreciated it, I'm sure."

Another life lost. For nothing. Though at least when I dream of this one I'll know it wasn't entirely my fault.

"Uh...Sheriff?"

I look back at Hendricks.

"You just going to leave her here?"

I'm about to argue with him, but it slowly dawns on me that he's right, that I'd have asked the same question. Hendricks, unlike me or Kyle, still has a life, and I don't reckon we should leave a dead whore on his couch to remind him why we're different.

"Sorry, Doc. We'll take her back to Eddie's."

Hendricks looks confused. "Eddie's? Why there?"

"Because it's quieter than any graveyard. Most of the time. We can bury her out back right next to Eddie himself. I figure he deserves the company after all the shit we've done under his roof. Besides," I move close to the girl. "We've got some burying to do anyway."

"Who else died?" Queenie asks, her first words to us since we arrived.

"The Reverend."

"Oh."

I smile at the lack of emotion on her face. "Yeah. Ticker gave out on him while he was preaching to us about the evils of drink."

Hendricks shakes his head. "Man had way too much time on his hands."

"You got that right, Doc."

We stay for a while, exchanging the kind of uneasy banter unique to folks who're waiting for one among them to die. Kyle paces, torn between refusing to accept that the girl is gone, that we couldn't save her, and eager to be in a room larger than Hendricks' parlor so he doesn't have to be within touching distance of me.

At last there comes a single hitching sigh. The girl frowns, as if in her dreams she's stumbled upon something dangerous, then she shudders once, and that's the end of it.

No one says anything for a moment. We all just stand there, trying to read the story of the dead girl's life from the lines on her face, the punctuation marks on her arm, the commas at the corners of her mouth from too much time spent grimacing in pain. I reach down and brush a strand of hair away from her face.

"C'mon, Kyle."

For the second time that night, we load the girl into the truck. I imagine she feels lighter, that the soul, or whatever leaves us when we die, has weight, and hers is somewhere better now, somewhere no one can touch it, and use the stains on it against her.

Our drive back to Eddie's is a silent one. There's plenty that could be said, but no need to say it.

At least, not until we see the fire.

"Aw *Christ no...*" Kyle says and is out of the truck and running before I have time to draw a breath.

CHAPTER SIX

Eddie's is in flames, a funeral pyre burning against the dark, turbulent maelstrom of the night, and though the rain is still beating down and pockmarking the mud, it's not doing much to put out the blaze.

My first thought is that Gracie has finally had enough, that the Reverend's death is the catalyst she's been waiting for, the escape she's longed for all these years. I imagine her chasing everybody out, leaving the Reverend's body and Brody where they are, dousing the place from top to bottom with kerosene or spirits, then standing in the doorway, flaming rag in her hand. I see the light burning away the shadows on her grim face, making her seem young and innocent again. Then she tosses the rag, and the fire races across the floor and up the walls, a raging thing, but pure, and cleansing.

But as I watch the lithe silhouette of my son racing toward the inferno, I remember what I thought when I stood in there looking down at Hill's body, waiting for him to suddenly resurrect himself. Cold dread grips my heart. Is this the surprise we expected from him? Did he burst into flame moments after Kyle and me left the bar? I picture his almost headless corpse erupting into bright searing flame, claiming the lives of those standing nearest him first before they're even aware what's happening, then spreading out and cooking the rest as they try to escape.

And then I think of Cobb.

I pull the truck to a halt in the parking lot. Flames rise up, licking the sky; the rain falls down. Glass shatters in the heat and I have to shield my face. Not before my eyebrows are singed away.

Kyle is not alone, and his company is not a decapitated burning thing. I make my way over, all but blinded by the light from the fire. It isn't until I'm right there next to Kyle that I see it's Cadaver who's with him. His eyes are narrowed against the glare, but still there's an odd look on his hollow face, almost like reverence.

"Cadaver, what happened?"

Kyle looks like a ghost, his eyes filled with fire. "He says Cobb did it. Just after we left, he went crazy and torched the place."

Cadaver nods, but adds nothing. I notice his little microphone is absent, which explains his silence. Just like Brody must have thought when the old man hunkered down next to him, Cadaver looks like death. More so now than ever before, the orange-red light only adding deeper shadow beneath the sharp outcroppings of his cheekbones.

"Where is everyone?" I ask, afraid of the answer, because I've surveyed the area more than once on my way up here and I'm surveying it now again, and I don't see anybody here but us, and that feels to me like a brand new nightmare fresh from the devil's womb, waiting to be christened by the ignorant.

Kyle looks at me, and the flames shimmer in his eyes. "Gone," he tells me. "Cadaver says they're all gone. All but Brody."

"And where's he?"

Cadaver nods in the direction of the burning building, off into the shadows the fire is weaving to the side of it. I don't see Brody, but I trust that he's there.

"Jesus." I put my hands to my face to block out a reality that seems to be getting darker by the second.

There's a story here, I suppose. Cadaver must have seen it all from his place by the window, before he hotfooted it the hell out of the burning tavern. He might whisper to me of Wintry's bravery, how he tried to carry as many people as he could out of the place before one of the big timber beams came down and cracked his head open like an egg, dropping him and suffocating beneath his weight those he'd carried in his arms, his beloved Flo among them. He might tell me the details of Cobb's descent into madness, how one minute he was a sobbing wreck, the next a raving lunatic, whooping and hollering and raging, spinning like a top with spirits flying from the open bottles in his hands. Then a match, the smell of sulfur, and a small flame ready to birth an all-consuming fire. He might say that Gracie fought Cobb to the end, maybe cold-cocked him with one of those bottles, or gutted him with the sharp end of a broken mop handle before the smoke took them both, laid them down for the fire to burn them in their sleep.

Good for Gracie.

Cadaver might tell me these things, but I don't want to hear that choked whisper from his cracked lips. My imagination is louder anyway.

"Is there a chance anyone else survived?" Kyle asks the old man, who shrugs and looks at me.

Like Wintry, there's more truth in his eyes than could ever roll off his tongue. But I'm stubborn, and what pitiful little sleep I have these days will be robbed from me tonight if I don't see for myself. There are no screams from Eddie's, no sound of anyone begging to be saved, but then we've all been damned for longer than we care to admit, and we've never cried for salvation.

I start moving toward the bar.

Kyle's hand falls firmly on my shoulder.

I start to turn, and the roof caves in. It sounds like a tree falling, a splintering crash that sends a plume of dirty smoke up before fresh fire rushes in to fill the hole, fed by the air that has tried to escape.

"Sonofabitch," someone cries out from the dark, and finally I see a shape rolling around in the shadows, batting at sparks that are trying to ignite his clothes. If the kid's able to roll, then could be his injuries are no more. We'll have to wait and see.

Crackling, spitting flames, but still no screams. On some level I know I should be thankful for that, and for the fact that this atrocity was not the Good Reverend's work, but I'm not. Not just now. Kyle is weeping, and as his hand slips from my shoulder, Cadaver's hand finds his before it occurs to me to comfort him.

"This shouldn't have happened," I say, without knowing whether or not I'm even saying it aloud, or who I think I'm saying it to if I am. "They didn't deserve this."

Another dumb, obvious statement in a night loaded with them.

"We should call someone." Kyle walks away and sits down, his back to the rickety wooden fence that separates the parking lot from the grassy slope down to the road. I start after him, rehearsing words of comfort that sound wooden, and useless, like pretty much everything I've ever said to that kid. He wants his mother back and he won't get it; he wants his father dead, and he can't get that either. If early life experience scars you for the rest of it, then Kyle's nightmare hasn't even started yet. He raises a hand as I draw near. It's as good as a signpost saying ROAD CLOSED, and all I can do is stand there feeling helpless, which is exactly what I do until I hear a sound I never thought I'd hear again.

The sound of pennies being counted.

"Cadaver?"

He's still facing the fire, but his head is bowed, all his attention on his upturned palm. I give the kid one brief, regretful look, then head back to the old man. Back there in the shadows, Brody's still cursing.

As I draw abreast of the old man, I see there's only two pennies in his palm. I guess the fire took a little something extra from him. But when at last he raises his head, not only does he seem calm, he's almost smiling. A thin thread of blue-gray smoke drifts from the small hole in the box in his throat. Opaque eyes settle on mine, and they look ancient.

The smile.

The pennies.

It dawns on me then, the not-so-quick-witted Sheriff of a town on life support, that there was something to Reverend Hill's threat after all. It was there right from the beginning. We were waiting for a great black winged demon to come bursting up from below, or the devil himself to come strolling in the door with a brimstone smile and eyes like glowing embers, all those peachy images the Good Book tells us we should be watching for, when we should have been looking at that ever-present patch of darkness in the corner. To the man counting his change.

Fear overwhelms me, and my legs, which have done a respectable job of holding me up through the madness, finally give out. I stumble. Cadaver's hand lashes out and clamps on my arm, somehow keeping me upright.

"You all right, Sheriff?" he whispers, head cocked slightly in an admirable impression of genuine concern.

From the fire comes a great hiss. It might be a serpent; it might just be the rain meeting flame. I'm not so certain of anything anymore. Only that Cadaver's the reason the air smells like burning flesh.

"'Just counting what's left'," I say, recalling his words to me before we left the bar. "You were talking about us."

He nods, glances back at Kyle, then steps closer. There should not be enough strength in his old bones to keep me from falling, but there is. His hand on my elbow might as well be a metal brace.

"There's no accountin' for human emotion," he says, his whisper tinged with sadness, aided by the expression of regret on his worn face. "Especially the love of a frustrated old woman for her shameless husband. Because of Eleanor Cobb, everythin' went sideways on us. You were right. This shouldn't've happened."

"But it did."

"Yes it did, and that's a shame." He closes his fist around the pennies. "If it means anythin'—and I don't expect it will, at least not for a while—this isn't what I wanted. They were my friends too."

I'm bitter, and scared, and more than ready for him to reach inside my tired body and wrench out my soul, whatever's left of it. "Am I supposed to believe that? Or is it just customary where you come from to burn your friends alive if things don't go according to plan?"

He purses his lips, then squints at me like a short-sighted man trying to read the fine print on a legal document. "The Reverend got what was comin' to him. They all did, unfortunate as it is. Wintry..." He shook his head, a wry smile on his wrinkled lips. "He can talk you know. He just chose not to after—"

"I don't want a litany of their sins," I interrupt. "It hardly makes a damn bit of difference now. All I want to know from you is what happens to Kyle."

He nods his understanding. Anyone looking might think we were discussing the latest decisions of the coaches of our favorite football teams. "Repentance is the name of this game, Tom. Don't matter whether I influence it or not, or whether you both live to be a hundred and ten or die tomorrow, the debt's got to be settled. It's the price you have to pay for makin' the wrong choice when both were available to you."

"You didn't answer the question."

He sighs. "I'm a reasonable man, Tom."

I can't help myself. I laugh long and loud at that little nugget of absurdity. The contradiction to Cadaver's claim is burning high and bright before us. Sure, he didn't strike the match, but if not for his influence, none of us would have been there to begin with.

He releases his grip on me. I don't fall, but there's not a whole lot of strength left in me. I stay standing only so I can look him in the eye when he tells me what's going to become of my son. And maybe when he does I'll have just the right amount of energy left to punch his fucking face in.

But he doesn't answer right away. Instead he grabs my left hand, forces it out of the fist that I've made to follow up on my unvoiced threat, and drops his two pennies into my palm.

I look up at him.

His eyes probe mine, and my guts squirm as if a surgeon has put his cold fingers in there. I'm afraid I'm going to be sick. "Consider it a loan," he says, and closes my fingers around the coins.

"Why?" I ask, as he starts to walk toward the burning building, the smoke whipping itself into specters that chase each other around the flames. Sparks dance like giddy stars.

At the threshold to the inferno that used to be Eddie's Bar, he stops, seemingly unaffected by anything but the light from the blaze. He squints back over his shoulder at me, and though his voice is still a whisper, I hear it as surely as if he's said it right into my ear.

"It's all I have."

STORY NOTES

"The Grief Frequency"

If William Schafer of Subterranean Press hadn't, in a rare moment of delirium, offered me a prized slot in the premier issue of his (at the time) soon-to-be launched flagship magazine, *Subterranean*, alongside such luminaries as Harlan Ellison, Joe R. Lansdale, Norman Partridge, George R.R. Martin, Peter Crowther, Mark Morris and Terry Matz, then rejected my first two attempts at trying to fill that slot, this story probably wouldn't exist. Back then, such opportunities, at least for me, didn't grow on trees, and having two stories bounced left me frustrated, and all too well aware that the third try was probably going to be my last. Determined, I opened a new Word file and typed the first sentence of "The Grief Frequency" with no idea where it was going to go from there, but, like the tale's inciting incident, it was pretty much a headlong collision with inevitability. It's a grim tale, and represented a turning point in my fiction. Rarely, since the inception of this piece, have I let the sunlight penetrate too deeply into my work. Even when it does, it most often comes with a price most of us would not be willing to pay.

And yes, fortunately for my sanity, the story made it into the magazine.

"The Number 121 to Pennsylvania"

Another first. This time the magazine was *Cemetery Dance*, a market I'd been trying to crack for ages. A series of rejection slips from publisher Richard Chizmar, each one more encouraging and positive than the last, proved inspiration enough to get this tale of a ghost train, and old man, and an old bargain, set both where I live now and where I grew up, out of me and into the pages of CD. Richard (along with then co-editor Robert Morrish and the fine CD crew) would go on to publish many more of books, inlcluding the limited edition hardcover of the very book you're reading now.

"Mr. Goodnight"

I had just finished writing my novella *The Turtle Boy*, my brain still full of summer and children, when the title "Mr. Goodnight" sprang to mind. As a basic storyline simmered in my brain, I looked out the window and saw my stepson and his best friend (who I also used as the models for Timmy and Pete in *The Turtle Boy*), digging a hole in the bottom of the yard in the shade of a walnut tree, working with the kind of fervor you'll only ever see in kids who are convinced they're bound to find treasure. I revisit such moments as often as I can in my fiction, because it's really the only way to recapture it now that adulthood has all but dispossessed me of such cherished beliefs.

One might speculate that in this story, the titular entity is a fictional embodiment of maturity and the things it steals from us.

Or, it could just be a monster story...assuming there's a difference between the two.

"Empathy"

Unlike "The Grief Frequency" which almost didn't get written, "Empathy" *had* to be written, or it's very likely the only writing you'd be seeing from me these days would be graffiti on the padded walls of my cell. It remains the most difficult story I've ever had to write, and one of the things I looked forward to least when putting together this collection was rereading it to ensure it was suitable for inclusion and devoid of errors. "Empathy" is a horror story, and by far one of the most horrific pieces I've written, maybe more so for me than you, Dear Reader, because a lot of it is true.

During the second Gulf War, I was emailed a link, and like all links that come from friends, I clicked on it, assuming it harmless. It led to a site much the same as the one in the story. At this point, any sane human being would realize where they've found themselves and make a rapid retreat. Not I, friends, operating under the assumption that there couldn't be anything worse here than what I'd already seen on the news. I was wrong. But whatever disgust my callous morbidity may inspire in you, bear in mind that I've paid a heavy price for my curiosity, one that very nearly destroyed me.

In "Empathy" Will Chambers continues to suffer on my behalf. Consider it a cautionary tale.

"Peekers"

Not much commentary needed on this one. I was asked for a short tale, not more than 2,000 words, which I took as an opportunity to write a flat out scare-story that didn't need to concern itself too much with backstory or an intricate plot. It would be simple, straightforward, and creepy as hell. It was initially inspired by a photograph I took in which a shadowy face peered out from the bottom of a partially open where a face has no business being unless there's something not quite right about the body it's attached to...

The story proved overwhelmingly popular, and was adapted for the screen as a short by veteran novelist Rick Hautala and director Mark Steensland. You can see the chilling result of their efforts on Youtube.

"High on the Vine"

In the introduction to "From Hamlin To Harperville"—my warped riff on *The Pied Piper of Hamlin*—in my previous collection *Ravenous Ghosts*, I discussed how writers, particularly horror writers, like to mangle fairy tales. There's something about them that holds endless appeal. So for this collection I thought I'd take a stab at another one, and I have to admit I had more fun with "High on the Vine" than any other tale in the collection. It's uncharacteristically lighthearted, but I figure if you've read any or all of the tales which precede or follow it, the break from the darkness is probably a welcome one.

"Tonight the Moon Is Ours"

I've been asked more than once why I never set any of my stories in Ireland, given that I'm from there. The answer is: I have. My novel *The Hides* was set in my home town of Dungarvan, as was another story in this volume "Prohibited", and a crime story called "The Acquaintance", and there are a few stories that have never been published (and never will be) that used various locations in Ireland as the stage for all manner of unsavory goings on. But the real answer is that I tend to write about where I live. When I lived in Ireland, almost all my stories took place there. Then I moved to Ohio, and now the majority of my tales unfold here. Occasionally, though, I'll get an idea for a story that couldn't have just happened anywhere, and "Tonight the Moon Is Ours" is one such story. Almost everything that happens in the tale—with the obvious exception of the supernatural elements—is true. The Irish countryside is an ancient and spooky place, and it's hard to be cynical about ghosts or anything else if you've spent any time among the locals or the endless fields that surround the villages. As a child, this is where I spent most of my time.

"Prohibited"

Blame me for my native country's decline. It seems as soon as I left Ireland they implemented a series of laws to ensure I wouldn't come back. Among them was their "No Smoking in Pubs" rule, which for a population consisting mainly of smokers, seemed a bit much, even more so when they started imposing fines on publicans who ignored the rule, and sent regular patrols of cops in to ensure the law was being upheld. The only real result was that pub owners lost tons of money as their customers simply stayed at home and drank. And smoked. When at last I did go back, I found that the citizenry had finally returned to the pubs and the nightlife was thriving. And every pub had a smoking room out back. If there's one thing that will never take in Ireland, it's prohibition, unless of course they adopt the tactics my government uses in this story.

"Underneath"

This one sat forgotten in a drawer for a long time after I finished it, because it was so different from most of what I'd written to that point, I had no idea if it was any good. Then Richard Chizmar asked if I had a story he could look at for the third volume in his excellent *Shivers* series of anthologies, and, embroiled as I was in a new novel, I didn't have time to write a new one. So, I dusted off "Underneath" which, like "Empathy" was written as cathartic therapy (there never was a scarred girl, but if you ever meet me, ask, and I'll show you my scars), and found it to be a pretty good story. It appeared in *Shivers III*, got some great mentions in reviews, and has recently been optioned for film. Not bad for a forgotten story!

"Snowmen"

I wrote this one late at night, the house creaking and settling around me, a full moon revealing the sad, half-melted remains of my stepson's snowmen in the yard outside my window. It's an E.C. comics-type tale, and was reprinted in illustrated format in *Grave Tales* magazine, itself inspired by magazines like *Tales from the Crypt*.

"Will You Tell Them I Died Quietly?"

I was sitting at home watching TV when the title of this story came to me. I quickly wrote it down, then forgot about it. A few months later, my grandfather passed away, and as a result of the grief I felt at losing him, and the guilt at not being able to travel home for the funeral, I found myself imagining the old churchyard in which he was buried, presided over by a small church in a village that sits in the shadow of a mountain range. My grandfather used to ring the church bell at six o' clock every evening, and early on Sunday mornings to call the parishioners to services. Somewhere along the way, my imaginings took a decidedly bleak turn, and I made the funeral after all. It just wasn't his.

"The Last Laugh"

This story was inspired by an interview I read with a prominent standup comedian in which he talked about the early days of his career—the seedy clubs, the crummy pay, and the unpredictable audiences. It was his contention that no two audiences are the same. Sometimes they love you, and sometimes they don't, and they're never afraid to show it. Before every show, the comedian would be filled not with humor and confidence, as I'd always assumed, but fear and doubt. It is, I suspect, why some comedians are so depressed in real life. Making people laugh becomes the most important thing in the world, because if you don't, you're considered a failure. In this story, I took that harsh reality a bit further.

"Cobwebs"

I was on the way home from town one fall evening when I glanced out the window just as we were passing a rest home. The sun was going down behind the building, enabling me to see through one of the windows, the silhouette of an old man sitting very still. I was struck by the need to know what that old man was thinking in that moment, if he was content, or missing the life he had once known, if he was bitter at having to spend his time in a home, or if he had created a new life for himself there that gave him joy. I wanted to believe the latter to be the case, but perhaps I'm too cynical for such optimism to ever stand a chance of taking hold. As a story began to form based around these questions, I found myself exploring a fear I believe everyone shares— the fear of being forgotten, or of being alone with no one to remember you.

There is a reference in "Cobwebs" to another story in this collection. I included it as a kind of afterthought, assuming nobody would ever spot it. I should know by now my readers are savvier than that. Hint: *choo-choo.*

"Saturday Night at Eddie's"

One of my favorite television shows of yesteryear is the oft-lamented *American Gothic*, created by Shaun Cassidy (yes, he of *The Partridge Family*). It is, in my opinion, one of the better genre shows, with Gary Cole on top form and chewing his way through his lines with malevolent glee.

Good performances, good storylines, and weirdness aplenty made this Must-See TV during my late teens. And then, sadly, like a lot of shows, it was canceled before it reached its full potential. However, we're living in a time when petitions to television studios can get a show put back on the air, and, while it wasn't revived, the entire (if woefully brief) run of *American Gothic* did get a new lease of life on DVD a few years back.

I was first in line.

I'd just finished watching the show, which turned out to be even better than I remembered it, and had also, right around the same time, just got done reading a pair of novels that I heartily recommend: Norman Partridge's *The Crow: Wicked Prayer* (which he would rather you didn't judge by the atrocious movie they made of it), and the late Jack Cady's *The Hauntings of Hood Canal.* The combination of *American Gothic,*

Partridge's dry dusty western disguised as a Gothic revenge tale, and Cady's deceptively gentle look at the something plaguing a small Washington town through the eyes of the barflies at a local tavern, left me with no doubt what kind of a story I wanted to try my hand at next.

And though I know better than to claim "Saturday Night at Eddie's" is anything near as good as the aforementioned works, I'm pretty damn pleased with it all the same. Shortly after I turned this novella in for the collection, I was left with a nagging need to know what happened next, and so developed it into a novel entitled *Currency of Souls*, which you can find in print or e-version on B&N, should you find yourself similarly curious.

ABOUT THE AUTHOR

Born and raised in Dungarvan, Ireland, Kealan Patrick Burke is an award-winning author described as "one of the most original authors in contemporary horror" (*Booklist*).

Some of his works include the novels KIN, MASTER OF THE MOORS, CURRENCY OF SOULS and NEMESIS, the novellas THE TURTLE BOY (Bram Stoker Award Winner, 2004), VESSELS, MIDLISTERS, and JACK & JILL, and the collections RAVENOUS GHOSTS, THEATER MACABRE, and THE NUMBER 121 TO PENNSYLVANIA & OTHERS (Bram Stoker Award-Nominee, 2009).

Visit Kealan on the web at http://www.kealanpatrickburke.com

Made in the USA
Coppell, TX
10 May 2020

24905364R00150